CITADELS
of the Lost

DAW Books Presents
TRACY HICKMAN'S
The Annals of Drakis:
SONG OF THE DRAGON (Book One)
CITADELS OF THE LOST (Book Two)

Tracy HICKMAN

CITADELS
of the Lost

THE ANNALS OF DRAKIS: Book Two

DAW BOOKS, INC.

DONALD A. WOLLHEIM, FOUNDER
375 Hudson Street, New York, NY 10014
ELIZABETH R. WOLLHEIM
SHEILA E. GILBERT
PUBLISHERS
http://www.dawbooks.com

First Printing, July 2011
1   2   3   4   5   6   7   8   9

Aknowledgments

I would like to thank Sheila Gilbert, without whose help this book would not shine so brightly.

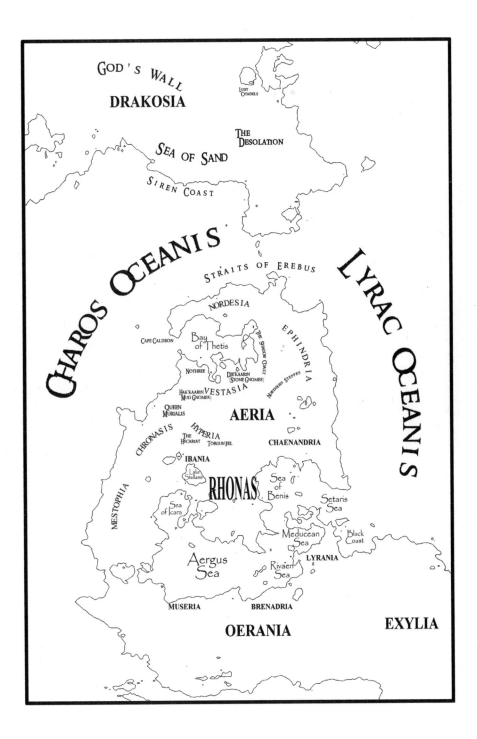

TABLE OF CONTENTS

BOOK 1: ROGUES

Book 1:

ROGUES

CHAPTER 1

Dragon Raid

T HE THROATS OF A THOUSAND DRAGONS answered the call.
Drakis took several steps back from the towering statue, awestruck by the shapes rising from the craggy peaks beyond. He glanced
back at the statue, the craning neck with the ridge of scales curving
down to the horn-spiked head with bladelike long teeth onto the ancient marble base, the enormous stone wings rising straight up over a
hundred feet, and the gigantic claws gripping the glowing crystal
globes. His gaze jumped back to the mountaintops and the shadows
pulling their way closer to him through the evening sky. Dragons . . .
real dragons! Even from this distance of several leagues he could
make out some details of the enormous monsters, their great wings
sweeping forward and scooping the air down and back with every
stroke. The sound of their shrieking calls rolled down the mountain-
side and shook the wide pedestal on which he stood, carrying away
with it every other sensation. It encompassed him, shot through him,
and drowned out everything else. Somewhere nearby the muffled
voice of Urulani shouted through the noise, calling her men to gather
closer around the statue and ready their weapons. *What were their
names?* he vaguely wondered. The dwarf, he knew, was also shouting
nearby but his voice sounded more distant than the dragon calls and
his movements seemed slow. Ethis was pulling at the dwarf, dragging
him back onto the pedestal and closer to the fold—the magical portal

sphere of radiant blue light that had opened at the base of the statue. Beyond the portal fold and through its shining blue haze he could see a land of dense foliage and distant towers but it seemed so very far away. Mala lay sobbing hysterically at his feet . . .

Mala, his Mala . . . the Mala who had betrayed them all because Drakis had heard the song of these dragons and brought them here.

Drakis grabbed her arm, yanking her to her feet. The muffled, confused sounds filling his ears suddenly cleared, and he was at once keenly aware of his surroundings. He had been a warrior not so many months ago, even if that lifetime now seemed like the distant past; his training acted for him. He reached for his sword, pulling it from its scabbard and finding comfort in the sound of the steel blade as it cleared the leather.

"Urulani! Get everyone back to the ship!" Drakis shouted.

"We can't outrun that!" Kendai yelled.

"It's coming here," Drakis snapped. "It's coming for me. I'll stay here—cut back and forth through the fold—and keep them at bay until you can get to the ship and think of some way to get me out of this."

"I'm staying," Ethis said.

"We'll take them together," growled the dwarf.

Urulani opened her mouth, but Drakis spoke first.

"You have to get the rest out of here," Drakis said in the firm voice of command that he had heard so often before from his commanders and which he, in turn, learned to use on those under his leadership. It was a voice that carried its own authority. "You're the captain. You're the only one who can. Take Mala, the Lyric, and your crew, and get help!"

Urulani gritted her teeth and then turned to her men. "Yithri, you and Kwarae bring the Lyric! I've got the princess. We're going back to the *Cydron*! NOW!"

Kendai, Djono, Gantau, and Lukrasae did not require another word. All four bolted from the platform, following their footprints back across the sands.

"So, are you glad you came along, princess?" Urulani said, grabbing the arm of the auburn-haired woman, pulling her away from Drakis. The harder she pulled, however, the more firmly

Mala gripped Drakis as though he were her only jetsam in a sea of fear. Urulani, after considerable effort, managed to pull her free. "Let's go!"

"NO!" Mala screamed, her hands shaking as her head and eyes began darting about. "The monsters are out there! They've come from my dreams! They've come for my soul!"

"We don't have time for this!" Drakis barked, his eyes fixed on the dark shapes wheeling above them in the sky.

"You heard the man, princess . . ."

Mala shoved Urulani backward with a mindless, animal roar.

The captain quickly recovered her footing.

"Fair warning," Urulani said as she pulled back her arm and smacked a quick fist across Mala's cheek.

Mala, however, did not drop. She staggered backward several steps before her eyes went wide—and then Mala erupted into a fury. With a ferocity and speed that shocked Drakis, she clawed suddenly at Urulani's face.

Just as suddenly, the Lyric pulled her arms free of Kwarae and Yithri, leaping on Urulani's back.

"By the gods!" Drakis shouted, reaching over to try and pull the Lyric from the captain's back. "Get them out of here!"

"Gantau!" Bloody red streaks opened up along Urulani's midnight skin. "Get back here! Lend a hand!"

Gantau slid to a stop in the sand, turned, and rushed back to the platform. By the look on his face, Drakis knew the man was afraid but obeyed.

Drakis managed to pull the Lyric off of Urulani's back. He pushed Mala behind him but she was still sobbing and as afraid of the portal as of the approaching dragons. She pushed back against him from behind. Drakis struggled to keep his footing on the slippery marble.

"Good luck, princess!" Urulani said. "Men of Sondau! Let's get out of here!"

"It's too late, they're already here," Drakis bellowed. "Ethis! You and Jugar watch the sides and each other's backs! Urulani, get what's left of your men to form up with our backs to the fold. The plan's still good . . . we'll drop back through the fold if we need to and hold on the other side until your men bring help."

"What kind of help do you think they can bring against that?" Urulani asked, pointing to the sky.

Three of the great shadows in the deepening evening sky were ahead of the rest, their shrieking cries seeming to cut directly through Drakis' ears.

"When do we fire?" Kwarae asked, but there was a strange quiver in his voice.

The song returned to Drakis' head like a thundering chorus of a thousand voices.

Back to the homeland of fallen dreams . . .
Is this the prophet returned?
Wandering so long . . .
Wandering so strong . . .

"Wait, I . . . what?" Drakis stammered.

"Do we fire?" Kwarae repeated.

"No! We wait!" Urulani replied.

"What?" Yithri yelped.

"That's no welcoming party, lass!" Jugar growled.

"So you want to fire arrows into *that*?" Urulani pointed as the first of the dragons banked above the sands, its enormous leathery wings held tight against the air through which it rushed. Sweat was breaking out on her brow. "Do you see the scales? Do you really think we can do any damage to that at this range? We have to wait until it is closer!"

"I think it's already too close," Ethis shouted, "We've got to retreat through the portal!"

"NO!" Jugar yelled over the tumult of voices around him. "We don't know where the fold leads! It could be a thousand leagues from . . ."

"What does it matter where it leads?" Ethis shouted back. "How can it possibly be worse than this?"

Drakis barely heard the words around him. The song filled his mind and thoughts.

Come to the claw and the forehand . . .
Come to the land of the dead.
Come quiet stealing . . .
Come to the healing . . .

Mala screamed.

The dragon had turned above the sands, pulling at the air so hard that the dunes beneath it exploded upward in billowing, sunset clouds of sand. In an instant, the enormous gaping jaws, with razor-sharp fangs nearly as tall as Drakis, were closing on the platform. The fifty-foot wings of the beast struck down and forward, slowing the monster in mid-flight just short of the platform, the sudden hurricane gust knocking Drakis back two steps. The dragon's great, left fore claws extended down toward him.

It was the eyes that caught his attention, Drakis realized in the last moment. Slit pupils and a terrible yellow color yet focused, determined, alert . . .

Intelligent.

Drakis reached forward with his left hand, transfixed by the eye of the dragon.

The sound of crashing metal brought him out of his stupor. Urulani, Gantau, and Yithri had all charged forward. Their swords and weapons clashed against the open claws, slashing at the leathery flesh of the dragon's palm which soon welled up with blood. Beyond the dragon, Kendai, Djono and Lukrasae had drawn their swords, uncertain how to attack the creature.

"Kendai!" Urulani yelled over the ringing blows as the dragon drew in a great gasping breath. "Get back to the ship! Get help!"

The dragon's cry was deafening, causing everyone on the marble platform to involuntarily raise their hands to their ears. The dragon pulled back, landing with a resounding boom on its hind legs as it clawed at the air in pain and outrage. Its tail whipped frantically about, crashing through one of the statue's claws. Rubble from the broken leg of the statue flew across the platform, slamming into Gantau's chest and smashing him against stone at the back of the platform's statue.

Two more dragons landed with such force around the statue that the platform shook, knocking Drakis and all of his companions completely off their feet. Gantau lay unmoving in a growing pool of blood.

"Do you think we could leave *now*?" Ethis shouted.

"Out!" Drakis screamed as he grabbed Mala's arm once more. "Everybody out through the fold!"

Drakis got his feet under him just as the dragon's head once more thrust down in his direction. He pushed Mala through the glowing sphere and prepared to jump after her . . .

Something connected at his back, rushing him toward the sphere. His hands were pushed backward with the sudden rush and he could feel the smooth, hard and wet surface behind him.

The dragon's fang.

The dragon had lunged at him but misjudged his prey. The massive head was pushing him through the portal, rushing through it with him. Drakis saw the glow of the fold rush past him and he was suddenly surrounded by the broken stones of a ruined plaza and an impression of the astonished faces of his companions.

Just as suddenly, the rushing sensation stopped and he tumbled forward, rolling across the broken stones of the ruined plaza that cut at his arms and legs. The final impact with the ground forced the air from his lungs and he struggled to stand up.

The sight before him was not to be believed. The ancient plaza was illuminated both by the twilight sky above and by the quavering glow of the fold portal. The ruins of the plaza itself had been all but completely reclaimed by the dense, lush growth all around it, shadows illuminated by the fold as the day was ending. The only remaining feature that might have had any recognizable function from a more civilized time was a short altar near the glowing portal, a pair of crumbling low walls along the edges and several broken columns.

But there was no time to consider this vision. Out of the soft radiance of the portal sphere the head and neck of the dragon protruded. The horns of the beast were thrashing back and forth, its jaws snapping at Urulani as she tried desperately to avoid its deadly maw, horns, and the raw power of its attack while striking blows against it at the same time. Jugar was urging the Lyric into the jungle despite her protests. Ethis had also drawn both of his weapons and was attempting to distract the creature. This resulted in one of the dragon's horns connecting with his chest and flinging him with such force into a tree that he seemed to nearly be wrapped backward around its trunk.

"By the gods," Drakis muttered as he sucked in air and adjusted the grip on his sword. "How are we supposed to deal with that?"

Drakis charged the front of the head, then dodged to the side, trying to strike but the dragon reacted swiftly, knocking Yithri into his path. They tumbled into each other, ending up on their backs desperately scrambling to get up again. He had barely found his footing when he was forced to leap suddenly to his right to avoid one of the many spiked scales protruding from the monstrous snout. There was a strong smell of sulfur in the air that struck Drakis as out of place, but he had no time to think about it.

"Yithri! Kwarae!" Urulani shouted. "Stay over on the right!"

"My right or the dragon's right?" Yithri yelled back.

"Your right, you stupid . . . watch out!"

The dragon was fast, faster than Drakis would have thought possible in a monster its size. Yithri had just leaped toward the beast, his ax raised over his head when the maw of the beast snapped in his direction.

Yithri's scream was quickly choked off as the massive, razor-sharp fangs and teeth plunged through his body. The dragon's head jerked back in distaste, rising up high above the plaza as it pulled in a great breath through its flaring nostrils.

"Take cover!" Jugar yelled just before diving behind the remains of a pillar at the edge of the plaza.

Drakis caught a glimpse of Mala standing shaking in front of a low wall. He leaped, catching her shoulders and pushing her backward over the broken stones.

Drakis felt the blistering heat against his back and saw the flash in his peripheral vision. He could not help himself. He had to look.

The dragon was spewing fire from its upturned maw, a churning conflagration that exploded through the entire large plaza with roiling flames. The center was a brilliant blue color, a place hotter than Drakis had ever known. The strange trees, brush, and foliage encroaching on the far side of the plaza erupted into flame, their own heat adding to the conflagration.

What remained of Yithri lay across the plaza, the stench of burning flesh filling the air.

Proud are the dragons who hear the call
Come at the sound of the song.
Why come attacking
in discourse lacking?

Drakis stood up.

Mala sat quivering, her knees drawn up to her chest and her back against the wall. "Drakis," she whimpered. "Stay with . . ."

Drakis stepped over the wall, his sword swinging loose at his side as he walked directly toward the creature.

The eyes of the dragon fixed on him, its spike-crowned head turning at his approach. Drakis was barely aware of Ethis, the four-armed chimerian, running across the plaza toward him with the dwarf Jugar at his heels.

The song in Drakis' head was overwhelming.

Come is the brother of ancient day
Come to the land he once lost.
Why come in anger?
Who was the traitor?

The dragon's flame choked off and its eyes focused on Drakis. The head flashed downward.

The fold vanished.

The neck and head of the dragon crashed down onto the shattering stones of the ancient plaza, blood rushing from the cleanly severed neck.

Drakis stood still, blinking at the sudden change of events. The thunderous song in his head had suddenly vanished, leaving him disoriented in the sudden silence of his mind. He glanced uncertainly at his blade.

"Help!"

Drakis looked around.

"Help me out!"

It was the dragon . . . the dragon was speaking a good deal like Jugar.

Drakis walked toward the dragon's head. The eye that had so enthralled him had gone dull now that the creature's life had fled.

"Jugar?" Drakis asked.

"Get this beastie off of me!" the dwarf yelled.

The lower jaws of the dragon lay across the legs of the dwarf, pinning him against the fitted stones of the plaza with the rest of his body unfortunately now situated in what had once been the mouth of the mammoth creature.

Drakis examined him for a few moments. "This is awkward."

"Awkward?" Jugar yelled, his face purple with rage. "I think the damned monster has broken my leg!"

Drakis looked around, still feeling dazed. Urulani was picking herself up off the stones as Kwarae rose to his feet uncertainly. "Kwarae! Give me a hand here . . . we've got to free the dwarf."

Ethis came to stand next to Drakis.

"You all right?" Drakis asked in flat tones.

"Yes, I'll be fine," the chimerian replied. "Although I'm not certain for how long. We had better find some shelter—defensible shelter—and soon. We've already run out of daylight, and I suspect this will not be friendly territory in the night."

"That should keep anything too curious at bay for a while," Drakis nodded over toward the still raging fire in the forest at the northern end of the plaza.

"And the smoke will attract them in the morning," Ethis replied.

"I don't suppose you know the way back to the ship?" Drakis asked though he already suspected the answer.

Ethis actually chuckled as he looked around. "No. The dwarf was right about one thing: that portal could have taken us a thousand leagues in any direction. Jugar might have better luck with knowing where we are by morning—dwarves seem to have an innate talent for that sort of thing—but if you're asking my opinion, I believe we're lost in a land of legend . . . and a dangerous one at that."

"You're all the crew I have left to me," Urulani looked at Kwarae. "Stay close."

CHAPTER 2

Burned Bridges

"**Y**OU *WHAT?*" THE DWARF SHOUTED, his body shaking with rage.

"I closed the portal," Ethis repeated calmly. "You were running toward the pedestal, too. I thought that was what you were trying to do as well."

"What I was . . . I was trying to get Drakis out of the way of that fell beast before he got himself eaten," Jugar sputtered. He sat with his back propped against the wall near where the thick forest was still burning, the fire luckily blazing up along a hillside and away from the plaza. "The *last* thing I wanted was to close that portal!"

Drakis stood over the dwarf with his hands on his hips. Urulani's gaze searched the perimeter of the small, shattered plaza. Mala kept apart from all of them, pacing listlessly back and forth.

Satisfied that they were safe for the moment, Urulani knelt next to the dwarf, examining his leg with a critical eye. "It's definitely broken. We'll need to set it and splint the leg if it's going to heal properly."

"I do not see why you are so upset," Ethis said, raising his expressionless face slightly as he crossed both sets of his arms across his chest. "Our efforts were not gaining us much success against the dragon. Closing the portal seems to have been quite effective."

"It was our only way back home!" Jugar wailed. "I would certainly beg pardon for upsetting the sensibilities of our fine ladies present . . ."

Urulani glanced around in mock surprise. Drakis allowed himself a veiled smile. The "ladies" present consisted of a traitorous House slave, a madwoman who changed her identity more often than her clothing and the warrior captain herself. The idea that the dwarf should be worried about the "finer sensibilities" of these three apparently amused Urulani.

". . . But thanks to you we are now deep in the stew, as the dwarven mothers like to say. You see those peaks to the south?"

Drakis was having a hard time seeing anything to the south or in any other direction through all the smoke and the brightness of the burning trees to the north.

"Those are the same mountains where these infernal dragons flew at us from the *north*," the dwarf continued. "We're on the other side of them."

"So you're saying that this portal *did* take us thousands of leagues out of our way?" Ethis' chimerian face betrayed nothing but Drakis detected an edge of goading in his voice.

"No, of course not," Jugar huffed, folding his thick arms across his chest. "But we *are* at least a hundred leagues farther north than where we started out the evening—and likely well over two hundred leagues north of the coast."

"So you *do* know where we are?" Drakis asked.

"I do NOT know where we are!" Jugar roared, then cried out in agony.

"You insist on getting upset like that, dwarf," Urulani said, "and you'll make that leg worse."

Jugar growled through gritted teeth, closed his eyes, and continued with all the calm he could manage. "I have a general idea where we are because of the mountains and the stars overhead . . ."

Drakis glanced up. He could not see a single star through the smoky haze.

". . . but as to the specifics of this cursed land, none of us has a worthy map by which we might guide our way. All that's left is legends and stories and that's no way to set your compass, boy. When Ethis here got it into his head to close the portal he burned our bridge behind us, so to speak."

"And you would have preferred we all be eaten, I suppose," Ethis said through a false smile.

"Dragons don't eat people!" Jugar grumbled.

"I don't know as Yithri would agree," Ethis observed coolly.

"It spit him right back out, didn't it?" Jugar yelled then sat back quickly once again as pain shot up his leg.

"Both of you just shut up," Drakis barked. His mind was still reeling from the day and this ridiculous argument was rubbing his nerves raw. "So how do we get back?"

"We don't," Urulani said as she stood up.

"We don't?"

"Well, not the way we came, anyway," Urulani sighed. "And not right away. If what the dwarf says is true—and I'll admit that is a big if—then we're weeks from getting back to where the ship is now. We'd have to cross those mountains to get there which, it seems, are filled with what I would think are very angry dragons right now. I left the ship with Ganja and Dakran. Kendai knows what happened to us and about our plan to use the fold."

"If he survived, "Ethis pointed out.

"They'll be looking for our return," Urulani corrected the chimerian. "They will wait for us."

"And just how long will they wait?" Ethis asked.

"As long as it takes," Urulani said through a tightened jaw.

"Two weeks? Three?" Ethis speculated. "We still could not reach them in such a short time."

"Then what about the portal itself?" Drakis asked. "Can't we bring it back—make it work again? I seem to remember a dwarf who has demonstrated some rather impressive powers of his own in that regard lately."

Jugar turned his head away. "It doesn't work that way, lad."

"Enlighten me," Drakis said, and his tone made it clear that this was not a request.

Jugar looked up. "There are basically two kinds of magic—Aer and Aether. Aer magic is that of nature: it comes from the ground, the rocks, the trees, the water, and the wind. It is within each of us, actually. The stories of its origins among the dwarves are some of the oldest and most fascinating tales ever told either under the mountain or above it. It all began with Thel Gorfson who . . ."

Drakis reached forward and knocked several times on the dwarf's head.

"Ouch! Well, yes, then . . . the point is that Aer magic wells up naturally from the ground. It is a relatively weak force and must be gathered to the wizard over time. The wizard's job is then to retain the Aer magic, cultivate it within himself, and add to it as time passes. Aer wizards absorb the power of the world slowly and naturally then channel that power to their wills."

"I'm guessing that's not the case with Aether magic?" Drakis replied.

"Aether magic . . ." Jugar began.

"Aether magic is a higher form of magic," Ethis answered. "It is built on the foundations of Aer magic but it uses mystic technologies—like the crystals of the Aether Wells—to pull the power of Aer out of the world rather than wait for it to come naturally. It is more powerful, more focused in some ways but also more fragile because of its dependence on physical devices. Still, that didn't stop the dwarves from dabbling in it, too, did it?"

Jugar was silent.

"That 'Heart of Aer' that you keep avoiding talking about," Ethis said, his eyes fixed on the dwarf. "The vaunted Nine Kingdoms who had built their nation on the power of Aer had come at last to dabbling in Aether, had they not?"

"The point is," Jugar said suddenly, "that I can no more activate that portal than . . . than . . ."

"Float?" Urulani suggested.

"Ye are a vicious woman, Urulani," the dwarf grumbled.

Drakis threw his hands up in disgust. "So that means we have to find another way back."

"No, what this means," Ethis responded, "is that we have to find shelter and food. That is the first priority. We have the supplies we brought with us in our packs but those were intended to last us through two or three days. With rationing we can extend that, of course, but that won't be nearly enough time to make our way back to Urulani's ship. I have never been in this territory or anything remotely like it and I doubt that any of the rest of you have either. Palm trees were new to you just a few weeks ago, Drakis. We'll never survive several weeks' march anywhere until we figure out what we can eat and drink and reasonably anticipate the dangers of the way."

"So you want us to just set up camp here and wait?" Drakis fumed. He did not trust Ethis. The blank face of the chimerian had fooled him too many times and his ability to mimic other people's forms with perfection had cost him more dearly than he cared to admit. Ethis was playing his own game, and until Drakis completely understood what that game was, he would remain on his guard against his former comrade in arms.

"I am saying that it would be better if we didn't just charge off into the brush without preparing for it," Ethis said. "You insisted on bringing both Mala and the Lyric with us on our little expedition to the God's Wall because you were so keen on proving that dragons did not exist and that you were not the fated one of the prophecies. Well, here we are, Drakis . . . the dragons most definitely *do* exist. If you have any further doubts to express then perhaps you and I can go right over there together and kick that huge dead head of that nonexistent . . ."

Ethis stopped short.

"Where is it?" Ethis said, blinking.

Drakis turned, then, without thinking, drew his sword.

"Where did it go?" Jugar breathed.

"They took it."

Everyone turned to face the Lyric.

The jaw of her thin, pale face was set, her eyes determinedly fixed on the space before the broken altar. She strode determinedly across the plaza, her body leaning forward and her arms held slightly away from her body. Drakis, Ethis, and Urulani fell in behind her.

"Who is she today?" Ethis said sotto voce toward Urulani.

"I haven't a clue," she answered back.

"Who I am is unimportant," the Lyric answered, her voice more husky than usual and her demeanor disdainful of her followers. She stopped next to the altar, pointing at the ground. "See the blood trail? They came from the edge of the stones, out of the jungle with worthy silence. They dispatched the one you called Kwarae without a sound . . ."

"Kwarae!" Urulani called out. "Where is Kwarae?"

"He was right over there," Drakis pointed toward the side of the plaza opposite the burning jungle. "He should be . . . Look!"

The massive bloody trail led directly to where Kwarae was expected to stand his watch. There was no Kwarae.

"They took the head with them," the Lyric said as she knelt next to the bloodstained swath.

Ethis drew in a deep breath, pointing with several of his hands at once. "Their footprints, Drakis. There are five toes but look how long—more like claws. And how many!"

The Lyric stood up suddenly and ran back across the plaza to where the dwarf still sat.

Drakis and Ethis were just getting back to the dwarf when they heard him cry out in pain. The Lyric had stopped only momentarily before she reached down and with unexpected strength rolled the dwarf over facedown against the ground.

"What are ye doing there, lass!" Jugar howled. "Oh, please stop! Will someone stop her?"

The Lyric placed one of her feet firmly against the dwarf's rump, then, grabbing his broken leg with both hands, she pulled it out straight. The bone set with a snapping sound, and the Lyric carefully laid the leg back flat against the ground.

"Help me turn him over!" the Lyric commanded.

Urulani and Drakis both bent down as the Lyric held the leg, rotating the dwarf onto his back.

"How are you," Drakis asked.

"Oh, you know, I'm feeling rather . . . not much . . ."

The dwarf smiled slightly and passed out.

The Lyric stood up, pointing to Urulani. "Splint that now and bind it well. Have everyone stay close, and we'll be better for keeping near the fire tonight."

"What did you see, Lyric?" Ethis asked quietly.

"They came for the meat," the Lyric said in a tone that dared anyone to contradict her. "There will be enough to keep them through the night. I do not think they will stomach daylight. If we are still here by first light, we should leave this place and go as far as we can, our broken dwarf permitting."

"Go?" Drakis was astonished. "Go where?"

"Down the ancient road," the Lyric replied as though the answer were obvious. "We must find a safe place to hide . . . a place where we can protect ourselves."

"Why?" Mala asked quietly as she, too, joined the closely gathered group.

"Because they are hunters," the Lyric replied, "like me."

CHAPTER 3

Pythar

IT WAS BARELY A ROAD. Grasses and vines choked their way across what remained of its surface, the fitted stones occasionally giving way altogether to the thick foliage. The sky was brightening with the dawn as they hurriedly picked their way between islands of fitted stone, broken pillars, and fragments of wall. The dwarf bounced along behind Ethis and Drakis as they dragged him on a litter, his loud complaints and cries ringing out with every jolt across the uneven ground.

It had been a long and difficult night, filled with noises from just beyond the edge of the great fire that the dragon's breath had ignited the evening before. None of them had slept except the Lyric—who snored quietly through the night. By the time dawn began to brighten the sky beyond the fire still burning furiously nearby, Drakis felt tired but he could still hear the words of his old commander ChuKang, urging him on . . .

"To stand still on a field of battle is to invite death to find you."

So he got everyone moving.

The Lyric bounded ahead of them, scouting their path and urging them onward. "Quickly! Daylight is short and we've a long distance to cover!"

"How does she know that? Where are we even going?" Drakis said through his hard breaths. He was sweating profusely. Never had he been in a climate where the air itself was so thick and wet.

Ethis glanced around at the thick jungle that surrounded them. "They are out there, Drakis. They're following us."

"I've seen nothing that would pass for shelter, let alone provide us any defense," Jugar said, gripping his splint to relieve the pain of the nearly constant jostling. "If they catch us in the open . . ."

"Who? If *who* catches us in the open?" Drakis snapped as he pushed through a group of ferns only to trip over a pedestal fragment hiding beneath it. "Ouch! We can't fight what we can't see—and we don't even know what we're looking for!"

"Quiet, both of you," Urulani said as she moved past them. She affected a deep calm, but her eyes were constantly shifting to peer into the long shadows of the forest around her. "You're scaring the women."

Ahead of them, the Lyric stopped at the top of a small rise in the road. She climbed up onto a pile of stones from a fallen wall and pointed, the bright salmon color of the sunrise sky casting the lithe woman in a warm glow as she gestured.

Drakis followed Urulani and Ethis as they hurried to the top of the rise. They all reached the crest of the broken road and stopped.

Drakis caught his breath.

They were looking across a narrow valley. Here, the road they had been following joined a much broader thoroughfare that time and nature had not yet so completely erased. This wide avenue ran straight across the valley to the base of a long mesa that jutted out like a gigantic ship whose stone hull was sailing through the jungle sea below. Here and there along the top of the mesa Drakis could see a finger of brilliant white pierce the sky. It appeared to have once been a tower or the alabaster walls of a building that had all but been reclaimed by the relentless growth. The vertical cliff face was draped in vines hanging from the flat top of the mesa above it, but here and there Drakis caught a tantalizing glimpse of the city that once was. Delicate towers, walls, concourses, and gateways remained visible where they had been carved into the cliff face, transforming the stone of the ridge itself into what must have been a grand and imposing mixture of art and function. Near the end of the mesa to their right, a great tower rose up from the concourses, its ornate curved walls soaring up past the top of the mesa plateau, where it appeared to be broken off.

The great avenue rose slightly near the base of the cliff, as though reaching upward toward the carved city and its tower in the cliff wall. Drakis could see that the road extended directly into the cliff, where it continued into the darkness. But the causeway that had once lifted the great road had crumbled and in so doing had opened a great gap of rubble at the base of the sheer walls.

"Look!" Urulani said as she pointed toward the base of the cliff. "Just to the left there."

Drakis squinted into the brightening daylight.

The cliff-city was isolated but not inaccessible.

There was a stairway carved into the cliff face.

"Who do you suppose is living in there now?" Ethis asked.

"Whoever is in there," Drakis answered, "cannot possibly be worse than whoever is out *here*. Let's go."

The valley was wider than they had anticipated; crossing it took most of the day. The sun had already lowered toward the horizon and was beyond the towering mesa, casting the face of the cliff and its carved city in afternoon shadow. The ruins at the base of the cliff were more extensive and difficult to pass through, the debris from the fallen walls choking the ancient streets and making their footing uncertain.

If any of them entertained thoughts of stopping, however, the shadows that moved with them, flitting from dark place to dark place in the ruins quickly changed their minds.

At last, the Lyric led them to the stair carved from the cliff itself. Clouds were gathering in the afternoon sky.

"I would not have believed it possible," Drakis said.

"Yes, it is magnificent," Ethis answered, gazing up the cliff face at the delicate relief carvings towering nearly a hundred feet over them.

"I meant I would not have believed it possible for the air to become any wetter," Drakis answered, laboriously climbing the stairs. Sweat was pouring off his face. "How did anyone ever live here?"

"You need to drink more water," Ethis said, eyeing the human critically.

"Just what I need," Drakis said with a tired laugh. "More water."

"You might be surprised," Ethis answered, "just how much water you're going to need in this climate."

The stair doubled back on itself as it climbed the cliff face, presenting a landing at each turn. Drakis was having trouble keeping up with the Lyric, who continued her climb ahead of them on the stairs, while the warrior pulled the dwarf's litter along behind him and urged Mala along before him. She had grown listless and sullen through the day, choosing not to speak. Her auburn hair was flattened by the humid air around her face and was stained dark with sweat.

Drakis glanced down over the side of the seemingly endless staircase to the valley far below. The distance gave him pause, and for a moment he thought dizziness might overcome him. It was a sheer drop down into the ruins nearly three hundred feet beneath them. From this height he could make out the old pattern of streets and alleyways that had once made up the civilization that had nestled against this mountain but which was defined now only by the crumbling foundations and, Drakis guessed, not even that after a few more short decades.

At last the stairs ended in a wide landing on the first concourse.

"Never before to my eyes," Urulani breathed in awestruck wonder.

The wide concourse led to delicately carved walls of buildings— each one from the same stone but unique in expression and design—a patchwork of individuality in art that rose a hundred feet above them. The entire structure was a melding of the natural cavern and the opulent architecture of its former inhabitants. A colonnade of pillars ran across the face of the cavern opening, supporting a second concourse overhead. Two of the pillars were broken and had toppled onto the wide concourse but those that remained were exquisite in the carvings of human faces mixed with those of dragonlike features. Each face was different from the next as were the animal depictions, some of which were strange and unknown to Drakis' eye.

Drakis turned back to gaze at the ornate wall of building carvings. Doorways and windows in the structures were largely unobstructed—

the wood that once fitted their doorframes or windowpanes having rotted away and vanished, leaving only faint marks in the stone to show that woodworking had been here at all.

"This will do well for us," Ethis said to Drakis, nodding with approval as he gestured with two of his four hands. "I'll search some of these ruins to make sure they're cleared of any troublesome inhabitants and find us a defensible position. Then we can concern ourselves with food and water."

"Very well," Drakis answered. "Urulani?"

Urulani stood staring at the base of one of the pillars, transfixed by the many faces, each with different aspects and expressions, that seemed to be staring back at her with their stone eyes.

"Urulani?" Drakis asked again.

The raider captain shook herself. "Yes! What is it?"

"We need to set a watch," Drakis said, walking over to her.

"Watch?"

"Yes," Drakis insisted. "Someone to watch the stairs to make sure that no one follows us here and another to . . . is there something wrong?"

"No!" Urulani said at once as her eyes suddenly focused on Drakis. "I'll take the first watch. Set the dwarf over here while I keep an eye on those stairs."

"Will someone get me off of this horrible contraption!" Jugar howled. "Bad enough that I should be dragged through the forest like a fireplace log, but to be tied to this . . . this *thing*! It is too much of an indignity to be borne by man or dwarf!"

"Relax, Jugar," Drakis said, wiping his brow as he knelt to undo the straps securing the dwarf to the litter. "You're not going anywhere for a while without considerable help on our part, so you might as well get used to being polite."

"Polite, is it?" Jugar sniffed. "Dragged into the wilderness of a forsaken land because some Ephindrian jelly-man had to shut the door on our only way back home! Having a dragon's head fall on me and who nearly *ate* me *after* he was dead! Considering the events of the day, I believe I have been the very epitome of polite!"

Drakis chuckled to himself, then shook his head. "Well, perhaps you might extend your famous patience a bit longer and help us. We can hardly know where we're going until we're sure of where we are now."

"Well, it's written right in front of you!" the dwarf groused.

"What is he talking about?" Urulani asked.

"Those columns," the dwarf yelled, pointing with his broad, right hand. "Those aren't just pretty carvings, you know! It's the ancient script, used from before the Shadow Wars in the time of the Age of Mists. That was after Drakis Aerweaver—the first Drakis, mind you—fought the dragon Kopsis south of the God's Wall Mountains and created the Desolation of the Sand Sea. That was nearly two thousand years before . . ."

Drakis held up his hand to stop the dwarf's mouth.

"Just tell us what it says," Drakis demanded.

"Reduced to reading for the illiterate, eh? Fine!" Jugar flushed red but held his temper. He turned toward the pillar and pointed again. "This says, 'Hekrian, Seer of our Goddess Quabet, bids all seekers . . .' or, maybe that's sojourners '. . . welcome to the peace and beauty of Pythar—City of Unification.' Then there's some religious nonsense about 'seeking the higher way,' and finding 'peace in the one.' I like the way it finishes, however. Right here it reads, 'Behold the eternal might and glory of Armethia, where man and dragon rule as one in their terrible might and justice.'

"Witness my polite compliance." Jugar gestured around him as he gazed on the ruins, "as I behold the eternal might and glory of humanity and the dragons that protected them so well."

"I am looking, dwarf," whispered Urulani, her gaze following the ornate column upward and then out over the ruins of the city now so much more evident below them. "I had never supposed that we were once so great a people."

"Once, perhaps," Jugar replied. "But no more."

"But we could be again," Urulani said with sudden conviction as she turned toward Drakis. "The prophecies! I had not believed . . . had not *dared* to believe that they could have been true. Yet here I stand in the land of legend, my hand touching the lost glories of our past and looking at the man who could make all of those things once lost come to be once more!"

Drakis groaned, shaking his head. "Not you, too?"

"You could be this man, Drakis," Urulani said, stepping toward him with conviction. "I do not know of any gods but I do see what is around me. The legends told of this place, and here it is. Those same legends spoke of a man named 'Drakis,' and here you stand!"

"Here I stand?" Drakis said in astonishment. "I stand here because our choices were to either retreat through a fold portal or die. How can you, of all people, believe what this dwarf has been selling?"

"How can I not believe it?" Urulani said, her voice rising with her temper. "All the signs of the legend being fulfilled . . ."

"Make any prophecy vague enough and it's bound to be fulfilled in someone's eyes," Drakis countered.

"But that same prophecy is found everywhere in the southern lands," Urulani said fervently, conviction growing in her as she spoke. "From farthest Exylia to the Straits of Erebus, from the shores of the Lyrac Ocean in eastern Ephindria to the rocky coasts of Mestophia on the Charos Ocean, the story is told of the coming of Drakis and the rise of a new day of freedom, peace, and justice."

"Everyone wants to make me into this marvelous godlike hero who will come riding out of legend and save them. But no matter how hard they try—no matter how hard they believe, Urulani—I'm still just *me*. I'm just a slave who happened to be named Drakis and got mistaken for someone important."

"No," Urulani shook her head. "I was there. The Iblisi came for you—slaughtered entire villages to find you—they came because you *are* that Drakis, and above all they fear you."

"No, Urulani," Drakis said quietly. "They came after me because they made a mistake. Now that we are so far from them, I don't think any of them cares what happens to us or even knows we're gone."

CHAPTER 4

Proper Orders

RHONAS CHAS WAS THE ETERNAL CITY of the Rhonas elves and the very life's-heart of the Rhonas Empire . . .

. . . And Sjei-Shurian of the Order of the Modalis was determined to make sure it stayed that way.

He stood before an awning-covered stand in the *Paz Rhambutai*—the Plaza of Sweetness—in the eastern section of the Old City and surveyed the ordered patterns of various colored fruits with an indifferent eye. Sjei was an elf of such common features as to defy description. His head was elongated as was common with his race but not so elegantly formed as might call attention to it. His nose was hooked but not so sharply as might be thought attractive to his kind. His eyes were black, but the shape of his drooping eyelids shuttered them and made them unremarkable. The tips of his pointed ears dropped slightly, and his mouth was small, hiding the worn tips of his pointed teeth. He was neither fat nor thin . . . tall nor short for his kind. His single distinguishing mark was a scar that cut through his right eyebrow, yet even this noble mark was so small as to be barely noticeable unless one were looking for it. His robes denoted that he was of the Order of Vash but the commendations, ribbons, and medals it sported were absent any of the more spectacular awards. Those he eschewed in favor of the more common types that dealt largely with mundane achievements. In all, Sjei had the most remarkably unremarkable appearance imaginable in an elf of one of the military orders; someone who would easily be mistaken for one who had never drawn a weapon in all his years of service.

Any elf on the streets of Rhonas—as happened commonly every day—would forget his face within three steps of passing and never give him another thought.

And yet, next to the Emperor, he knew himself to be the most powerful elf in the entire Imperial City—and by logical inference, in the entire world beyond. Sjei-Shurian was the *Ghenetar Omris* over the Order of Vash. This post as the "general of unity" over one of the three warrior orders of the Empire would have been enough to have secured his place of power within the treacherous and ever shifting landscape of Rhonas Imperial politics but he was also Master of House Shurian. He was, in addition, a member of the most elite of all elven Orders, the Modalis.

The Modalis was, so far as its public face was concerned, a largely philanthropic organization with impressive public holdings north of the Old Keep of the Iblisi and well situated inside Tsujen's Wall east of the Mnera Gate. Nearly everyone in the city knew that there was far more to it than that, but it was a pleasant fiction that all the Rhonas elves found advantageous to maintain as the truth even without the encouragement of the Iblisi. The true center of the Modalis lay in the rather unpretentious and otherwise unmarked building just behind Sjei on the eastern side of the *Paz Rhambutai* northeast of "The Ministries" and situated nearly equidistant from every other Order, Forum, Guild, and Ministry that struggled for dominance in the Imperial City. It was known simply as "Majority House" which was something of an irony considering the elite and exclusive nature of its occasional occupants.

Sjei, after considerable deliberation, picked out an apple from the cart and paid the groveling Fifth Estate market vendor with carefully and precisely measured coins. He then turned, holding the apple gingerly in his left hand as he looked across the square to the building occupying his thoughts.

He smiled slightly, baring a minimum of his teeth. He felt a kinship with Majority House. It, too, was unassuming in the extreme if one might be forgiven for describing mediocrity in imperative terms.

The subatria was narrow and high, appearing to be almost hidden behind flanks of vertical shops and market stalls in the plaza. That those shops were either owned or controlled by the Modalis was an open secret, and the height of the walls and location of the shops were a part of a carefully orchestrated design for its defense and safe-keeping. The avatria floating above it was small and unassuming, dwarfed in comparison to the monumental extravagances of the surrounding houses, each of which vied for supremacy of ostentation. That was also to Sjei's liking: the idea of hiding in plain sight appealed to him.

Sjei lifted the apple and sank his teeth into its crisp flesh, pulling it away with a satisfying snapping sound. The plaza was filled with elves moving in the labyrinthine spaces between the stalls of the market. A cross section of the Empire was well represented there: First Estate Imperators anxious to get through the crowds and on with their business in The Ministries; Second Estate masters and mistresses of the Aether simply taking from rather than bargaining with the Fourth Estate vendors who were dependent upon their magic to maintain the yield of their client Fifth Estate farms; Third Estate noblewomen on their shopping expeditions with their slaves and guardians in tow . . . all these moved through the plaza with their eyes casting about or staring at their feet. Not one of them gave so much as a casual glance upward toward the unassuming building that held their fate within its common-looking walls.

Sjei tore another large bite from the apple, his grin allowing some of the juice to run down the side of his chin. He was more than a member of the Modalis; he was the *Sinechai*, the Quartermaster whose charge was to conduct the meetings of the Modalis. Some had more rank and some had more seniority in the House Forum, but he alone controlled the agenda of those meetings, steering the discussion in the direction he felt necessary. It was a power that required finesse and a subtle touch. It also was a power that was best used sparingly, tactically, and emphatically.

Today, he knew, was a day when all his skills would be required. Playing the Modalis council members was a dangerous game with stakes deadly high, swift, and permanent. Still, one didn't begin with the Modalis unless one was sure all his pieces were in place and that all the dice were covered.

Besides, he loved a good game.

"Kyori-Xiuchi," Sjei said with quiet dignity. "You have summoned this assembly. It is for you to state your cause."

In truth, Sjei had exerted considerable effort in influencing Kyori into calling this gathering. He could only hope the doddering old patriarch of the Occuran would actually remember the reason he had been given for summoning everyone to the Modalis forum.

Smoke from the incense braziers drifted through the large room. To Sjei, the smell was cloying, but it seemed to please Liau Nyenjei, the Minister of Thought, who was very much enamored with such recent fads. The walls were partially hidden behind layers of shadow and smoke. Only a single shaft of light from the open circle in the apex of the domed ceiling illuminated the center of the room. The elven figures sat in their appointed chairs facing toward one another just within the shadows around the bright center of the floor—as they each did in their dealings as the Modalis.

Kyori stood very slowly.

Play your part, you old fool, Sjei thought.

"A most troubling report has reached the Occuran regarding the Western Provinces," Kyori began. "It seems that there has been a disruption of the Aether Wells across most of the province. Several Houses fell completely, their magic failing and their Impress slaves released from the bondage of the House Altars."

A low murmur rumbled through the forum space from the other Modalis masters.

"As control and trade of the Aether is the lifeblood of our Order, this constitutes a threat to the Modalis as well as the Empire at large—making our interests allied with the Imperial Will. I therefore forward the discussion and resolution of this matter before the assembled . . ."

"I beg a question."

Sjei frowned. It was Wejon Rei, the Fifth High Priest of the Myrdin-dai and councillor to Master K'chok Valerisom, the Grand Master of their Order. He was a stooped, round-shouldered elf, shorter than most, who had an unfortunate tendency to interrupt others with what he believed were more important or pertinent thoughts of his own. His voice, however, was like honey: smooth, rich, inviting, and occasionally overpowering. It did not help that the Myrdin-dai were still basking in the favor of the Emperor, as Wejon seemed talented at keeping his particular brand of sunshine blinding the members of the Imperial Court. The darker truths of the disaster in the Western Provinces were still effectively hidden from the Emperor's eyes. So Wejon could afford to interrupt the senior Kyori of his rival Order without fear of reprisal for the time being.

If Wejon had no fear of the Occuran, then he certainly had no fear of opposing Sjei.

"The Myrdin-dai have already addressed this matter," Wejon said with smiling condescension. "We were first aware of this incident in the Provinces and our illustrious Grand Master Valerisom took decisive action that should serve our interests. Our Iblisi brothers . . ."

Sjei could feel Kyori stiffen. The Iblisi were allied with Kyori's own Order. Wejon was rubbing the aging patriarch's face in the recent changes of favor at court.

". . . investigated the matter at our request and have since provided us a most satisfactory report in all its particulars. The reports of trouble in the Provinces have been greatly exaggerated and the problem has been fully contained through the mutual efforts of the Myrdin-dai and the Iblisi. I put forward the dismissal of this discussion and the adjournment of this forum."

Wejon turned toward Sjei, flashing a syrupy smile as he bowed.

Kyori glared at the short elf opposite him.

"I am compelled to remind our brother Wejon Rei," Sjei said with a courteous nod of his own, "that no member of the forum may put forward either discussion or action before the assembly when begging a question."

Wejon's smile dimmed even as his eyes brightened.

"Our brother Kyori holds the attention of this forum still and . . ."

"Then I would urge this forum," Wejon's voice cut across the hall, "to reject my brother's suggestion that the great members of the Modalis should concern themselves with a matter that has already been resolved!"

Sjei's eyes narrowed. The Myrdin-dai must be very sure of themselves if Wejon thinks he can interrupt the Sinechai of the Modalis. *You're getting careless,* Sjei thought. *It will cost you dearly.*

"I beg a question!"

Sjei turned toward the high, nasal voice two seats to his left.

"Your question, Brother Liau?" Sjei said, turning away from Wejon. Liau Nyenjei was the Director of the Ministry of Thought and, ironically, rather slow-witted on his own but his timing was impeccable.

"Unlike our brother," Liau tossed a sneering nod in the direction of Wejon, "I actually *do* have a question. Is there any evidence of what actually happened out in the Provinces? All due respect to our brother and the incomparable thoroughness of the Iblisi, the failure of Aether Wells over such a wide area as we have come to understand warrants more consideration than vague and simple assurances from our brother Myrdin-dai . . ."

Wejon jumped to his feet, his black eyes flashing in the column of light striking down from above. "Does our brother insult me thus? Am I to endure this outrage without the satisfaction of his blood?"

Liau did not move from his chair but only turned his head slightly in the direction of Wejon. "No matter how strong the wind, the stars remain fixed. Blow all you like, Wejon, but it is unbiased confirmation that we lack."

Wejon reached for the handle of his sword.

"If the assembly will indulge me . . . I have evidence to present in the matter."

Sjei turned his solid-black eyes languorously toward Ch'dak Vaijan. He was the Imperial Emissary from the Ministry of Law—a middle-level position, but his family's influence was beyond reproach. He was the one member of the Modalis that everyone in the forum knew to be beyond influence.

He was the first elf Sjei had learned to manipulate.

"Will Kyori yield the forum for evidence?" Sjei asked the elder Occuran who was still standing, waiting to present the rest of his motion.

"For evidence," Kyori said carefully.

Sjei nodded then turned back to Ch'dak. "The forum is yielded to Ch'dak Vaijan for evidence."

"What is the nature of this so-called 'evidence'?" Wejon hissed through his bared, sharpened teeth.

Ch'dak stood and stepped into the light in the center of the forum. "The best evidence. I have a witness."

"A witness?" Wejon mocked. "What witness could you possibly present?"

"One who was there at the very heart of what happened," Ch'dak continued. He lifted his hand, gesturing to the guardians at either side of the forum doors. "One who can tell us who is responsible for what we believe to be the worst disaster to befall our Empire in over a hundred years. One who comes to warn us of even greater disasters to be visited upon our Empire unless we act quickly and decisively. One who can tell us the truth of who is responsible . . . and help us to know what must be done to stop them. Hear her now!"

The doors at the end of the hall opened and a thin elven figure with a bowed head walked into the forum. It was a female elf, young by the look of her build, but her face was careworn. She lifted her head as she stopped in the center of the circle of light.

"I am Tsi-Shebin, daughter of Sha-Timuran of the fallen House of Timuran," the young girl said, her voice clear and her black eyes shining in the light. "I was there."

Chapter 5

Mutual Interests

SHE WORE THE SAME STAINED and tattered dress that she had been discovered in amid the ruins of her household. Some of the rips in the cloth seemed a bit too strategically located to have occurred entirely by accident, showing off her young figure to better advantage. *She put them there herself,* Sjei thought. *And the stains are still in the cloth. Surely the brothers of the council are not so gullible as to think she's worn this same dress for the last two months since her House fell. Her face is even smudged! Still, it is an excellent bit of theater . . . and just look at them; she's got their sympathies already.*

Ch'dak stepped to the edge of the light, his features cast in stark relief. His voice was firm but had a soft edge to it. "Tell us, child, what happened to you in the Western Provinces."

Tsi-Shebin raised her head, lifting her chin with seemingly enormous effort. "My father took us some years ago to establish our House in the Western Provinces. He was a devout citizen of Rhonas. We moved there so that my father might better serve the Emperor's Will."

Sjei smiled inwardly. *Everyone who knew him reported that Sha-Timuran was a crass, opportunistic fool with a violent temper and delusions of grandeur far above his Estate. He was generally despised at court and only moved to the frontier when no other form of easier social advance was available to him.*

Ch'dak continued. "And where do you reside now?"

Sjei glanced at Ch'dak with a slight frown. The answer to that question might prove awkward to the Quartermaster.

"I am currently living off the graces of my remaining relatives here in town. My home is gone, our estate is in ruins, and I have lost everything in the fall of my father's House from the wanton and utter destruction of our Aether Well."

Sjei raised an eyebrow, drawing in a relieved breath. Shebin had not only avoided divulging her living arrangements but had brought old Ch'dak back to the point of the performance. This young girl was proving more adept at this game than he had hoped. In the next moment he realized that he would have to reevaluate her strengths in this regard—and take care to never underestimate her again.

Ch'dak nodded at the response. "And you were there when your House fell?"

"Yes, my lord," Shebin's whisper carried clearly throughout the hall.

"Then tell us what happened," Ch'dak spoke gently.

Shebin raised her eyes toward Ch'dak but seemed not to see him as she spoke in flat, distant tones. "It was during our evening Devotions. Father had heard the report from a few of his returning Centurai warriors early that afternoon in his court. They were the first to return from the Dwarven Wars and had been expected as their trophies from the war had arrived earlier in the day. Father was angry with the Captain of the First Octia because he had lost the great prize in the final battle and had only returned with meager and unimportant dwarven trifles . . ." Shebin's voice trailed off to nothing.

"You say this warrior had lost a prize?" Ch'dak prompted.

"Yes," Shebin said, gaining her voice once more. "The warrior had reached the Crown of the Last Dwarven King and held it in his hands. Then he had thrown it away."

"Thrown it away?" Arikasi Tjen-soi chuckled loudly. Arikasi was the Minister of Occupation whose concerns largely touched on any of the conquered lands beyond the traditional borders of Rhonas. Once, many years before, he had been a warrior subjugating those lands—now, by the look of his growing midsection, he preferred to administer them from a distance. The fall of Aether Wells in the Western

Provinces was of peripheral interest to Arikasi who preferred distant maps to nearer territories. The conquest of the Ninth Dwarven Throne and its associated crown, however, was firmly within his purview and seemed to awaken him. "You are mistaken, child. That crown was the expressed objective of the campaign, burned into the Devotions of every Impress Warrior taking the field that day. None would have been capable of doing such a thing."

"My father believed that it happened," Shebin replied, lifting her chin with just the right mixture of pride and hurt in her expression. "The other warriors who were with him confirmed it . . . and I heard it from his own lips."

"But why?" Arikasi pressed. "Why would a slave so willfully break the bounds of his Devotions?"

Sjei frowned. Arikasi was derailing Shebin's narrative with unnecessary issues. The Sinechai leaned forward, opening his mouth to speak.

"I cannot say, Master," Shebin responded. "Perhaps it was his first willful act of rebellion . . . the moment when the Captain of the First Octian conceived the tragedy that destroyed my home, saw my father torn limb from limb and my mother's charred remains impaled atop the ruins of our subatria wall with a spear."

Sjei leaned back slowly. Shebin was good indeed. In a stroke she had both answered Arikasi's question and put him back on the point of this entire performance.

"Go on, child," Kyori urged quietly into the short silence that followed. "Tell us what happened."

"It was during evening Devotions," Shebin said quietly. "All of the household and most of the slaves had already received their Devotions. We were all in the garden courtyard. I was down near the center next to the House Altar with Father and Mother—just next to the Aether Well. We heard sounds—shouts and screaming, I think—from the edge of the courtyard. I looked up with alarm and saw one of the slaves—that same Captain of the First Octian—brandishing a sword and threatening my mother and me."

Sjei glanced around at his fellow members on the council. There were conflicting accounts as to exactly what happened in the Timuran House courtyard that night and not one of them corroborated the story Shebin told. It did not matter what the facts were—what would the council believe? Did Shebin's story go too far?

Not even Wejon challenged her.

"The House Guards approached him at once, and my father rushed to help them but it was too late," Shebin continued. "Drakis turned toward the Aether Well . . ."

"Drakis?" Arikasi asked. "Who's Drakis?"

"The Captain of the First Octian, Master . . . the human warrior-slave," Shebin replied. "He turned toward the Aether Well, held out his free hand, and then there was a terrible bright flash of light and the sound of a thousand thunders. Pieces of the Aether Well flew . . ."

"Pieces?" Kyori exclaimed.

"Yes, Master," Shebin shook visibly as she spoke. "It shattered—like dropped glass—its pieces falling like bright rain all about the courtyard.

Ch'dak turned to speak to the Modalis. "The Well not only was broken but exploded. I have seen the reports from the Iblisi Quorum who investigated. An Inquisitor by the name of Soen Tjen-rei reported that there were no pieces of the Aether Well remaining that were much larger than a finger of his hand. It was this event that caused Wells all across the Western Provinces to fail in turn. It was only by fortune that these cascading failures did not reach Rhonas itself."

A murmur rose in the hall at this statement. Sjei raised his hand. "Brothers! Order! Let us proceed."

Ch'dak turned back to face Shebin. "What happened next, child?"

Shebin's lips began to quiver, her black eyes shining under the light from above. "The . . . the slaves all went mad. It was like Drakis had cast a horrible spell upon them all. They began raving . . . murdering . . . they wouldn't stop. The . . . the avatria started to fall and our Tribune Se'Djinka pulled me out from under it. I saw my father. He was fighting with his sword, but there were so many! I couldn't see my mother at all. The slaves tore at me, tried to pull me among them, but Se'Djinka kept them away . . ."

"Who is this Se'Djinka?" Arikasi blurted, trying to follow the narrative.

"The House Tribune," Ch'dak offered. "He commanded the Timuran Centurai at the Battle of the Ninth Throne."

"Wasn't there a Ghenetar by that name?" Arikasi mused. "Fought in the Benis Isles campaign years ago."

"I believe your memory serves you too well," Sjei said quietly. "It is the same elven general but some history is best forgotten. Please, Tsi-Shebin Timuran, continue: what did Se'Djinka do?"

"He pushed me back toward the Hall of the Past. The avatria crashed down into the garden and fell over. It crushed so many . . . He pushed me into a hidden room . . . a room I'd never seen before . . . and told me to stay there until he came for me . . . Until he came for me . . ."

Shebin's voice trailed off, her eyes unfocused.

Ch'dak nodded. "How long were you there?"

Shebin's mind seemed to have taken her to a place far removed from the chambers of the Modalis. "The sounds were so chilling . . . the screams went on and on . . ."

Ch'dak tried again. "Shebin, how long were you there."

"What did you . . . what?" The young elf girl blinked, trying to focus.

Ch'dak drew in a long breath between his sharp teeth.

"He found me, you know," Shebin suddenly whispered across the silence with just enough strength to be heard clearly throughout the hall. "With the house burning and my parents dying somewhere out in the ruins—he found me in that filthy little room. The Aether was gone. I . . . I had no magic to defend myself and there he was coming toward me with that . . . that terrible grin on his face! I tried . . . but he was a warrior . . . a warrior, you see . . . and he kept touching me and pulling at my dress . . ."

Ch'dak looked away from her.

Sjei did not move. He knew this part was an outrageous twisting of the truth, but he could read the faces of his fellow council members. *We've got them,* he thought.

"My dress," Shebin murmured, fingering the tears in the cloth. "It used to be so beautiful . . . and he had to ruin it all."

"Who?" Ch'dak said as if on cue. "The slave who did this, who was it?"

"Drakis," Shebin said through stuttering breaths. "The human slave named Drakis."

"Thank you, Tsi-Shebin Timuran," Ch'dak said in quiet respect. "We hear your words and shall deliberate on your justice."

Shebin nodded hesitantly and then walked quietly from the room, her head bowed. The dark doors closed quietly behind her.

Wejon barely waited for the sound of the latch before his voice filled the hall. "What is all this to us? There is nothing new in this report that was not known to us."

"To what are you referring, Wejon," Liau observed coolly, 'that all the Aether Wells collapsed at once in the Western Provinces or that it was all caused by this one human named Drakis?"

"It's one escaped slave!" Wejon squealed, his voice echoing in the hall. "That House Timuran fell is a tragedy. I feel nothing but the deepest of sympathies for this unfortunate young woman who has stood before us. Sad, indeed, is her tale. More tragic still are the hundreds perhaps thousands of others who did *not* survive this unfortunate accident to come and tell their tales to us as well . . . but we are still talking about a single, unimportant slave!"

"A slave who caused the fall of all the Western Wells," Liau replied with, for the first time in Sjei's memory, an edge of anger in his voice. "The power of the Aether is what supports the very foundations of this entire Empire. We maintain control of our slaves by it. We command our armies through it. All trade is built upon it. Our lives are sustained by it. Our very walls are supported with it. Your own Order's *only* purpose in existence is the distribution of this power and your enrichment through it yet when all of this was shaken by the hand of a single slave, you consider him 'unimportant'?"

Wejon bristled once more. "It was not *our* Wells that failed, but those of our Occuran brothers. Is it our fault that their poor craft left the Western Provinces in such a state that their Wells threatened the Empire itself?"

Kyori's hands gripped the rests of his chair until all color had left them, but a single warning look from Sjei kept him in his place.

"No," answered Kyori with barely restrained fury. "But it seems that the efficient auspices of the Myrdin-dai managed to facilitate this 'unimportant' slave's escape."

"It is a lie!"

"I have seen this same report from the Iblisi, my brother Ch'dak," Kyori said in even tones. The Occuran could smell Wejon's panic at being cornered. "It further states that this 'unimportant' slave Drakis used the Myrdin-dai folds to escape northward and beyond."

"But is this not what your friends the Iblisi do . . . capture escaped slaves?" Wejon snapped. "If they had escaped into the northern lands, then it was the Iblisi's responsibility to retake them."

"And so they tried," Ch'dak said.

"Tried?" Liau asked.

"This same Soen Tjen-rei . . . this Iblisi Inquisitor whose report has been quoted . . . left to do exactly that several weeks ago," Ch'dak said, shifting his gaze to the elf from the Ministry of Occupation. "Arikasi, you remember Soen . . . he was the Iblisi representative at court at the time."

Arikasi considered for a moment behind a frown. "Yes, I remember him. Unpleasant and always moving about."

"That's him," Ch'dak continued. "His reports refer to an ancient prophesy about a human named Drakis and how he would return to oppose the Empire. It's all nonsense, of course, but a large number of the Sixth Estate believe in it. They are all looking for some prophet to save them. Shortly after studying these prophesies, Soen went north to hunt down those slaves—and was followed immediately by a full Quorum of Iblisi who had orders to kill him."

Sjei raised his eyebrows slightly. This was something he had not known—and he hated surprises. They always had a tendency to bite you when you were not looking.

"Not only did this Drakis escape again but Soen has vanished as well,' Ch'dak continued. "The Iblisi believe that Soen may have joined this Drakis. They have secured an Imperial Edict for his execution although from what I understand of this elf, asking for his death will be far easier than obtaining it. They're looking for both this Prophet and Soen now and appear to be going to great lengths to find each, but so far without success."

Sjei turned to the Minister of Occupation. "Have you heard anything from the northern marches about either of these persons?"

"Wait a moment," Arikasi said. "Someone said something just the other day . . ."

Come on, you used-up old fool, Sjei thought. *Make the connection!*

"A Prophet! I remember!" Arikasi exclaimed. "A trader working the Northmarch Folds told the Paktan guildmasters that there were mass migrations in the north . . . entire villages of Sixth Estate races just picking up and leaving. Everyone was moving past the Shadow Coast up toward Nordesia. Something about a gathering to a prophet who would free the slaves."

Liau breathed out a sigh. "It's Drakis . . . all those migrations . . . he's raising an army in Nordesia."

Arikasi suddenly sat forward. "Rebellion? In Nordesia? It must be put down at once!"

The Modalis all turned to Sjei.

"What should be done?" Kyori asked the Sinechai.

Sjei had engineered this moment and, despite a few unexpected bumps along the way, he had never doubted it would come.

"If it is the will of the Modalis," he said with practiced modesty, "I believe I know what to do . . ."

CHAPTER 6

The Victim

THE SMALL SIZE OF THE ELVEN COURTYARD was more than compensated for by the elegance of its execution. Graceful curves formed the three walls around the central space, beautiful sweeping lines that spread like beckoning arms to the weaving, broad lattice-work of pale pink that held the carefully beveled panes of glass rising from the floor to arch overhead. The glass was imbued with Aether, making each pane completely transparent from inside the courtyard looking out. When viewed from the outside, however, the panes perfectly matched the opaque, dull white pattern design that formed the peak of the understated avatria above "Majority House." The avatria rotated specifically to the whim of the current occupant, allowing just the right amount of brightness by day to come into the central space and the perfect view of the streets and lights of Rhonas Chas at night. Raised gardens were set with exquisite taste in elegant harmony, their flowers, herbs, and greenery in delicate and perpetual balance. It was a study in peace and tranquility, spotless and perfect.

It was a wonderful illusion, Sjei thought as he stepped into the garden. One could stand here in relaxed serenity and not suspect that this place had seen more violence, blood, and death than any other rooms combined in all the Rhonas Empire. Where better to do away with one's problems than with a quick blade in a place that no one knows exists at all? All that is left is cleaning up the mess . . . and cleaning up messes was one of the things that Sjei did best.

Looking at the lithe figure standing like another statue in the garden, Sjei actually hoped that it would not come to that most final of conclusions in this case. She was young, to be sure, but she had a fine, narrow frame and long hands. The taper of the back of her head was extremely becoming and her silver-white hair—earlier fallen around her shoulders in dirty strands—was now washed, soft and pinned up over the bald area of her crown. The hair exposed her elegantly pointed ears and framed her angular, pinched face perfectly. Her white silk gown had a neckline that plunged between her small breasts down to the clasp belt at her waist, exposing the bony ridges of her chest. She was striking, Sjei thought, and as cold as the stone under her bare feet.

"Is it done?" she said.

"Yes, it is done," answered Sjei, removing his outer mantle and folding it over his arm. "All the pieces are in play, Shebin, and they are all moving in the same direction."

Tsi-Shebin Timuran turned only slightly toward the Ghenetar Omris. "That should please you."

"That should please us both," Sjei said lightly. "The Modalis exists for profit . . . but won't mind investing a bit in you as fair exchange for your help."

"So you have your war, then?" Shebin said with her featureless black gaze fixed on the view of the Imperial City spread beneath her.

"Yes, thanks to your most convincing performance," Sjei sat down on the edge of one of the raised gardens. The flowers recoiled slightly from him, but he was used to the reaction after so many years. "A nice private little war without a lot of Imperial fuss and division of the spoils. You have provided us with a sufficiently frightening specter in this Drakis character to provide me the excuse I needed. Arikasi will make sure that what we're doing in Nordesia remains quiet until we have succeeded. Ch'dak will keep the courts out of it, and Liau will manage what everyone hears and thinks. Kyori and Wejon are so worried about each other that they will provide us all the power we need to support the army. In the end, the story will be that the warriors of the Blade of the Northern Will were dispatched to the Northmarch

Folds for training, discovered a seditious army formed in rebellion against the Imperial Will by a runaway slave named Drakis, and pursued it until it was crushed—conquering considerable northern territories as part of their prize."

"And Drakis?"

"He's nothing," Sjei shrugged.

"No, Sjei," Shebin's head swung sharply around, her black eyes fixed on the Ghenetar Omris. "He is everything. He *is* our bargain. I gave you the excuse to search for him and start your little war. You will deliver him to me."

Sjei stood slowly, allowing time to let the urge to strangle her slip from him. He might yet need her to justify the war before the Emperor. Still, he was not used to being told what to do by any citizen of lesser class, no matter how beautiful or cunning they might be. "Why do you want this one human slave so badly? I could go out in the streets right now and buy you half a dozen human males—each one named Drakis. Indeed, I think I'd be hard-pressed to find a human male *not* going by that name."

"No, it is *this* Drakis who must be found and brought back to me," she said, her eyes unblinking. "He is to be brought before me whole and unharmed."

"Why?" Sjei asked in an easy voice.

Shebin turned once more to look out the window. "He owes me something . . . and I will have it from him."

"I don't suppose you have any suggestions as to just how we might find this one and only Drakis human in all the northern lands?"

"You said there were Sixth Estate trash gathering toward this 'prophet' in Nordesia," Shebin answered. "Follow them!"

"That was information I should not have told you and which you had best keep to yourself . . ."

"Then find Soen!"

"Soen? The Iblisi Inquisitor that's disappeared? You must be joking!"

"He was tracking him before, and for all we know he still is," Shebin continued. "I met him, you know. He was the one who found me in . . ."

Shebin's voice caught slightly before she continued.

". . . He led the Quorum that found me. If the Iblisi are hunting him, then it's because of Drakis. On the other hand, if Soen has joined Drakis, then he'll be near him. Either way, if anyone knows where Drakis is, this Soen will."

Sjei shook his head, his lips curled back around his sharp teeth. "I'd think it easier to find your human slave with a blind-and-deaf dwarf than to find an Inquisitor who doesn't want to be found. He'll be a shadow."

"He'll be a shadow being chased by shadows," Shebin replied. "The Iblisi won't give up their hunt for him. I would think they could tell you where they're looking. That would be a start."

Sjei nodded. "That is true . . . at that point it would be better for Soen to find us than for us to find him. If he is looking for Drakis, perhaps I could arrange a little detour for our friend Soen . . . allow him to cross our trail so that we might find his?"

Shebin's face and posture suddenly changed. The chill that Sjei had felt from her evaporated into a stunning smile and bright, shining black eyes. Her rigid frame dissolved into the soft curve of an easy stance, shifting the folds of her gown in a way that made her stunningly pretty all at once. It was startling to see the cold and calculating Shebin transform in a moment into a warm, endearing young elven woman.

Sjei felt a strong shiver go through him. He had fought in countless wars and seen unspeakable horrors, but nothing had shaken him quite this way.

"Oh, my dear Sjei," Shebin cooed. "I know you can do it. You *are* the Modalis and I'm here to help you. I'll be anything you need me to be—anything at all. If you want me to be the poor, helpless elven maiden savaged by the brutal slave . . . well you've already seen how good I can be in that role! If you want me to be the strong, defiant elven woman in search of justice for her wronged family and their honor; why, I can do that, too. How about a warrior woman? Would you like that as well?"

Shebin stepped softly over toward Sjei, her hands reaching up and resting on the front of his tunic.

"Who are you, Shebin?" Sjei asked quietly.

"I am whoever I choose to be," Shebin smiled, the lids of her eyes closing and opening with languid motion. "And I choose to be more than I am."

"Higher Estate, perhaps?" Sjei offered.

"Oh, certainly," Shebin purred.

"Power and wealth restored," Sjei continued.

"Oh, no," Shebin smiled. "I wouldn't settle for some Provincial House on the frontier. No, I have more in mind."

"Indeed," Sjei said. He suddenly reached up and gripped both her thin wrists so strongly that she yelped slightly. "And just what did you have in mind?"

"Bring me this Drakis," Shebin hissed through her sharp teeth, "and I think I can give you the Emperor's Throne."

Sjei looked down into the young woman's face. "You shouldn't speak such things . . . not even here."

Shebin eyed the various rooms branching off from the courtyard that formed the suite. "If not here, then where do you have in mind?"

Sjei slowly pushed her away. "Aren't you a little young for that sort of play?"

"Maybe I'm older than you think," Shebin smiled.

"Maybe I'm smarter than I look," Sjei smiled back. "This Drakis didn't assault you after the avatria fell. I read Soen's report—the real one and it cost me dearly to get it out of the Lyceum. Se'Djinka's body was slumped in front of the door when he found you. I very much doubt that he ravaged you and then took the time in a burning and collapsing building to carefully prop a corpse up just to confuse me."

Sjei could feel Shebin's spine stiffen through his grip on her wrists.

"Yes, maybe you are older than you look," Sjei smiled as he released her. "But I am going to do everything I can to find this Drakis. I'm going to make you the most sympathetic victim ever seen in the eyes of the Empire. You are going to be showered with the love, adoration, and outrage that our Ministry of Thought can inspire. Your name will be known in every corner of the Empire, your higher caste will be assured, wealth will flow to you, and, yes, I will bring this

Drakis to you for the raw spectacle of it because it could, indeed, bring me the Imperial Throne."

"Bring *us* the Imperial Throne," Shebin corrected.

"Of course," Sjei replied. "All we need is your precious Drakis."

"And if you can't find him?"

"Then let us make offerings to the gods that we find this Soen before the Iblisi do."

CHAPTER 7

Temple of Whispers

MALA SAT UP IN THE DARKNESS of the room, holding her knees as she peered into the night. The rain clouds that had gathered in the early evening burst with torrential rain as the sun went down. Water from the mesa above them fell now in waterfall sheets across the cavern, spilling in a river down the steps they had climbed earlier in the day. They were all gathered in what had once been the front of a small shop—a fish shop according to the dwarf. Now the roaring cascade and the rain filled her ears with noise. The darkness was complete as they had forgone any fire that night out of fear of what it might attract and from the more basic fact that they could not find anything to burn in the immediate halls, rooms and warrens of the stone-cliff buildings. The only illumination they were afforded was the lightning of the storm, which, in its fury, was nearly constant, its flashes piercing the darkness of the doorway, followed by the rumble and the crash of thunder. It was a tumultuous night, but the dwarf was snoring loudly against the far wall and everyone except herself and Ethis, who now standing guard just outside the entrance, had managed to make themselves comfortable enough for rest.

Mala watched Drakis sleep, catching images of him in the flashes of light through the door, her own thoughts as tumultuous as the storm outside.

I'm falling through pain long remembered . . .

He is smiling with his fangs.
Longing and lusting . . .
Never entrusting . . .

Mala's mind had refused once again to quiet into the longed-for oblivion of sleep. Her thoughts spun unbidden through her mind, pounding like the thunder, tumbling in a roiling cascade of pain, hope, hate, longing, and fear. A waterfall of memories refused to retreat, thundering through her consciousness in a wild, uncontrolled torrent.

Elven house gardens were flowering . . .
Blood red the petals of pain.
Come and forget them.
Come to forgive them . . .

Forgiveness was not in her, and she devoutly wished the voices would go away and leave her alone. The elves had put them in her head, she was sure. Voices to call her back home to them at any cost. Voices that called her to a bliss-filled forgetfulness that she longed to be a part of once again. She wished everyone would go away and take her shame and her loathing with them.

Mala sat only a few feet from Drakis and hated him for who she had become.

She remembered those days in the Timuran House where she pleasantly tended the gardens and kept the house spotless as much for her own pleasure as that of her overseers and the House Mistress. Her hands moving through the warm earth while she planted flowers was a joy to her. She remembered the smell of freshly baked bread coming from the kitchens in the back of the subatria. She remembered, too, the smiles she had shared with Drakis and the desires they felt; how she had thrilled at his brushing touches and all the dreams, day and night, she had involving both of them together.

But then he had returned from the War for the Ninth Dwarven Throne, and she was forced to remember *everything else.* He had taken her from her lovely, safe garden and she hated him for that . . . and she loved him for it, too.

She tried to remember again that moment when she had awakened to all her memories in that fallen garden so far away. It was difficult to consider, for her mind only allowed her glimpses of understanding. She recalled her mind thrown into chaos, unable to reconcile one memory with another as the continuity of her ordered life unraveled in a single moment. She was in a freefall of thoughts, the cord of her mind unraveling until she slammed into a place in her past experience that had been specifically planted there for just such an eventuality. She saw it, embraced it as she had been trained to do so many years before, and a new purpose came into her mind.

This memory was a dark one and impenetrable by her conscious thought. It called her to do anything, say anything that would ensure the discovery and recovery of her fellow slaves should the spells of the Devotions be broken. It was not a thing planted there by the Aether since that would have been unraveled, too, should the magic fail. This was far more direct, far less subtle and far older than the Devotions. This was conditioned though through unspeakable means that would bend the will of a slave even against her own interest. She was a *Seinar*—a beacon—and even as the avatria of House Timuran was falling to crush her beloved garden, she knew she would betray any of her fellow slaves just to keep the demons at bay that threatened to tear her mind apart.

She saw the avatria collapsing over her. She wondered in that moment if perhaps it were best for the entire structure to fall upon her, crushing her into oblivion and ending her pain.

It was just as these thoughts were coming together in her that Drakis had appeared before her.

"Come with me . . . I'll take you somewhere safe."

She had recoiled from his touch . . . longed for his touch. He was leaving the House. He was taking her with him.

"Take me?" she had said and had begun to laugh hysterically.

Laugh because it was so terribly funny! Here he was, the great hero of House Timuran and the man that she loved dragging her to safety as though she were some distressed elven princess and she knew—*knew*—that she would betray him to his captors. Who wouldn't laugh, she thought, that the one person in the entire household who was willing—no, not just willing but compelled—to rob him of the very memories and life he had just won was the same woman that he loved and was trying to free. She'd been trained since she was fourteen years of age to do anything and everything that would en-

sure his capture—and for him to lose those same memories and that
same life he had just won. Take everything from him he ever wanted
in his life—including her.

Wasn't that funny, she thought, shaking in the corner as the dim
pulse of distant lightning flickered into the room.

The journey to peace and a purpose,
Is never trodden alone
When the heavens wake
And your body breaks . . .

"Mala."

She blinked in the darkness, uncertain she had heard her name.

"Mala!" came the urgent whisper in her ear.

She jumped at the sound, the closeness of the breathed whisper
shifting the hairs at the back of her neck. She flinched, turning at
once.

The Lyric grinned back at her, her gaunt face filled with contrast
from the cold light of the lightning outside.

"Come on!" The Lyric grinned. "She's waiting."

"Who?" Mala whispered.

The Lyric was already moving to the back of the shop, picking her
way carefully among their sleeping companions.

"Hurry!" she whispered.

Mala stood carefully in the uncertain flashes coming through the
doorway. She could see the Lyric standing against the back wall of the
shop, her hands set against the stone. The darkness engulfed them for
a moment, robbing her of her sight until the next flash.

There was a doorway in the wall where before there had been
none.

And the Lyric was stepping through the opening.

"No!" Mala said, restraining her voice, fearful of waking the others. "Come back!"

But the Lyric only grinned back at her and beckoned her on as
she stepped through the portal, whispering as she left.

"Come with me," she said so quietly that Mala was not sure of the
words beneath the rolling thunder. "I'll take you somewhere safe."

In the next flash of light, the Lyric was gone.

Mala stepped quickly between the sleeping bodies, desperate not to disturb them. She made her way to the doorway that had appeared in the previously solid wall at the back of the shop and stuck her head through the opening.

Circular plates in the ceiling of a long hall glowed dimly overhead, pulsing slightly with each flash of lightning outside. They did not fade so quickly nor was their light so suddenly bright, as though they held the light for a time in their grasp before releasing it. They lit the way down its length, plunging directly back into the mountain. Arched portals lined the hall, ink black and forbidding. Yet the Lyric skipped past them, her strange giggle echoing back down the hall.

Come past the dead in the dying light . . .

Come to the bliss of the night.

Mala took a tentative step into the hall.

Face now the truth

And the death of your youth . . .

Mala rushed down the hallway, the pulsing glow from the distant lightning lighting her way.

"Stop, Lyric!" she called out, but her voice was swallowed up in the continuous crash of thunder outside.

She rushed after the other woman, desperate to catch her and bring her back to the safety of their group. In front of her, the Lyric laughed at the game, and kept ahead of her with frustrating ease. Quite suddenly, Mala realized that the woman had led her into a complex warren of subterranean rooms—some lit by the same ceiling panel arrangement as those she had just passed—and that the Lyric was taking her deeper into the ruins beneath the mountain. The hall turned, opening into a room where one wall had completely fallen, a raging stream of water rushing out from behind it and coursing down across the dim mosaic that covered the floor. The Lyric was still ahead of her, running now, splashing the water up behind her. Mala quickened her own pace, following the madwoman through a succession of several rooms. Brilliant light suddenly surrounded her, followed in an instant by an explosion of sound. Mala screamed, cowering by instinct from the overwhelming noise and glancing upward in fear. The fading light showed a circular shaft that ran up through the mountain, vines reaching down toward her from the opening several hundred feet overhead. The walls were lined with stone balconies and black doorways, each looking down on her. Rain fell straight down the shaft, soaking her hair and clothing before she recovered and rushed into the opposite opening where the sound of the Lyric's laughter echoed its taunt in her direction. The water in this room pooled above her ankles as she ran toward the arched hall on the other side. No lights penetrated this darkness, but the laughter led her on, Mala's fingers running against the smooth mosaic tiles of the curving hall. She stumbled on something that clattered at her feet but kept on, believing that the voice of the Lyric was closer now. She could see something now as she continued: the end to the curving tunnel and a grateful return to the light.

She stepped into a great circular plaza. A curving staircase descended from an upper level. This plaza, too, was open to the sky above where the great overhead dome had cracked and part of it had fallen, its stones having crashed into and ruined the finish of the polished stones that formed the floor. This open fissure extended across the ceiling of the plaza where one wall had collapsed into the courtyard, revealing an enormous room more than thirty feet wide and a hundred feet deep. Its arched ceiling rose up nearly a hundred feet to where it was split by the end of the overhead fissure to one side, cascading water down one wall and illuminating a gigantic statue at the far end. Water also tumbled down the staircase and flowed across the floor, washing away the dust and revealing the ancient shine under the pulsing flashes penetrating from overhead.

The Lyric stood before the statue, gazing up at it as she swayed back and forth.

Soaked to the skin, Mala carefully climbed over the rubble of the fallen wall and entered the enormous arched hall. There were stone benches set in rows here, all facing the statue which lay in shadow at the curved back of the room. The lightning had subsided for the moment and Mala found it difficult to see.

"Lyric?" she called. "Come back with me. It isn't safe here."

The figure standing before the statue lifted up her arms slowly but did not turn around.

"Please, Lyric . . . or whoever you are," Mala called, her voice quivering and uncertain. She remembered that who the Lyric thought she was could change at any moment and without notice. If she was to respond at all, Mala remembered, it was occasionally prudent to ask the strange woman who she was and then hope to navigate the conversation based on whatever story she was reenacting that day. Mala decided on a different approach. "I mean . . . excuse me, can you help me?"

The Lyric turned, barely discernible in the darkness. "Yes, Mala," she said in a deep, warm voice. "I can help you."

Lightning flared above the fissure.

The statue towered over them, brilliant in the flash. It was a woman carved from marble, but her face was staring directly at Mala. It was a face more beautiful than she had ever seen, the form of her body so exquisitely perfect that it filled Mala with wonder just to look upon it. Her arms were outstretched toward Mala. There was pleading in her eyes.

The vision faded with the light.

Mala had to remind herself to breathe again. She had to force herself to look away from where the statue stood and back toward the Lyric. "I want . . . excuse me, but if you want to help me, you need to come with me back . . ."

The Lyric was silhouetted against the dim flashes of distant lightning. She shook her head and spoke, though, through some trick of the hall, Mala thought, the voice seemed to be coming from everywhere at once.

"No, Mala, there is no going back."

"But they are waiting for us," Mala insisted, reaching out for the Lyric. "It isn't safe here. Those creatures—the hunters—from the forest could be anywhere in these . . ."

"The drakonet will not bother us here," the voice replied. It seemed to be coming from the Lyric, but Mala could not be certain. The Lyric was moving her lips yet the sound seemed to come from everywhere at once. "They know that this place is mine and that I do not approve of them wandering my halls."

"As you say," Mala responded carefully. She was uncertain of her own sanity and quite certain that the Lyric had none. "Then we should get back to the others. They will be looking for us . . ."

The lightning flashed again.

The statue struck Mala as appearing differently than she had first supposed. The face of the beautiful woman now seemed stern and resolute, looking not at Mala as she had first supposed but into the distance. Her hands were still outstretched but now appeared not to be inviting but defiant and expectant of a struggle.

The flash faded and the statue fell into night's shadow once more.

"Yes," came the deep and sad reply, "They are gathering and they look for your return. Warriors and hunters rise up against them. The might of many against the will of the few, and who shall save them? In whom will they trust when trust is forgotten and betrayal at hand?"

Mala took a step back from the Lyric and stumbled, nearly falling over a stone bench. The Lyric stepped toward her, grasping her by the shoulders.

"You think you are lost," the deep voice echoed through the hall. All Mala could see was the silhouette of the Lyric against the dim pulsing illumination of the great statue beyond her. "You think that everyone hates you because you hate yourself more than any of them. Who will love you when you are so undeserving of love? Who will gather you home, Mala Timuran? When the truth is known and the fallen citadels rise again . . . who will bring you home?

The Lyric gripped Mala's shoulders with incredible strength. "I know your heart, Mala Timuran. You are lost and do not know your own way."

Mala shivered. "I just want to go home."

"Home? What do you know of home?" the voice gently mocked her. "Home to you is a forgetful nothing, a blind eye and a deaf ear. Home is a dream from which you never awaken while sleeping in a bed of devouring roaches. You know nothing of home."

A quick flash illuminated disdain on the statue's face.

"But there is a place within you that remembers what home truly is," the low voice echoed through the hall. "Find yourself . . . and I will bring you hope. Find that memory . . . I will bring you home."

Mala shook uncontrollably. "By the gods!" she stammered.

The lightning flashed again near the top of the mesa high above them, the crack of thunder following almost at once. The brilliant light bathed the statue once more.

The carved face smiled back at Mala with a horrifying grin. The face was now deformed, with an elongated snout and sharp teeth.

Rusting iron bands had been bound across the statue's chest, fixing torn, leathery wings to its back.

In the sudden darkness that followed, all Mala heard was the voice surrounding her.

"Yes . . . by the gods . . ."

CHAPTER 8

Spirits

DRAKIS PEERED DOWN the dark curving hall, griping his sword nervously in his right hand. The splash of his footsteps echoed loudly around him no matter how carefully he stepped. He heard rather than saw Urulani behind him, her footfalls overlapping his.

"*Mala!*" Drakis called out in a hoarse whisper as loud as he dared. "Mala!"

"We should be going back, Drakis," Urulani said quietly.

"You said she came this way!" Drakis snarled back at the warrior woman behind him.

"There were marks leading into this hall and they must have been in a hurry, judging by the scrapes," she replied. "The Lyric's tracks are more pronounced—almost as though she wanted to be found—but the rain and the water have washed much of their passage away."

"But you can still track them," Drakis urged. "What is the problem?"

"We are getting deep in the mountain," Urulani said, an unusual nervous edge in her voice. Were her teeth chattering? Drakis wondered. "Whatever was tracking us in the jungle may have come in here as well. We should get the others if we are going to go farther in."

"How long?" Drakis said, stopping in the dark, curving hallway but reluctant to go back.

"How long until what?" Urulani asked.

"How long since they came this way?" Drakis' voice echoed hollowly in front of him. The water around his boots was settling into an undulating sheen from the scant light coming from one of the oddly glowing panels in the ceiling behind him. Ethis had noted earlier that the panels dimmed and flickered occasionally as though they were set in the shadow of trees blown by the wind or clouds passing between them and the sun in a clear sky. That they were originally intended to bring light to the depths of the ancient human ruins seemed a reasonable conclusion, but how such a mechanism could survive down the centuries to continue its work was a mystery to them all.

"By the signs of their initial tracks, and assuming neither of them was ill at the time they left," the raider woman replied in cool analysis, "I would say both of them have been gone more than an hour— perhaps longer."

"An hour . . ."

"Most likely longer . . . which means they could be anywhere by now," Urulani said, her voice strained and uncomfortable. "I don't know why the Lyric went with her—who knows why that woman does anything—but Mala's run off, Drakis; left us to go back to her slave masters."

"No," Drakis said, shaking his head. "She wouldn't . . ."

"Wouldn't what?" Rising anger flooded into Urulani's words. "Wouldn't abandon you? Wouldn't sell us all out to Death itself if it meant running back to her precious elven keepers? She already *did* that, Drakis, but you don't see it because you don't *want* to see . . ."

Urulani stopped speaking, raising her own sword and crouching slightly in anticipation. Her large, dark eyes shone in the faint light from the panel above.

Sounds, jumbled and blurred by their own echoes tumbled from in front of them down the darkened corridor.

Drakis glanced over at Urulani.

There came the distinct sound of splashing steps . . .

The noise of bright laughter.

Drakis charged forward at once, plunging into the darkness. Urulani was momentarily surprised by his sudden action, but followed quickly in chase.

Drakis followed the wall of the gently turning corridor with his left hand extended, his right hand gripping the hilt of the sword. He could hear, farther back, the echoes of Urulani's footsteps in the water mixed with the mumbled "Wrong!" she uttered with every step. The corridor was brightening before him; he could make out the moss-covered walls now and could hear the tumble of water ahead of him. He quickened his pace with his increased ability to see and was at a full run when he emerged from the vine-covered arch and into the circular chamber.

It was actually the bottom of a shaft, he realized as he came into it. Water gushed from high over a broken wall on his left side, cascading down the fallen stones and across the shattered mosaic that once covered the floor. There was another arched opening on the opposite side of the space nearly hidden by the hanging vines, which extended up the hundred-foot length of the shaft overhead. At the top, the shaft opened into gray clouds filtered through the jungle canopy; a dappled, slanting column in the mists which, in the youth of the day, barely entered the space.

Mala sat on a segment of broken wall next to the base of the falling water, her laughter echoing up the shaft in hysterical peels, as the Lyric stood over her.

Drakis walked quickly through the rushing water, nearly losing his footing on the slick tiles beneath his feet. He sheathed his sword in its scabbard and squatted down to look into her face.

"Mala?" he asked.

Mala turned suddenly toward the sound of her name as though she had been slapped. Her eyes were bright as they looked more through Drakis than at him. Her laughter had stopped just as suddenly. She shook visibly now.

"Drakis?" she said. "Did you see it? Did you hear it?"

Drakis took in a breath. "See what, Mala?"

She tried to focus on him but her eyes seemed to be looking beyond him. "I'm going home, Drakis! She's going to take me home! We're all going home, my beloved! You can come, too! I know the way!"

Drakis was shaken. He glanced up questioningly at the Lyric.

The Lyric looked back sadly and shrugged. She raised her hand, pointed to her own head and made circles as she looked down on Mala.

"We've got to leave!" Mala said, her hands grasping the armholes of Drakis' leather chest piece on both sides, dragging his attention back to her. "We have to get out of this place. We have to leave!"

"What do you mean we've got to leave?" Drakis said in frustration. "We just *found* this place!"

"I know it seems wrong," Mala protested, her speech rushed as her words seemed to outrun her thoughts. "This place seems safe enough and we're sheltered from the weather—I know everything you've done makes sense to you, but we're in danger here and we've got to get out while we can."

"Of course we're in danger here," Drakis rolled his eyes. "But at least we've got some chance to defend ourselves in these ruins. Telling us to dash back out into *that* jumble of a wilderness"—he gestured up past the moss-and-vine obscured walls, broken balconies, and dark openings toward the gray rain and mists nearly obscuring the jungle-choked ruins below them—"is *not* going to make us safer! We don't even know what monsters were tracking us in that choked mess, and you want us to dive back into it by giving up the one place we've found where at least we can see trouble coming before it takes our lives?"

"The Pythar are coming and we have to take the Living Road before death finds us!"

"The dwarf said this place was called Pythar," Urulani frowned. "What is she raving about? The living road? *What* living road?"

Drakis could not remember how long it had been since the recently sullen Mala had shown much of an interest in anything, and her sudden fervor inclined him to believe her. The unexpected existence of a back entrance to the shop rooms they had previously felt were so secure gave both credence to her strange tale and concern for the safety of their cliff-face warren, heightened by the disappearance of both Mala and the Lyric. But now, with the gray light of dawn, and having found both women not only alive but apparently only having wandered off on their own, Drakis' fears were damped down. The rush to action was slowly ebbing into a desire for rest and, he thought, perhaps more lengthy and reflective deliberations.

Drakis stood up, dragging Mala to her feet with him.

"All right, Mala. Let's get back with the others, and we'll talk about what to do."

"Talk?" Mala was indignant. "There's no time to *talk*! We have to leave—right now! Our lives are . . ."

The bellowing sound of a dwarf and the distant clash of steel came from the curving hallway they had just left.

"Maybe she's right," Urulani said, shrugging her shoulders as Drakis, Mala's hand gripped firmly in his own, rushed back into the corridor and toward the shop.

"I'll have that back, you black-hearted scoundrel, if I have to cut it out of your rubber hide!" Jugar roared. The dwarf was leaning heavily on his good leg but still standing, his short-handled battle ax held in both hands as he spun unevenly around on his good leg. "Give it back now or I'll cleave you in twain!"

Drakis rushed through the previously hidden doorway, his sword at the ready but then stopped short.

The hobbling dwarf appeared to be chasing Ethis about the small room with his war ax.

Urulani slid to a stop behind Drakis. "Chimerian! What's the meaning of this?"

"Theft and thievery, that's the meaning!" the red-faced dwarf howled. "Piracy, by Thorgrin's beard, coldly calculated and expertly performed!"

"I regret to inform you that the dwarf appears to have gone insane," Ethis replied, dodging a strong slash across the center of his body.

"What happened," Drakis said wearily.

"I was on the concourse—on watch," Ethis replied. The dwarf was taking another lunge at him, but the chimerian managed to extend his arm, grasping the dwarf's head and holding him far enough away to avoid the blade. "I must admit that the architecture interested me considerably and may have distracted me—but not for long."

The dwarf howled, and Ethis quickly withdrew his arm before Jugar could cut it off.

"Now he claims I stole his precious rock from him," Ethis concluded, jumping deftly out of the way as the dwarf charged forward, stumbled, and fell flat against the stone floor.

"It was absorbing the Aer through the stones," the dwarf wailed. "Drawing it out of the ground in ways you cannot possibly understand!"

"You have no magic at all without the stone?" Drakis asked.

"Aye . . . all living things are imbued with Aer," Jugar said, rolling painfully to sit up, "but it's like comparing a trickle with a river. I would have had my leg healed in days with that stone. Now it will take me weeks!"

"He's convinced I took it," Ethis said. "However, before he became belligerent, he insisted on searching everyone's packs."

"Everyone's packs?" Mala was indignant.

They had been so intent on the battle between Ethis and Jugar that none of them had noticed the contents of their packs spilled across the floor.

Jugar painfully tried to pull himself into a better position.

Urulani pushed her way past Mala and the Lyric who were crowding in the doorway at the back of the shop, raising her elegant head slightly as she stepped around Drakis. "Jugar is not just being unreasonable. It appears we've all got something missing."

The chimerian frowned then fell forward, catching the ground with all four of his hands spread out before him at once. His body contracted slightly and he looked more like a spider as he lowered himself close to the ground. Even the heavy-breathing dwarf stopped his rage at the sight. Ethis moved quickly along the ground and then rose upright, extending his torso into the more familiar form to which they were all accustomed.

Ethis placed two of his fists firmly on where his hips would have been. "It *was* a human . . ."

"See!" Jugar shouted. "I told you . . ."

"But it wasn't one of us," Ethis concluded.

"What do you mean?" Drakis asked, returning his blade to its scabbard.

"The markings are not obvious, but they are there," Ethis continued speaking with a distracted air as much to himself as to those around him. "There are footprints all through here. Most of them are obscured by the unfortunate ravings of the dwarf, but there are enough remaining for me to be sure. It was a human . . . barefooted, too . . . a male of your kind of approximately fourteen years or female of fifteen. It's difficult to tell from what remains."

"Could it be one of the monstrous predators that dragged Kwarae off?" Drakis asked.

"No, there's no heel spur like the ones we saw before, and the toes are not long enough," Ethis shook his head, looking out the front door of the ancient room into the gray mists beyond. He came in and left through that front opening, too. An amazing feat considering I was standing not thirty feet from the opening."

"Then we've got to be finding him at once!" Jugar demanded. "He's got my Heart!"

"One cannot steal what was never there," Ethis sniffed.

"You'll answer for that one day, bendy," Jugar snarled. "Although I would be willing to forgo the matter entirely, if you'll just move your rubbery cheeks and track down this thief and recover my property no matter what his age!"

Drakis moved to his own field pack and quickly undid the toggles securing the top flap. "Well, I've a dagger missing. Do you suppose everyone else has something gone as well?"

"Certainly," Ethis agreed, "although it seems the thief didn't discriminate in what he or she took. Value didn't seem to be the motive behind the theft."

"Well he took something of inestimable value from me," the dwarf shouted as he struggled to stand on his good leg. "We've got to get it back!"

"The dwarf is right," Drakis said. "It's the source of the dwarf's magic and it may be our best chance at getting out of this nightmare. Can you track this person?"

"Yes," Ethis answered. "Now that I know what to look for, I can track him, but we'll have to hurry."

"Why?"

"Because we need to find this thief for a better reason than the dwarf's magic stone," Ethis said, gazing out from the front opening beyond the concourse to the gray mists beyond. "We have limited food in a land where we do not know what is edible for foraging. If there is a human surviving here, then we need to find him and learn from him how to survive here as he does. And there is another compelling reason for us to leave whether we find the thief or not."

Drakis finished securing his field pack. "And that would be?"

"Because I've also found other tracks all over the concourse," Ethis said. "Whatever hunted us yesterday has been in here before and, I suspect when the rain stops, they'll be coming for us."

Drakis thrust out his lower lip in thought. "Mala said we had to leave . . ."

"It would seem she is right," Ethis nodded.

"And you can track this person?" Drakis asked again.

"If we hurry," Ethis repeated.

"So you're a tracker, eh?" Drakis said cautiously. "Odd you never mentioned this before. You seem to be a man of inestimable hidden talents, Ethis. Anything else about yourself you'd care to share with us?"

"Not at the moment," Ethis said. "We've not the time."

CHAPTER 9

Death's Shadow

"THIS IS MADNESS," Urulani huffed.

"And to what particular aspect of this madness are you referring?" Drakis responded. The air weighed down on him, laden with the moisture from the night's rain. He was sweating profusely and having trouble keeping the salty liquid out of his eyes. The clouds had cleared with the rising sun but the warmth only served to increase his discomfort. "The fact that we are here at all? Or perhaps that we actually believe we can survive a thousand leagues from any help? I can think of a number of different ways that our situation would qualify as insane."

"Did you include the fact that we're following a chimerian into ruins which we know to be deadly," the captain said, sweat beading on her dark forehead, "in order to give a dwarf back a piece of rock? How about that we have happily left our stronghold because a proven traitor among us tells us some goddess none of us have ever heard of told her so? Was that on your list?"

"Well, we're apparently not *all* happy about that," Drakis answered, pushing aside a massive fern frond, trying to keep Ethis and Mala, both of whom were ahead of him, in sight. "And I'll even admit that it was on my list."

"She cannot be trusted, Drakis," Urulani said as she followed at his heels. "Even the Lyric thinks she is insane."

"This isn't the time, Captain."

"We may not *have* another time," Urulani snapped back. "I'm beginning to wonder if all you southlands humans are lunatics."

What a horrible place, he thought, as he made his way around a fallen pillar jutting out of the shattered stones of the nearly obliterated roadway. *Who in their right mind would want to live here? Who out of their right mind would want to live here either?*

A quick smile flashed across his face. There were certainly enough people here to ask that question and get an answer with authority. The Lyric had not been in her right mind since House Timuran fell and it was beginning to look as though Mala had joined that particular tribe as well. Mala's new obsession with having seen a goddess and fleeing back into the jungle ruins looking for some "living road" made just about as much sense as the Lyric. Maybe they were all destined to that fate, he thought as he struggled to keep his footing over a pile of loose stones between a row of bushes with thorns nearly as long as his hand. Perhaps it was an inevitable result of breaking the magical bonds that had held him in a blissful state—innocent of the true horror of his life as a slave. What had his freedom won him except misery, suspicion, and a journey that had brought him to die in a land far from anything that he had ever known? All this because his name happened to be the same as the one mentioned by some long-dead poet and because everyone else, it seemed, wanted the story to be true.

"Well, if I am insane," Drakis said, entering a small section of the road where the cobblestones were fitted so tightly together that they had kept the jungle foliage at bay, "I wish it were in a more pleasant climate. What do you think, Captain? Does the fact that I would rather die in more pleasant surroundings prove me sane or not?"

Urulani smiled slightly. "I think that leaves the entire question open."

"Well, Ethis must be crazy," Drakis stated looking ahead of them. "He's carrying the dwarf."

Urulani looked up as well, peering through the jumble of broken walls, street, and plants. Jugar was strapped to the back of the chimerian, lashed down like scowling cordwood being hauled to market. "He's the only one who could shoulder the little fool. The dwarf's none too happy about it, but his comfort is the least of my concerns."

"What about the Lyric?" Drakis wiped his brow again but it did not seem to help.

"She's ahead of us, too," Urulani reported as she scanned the thick undergrowth around them. "The Lyric seems to be keeping up better than I am. I'm more comfortable with a deck under my feet. Land is hard for me. What about your wondrous goddess-talker?"

"Up ahead," Drakis replied.

"With Ethis?" Urulani said, raising one dark eyebrow.

"Yes," Drakis nodded, not wanting to be drawn into that particular argument. "With Ethis."

The roadway they were following could barely be discerned as having ever lived up to the name. Ferns and thick brush, as well as a number of towering trees, had laid claim to the ancient path. From roots to leaves they had broken up the evidence of man's ordered mind and handiwork over the centuries, until only scattered pieces remained. If there had once been far-seeing towers, they were now obscured by the enormous trees growing in thick succession. Only jumbled fragments remained. The ruins of Pythar were, to Drakis, a metaphor for madness—like making one's sad way through the remains of greatness that no longer functioned or even made sense.

They had left the cliff-city as soon as they could gather what remained of their belongings. Ethis asked them to go down by the same stairs they had come up the previous day. Their intruder had apparently come to them some other way, which Ethis believed too dangerous for Mala or the Lyric to traverse. He had gratefully left Urulani off of that list as Drakis was coming to appreciate the captain of the Sondau Clan and knew that any inference of her being weak might well have ended in blows exchanged. Ethis said the trail led downward and that he and the dwarf would meet them at the base of the stairs once he knew where the trail went. Drakis half believed the chimerian would dump the dwarf and disappear altogether, abandoning them, but Ethis arrived as promised. He showed them a passage to the other side of the broken bridge and onto what once had been a wide boulevard, now choked with vegetation.

Ethis, followed closely by the suddenly enthusiastic Mala, led them down the broken avenue. They passed several ruins whose remains made Drakis' heart ache for their lost and ruined beauty: a partial wall with frieze carvings across its face forming compelling patterns within patterns; a fountain which, though long since non-functioning, intermingled its own perfectly crafted stone leaves with those of the surrounding plants; or a staircase, rising to nothing with stone riser posts formed to look like jumping fish. In each case, Drakis felt the ghostly presence of artisans who were long dead. Who carved that frieze, he wondered? What hand held the hammer and the chisel? To whom did they go at the end of their day's labor? The evidence of their hands was everywhere, and Drakis struggled to comprehend their loss.

Four separate streets intersected the boulevard. Ethis paused for a moment, his head and body rising slightly as he turned around. His voice was lowered when he spoke, "They're back."

"Back?" Urulani said. "The hunters, you mean . . . or whatever they're called?"

"Yes," Ethis said.

"Can we get back to the cliffs?" Drakis asked at once.

"No," Ethis said, shaking his head. "They're coming from the cliffs. The markings lead this way. Come on!"

He dashed down the avenue to his left, weaving across the fitted stones among grass blades that were nearly ten feet tall.

"Where are we going now?" Urulani asked as she adjusted her grip on her sword.

"One foot after the other, Captain," Drakis said, drawing his own sword. "Anywhere but here."

They both ran after the others into the opening formed by the remaining stones of the road. It was a ragged course, but Drakis soon realized that it *was* a path. In places, he noticed, the stones did not fit the pattern of the remaining road. There were large, flat stones laid across the ground that bridged the grass between sections of the old avenue.

A loud rustling sounded behind them. Whatever was following them had plunged into the tall grasses. Either they did not know of the path or they were heedless of it. Drakis glanced back and could see the tops of the grass blades violently shaking behind him and to his left.

He gritted his teeth, concentrating on the path before him and the back of Urulani, who was running the twisted way in front of him.

With shocking suddenness, they emerged from the grasses into another clear intersection. This area appeared to be burned, as though a fire had passed through a few seasons before. Ahead of them, the Lyric and Mala were running toward a black thicket of brush that looked as though it were spilling from one of the branching alleys. Ethis was standing in front of it, waving them on.

There was an opening in the wall of brush. Mala and the Lyric had already passed into the opening.

Drakis and Urulani ran across the space quickly and ducked into the low opening, passing Ethis. There was an obvious path beaten into the ground, again weaving back and forth deeper into the thick brush.

"Ouch!" Urulani exclaimed quietly.

Drakis looked at her.

Her arm was bleeding near the shoulder. The brush was filled with razor-sharp thorns.

Ethis came in behind Drakis, pulling a woven patch of the same thorny materials behind him and sealing the way behind them. As Ethis turned, the dwarf strapped on his back swung toward Drakis.

"I have *never* suffered such indignities in my life!" Jugar was almost purple with rage, his spittle flying at Drakis' face, only a hand's breadth between them. "Slung to the back of this thieving bendy like I was one of his rubber-bottomed offspring . . ."

"Silence, fool," Ethis hissed. "We're not alone."

Straw-thin rays of sunlight were all that penetrated the thicket, the branches of the thorn-covered brush so thick around them that it was impossible to see anything beyond. Ethis raised one long hand, holding his palm toward Drakis and Urulani.

The thicket shook suddenly with several impacts, each followed immediately by whooping and screeching sounds that they felt as a chill in their bones. Shadows moved across the face of the thicket, blotting out shafts of light back and forth. Ethis turned to Drakis, his expressionless face registering concern for the benefit of his companions. Then he motioned with his hand for them to continue farther into the thicket.

"This path is no accident," Drakis whispered to Urulani.

They emerged from the thicket into an enormous plaza, its

grounds also burned to stubble where the grasses were just starting to reestablish themselves. Broken columns on either side lined the area that was nearly fifty feet across and more than three hundred feet in length. At the far end stood a wall nearly three stories high with additional crumbling walls and structures holding it vertical. The remains of buildings lined the great square. The rest of their companions were waiting nervously for them.

The terrible whooping sound came again from the left. Others soon joined it in chorus, beyond the ruins across the square and from the ruins to their right.

"Now where?" Drakis demanded of Ethis.

The chimerian's head moved in swift jerks as he took in the area around them. "That way," he said, point to their right. "Down the length of the plaza! Run!"

"Oh, no!" cried the dwarf. "Not RUN!"

Ethis plunged ahead of them, all four of his arms swinging with the effort of his dash, the dwarf roaring now in pain with every step. Drakis had the Lyric by one arm as they both dashed down the center of the plaza together. Mala ran alone, her auburn hair bouncing in the wind behind her.

Ethis suddenly skidded to a halt in the center of the plaza.

Drakis nearly fell over trying to stop short of running into anyone. "What is it?"

"It ends," Ethis said in blinking astonishment.

"What ends?" Urulani demanded.

"The trail," Ethis said. "It ends right here!"

"I think you may be right for once, chimerian," Jugar said after drawing a deep breath. "Look!"

They were swarming over the ruined walls.

They might have been mistaken for humans except for the long, barbed tails. Their legs were different, too, double segmented with both forward and backward knee joints. Their feet had a heel claw and elongated toes with long claws at the end as did the hands at the ends of their immensely powerful arms. The bones of their faces were angular, ending in jutting spiked bones. Their wide mouths were filled with long, sharp teeth.

Their scales shone in the sun as they screamed.

They flowed like a tide over the ruins from all directions at once, surrounding the plaza. They crept forward, crouching down on all four appendages, coiling muscles to strike.

Drakis raised his sword, wondering just how tough the hides of these horrors would prove to be. There would be no time for words. Even if there were, he had nothing to say.

The stone beneath their feet suddenly shifted, tipped, and dropped beneath them. Caught off-balance, they all tumbled into each other, sliding sideways down the stone into the darkness.

The monstrous horrors screamed as one, leaping forward toward their prey, but it was too late.

The stone had already risen back into place.

Their prey had vanished into the earth.

CHAPTER 10

Ishander

DRAKIS ROLLED OVER QUICKLY, his right hand desperately searching for his sword.

"Hey!"

"Sorry," he said, moving his hand in a different direction across the stone floor.

"Touch me again with that hand and you'll lose the arm that goes with it!" Urulani snapped.

Drakis' fingers felt the familiar bite of a cold, steel edge. He lightly followed the side of the blade to the grip and snatched it thankfully. The muffled sounds above him sent a shiver through him. "Now they're angry."

Quickly pushing himself up to his feet, Drakis looked around him. A single, bright patch of light lit the vast subterranean room. Massive columns, wider than Drakis' reach, marched in seemingly endless procession into the darkness. Opposite the light and behind him a great device towered from floor to ceiling. Drakis took it all in at a glance—a hopeless complex of spiked wheels, rods, and cords that the warrior found completely incomprehensible.

A shadow passed over the device, and the light was momentarily blocked near its source.

"Ethis! Urulani!" Drakis shouted. "Get up! There's someone else down here!"

The screeching above them was getting louder, as was the pounding on the stone above. Sand, shaken loose, fell in thin veils around them. The great device creaked.

"Where do we go?" Mala cried as she scrambled to her feet.

"Toward the light," he said. "Come on, everyone! Let's move! Now!"

They started their run toward the square of light at the end of the enormous room. A shadow again flickered against the intense light.

"Did you see that?" Urulani shouted.

"Keep running!" Drakis urged. "Run through it if you must, but don't stop!"

The rectangle of light was getting closer; Drakis' eyes were adjusting to the change. There were trees and sky beyond. Fitted stones of a plaza and . . .

They burst into the open stone court beneath a towering city wall behind them. The sounds of the monsters were beyond the wall, but Drakis doubted that it would hold them back once they caught the scent of him and his companions. Yet that was not what astonished him.

The plaza sloped down, forming a quay that jutted into a wide, green river.

More astonishing still, two long boats formed from bundled reeds were tied to the end of the quay. One held a few provisions. The other was nearly empty except for one very interesting occupant.

No longer a child but not yet grown into his beard, a young male human stood at the front of the boat a long pole in his hand. He wore a leather loincloth and vest but little else, his feet being bare. His skin was a deep brown color, but his hair was straw colored, long and pulled back into a thick braid. The pole he held extended down into the water where the youth was holding the boats against the current next to the quay. He stared at them expectantly.

Waiting.

"Ethis, I think we've found your thief," Drakis smiled.

The tied-togther boats drifted down the center of the river. The young man—he looked to be about fourteen years old—piloted the boats with his long staff. When the boy had pulled the staff from the water earlier in the day, Drakis discovered that the pole actually had a flattened, wide end at the bottom that allowed him to use the implement as a pole and as a paddle or rudder, depending on the needs at the time. It proved to be a most effective tool in keeping their course steady down the serpentine convolutions of the river's passage.

"He doesn't say much, does he?" Urulani observed from the front of the reed boat. She seemed more relaxed now that they were on the water although Drakis suspected that she was a bit restless over not being in command of the ship. She continued watching the river as they drifted with the current, affecting a pose of being in charge of a craft over which she had no authority or control.

"He may not speak our language," Ethis said. The chimerian was sitting at the front near where Urulani stood, his back to the direction of travel as he inspected and repacked his gear in his field pack. "It has been more than five hundred years since the Unified Tongue was spoken in these lands. Their language would almost certainly have been corrupted by now. For all we know they may have even lost the ability to speak altogether."

"Altogether," the Lyric said.

Ethis glanced up at her. She was sitting in the back of the boat near the silent young man. "What did you say?"

"I said, 'altogether,'" the Lyric replied.

"Why?" Ethis asked.

"Because you wondered if we had lost the ability to speak it," the Lyric replied.

"I don't understand," Ethis said, shaking his head.

Drakis chuckled. "Ethis, may I introduce you to Litaria; a relatively minor character . . ."

"I am not a minor!" huffed the Lyric.

". . . from the Rivaen Sea Tales. She was renowned for taking everything said literally."

"Charmed," Ethis said without enthusiasm.

Drakis watched the deep jungle drift past, its thick brush occasionally giving up a glimpse of some piece of ancient, fallen structure. "There are many ruins along the river."

Following Drakis' gaze, Urulani looked over at a broken tower foundation around which the river waters swirled. "There will be more ruins along the river than inland. Civilizations tend to follow the course of rivers. They offer water to sustain life and irrigation for crops as well as an easy source of sanitation so long as you don't give much thought to those who are downstream. They also offer the benefit of easier and faster travel over longer distances. If you are ever lost, a river will always take you somewhere."

"Well, we certainly are lost," Drakis said, looking back past the young native boy to the second boat tied behind them. The prow and the stern of each boat curved upward where the reeds were bundled and lashed together. Mala lay sleeping in the front of the second boat, with her head against the raised prow. Jugar was also in the trailing boat, Ethis having rigged what remained of the canvas he had used to haul the dwarf all morning as a shade for him. The dwarf had been knocked cold by the fall through the trapdoor in Pythar and still lay unconscious in the bottom of the boat. Drakis considered Mala for a moment before he spoke again. "It's a road, isn't it, Urulani. This river, I mean. This is Mala's living road."

"Perhaps," Urulani replied, turning back to watch the river ahead of them. "Or she may just be crazy. Even the Lyric thinks so."

"Whether providence, fate, or just luck brought us here is unimportant," Ethis said. "The question is what do we do next? This river eventually could take us to the sea."

"Which sea would that be?" Urulani chided.

"*Any* sea, I would think," Ethis answered back. "You *are* supposed to be a renowned captain, are you not? Sail along the coast until we find familiar waters and then head back south from there— back to more familiar lands."

"What, in *these*?" Urulani gestured at the reed boats. "I may be a fine example of my craft, chimerian, but not even the gods of the ocean depths would attempt an open-water crossing in one of these reed sponges."

"Quiet, both of you," Drakis said. "The most important thing is to find a way to make contact with this native boy's people and find a way to survive. Then we'll worry about building ships and crossing oceans."

"And what makes you think we can trust him?" Ethis asked.

"He could have left us back there," Drakis said. "Someone made those paths, and as good as he was at sneaking into our camp and taking our things, he was waiting there for us by the quay when we were all but dead. If it hadn't been for him, we would have been a quick meal for those . . . those . . ."

"Pythars," the boy said.

"Yes, Pythars, when they . . ."

Drakis stopped speaking.

They all turned to look at the boy, who continued working his oar against the river, shifting them again toward the center.

"You speak our language?" Drakis asked cautiously.

"No," the Lyric sniffed. "We speak his."

The boy laughed. "She funny."

"Just . . . wait," Drakis said, shaking his head as though it would somehow help him to embrace this new thought. "We've been talking here for the last four hours and you've understood everything we said?"

"Most," the boy replied. "You are much entertaining. I learn your secrets—that is the way of my duty, the way of my glory. Save you did I! Hero am I! Far-runner am I!"

"A Far-runner?" Ethis said carefully. "Tell us, what are Far-runners?"

The boy's face broke into a sneer. "The four-armed man is from a far land, indeed, if you do not know about Far-runners. We leave the Clan, master rivers, run far to the ancient places, and brave the Citadels. We gather our past from the fall of the proud and bring them back for our clan. My father was a Far-runner. My father's father was a Far-runner. I now am a Far-runner!"

"So you rob the bones of the dead," Urulani said, recovering from her astonishment at the boy speaking.

"The dead brought down their doom on their own heads," the boy shrugged. "They have no more use for their things."

"Why not just live in the Citadels?" Ethis asked with a shrug of all four shoulders.

The boy glared at him. "The four-armed man is a child!"

"Yes," Ethis said carefully. "I am a child . . . teach me."

"Citadels are cursed!"

"So you bring back cursed items to your tribe?" Drakis asked incredulously.

"No, foolish man!" the youth spat back heatedly. "Cursed magic we leave to die with the Citadels. Only Far-runners are blessed by the gods to go there and find those things not of the magic. It is our honor. It is our glory."

"And yet we were there," Ethis said evenly. "We, too, braved the cursed Citadels."

The boy's lips curled in disgust. "You were lost! You would have been eaten by the Pythar if I had not led you to the river. You are children fallen in a pit of dragons crying for help."

"And you are most brave," Ethis continued. "So brave that you stole our things from us."

"Yes! I took your things!" the boy said proudly. "It was to my honor and your shame!"

"Yes, you are brave," Drakis said. The boy was in this way over his head, no matter what his boasts might say. The boy was quick, certainly, and dangerous, but any one of them would be able to take him in combat, let alone all of them at once. "We are shamed before you. We would like our things back now."

"They are mine!" the boy said, thrusting out his jaw. "I have taken them as is the Far-runner's right!"

"Yes, they are," Ethis took up Drakis' thought. "But I am surprised that you would bring a great magic thing back to your clan."

"You are talking foolish again," the boy said dubiously.

"No," Ethis continued. "You took a stone from the dwarf—a black stone. It is great and terrible magic in disguise . . . and you have brought it back with you."

The boy's eyes went wide. He suddenly tossed his long pole at Drakis who barely had the reflexes to catch it. The boy jumped down, shoving the Lyric aside so violently that she nearly fell out of the boat. Frantically, the boy pawed through his sack and pulled out a black, faceted stone.

He drew back his arm as though to pitch it with all his might into the river.

Ethis lunged forward, snatching the stone out of the boy's hand before he could let loose his throw.

"Do not worry, friend Far-runner," Ethis said, steadying the boat as he sat back down. "Four-armed men are immune to the curse. I will take care of it for you and protect you and your clan from its effects."

The boy blinked, uncertainty in his face for the first time. His lower lip quivered slightly.

"The honor is still yours, Far-runner," Drakis said quietly. "I am Drakis. This is Ethis. The woman at the prow is Urulani and this woman we call the Lyric. We are your prize and we will not trouble you. May we ask you your name?"

"Ishander," the boy said. "I am Ishander."

"Then, Ishander," Drakis said, handing back the long pole. "We are trying to find our way back home. Where are you taking us?"

"Home," Ishander answered. "My home. But your people . . . if you are lost, will they not come looking for you?"

"No, Ishander," Drakis said with a sigh. "No one is looking for us at all."

CHAPTER 11

Hunter and Hunted

SOEN TJEN-REI THE RENEGADE, elven Inquisitor whose capture and death was decreed by Imperial Will throughout the Rhonas Empire that he had faithfully served, sat wearily down at the crest of a small knoll, leaning his back against the sloping broad trunk of a tree as he gazed back down at the length of road he had just taken.

Looking behind him had become a necessary habit. He was verging on the far northern reaches of the Empire as far from the Imperial City of Rhonas as possible . . . and he knew that it was not far enough.

The Scheliss Field Road wound its way among the gently rolling mounds of the Northmarch, an unhurried path for traders who came eastward from River Town. At that walled village the road split, the Coast Road following the river to the ports of the Shadow Coast to the west. Gnomish goods from Cape Tjakar on Manticus Bay traveled this road as well as goblin spices from Nordesia's Gorgantia Bay far up the coast. He knew this because he had journeyed with those cargoes, quietly working his passage on a gnomish galley and helping shift their jars in Shellsea to the transport wagons. Shellsea was an elven settlement requiring that Soen take more care to not be recognized for either whom he now was or who he had once been. He had covered many leagues since discarding the robes that once heralded him as an Inquisitor of the Iblisi, taking instead the more common robes of a Fourth Estate merchant as he reinvented himself and his false past. His Matei staff—powerful symbol of his former calling—he disguised as best he could from the eyes that occasionally might be cast in his direction. He never considered discarding it though its discovery in his hands would certainly expose him; it was too powerful a weapon to be without.

In his mind, Soen saw the farther reaches of the road branching south from River Town to become the main trade route down through the Northmarch connecting with the Imperial Folds—the magical transportation portals that were the backbone of Rhonas commerce, communication, and might—just outside an otherwise inconsequential village called Char. Through those portals he had passed freely only a week before—a master on a mission sanctioned by the Imperial Will and blessed by Ch'drei, the matriarchal head of the Iblisi Order that he faithfully served.

What a difference a few weeks can make, he thought.

He drew his mind back sharply to the present and again studied the road below him at the base of the knoll. It was a well-traveled road as it made its way east toward the town of Scheliss Field at the base of the Whispering Hills, just two leagues ahead. Scheliss Field was one of several towns established just short of the borders of Ephindria, the silent, reclusive land of the chimerians. Those strange, four-armed creatures with their blank, nearly nonexistent faces came to Scheliss Field for trade—leaving their own borders closed to any-one not of their race.

The Scheliss Field Road was not wide or well maintained because those who normally traveled it, while constant, were few. Recently, however, some great movement had flooded over the boundaries of the established road. The new ruts had not yet sunk deeply into the hard ground despite the evidence of a large number of travelers—all moving northeast. The predominance of tracks were manticorian—lion-men inexplicably now moving from their traditional clan hold-ings in the Steppes of Chaenandria up this road and probably far past the Whispering Hills. Such a migration was without precedent, but it was not manticorians alone; also mixed in with the tracks were those of Plains gnomes from Vestasia and an unusual number of goblins who where rarely, if ever, seen this far south of their Nordesian lodges.

"Whole nations on the run, and I'm running right along with them," Soen sighed. "All because of a few broken slaves."

Soen gazed down again at the dirt road. The number of manticorian tracks was dizzying.

And I have to find one among an entire nation of manticores, Soen thought. *"Just a single broken, crazy, bolting manticore slave by the name of Belag. Find him and I'll find the human Drakis . . . find Drakis, and perhaps then I'll have the means of convincing the devout members of my former Order that there is more value in my life than in my death.*

Soen was both the hunter and the hunted; the game was which role he would fulfill first.

Someone below him had left the road and was climbing toward him up the knoll. Any new acquaintance could be the harbinger of either his salvation or his doom. Soen always found his interest piqued to discover which of the two was approaching.

"Good noon to you," called out the other as he approached.

"Good noon to you as well," Soen called back. He could easily make out four arms and the featureless face that marked the approaching creature as a chimerian. This approaching citizen of Ephindria held walking staffs in two of its four hands. As to its gender, Soen knew that determination would have to wait until the creature was closer. Most elves could not tell whether a chimerian was male or female until the creature specifically let them know during conversation. Even as a trained Inquisitor, Soen had difficulty knowing at a distance. "What news do you bring?"

"News enough!" the chimerian replied. "And good news at that. I come from the Shadow Coast and the cities are alive with the most amazing talk."

"Come share the shade of my tree," Soen coaxed with a practiced smile, his hand resting with studied ease on his disguised staff. Fire and death spooled in the back of his mind, his hand communicating his murderous intention to the staff that warmed beneath his hand. "I long to hear what is happening in the world."

It was a lie. Soen had himself just come from the Shadow Coast and knew better than most what was truly going on there.

"Thank you, noble elven lord," the chimerian said as he stepped up to the tree, paying the deference to the elf that Rhonas demanded of everyone else in the world. "Your generosity is great and does honor to us both."

"I am Thein Tja-kai, of late a merchant of the Fourth Estate and of the Order of Paktan," Soen lied again. When conversing with strangers, he knew, the more distant his location was from the heart of the Imperial Will, the more politic it was to distance himself from the Empire in every way. "I have come to seek a better destiny here in this wild land than I found in the stifling and rotting courts of Rhonas. And you?"

"Ah," the chimerian replied. "Then the Shadow Coast is just the place for you—or perhaps even the Mistral Peninsula itself far beyond the Mournful Mountains. There are great opportunities there. I should know; trade was once my profession." The chimerian extended a free hand. "I'm called Vendis."

This seems to be the season for changing professions, Soen thought but instead reached up with his own free hand, grasped Vendis down near his elbow, and said, "And what do you do now, Vendis?"

"Why, I believe I am a pilgrim!"

"You're a . . . I'm sorry, I'm not sure I understand."

"I am a pilgrim . . . I am on a spiritual journey," Vendis said, leaning on both his walking sticks. "You asked for my news. Have you heard the stories of the Prophet?"

Hunter or hunted, Soen thought though not a muscle moved in response, his left hand still resting on the *Matei* staff. *I've heard of nothing but this "prophet" Belag since tracking the manticore all the way to Port Melthis,* he thought. *The more immediate question has more to do with Vendis. Do I use this chimerian or kill him where he stands? Is he a predator or the prey?*

"A Prophet?" Soen replied with carefully feigned interest. "Is there such a thing?"

"All the winds of the Shadow Coast could not match the force of the words being whispered about him from Shellsea to Gorganta Bay. Surely with so many stories, he must exist."

"The weight of tongues never adds to a truth—it only detracts." Soen said. "But please go on. Tell me about it."

"I have heard that it began many centuries ago . . ." The chimerian stopped. "Surely my noble lord has heard this tale!"

"Not at all, I assure you," Soen lied again. He had heard variations of this tale—some wilder in their miraculous attributions than others—in every town, village or hamlet that he had entered. Each one had grown with every telling. But he was trained as an Inquisitor and so he took in all variations of accounts . . . knowing that often the truth was found in the smallest, barely included detail. "Please, continue."

The chimerian's face twisted into what almost passed for a smile. "Well, I have heard that it began many centuries ago when the *hoo-mani* ruled a great nation across the northern sea. There the might of terrible Rhonas came down in its wrath upon the *hoo-mani* and crushed their brittle bones back into the dust of their land. But as their great priest died on the altar of their citadel, he wrought a great prophecy that one would come afterward who would bring down the towers of the unjust and avenge the bones of the *hoo-mani*. Rhonas would fall before the thunder of his words and the fire of his mouth. And his name would be called Drakis."

"I believe I have heard something of this tale," Soen coaxed. In truth, he had studied the original Prophecy texts in the deep libraries of the Iblisi Lyceum. The Prophecy itself was far more complex than this simple telling and more disturbingly—almost grotesquely—detailed. This was a children's version, but he had to know who this chimerian was and why he had approached Soen searching for the same Belag he sought himself. "It is very old."

"But he has come," the chimerian hissed quietly. "This Drakis has come at last. It is said he broke the chains of his enslavement through the power of his own hands. He vanished before the eyes of the Iblisi who were sent to recapture him—destroying a Legion of their ranks with the wave of his hand—and weeping for their loss afterward. He walked the forests of faery and emerged whole and untouched from the other side. This *hoo-mani* Drakis is the prophesied one. He has fulfilled the prophecy in every particular!"

That was certainly *not* true. Soen and three remaining members of his Quorum had chased Drakis and his companions down the wide length of the Hyperian Plain only to lose them when they crossed into faery lands. That move had cost him the lives of his two Codexia and nearly that of the Assesia his master Ch'drei had sent to spy on him. *Would that he* had *died then,* Soen thought. *I managed to track Drakis again on the Thetis Coast only to lose him when the fool Jukung showed up to kill us both and ruined it all.*

"So this Drakis is the Prophet you are looking for?" It was a deliberate error meant to bait Vendis. Soen knew very well who the Prophet was supposed to be.

"Oh, no," the chimerian answered gently. "The Prophet is the one who tells the stories of Drakis. He is the one who comes ahead of Drakis, preparing the way for his return . . . at least; those are the tales that are being told on the Shadow Coast. I have not met this Prophet and am curious as to what sort of a creature he is . . . that is why I have become a pilgrim, that I might discover the truth."

"A worthy ambition," Soen nodded. The Iblisi had been the guardians of truth for centuries. It was their job to keep the truth safely hidden away. In an empire where history itself was modified to suit the whims of the moment, only the Iblisi kept the sacred difference between reality and expedience. Truth—or the safekeeping of the truth—was, therefore, his business. "To find the truth of a thing is of value indeed. I think I might like to hear what this Prophet has to say as well. I am on no otherwise urgent business and am searching for a better truth—just as you seem to be. I don't suppose you know where this Prophet might be found, do you?"

Vendis opened his mouth as if to speak . . . but hesitated for a moment. "He is, they say, a most generous being, but those who are close to him keep his location closely guarded for fear that the Emperor might wish him ill. But those who told me the tale also told me where to seek him."

"I am an elf as you can clearly see," Soen said. "But is not the truth for all creatures—even the elves under whose doom we quake? Is there no elf who might hear the truth and, knowing it, follow it, too?"

Vendis thought for a moment and then nodded, smiling his strange smile once more. "Then Thein Tja-kai come with me into

Scheliss Field, and we shall decide together how best we may find this prophet!"

Soen did not for a moment believe that this Vendis of Ephindria met him by anything like coincidence. Only fools believed in the providence of the gods arranging such an obvious and fortuitous meeting.

Hunter or hunted? Stalker or prey?

Soen stood up, his Matei staff still ready.

An interesting game, he thought.

CHAPTER 12

Prophet for Profit

"**I**T'S ABOUT TIME, YOU GOT IN!", the goblin innkeeper huffed, his brick-red arms folded across his sunken chest. "I was beginning to wonder myself what I'd be able to find for my own supper—let alone anyone who's left with coin."

Soen stood in the shadow just inside the open doorframe. The contrast made it hard for the goblin to see him from his perch atop a tall stool behind the inn's ledger desk. Soen hung back to observe as Vendis dealt with the creature behind the desk as well as his own mounting frustration.

"Good innkeeper," Vendis said after a deep breath, all four of his narrow hands gripping the front edges of the desk as he spoke in controlled tones. "For the last time, we are NOT the teamsters you are expecting. We do not have any shipment for delivery . . ."

"Well, then what good are ya?" the goblin yelled as he leaned his face forward until his hooked nose nearly touched the chimerian's face. His nasal, high-pitched voice was grating even on Soen's ears. "I've got nothing to EAT! Sold it all down to the last pickle and THEN sold the barrel they come in. I'll bet they ate THAT, too!"

The chimerian gripped the desk edge harder. "We're NOT merchants . . . I mean, we *are* merchants but we're not *your* merchants . . . That's not why we're here. We just want to ask you if . . ."

"So you're merchants but NOT merchants when it comes to me, eh?"

"We're travelers. We just want to ask you . . ."

"No!" the goblin innkeeper said emphatically, its brown ears waggling as it shook its head. "We are taking on no boarders! I appreciate your patronage, but there ain't naught to eat nor buy left in all of Scheliss City."

Soen stifled a laugh, turning his head away momentarily. "Scheliss City" was what the locals had started calling their collection of huts, lean-tos, and shacks. It was difficult for Soen—who had spent far too much of his life in the broad, cobblestone streets and magnificent towers of Rhonas itself—to put the image of this random collection of hovels in the same category of city. Not even the glorified mounds behind the village— the Whispering Hills—were as impressive as their names might sound. The rounded tops seemed to rise reluctantly from the plain, lacking sufficient enthusiasm to push to any truly inspiring height.

Granted, he mused, they were standing in the finest structure the town had to boast of—the "Gobble Inn"—but the name itself all too perfectly demonstrated the refinement and taste of the establishment itself. It was both pretentious and tawdry at the same time: too much statuary and all of it bad reproductions of more elegant and famous pieces. The massive fireplace that took up an entire side of the common room opposite the desk was elaborately carved from stone into the enormous shape of a goblin's head, its gaping mouth forming both the inner hearth and the hood. The stonework, Soen noted, was impressive, carved from a single piece and probably by dwarven craftsmen by the careful and delicate detail work it demonstrated. It was unquestionably an exorbitantly expensive feature especially considering its remote location from Imperial trade. Yet the overall effect of the gaping maw containing the fire was, despite its expensive craftsmanship, in hideously bad taste and completely uninviting. Soen had not yet decided if that was, in fact, the intention of the goblin innkeeper—who seemed not just indifferent to the clientele standing before his desk but remarkably hostile.

Soen smiled to himself, baring his pointed elven teeth. He moved forward.

"Innkeeper . . . I beg your pardon, but I have forgotten your name," Soen said, stepping up to the ledger desk.

"Gobekandrus," the goblin answered indignantly. "And what business does a 'long-head' have traveling with a 'bendy' anyway?"

Soen ignored the multiple insults implied in the remark. "Master Gobekandrus, you have found us out."

"But . . ." Vendis began.

Soen turned to the chimerian. "It's no use, Vendis, I told you that this goblin looked far too obtuse and puerile for our scheme to get past him."

"Scheme?" Gobekandrus asked.

Vendis turned to face the elf. "You're right; he is the very embodiment of puerile."

Soen nodded, "Not to mention obtuse. And we could have made such a fabulous profit!"

"Profit?" the goblin squeaked. The elf and the chimerian were ignoring him in their conversation, but he was hanging on their every word. "What profit?"

"When will the shipments arrive?" Soen asked.

"Oh . . ." Vendis pondered. "Perhaps . . . tomorrow?"

"That soon?" Soen asked with astonishment.

"Well, that may be a very optimistic expectation . . ."

"WHAT SCHEME?" Gobekandrus leaped up onto the ledger desk, reached out and grabbed both the elf's cloak and the chimerian's collar with each of his bony, red hands.

Soen turned his black, featureless eyes on the goblin. "Why, we *are* merchants and we *have* brought goods. We need information to make the scheme work; however we should have realized that you are far too verbose and intractable for us to have fooled you. However, perhaps you would be interested in a business proposition . . . a sharing of our abilities for our mutual profit."

"I've already got money," the goblin said, letting loose his grip and drawing back slightly.

"As one can plainly see," Soen continued, his black eyes shining in the dim light of the common room. "It's goods you need . . . and those are what *we* have."

"What's your plan," the goblin asked quietly, his red eyes fixed on the elf.

"We are interested in moving these items quickly," Soen contin-

ued. "Most of the crates were mistakenly addressed to another destination, and we would just as soon sell the items quickly before anyone
makes any kind of trouble over a few mistakes on a cargo manifest."

Vendis glanced sideways at Soen, but, being a chimerian, there
was no appreciable change in his face.

"I'm not concerned with where things were supposed to go," the
goblin said through a sneer, "just with where they end up."

"Then I think we are in agreement," Soen smiled, his lips pulling
back over his sharp teeth. "I heard the pilgrims passing through were
a good market."

"Good?" Gobekandrus smirked. "Them pilgrims came through
here like one of them plagues. Locusts couldn't have done a better
job cleaning out the town. They came up the south road happy as you
please—manticores singing their songs and what not—and before
you knew it, they were streaming through here like a flood and buy-
ing up everything that looked remotely like it could be eaten or
drunk. Sure, they paid and paid—good Imperial coin as well as some
of those Dje'kaarin trade notes and even a few Kingsrune Slate from
the Goblin Peaks. Price 'em high as you please and they just kept
paying. In the end, none of them town merchants would take coin or
notes . . . it all came down to gems, metals, and the like. Took it all
we did."

"Then what happened," Vendis asked.

The goblin started to laugh. "Well, then they left!"

"Left?"

"Aye! Every last one of them and took every morsel with them!"
Gobekandrus roared with mirth. "The town's full of money . . . bustin'
at the seams with it . . . and you can't buy a loaf of salt bread or a
bottle of mulled wine for less than a king's ransom! Hahaha!"

Holding his belly, Gobekandrus rolled onto his back. Soen and
Vendis just stared as the hilarity overtook the goblin. "I could just
about buy this city with a crate of apples! Hoohoo! Elected king for a
barrel of wheat! Heehee!"

"Exactly . . . exactly our point," Vendis said, trying to bring the
goblin back to the subject. "If you can tell us where these pilgrims
went, then we'll know where to take our goods for sale to . . ."

"Ain't no point in that, boys," the goblin said, wiping his eyes as he stood back up on the ledger desk. "We already wrung them pilgrims out sure. You just bring the goods here to my inn—right here, mind you—and within a few days we'll have more business than even the pilgrims brought us."

Soen lifted his head back slightly. The points of his ears itched. "What do you mean?"

"The Blade of the Northern Will!" Gobekandrus said as though stating the obvious. "The Legions of the Rhonas Empire are coming this way—two or three days at the most!" The goblin leaned in, his voice conspiratorial through his smile. "You bring your wagons here to me, and we'll be the only game in Scheliss City! The Legions will pay far more than those religious fanatics—and in solid Imperial coin! I can guarantee that by the time *I'm* finished with your crates, there'll be no trouble with any manifest. We'll split the take in half?"

"Half!" Vendis exclaimed.

"I'm taking all the risk!" Gobekandrus snapped, his eyes narrowing. "All you have to do is count your coin!"

"One tenth," Soen stated.

The goblin snarled. "I'd rather sell them my inn."

"If you think they'll buy it, but knowing the Legions, they would just as soon burn it to the ground," Soen answered. "Without our goods, you have nothing to sell."

"One in three," the goblin said.

"One in five," Soen responded, "and I see that I can still walk right out your door."

"One in four!" Gobekandrus said as his eyes narrowed.

Soen turned to Vendis. "You know, I seem to recall a tavern up past that wreck of a smithy . . . that seemed to be a nice place . . ."

"Fine!" The goblin pushed out his bony hand. "One in five it is."

Soen smiled. "I'm sure you will not live to regret this, Master Gobekandrus. Are you certain the pilgrims are well on their way? War is always good for business but not if you're caught up in the middle of it."

"Nah, they went up the north road happy as you please four days ago. At their rate, they're probably crossing the Shrouded Plain as it is. Good a place to die as any, I suppose," Gobekandrus shrugged. "So what do you say? Have we a bargain?"

"You can trust me when I say that the moment our goods arrive,"

Soen said through his best sharp-toothed smile, "we will bring them straight to you."

"Thein Tja-kai," Vendis asked after they had stepped out into the dusty path that passed for the main road through Scheliss. "What was that about?"

Soen turned, answering to his adopted name without hesitation. *Hesitation always kills you,* he thought. "Friend Vendis, our new acquaintance and partner Gobekandrus has no intention of splitting anything with us. I suspect he would murder us in our sleep once the goods were delivered . . . fortunately for us, he will wait until we *do* deliver the goods and, since there *are* no goods to deliver, we should be reasonably safe before we leave this ridiculous excuse for a town."

"But why all the . . ."

"You want to find the Prophet, don't you?" Soen said as they walked briskly side by side. "*I* want to find the Prophet, too. All I did was to offer him one kind of profit in exchange for information on where to find the other kind."

"The Shrouded Plain?"

"A migration that size shouldn't be terribly difficult to track."

"So that's where we find him?"

"Perhaps . . . if we're quick enough. Now, it seems, that the Empire wants to find this Prophet as well, and I suspect that since they have sent the Legions to do the job, they do not have any expectation of treating him or his followers kindly. If we're going to ask this Prophet any questions, we're going to have to find him before the weight of Imperial Might does so."

"But the Shrouded Plain?" Vendis asked. "It's a terrible place. Why would anyone want to cross that?"

"I've got a better question for you," Soen replied as he hefted his pack to his back and shouldered his mundane-looking staff. "Why should the Empire send an entire Legion to deal with a migration of religious pilgrims?"

CHAPTER 13

Panaris Road

SCHELISS FIELD WAS NOT the last town on the north road but it certainly was the biggest. The settlements Soen and Vendis encountered as they followed the emigration trail along the western slopes of the Whispering Hills got progressively smaller—each barely more than a collection of a few houses huddled in proximity against the wild expanse around them. As they passed by these smaller, outlying farms, Soen occasionally saw their goblin residents standing by their doors and watching them with suspicion. They were never threatening nor did they come any closer to inquire about the passing strangers.

At least the trail was an easy one to follow. The wide swath that the emigrants cut both down the old road and to either side of it where possible would have been difficult to miss blindfolded. The smell of oxen droppings ground into the earth was pronounced—a sure sign of manticores on the move.

For once, Soen was glad to be on so obvious a course despite the inherent dangers it presented. It meant that he could concentrate on his companion Vendis. The chimerian remained irritatingly cheerful even at his most serious. He was also, unfortunately, a most affable companion on the road. For Soen, who was used to maintaining long silences as he strode the face of the world alone, the constant need to keep up a conversation that Vendis demonstrated was exhausting and demanding. As an Iblisi, few would have dared to approach him in dialogue and those who did—even in his own Order—would have preferred to keep their exchange short. But he wasn't an Iblisi to Vendis or, gods willing, anyone else for the unforeseeable future: he was Thein Tja-Kai, the wandering merchant of the Paktan in search of some Prophet of the North. He was supposed to be interested in the torrent of unending words coming from Vendis as they walked.

So, on those occasions when Vendis stopped and asked why the elf merchant was so quiet, Soen had learned to respond with something on the order of "Oh, I've just been thinking." To this, Vendis invariable and earnestly replied, "Thinking about what?" at which point Soen would have to elucidate on whatever subject Vendis had been chatting about. This, of course, would set Vendis off on another line of thought that, Soen fervently hoped, would occupy his companion for a long stretch of the road.

". . . As I've heard from some of the Ephindrians who occasionally make their way through this country, it has something to do with the rock formations at the northern end of the Whispering Hills. You can see them just up there beyond the rise. See how that granite upthrust splits in several places? Well, the wind crosses there pretty much throughout the day and night, and the currents and eddies through those crags make a peculiar sound very much like voices. For a time there were shamans who would camp at the foot of those crags, listening to the voices in the wind and interpreting their words for pilgrims who came to them trying to speak with their dead relatives or loved ones. That all started because of a legend the local goblins had from their ancestors who first settled here during the Age of Mists before the Shadow War. Have you heard of them?"

Soen cleared his throat, trying to bring his mind back to the conversation. "Heard of who?"

"The Shamans of the Whispering Hills?"

"No, I don't believe I have," Soen replied. Privately he wondered if Vendis was now referring to the original Shamans who initiated the cult during the Age of Mist or the revival Shamans who came to the area during the Age of Fire and twisted the rituals into a powerful death cult, or was he referring to the most recent incarnation carried on by the local goblins who used it as an easy source of money from those few travelers who either by mistake or design came upon them. The history of each was a separate subject tied together only marginally by the legends regarding the winds blowing across the rocks, and none of their histories was particularly interesting.

"Well," said Vendis after taking a deep breath, "there actually were three separate incarnations of the Shamans . . ."

Soen groaned.

"Are you feeling all right, Thein? Vendis asked.

"Yes, I am fine," Soen answered. "Something from my lunch did not agree with me."

"Oh! Would you like to stop?"

"No!" Soen said emphatically. Walking at least gave him something more to do than just listening to Vendis. The chimerian appeared to be taken aback by the strength of his refusal. Soen noted with satisfaction that the shadows had lengthened considerably. Soen tempered his voice. "No, I'm fine—the walking helps me feel better. We'll soon be stopping for the night."

"Of course," Vendis said with satisfaction. "I recall that there's a good spot just atop that next rise . . . Hey, where are you going?"

Soen broke into an easy run, putting some distance between himself and the four-armed chimerian. Maybe it was the road, he thought, that was playing tricks on his black, featureless eyes. The closer he got, however, the faster he ran. Then, abruptly, he stopped.

The red dirt of the road had been worn away. In its place lay a patch of gray granite stones, each fitted together with such precision that Soen could not have wedged the sharpest blade between them.

Soen smiled broadly, exposing his sharp teeth.

Vendis ran up behind him. "What is it?"

Soen smiled. "It's the Panaris Road. I didn't think it would still be here. This was built early in the Age of Fire and leads directly . . ."

Soen stopped talking as his gaze followed the road.

"Leads directly where?" Vendis asked.

"There, my friend," Soen pointed with his long, narrow finger.

Two lone figures sat on the broken stones at the side of the ancient road. One was a human male who, upon seeing Soen, scrambled to his feet. He was middle-aged as humans go, a remarkable feat considering he was wearing an incongruously shiny armor breastplate over his otherwise dull slave's tunic. His exposed head was shaved as was typical of all slaves. He was short and stocky in build with a great hooked nose and dark, piercing eyes that seemed fixed on Soen. He leaned heavily upon a staff with a crystal fixed at the top of its shaft.

The other was an elven captain. His long armored helmet gleamed among the blades of grass where he had set it next to him. The captain's pinched face had a long scar that ran from his forehead past the corner of his right eye and nearly to his ear. The right eye was a dull, graying color—now useless. One of the captain's sandals had also been removed as he sat vigorously rubbing his aching foot.

The human spoke first, his eyes fixed on Soen as he approached. "You've come at last, I see, but you're still behind. Will you ever catch up?"

The captain gave the human a quick kick with his bare foot, and then groaned from the pain he had caused himself. "Braun! Shut up!"

Hunter or prey, Soen thought. *Which is which?*

"My apologies for this fool," the captain said to Soen. "We found this Proxi wandering about the northlands a few days ago. My Tribune seems amused by him, but I don't find him quite so entertaining."

"No apologies necessary, valiant captain," Soen said with a slight bow. "I am Thein Tja-kai of the Paktan; this is Vendis, a merchant trader of these lands. We are all far from Rhonas, are we not Captain of the Imperial Will?"

"We are, Thein Tja-kai," the captain acknowledged through a heavy sigh as he gazed around at the open lands around them. "I am Captain Shuchai of the First Modalis Legion . . . and I feel as though I have walked every step of the road from Rhonas today. But I believe I have walked far enough."

The captain nodded toward the north.

They had crested the rise at the end of the Whispering Hills. The broken granite crags stood off to their right, but it was the vista before them that caught their attention. The plain sank down before them as though the thumb of some god had pressed down into the face of the world. There, in the last rays of the setting sun, lay the salmon-colored tops of clouds beneath them in the distance, holding close to the ground in a perpetual fog that extended beyond the northern horizon.

But it was the encampment that bordered on the near edge of the fog that held his fixed attention. It was a tremendous collection of tents, wagons, animals . . . nearly a mile wide where it nestled near the strange and permanent bank of fog.

"Then we take our leave of you, great Captain," Soen replied, "for it seems that our remaining road must, perforce, be one quickly traveled."

"If that road continues to the north," Shuchai chuckled as he went back to rubbing his foot, "then I might suggest a different road entirely."

"Your council is good," Soen replied. "We shall divert as soon as possible. Fare you well in the Emperor's grace."

"And you," the captain answered with a shrug.

Soen turned and continued down the road to the north, his eyes fixed on the encampment.

Behind him, the Proxi called after them in his strange, unhinged voice. "He isn't there, you know! But he will be . . . just you wait! He will be!"

Through it all, Vendis had not said a word.

It was almost thirty minutes before Vendis found his voice. "Who was that back there?"

"You heard him," Soen answered without breaking his stride. "He's Captain Shuchai of the Modalis Legions out for a stroll with his Proxi Braun. They won't be lonely for long, however. Within a few minutes of that captain getting the ache out of his feet, that same Proxi undoubtedly began propagating gate fold symbols all along that ridge. By now more Proxis from the following Centurai have propagated an exponential number of gate symbols. It won't be long before those two hapless servants of the Rhonas Empire have been joined by the entire Blade of the Northern Will—at least two full Legions— almost sixteen thousand warriors."

Vendis looked back. "I don't see any . . ."

"It's the perfect position," Soen continued, his gaze fixed forward as he walked with a brisk pace. "Deploy the army behind the rise so that it can be hidden from the enemy and then deploy the command tents along the ridge last so that you can command a proper view of the field of battle."

Vendis took several quick steps to catch up to the elf. "They mean to attack the encampment?"

"I believe we may have found your fellow pilgrims, friend Vendis," Soen said in an eager voice. "But I believe the Legions have found them as well."

"There must be . . . more than ten thousand in that camp!" Vendis stammered. "Surely they're mostly families . . . children . . ."

"Closer to fifteen thousand, I should think," Soen replied. "They are at least another three leagues away. Look there. The trailing elements have not yet caught up with the main encampment. You can see the dust still rising behind them, so they are still moving."

"What does it mean?"

"It means," Soen grinned once more, "that we are not stopping until we've reached that camp."

Twilight was nearly over by the time they approached the trailing end of the migration.

Soen had given considerable thought to their approach. He was not concerned about being a prisoner—indeed, it was part of his plan to *become* a prisoner. No, the real difficult part was not being killed in the process of becoming a prisoner. The signs on the trail had clearly indicated that they were following a huge encampment of manticores—lion-men of the Chaenandrian Steppes. They came from a fierce and proud warrior tradition where the family's status and honor were embodied in the ancestral armor that passed down through generations. Though the elders of the Manticas Assembly— the closest the clans ever came to a central government—had surrendered their conquered lands to the greater glory of the Rhonas Imperium, they had not surrendered their warrior hearts as well. Several of the clans had left the Assembly rather than submit to the elves, and one Imperial Eye was forever trained on Chaenandria where the fire may have died but the coals still burned hot in manticore hearts. These manticores had left their ancestral lands and journeyed beyond the boundaries of Chaenandria, taking everything they possessed with them into a strange and hostile land beyond the control of the Emperor or any respect for an elf.

As an Iblisi, he might have walked into such a camp without fear of protecting himself. However, as *Thein*, a lowly Fourth Estate merchant wandering about in the night on the edge of their camp, his fate might very well be in question. He held his Matei staff in his right hand but to use it would unequivocally expose his true nature. That would defeat the entire purpose of his journey.

Prey or hunter . . . always the same question.

"So, how do you think we should do this?" Vendis asked.

"Do what?" Soen replied casually. They were rapidly getting closer to the massive wagons of the manticores ahead of them, the dust from the eight-foot-tall wheels settling on their robes.

"Let them know we're here," Vendis said sotto voce.

"Oh, I wouldn't worry about it," Soen said easily. "I'm sure we already have. Will you do me a favor?"

"A favor?"

"Yes, a small favor really."

"What?"

"Would you just walk in front of me for a few minutes," Soen said pleasantly. "Just until we reach those wagons."

"Just until . . ."

"Yes, until we reach those wagons."

Vendis shrugged and then took a few quick steps forward. "You mean like . . ."

Something huge smashed against the chimerian, driving him forward ten feet and into the back of the wagon with a sickening splat.

Soen was already moving. He had felt the movement more than seen it, the thin hairs that circled his elongated head shifting with the air about him. At once, he fell flat against the ground.

The massive dark form flew over him, with a roar of angry disappointment, huge arms clawing at the darkness above him.

"Any gods who can hear me," Soen muttered, "pray this works."

Soen let go his staff, pushing it slightly away from him even as he felt the pounding feet of the enraged manticore charging toward him.

Slowly and deliberately, Soen pulled his knees up under him but he kept both of this hands flat against the ground, his face down and his eyes averted. Then he held very, very still.

He could feel the hot breath of the manticore on the back of his neck.

"WHO ARE YOU?" roared the manticore, its voice so loud in Soen's ears that he was actually startled.

I'm alive, Soen thought.

"I am a pilgrim," he answered.

The manticore laughed. "An elf pilgrim?"

"Is not one prophet the prophet of all?" Soen asked. His face remained turned down, his hands touching the ground before him.

Three full breaths from the manticore brushed against the back of Soen's neck before he replied.

"Perhaps," the manticore answered at last. "Get up."

Soen stood, picking up his staff.

"Give that to me," the manticore said at once.

Soen looked at the manticore. He was mature for his race but still an able warrior. He wore intricate armor of a very old design.

"This staff," Soen said carefully, "was given me by my grand-father—my father's father—and is the symbol of my family's honor."

The manticore snorted loudly. "It is a stick."

"Yes, but it is *my* stick and *my* honor," Soen replied.

"Honor is found in battle, long-head," the manticore snarled.

"I fight a different war," Soen answered, handing the staff to the manticore.

CHAPTER 14

Grahn Aur

SOEN FOLLOWED AFTER HIS CAPTOR—a manticore who had flatly stated that giving his name to the elf was beneath him—with Vendis at his side. Three more manticore warriors followed a few steps behind them, waiting for their own excuse to pounce on the captives and get a few battle strikes in of their own. The group wound their way into the interior of the encampment, down crowded paths between clusters of tents and wagons. Many of the covered wagons had rigged their canvas to form temporary shelters along the side of the towering wagon boxes. Now these were hastily being taken down and secured once more over the wagon's load. Everywhere Soen looked, there were creatures of many different races rushing in furious activity. The great majority was made up of manticores, but the remarkable thing in this for Soen was that they were in families. Manticores rarely allowed outsiders into their clan-prides or even to see their young, yet here Soen observed them all. Elderly lion-men with long, dusty manes stooped next to a fire by a wagon as they gestured in storytelling to a circle of cubs and their manticore mothers while their fathers readied their wagons to leave. A group of young lion-men struggled with a recalcitrant team of oxen while another group of young manticore women jeered at them from beside their own quickly harnessed team. Manticore males and females rushed to strike their recently made camps or to move the oxen out of corrals and take them back to their yokes.

Not just manticores, however, but other races packed the encampment as well. A considerable number of chimerians were also here in the camp as were a not insignificant number of dark-skinned humans and even a few lighter-skinned humans as well. In several instances, Soen observed these chimerians and humans working at a furious pace side by side with the manticores and they often seemed attached to a manticore family camp wagon. Hak'kaarin gnomes ran everywhere through the camp, stopping here to listen to a story and there to lend a hand or occasionally bumping into another gnome and chatting furiously before dashing off to some other parts unknown.

The paths were occasionally so crowded that it was difficult to tell where a camp ended and the path began. Everyone, however, quickly moved out of the path of the manticore warrior, their eyes fixed on the captives with a mixture of curiosity and suspicion as they passed. Their pace was only impeded by the occasional choke of oxen in the path before them who were not impressed by either the strange prisoners or the fierce warriors accompanying them.

"Just when were you going to tell me about the ambush?" Vendis asked testily.

"What ambush?" Soen answered.

"That ambush at the edge of the camp—the one where I ended up with my head smashed against the back of a wagon."

"Oh, *that* ambush," Soen said, delight playing about the edges of a smile.

"You and I need to talk more," Vendis huffed.

"Look," Soen said, "you're a chimerian. These manticores patrolling the perimeter of the caravan were obviously in the mood to kill us first and then ask who we were later. I needed time before being too dead to manage a proper surrender to the manticores. I knew you could take the blow of their initial charge because . . ."

"Because I'm a 'bendy'?" Vendis bristled at the implied insult in the word.

"I was going to say that you are more flexible," Soen corrected.

"Being 'flexible' does not mean that it doesn't hurt," Vendis replied. "Or that it doesn't *still* hurt."

"Then I am sorry for your pain," Soen answered almost truthfully. "Nevertheless, manticores prefer to strike first with their claws and fists . . . claws that would not cut deep enough to do you any lasting harm and the unusual telescoping bones and pliable sinews of your race would blunt their hammering fists. It takes a great deal to kill your kind, Vendis; very sharp blades and at the right puncture locations . . . or a knowledge of the nerve points that can paralyze chimerians long enough to allow for more permanent options."

"You sound a little too familiar with the subject," Vendis said.

Soen shrugged. "We are still alive, and I count that as something of a victory."

"For now," Vendis grumbled.

"Yes, for now."

The manticore leading them turned to the left and then right once more. The smells of cooking in the camp were becoming more pronounced: heavily laden with spices that were in turn enticing, exotic, cloying, and occasionally brought tears unbidden to the elf's eyes.

"Would you look at that!" Vendis exclaimed.

They were passing a small group of elves. These, too, had been repacking their camp and were just finishing.

"These pilgrims don't seem to be very discriminating," Vendis said with sarcasm.

"I did say I was sorry," Soen countered, but his mind was considering the implications. Not only had the encampment included the elves in their camp but indeed seemed at ease with them living among them.

"Where are they going?" Vendis asked quietly as they continued on.

"Toward the center of the camp, I should think," Soen answered, his mind still on the pilgrim elves. "The layout appears to be concentric even though the paths are mazelike in their design. A good proper defensive structure, actually, so I suspect we're headed for some sort of interrogation . . ."

"No," Vendis interrupted. "I mean, where do you think this camp is headed? They came from the south, so they wouldn't be reversing their direction. Ephindria lies to the east, and I know from personal experience that an incursion of a single outside individual over their border is cause enough for the chimerians to be outraged, let alone what looks like an entire small nation. If their objective had been the Shadow Coast, then there are much better and faster routes to the west that they could have taken at several places in their journey. That leaves north—the Shrouded Plain. That's no choice at all; it's said to be blanketed by a haunted fog more than a hundred leagues across—a place where ancient spirits continue to wander and exist only to lead others to their doom."

"Cheerful prospect," Soen chuckled darkly.

"So where are they going?"

The crush of the encampment suddenly gave way to a large circular clearing surrounded entirely by manticore warriors in full armor. In the center nearly one hundred meters from the edge of the clearing was a large, multi-chambered tent.

Soen grinned. "I suspect we're about to get the answer to your question."

The tent was not the most opulent that Soen had ever seen. Indeed, even by most manticorian standards, it was modest and a little austere. There were the usual compartments—small rooms all arranged around the large, central gathering room, but they were few in number and all of them had their partitions pulled back so that the elf could see the contents of each. A sleeping chamber with the expected ground mat and tubular pillows, a small dining table built low after the manticorian custom of lounging on pillows for formal meals and an ablutions chamber common to every household in Chaenandria. Curiously missing was the deity shrine that universally graced every manticorian household.

Their manticorian captor had preceded them into the tent and now stood in the center of the gathering room facing them. "Grahn Aur will arrive shortly. You will kneel when he enters the room. You will speak only when he gives his permission for you to do so. You will answer his questions when they are asked and keep your own questions to yourself. Stand where you are, and I will inform him that you are here. Do not move; do as I have instructed you, and you may yet live to see the stars again."

Vendis cast a sidelong glance at the elf. "Well, Thein . . . what's our next move?"

"My understanding is that we're to make no move at all," Soen replied, his eyes fixed straight ahead.

"What kind of an elf are you?" Vendis snarled. "You let me take a hit from behind so that you can properly surrender, several Legions of the elven army are about to display the displeasure of the Emperor in a most emphatic way against mostly the old, the infirm, and the helpless, and now you just want to stand here and wait? What happened to the defiant spirit of the elves that led them to conquer the world?"

"It's hard to conquer anything when you're dead," Soen observed. "Victory always consists of letting someone else die for their cause."

Vendis cast a baleful eye on Soen.

"You're still here, aren't you?" Soen replied. "Besides, if we're going to find this prophet you keep telling me about, who better to point the way than the leader of these pilgrims?"

Vendis sighed. "Do you always have to be right?"

"No, but I always am," Soen grinned to himself. He thought he also heard a low chuckle from one of the three manticore guards still standing behind them.

The sound of the tent flap being pulled aside caused both Soen and Vendis to straighten slightly. They felt more than heard the movement behind them before the large, stooped figure of a manticore shuffled around them with two young manticores assisting him on either side. The mane of the elder manticore was almost entirely gray, cascading back from the crown of his head down the back of the great ceremonial mantle that he wore. In his hoary left hand, he clutched a tall, intricately carved staff, the top of which was fashioned into a clawed hand gripping a fractured crystal globe. The ancient manticore squinted at the elf and the chimerian from a face filled with the deep folds of age and partially covered by a long, gray beard that had been carefully braided just below his chin and fell nearly to the center of his chest.

Under the critical gaze of the old manticore, Soen quickly remembered the instructions he had been given. He knelt down to the ground on one knee, followed quickly by his chimerian companion.

The wizened manticore kept staring at them even as he continued his shuffling walk toward the back of the tent, both manticores at his side in constant attendance.

Soen watched and waited.

The old manticore disappeared into the back sleeping chamber of the tent. The two manticores assisting him closed the flap behind them, shutting them off from all eyes in the central chamber.

A moment passed during which no one spoke or moved.

Soen sighed. "Well, I suppose our interrogation is over."

The quiet was broken by a resounding, deep bellowing sound that shook the tent poles behind them. Soen turned instinctively toward the resonant sound.

It came from a younger manticore wearing a plain tunic, leggings, and a cloth robe. There was genuine amusement in his eyes and perhaps a bit more, Soen thought, as he quickly examined the creature. He had the broad manticorian face though his mane was perhaps a bit short for his apparent age. This he kept pulled back tightly away from his face and bound in the back.

"I can see you have met Gradek," the young manticore said through a broad smile of his fanged teeth. "He's my captain of the evening watch. He's very good at his job, but I think he takes me a bit too seriously sometimes."

The manticore strode around in front of the kneeling elf and chimerian, extending both of his broad, strong hands. "Come! Get up. Let us talk quickly, for you are late arriving and there is much to be done."

"Late?" Soen asked, taking the manticore's offered huge hand, his own smaller hand nearly disappearing in its grasp as the manticore effortlessly pulled the two of them to their feet. "You were expecting us?"

"Of course," the manticore flashed another beaming smile. "We've been tracking you for several hours. I wanted to just bring you in but Gradek was concerned and suspicious. Of course, his job is to be concerned and suspicious, so I can hardly fault him. Unfortunately, you arrived just ahead of a much bigger problem, which I must address very shortly. I hope to have a much longer discussion with you both later, but there simply is not time to interview you now. For the time being, what are your names?"

The manticore's breezy manner had taken Soen by surprise. The lion-man race was little known for its humor, and it had often been said that they had practiced being dour until it was a fine art among them. "I am Thein Tja-kai, a merchant of the Fourth Estate and the Order of Paktan."

"A merchant who travels without goods," the manticore observed as he turned toward the chimerian. "And you?"

"I am simply known as Vendis, sir," the chimerian answered awkwardly.

The manticore nodded. "Well, I am Grahn Aur . . . the leader of these combined clan-prides on our pilgrimage into the land of the Chosen One."

"*You* are the leader?" Soen asked, his voice rising in astonishment. "But I thought the old one . . ."

"No," Grahn Aur said, a smile playing about his fangs as he spoke. "That is one of the Clan Elders. He is in need of some rest before we set out again, and I offered him my tent. It will not be a long rest, sadly, for our time is already short." Grahn turned to one of the guards. "Hegral, please remove Vendis and keep him company outside while I speak with the elf alone. I'll call for him when it is his turn."

Vendis barely had time to raise one of his four arms in protest before the powerful Hegral grabbed him and dragged him swiftly out through the tent flap.

"You can hardly blame them for being suspicious," Grahn Aur said with a deep sigh. He turned back to gaze at Soen. "Tell me, Thein Tja-kai, why does an elf come seeking so carefully the company of pilgrims?"

Soen looked into the bright eyes of the manticore and saw something familiar in them. "Because I, too, am a pilgrim, Grahn Aur."

"Indeed? And what do you seek, Thein Tja-kai?"

"A man of prophecy . . . a man named Drakis."

"It seems all the world is seeking Drakis," the manticore answered, his manner turning suddenly thoughtful. "And perhaps we shall find him together then, Thein of the Paktan. But first we must survive your brethren."

"The Legions?" Soen asked.

"Already assembled to the south and moving. I had hoped they would wait to attack in daylight, but that is not our fate," Grahn Aur nodded. "The order has already been given to break the camp. Our warriors are arrayed at the rear to cover our flight."

"Flight?" Soen exclaimed. "May I ask to where?"

"The only place the gods have granted us," Grahn Aur replied. "You come at a strange time, Thein of the Paktan. Do you believe in this Drakis that the prophecies foretold?"

Soen felt uncomfortable under the manticore's gaze. "I do not know, Grahn Aur. I only know that I seek him and must find him. That is the truth of it."

As close to the truth of it as I might speak, Soen thought.

The manticore smiled and nodded his great head. His eyes fixed on Soen for a few long moments as the lion-man thought before speaking again.

"You shall join with us, Thein. We shall seek him together," Grahn Aur said with some conviction. He snapped his fingers loudly. Hegral appeared instantly, his large hand on the grip of the sword at his waist. "Take Thein to find Captain Gradek. I believe he is holding a walking stick that was confiscated during Thein's introduction to our camp. Have him kindly return it to our fellow traveler."

"Yes, Master Grahn Aur," Hegral said in a snapping voice that was a little too loud.

"Thank you," Soen said, bowing graciously to Grahn Aur. "That stick means a lot to me."

Grahn Aur bowed in return. "So Captain Gradek has informed me."

Several minutes had slowly passed since Hegral and his elven charge had left Grahn Aur with the chimerian prisoner. During all that time, each had watched the other with interest but neither had spoken a word. At last, Grahn Aur spoke.

"Is he the one, Vendis?"

"I believe so, Master," Vendis replied with casual ease. "That he is—or was—an Inquisitor of the Iblisi is certain given that Matei staff he tries so hard to conceal. There are a number of their Order who are scouring the Northmarch, Vestasia, and the Shadow Coast right now, but I feel certain that we have the one."

"Soen Tjen-rei," Grahn Aur murmured. "An Inquisitor who appears to be out of favor with his own Order."

"Appearances can be deceiving, Master," Vendis said, folding the upper set of his arms across his chest while placing the lower set of hands on his hips. "Why do you let him so near you?"

"There's an old saying among my people," the manticore said. "Hold your enemies closer than your friends. You still do not know why he is seeking Drakis, then?"

"No, Master," Vendis answered. "I wonder if he does himself."

CHAPTER 15

Battle Lines

"GRADEK!" SOEN YELLED as he followed on the heels of the manticorian warrior. "Where is my staff?"

"I have more important duties than finding your stick for you," Gradek roared back as he stormed down the line of manticore warriors arrayed in a battle formation beyond the southern end of the encampment.

Soen raged inside. He could think of a dozen ways to kill the manticorian War Master on the spot with or without his Matei staff and had certainly done so to others with less provocation. Killing Gradek meant disrupting the chain of command for these warriors at a critical time, and Soen just could not bring himself to make a bad situation worse simply for his own satisfaction.

Not, he noted, that it would make much difference.

Gradek continued yelling at the warriors arrayed in front of him. "Maintain the line! They'll come at you quickly out of their magical gates. You've got to get to them before they can form up, then charge when you see your chance!"

Soen shook his head. It was a classic manticorian battle structure that had been passed down from generation to generation for the last thousand years and bent in more recent times to address the specific challenges presented by the difference in elven warfare doctrines.

It was also why the Legions of Rhonas had won every battle against the manticores in the last two hundred years.

"Do you even have a clan, Gradek?" Soen suddenly demanded as he continued to follow on the manticore's heels.

"Have a clan?" Gradek turned suddenly, baring his fangs as his eyes narrowed on the elf. "I am a warrior of Clan Hravash, you insignificant long-head! Who were your parents?"

Soen held both hands up, palms facing away from the manticore. "My apologies, War Master Gradek."

The manticore snarled and then turned once more to stalking the line of warriors.

Soen quickly looked around. Night had fallen but he knew that would not stop the Legions any more than the antiquated battle traditions of the manticores. He could see that there were elements of the camp that had started to move—incredibly toward the cursed mists of the Shrouded Plain—but it was like watching a river break up at the end of winter; the wagons and pilgrims closer to the battle line had to wait until the bulk of the camp in front of them started moving before they could move themselves. The edges of the encampment were over a hundred yards from the battle line, but that distance would be nothing for the Legions to cross once they smelled the blood of unarmed prey. Nothing among the pilgrims was happening quickly enough.

Then Soen saw what he was looking for—the battle standard of Clan Hravash. By tradition, such a standard flew in every battle the manticore clans fought and usually above the clan house that commanded the battle line. That it now flew above a handcart did not diminish its significance to the manticores.

Soen ran across the open space toward the rear of the pilgrim company still waiting to move forward. He could see hundreds of faces glancing backward toward him, uncertain and afraid. It did not distract him from his purpose.

He quickly closed with the battle standard and the cart next to it, sliding slightly on the prairie grass beneath his feet as he came to a stop. Gradek would not have trusted an item of honor to anyone else once he had given his word. Manticore battle traditions dictated that all his possessions be held in his home during battle and were considered sacrosanct in any conflict. But when a manticore no longer had a home, his possessions would be kept . . .

Soen suddenly stopped tossing Gradek's life possessions on the ground and smiled. His matei staff filled his hands with familiar warmth.

A sudden shout and instantly the air filled with a roaring cacophony of sounds. The Legions were on the march toward the manticore battle line and were within a thousand yards. Many in the first line were Impress Warriors but elven warriors were backing them up. The Blade of the Northern Will was a Modalis Legion and preferred to use their own warriors in battle in combination with Impress Warriors of the Sixth Estate slaves.

Soen quickly ran back toward where he could see Gradek once again yelling instructions at his warriors. The elf's mind spun the words in his mind, conjuring the power building in his matei staff. He could only trust that the darkness would help him.

Gradek had pulled out his signal horn, a small curving instrument with which the manticores issued their signals on the field of battle.

The former Inquisitor stopped behind the manticore commander and felt the release of the energy from both his body and the staff; the rush of the power through him. It was a momentary ecstasy, and he felt the customary emotional and physical drain when it was done. He glanced once behind him and, satisfied, spoke loud enough for as many of the manticores grimly arrayed before him to hear.

"Gradek! The encampment!" Soen shouted. "They've moved to the west!"

Gradek spun around, the horn already raised. "Now what are you . . . ?"

"They've shifted along the front of the fog," Soen said, pointing with his staff and hoping that the manticorian warrior would not notice that he had retrieved his own staff from the bottom of Gradek's cart.

The manticore's jaw dropped open.

The entire camp had somehow shifted behind him.

"Your battle lines," Soen said, pointing once more toward the warriors. "You'll be out of position! The clans will be undefended!"

Gradek shouted at once. "Warriors of the clans! Rise up! Charge right! Protect the clans!"

Gradek put the horn to his lips and sounded a series of thunderous blasts. Answering blasts resounded all down the battle line.

The manticorians stood up in confusion. The signal was not the one they were expecting. They were trained warriors though, Soen realized, many of them were still very young. They, too, now could see that their wives, children, brothers, sisters—their clans—had all inexplicably moved from behind the protection of the carefully placed battle lines and were now so far to the west that they could not longer be protected.

"Charge right!" Gradek bellowed, then sounded the signal again for the line to shift.

"Charge right!" the line answered and they began to run across the line of march from the approaching elven Legions.

Soen crouched down in the grass, his black eyes gazing with fixed intensity on the approaching line of the Legions. The magic he had conjured bent what little light there was from the stars above, making the image of the fleeing pilgrim company appear much farther to the west than its actual position. Shifting the battle lines to protect the false company was meant to draw the Legions away from the real refugees.

"Take it," Soen muttered toward the approaching Legions through his sharp, clenched teeth. "Take it!"

The front lines of the Legions wavered for a moment, and then started marching toward their right.

Soen smiled. He could not see the refugees behind him as his own spell prevented it, but he could see the image of them off to the west.

They were starting to move at last toward the fog . . .

. . . Still, not quickly enough.

Gradek's horn sounded again, this time with the signal every manticore warrior on the line expected. The manticores began their charge just as Soen arrived.

The Legions were within fifty yards of their lines. The lion-men surged forward as a tide, tearing over the ground with their battle roars resounding, their blades cutting the air as they ran.

Soen gritted his sharp teeth. He knew what was coming but he also knew that he could never have prevented it; never have convinced Gradek of the truth. He charged forward with them, struggling to keep up with the great lion-men in their onward rush.

The manticores slammed into the front lines of the Legions, smashing the Impress Warriors and dealing death to them in horrific numbers. The Impress Warriors, who had no memory of ever losing a battle because their elven masters had erased any such memories from their minds, suddenly panicked, broke ranks, and ran, trusting that the elven warriors behind them would cover their retreat.

The elves were not there. Unnoticed by either the charging manticores intent on their prey or by their own Impress Warriors on the front line, the elven warriors had quietly retreated back through the gate folds another hundred yards. There they had not formed a line but were arrayed in Octia clusters around the folds as though prepared to retreat through them again.

"Forward!" Gradek bellowed over the sounds of death. "Forward!"

Encouraged by their success, the manticores continued their charge in pursuit of the remaining Impress Warriors, running them down and continuing their charge toward what looked to them like the disorganized line of elven warriors ahead of them.

Soen kept glancing backward, dreading what was to follow and desperately trying to reach the still charging Gradek who remained yards ahead of him on the battle line.

Forgotten were the Proxis, most of whom had died in the initial charge; they had come forward with the Impress Warrior line and had, as instructed, inscribed the gate fold sigils at the farthest point of advance.

The gate folds flashed once more . . .

And several Centurai of the elven army emerged from the gates that had suddenly opened *behind* the manticorian line. No manticore warrior stood between them and the fleeing refugees. The elves charged at once toward the unprotected wagons, intent on inflicting as much death as possible.

Gradek heard the folds open behind him. He turned as Soen reached him, the manticore's face filled with horror.

More Centurai of the Legion were folding in all around them. The battle line was dissolving into chaos.

"Run!" Soen yelled at Gradek. "Sound the retreat!"

Gradek's eyes remained fixed on the wagons. A massacre was but heartbeats away.

"Gradek!" Soen screamed. "Charge to the *north*!"

Gradek's eyes suddenly focused. He pulled his horn to his lips and sounded the signal.

The manticore line had collapsed into chaotic melees. Groups of manticores fought elven warriors in a mass of confusion. Manticore blood flowed thick across the ground as the elven warriors' superior training was evident in their systematic and long-practiced slaughter. The sound of Gradek's horn was still answered from up and down the battlefield with repeating sound though far fewer in number than had answered before. Within moments, every manticore on the field of battle attempted to disengage from the enemy and charge northward toward the unrelenting, menacing fog.

The threatened pilgrim caravans suddenly vanished, the illusion dissipated. The confused elves, seeing their prey evaporate instantly before their eyes, were momentarily uncertain, but the Tribunes conducting the battle from the ridge three leagues to the south acted quickly. The elven Centurai quickly folded away, back to their original battle formations to regroup and determine what had gone wrong.

Soen ran with Gradek toward where the illusory caravans had existed only moments before. The elven folds were collapsing around them. The screams of the wounded manticores and elves behind them echoed in their ears, as did the sounds of the pounding feet of the remaining elven Centurai who now were chasing after the retreating manticores.

Soen ran into the fog and kept running, directly into its chill, smothering embrace.

CHAPTER 16

Silent as the Grave

SOEN SLOWED HIS PACE when he was nearly a mile into the mists. The ground was flattening out and seemed to be descending slightly beneath his feet. Normally, this would have allowed him to quicken his pace, but nothing about his surroundings struck him as normal.

Elves naturally have keen sight and hearing, abilities which had been honed fine by Soen in his role as an Inquisitor of the Iblisi, but his senses appeared to be failing him in this strange, blanketing mist. He could hear the sounds of those around him—usually muted but occasionally sharp and nearby—yet he could not discern their direction or precise distance. The elves also had a limited ability to see heat during the cool of night but this utterly failed him now. All he was left with was a strange, blue-green glow that was everywhere in the mists and increasing with each step. Soen wondered idly if the glow was always here or was created by the passage of living creatures through it. It was entirely speculation on his part, but the mental exercise helped keep him focused despite the haze all around him.

The enormous shape of a manticore shadowed the fog before him. Soen slowed even more, his Matei staff held at the ready. The former Inquisitor gritted his sharp teeth in preparation for battle.

The shadow emerged before him in the aqua-green glow.

It was a pillar of stone.

Soen let out his breath and ruefully shook his head.

"Looking for me?" came a voice sounding clearly in his right ear.

Soen spun into a defensive stance, his staff clearing the space around him, leveled to launch a deadly array of powerful magic.

A figure was retreating from him slowly into the glowing mists. Soen narrowed his lids over his featureless black eyes and frowned. It was about the size of an elf or human and moved like it could have been either. He made a mental effort to relax his grip on the staff and began pacing the figure through the fog, trying to get a better look at it as he moved across flat ground covered in anemic, yellowed grass. He tried to close with it gradually. While he felt he was getting closer, his prey somehow continued to elude him.

There was a building emerging from the mists ahead of them toward which the figure was walking. It was a tall, circular structure set atop a round foundation of shallow steps. Fluted columns supported a domed roof overhead. It was a typical structure of the old kingdoms, Soen realized; the frivolous sort of a building they used to call a "folly." It was ornamental, lovely in its architecture, and completely out of place. There was something about it that was both purposeful and useless all at once.

The figure stopped halfway up the steps and turned, pulling back the hood covering her head and obscuring her face.

"Ch'drei!" Soen breathed in a mixture of apprehension and admiration.

"How nice of you to remember me," the ancient female elf said, smiling back at him in the glowing mists. "You've been looking for me behind you since you left me your message on the throne of the Dje'kaarin and now you have found me at last."

"More accurately, you have found me," Soen answered though his lowered Matei staff never wavered. "But why come yourself? Killing was never a pleasure to you when it was done by your own hand. You always preferred to enjoy it as a spectator. Why bother to come yourself?"

"Come inside, Soen," Ch'drei smiled, her cadaverous face pulled back in a ghoulish grin. "Everything will be made right. Everything will be explained."

Soen raised his narrow, pointed chin slightly. "I think I would like to get this explanation right here, thank you all the same."

"Nonsense, my boy," the Keeper said with a sharp-toothed grin. "Come on up here and see for yourself. The answers are all right inside."

"I'd rather find my own answers," Soen replied. The wispy hairs at the back of his elongated head were twitching. Something was wrong here.

"You're looking for something that doesn't exist," Ch'drei said, her smile falling slightly. "Don't be foolish, boy."

Ch'drei turned away to step inside the folly.

Soen released the charge in his Matei staff. A white bolt shot from the end, encapsulating Ch'drei and suspending her in time. The Inquisitor did not want to harm the Keeper; he needed her alive if he was ever to get back into the graces of his Order. She was the most powerful member of the Iblisi, and Soen knew better than to equate her age with weakness. It had cost him dearly in the drain of the remaining charge in his staff but he knew he had only once chance. That Ch'drei had turned her back on him at all, making his attack possible, was an unusually rare mistake for her, and Soen had not hesitated to take advantage of it. He rushed up the steps of the folly toward the glowing spheroid of temporal stasis, stopping short of the top stairs.

The mystical globe surrounded with silent lightning was empty.

"Impossible!" Soen uttered.

"Come in, Soen," called the voice from within the folly.

Soen peered between the pillars. There was nothing but darkness within.

"I'm waiting for you."

Soen turned and ran with all his speed down the stairs and across the plain through the glowing mists. Many shadows appeared in front of him, and he remembered that he had directed the entire column of refugee pilgrims into the mists. Perhaps he had found them gathering together and trying to make their way as a group. In any event, they would provide cover for him against the pursuit of Ch'drei or any Iblisi whom she'd, no doubt, brought with her. He barreled in among the figures, rushing by their shadows in the fog.

They were not moving.

Soen quickly stopped, examining them more closely.

They were stone carvings—statues—all arrayed on the plain facing in the same direction. It was an army rendered out of rock. Some held swords with the short, broad blades of the Impress Warriors. Many were human though the majority were either manticores or chimerians. More striking still, Soen realized that they were all different, carved in the shape of individuals. In fact, some of their faces looked quite familiar.

Soen blinked.

He was staring into the face of a statue that was an uncanny likeness of the human he had met only the day before on the Panaris Road. The figure's arms were outstretched, and his face was upturned in a strange, rapturous grin. Soen struggled for a moment to recall his name. *Braun*, he thought.

He moved quickly past the figures, heading in the direction they were facing, subconsciously following their silent intention. There was the chimerian Vendis, his face turned away, unlike any of those around him, his four hands held up before him as if to ward something off. As he broke through the front ranks of the stone army, Soen saw statues of a manticore and a dwarf standing in front of the motionless ranks behind them facing across a river.

Beyond the stone manticore waited the folly.

Soen drew in a breath. He was sure that he had kept a straight line in his dash away from the isolated structure and yet here it was again, the same in every detail.

"Looking for me?" came a different voice from behind him.

Soen wheeled around and suddenly stopped the arch of his staff before it connected with the man standing there. More in anger than astonishment, the elven Inquisitor exclaimed, "You!"

"I've been waiting for you," said Drakis. The human didn't look much different from the way Soen had seen him last, fleeing in the ship of the Forgotten. His dark hair was roughly cut and his beard was untrimmed and wild. The dark brown eyes were unmistakable as was his stocky build. More particular was the shape of his ear, a unique feature among humans and, for members of the Iblisi profession, the surest way to differentiate humans from each other. He still wore his tattered slave's tunic but had managed to pick up pieces of leather armor along the way. None of it matched, of course, but it would serve better than no armor at all. Drakis deftly held the hilt of a sword casually in his hand, seemingly more out of habit than as a threat.

"I have been looking for you," Soen replied. "You've caused a lot of trouble in the world and no small inconvenience to me personally."

"And yet we both seem to be the prey at the moment, don't we?" Drakis said with a sigh. "I think we can help each other."

"We can start with who *they* are," Soen said, nodding toward the statues whose ranks faded beyond Drakis into the glowing green mists around them.

Drakis looked over his shoulder. "Them? They are the future, Soen. They are what is coming."

"The future?" Soen said with a nervous laugh. "Then they are not coming very fast."

"Faster than you think, friend," Drakis said as he walked past the Inquisitor and started toward the folly. "I can show you your future, Soen—it's just in there. You Iblisi are all concerned with keeping the truth, the guardians of truth—or is that the buriers of the truth, I've never quite understood the difference. Follow me, and I'll show you a truth no living soul has ever known."

Soen started to walk after Drakis. *How is it possible that I, an Inquisitor of the Iblisi should find myself over a thousand leagues from the Lyceum Halls of Rhonas and stumble through a blind fog to find the one human in all the Northmarch that I want to find? That Drakis should have changed so little and look exactly as I expected . . .*

"You haven't changed at all, have you, Drakis?" Soen asked casually.

"You would be surprised at how much," Drakis said. "You'll see as soon as we're inside."

"How good of you to remember my name," Soen spoke quietly.

Without warning, Soen swung his Matei staff. The sound of it tore the air with speed and strength, aimed precisely at the base of the human's neck.

Soen nearly fell off-balance as the staff passed unhindered through the neck of Drakis, ripping through the air on the other side. Yet in the instant of contact, a bone-chilling cold rushed up the length of the staff, shooting into Soen's fingers, running up his arms and driving frigid pain into his beating heart.

The Inquisitor stumbled slightly, recovering as the staff continued its powerful arc and nearly carried him over with it.

"Been looking for me?" Drakis turned around, facing Soen—but this time the dark eyes of the human were empty space. The apparition of Drakis grinned. "We've been *looking* for you!"

Soen ran past the folly, away from the stone army, leaving all of it to fall behind him. He found a river with an ancient, broken bridge and followed its banks to what he thought was the north.

The river led him to the folly.

Soen turned at a right angle to the river, pushing his way through a thicket of dead trees in the thick green glow of the mists. He came too quickly upon a precipice, fell over its edge and tumbled down the slope sliding at last to a stop.

He pushed himself painfully to his feet.

The folly stood before him, a mist-shrouded squat tower ahead of him in the green, glowing fog. Three shadowy figures were moving toward him out of the fog.

Qinsei, Phang, and Jukung—all fellow members of the Iblisi Order and all of whom Soen knew for a fact to have died. Jukung's face was disfigured as he had last seen him, including the great gash across his windpipe that Soen had cut for him. They shifted around to surround him, their own Matei staffs leveled at him, urging him toward the folly.

Soen bared his teeth.

A deep, resounding shock wave rolled across the plain, followed at once by a white, diffuse point of light in the fog to Soen's right. The dead Iblisi around Soen turned in shock toward the new, searing light. A second, deafening sound rolled over them as the fog was driven back, burned away by the light. The specters surrounding Soen keened horribly, their shrill voices in agony as their shapes collapsed into dust in the sudden wind.

On a rise over the plain, the single figure of a manticore stood. The light shone from the tip of the sword he held high over his head. Already, figures were emerging from the fog, held at bay by the light of the sword, and gathering around the manticore. Men, women, children of humans, manticores, chimerians, and others—many having even managed to keep control of their wagons and beasts—thronged toward the lone manticore at the top of the rise.

Soen turned and walked toward the light.

CHAPTER 17

Nothing but the Truth

SJEI-SHURIAN WAS OFFENDED by the rain.

He normally enjoyed a good downpour in Rhonas Chas. It allowed him to be even more secluded than usual as he passed down the streets of the great city, and he enjoyed having the streets largely to himself. Rhonas Chas was, he reflected, much more impressive without all the elves clogging the streets and spoiling his view. The rain washed down the streets, giving them a gloss under the leaden skies overhead. He preferred the softer light of the cloud-shrouded rainfall to the starker, glaring illumination of clear skies.

But today he found the weather an affront because it had been so ordered at the Emperor's whim. The Imperator of all Rhonas was melancholy, and High Priest Wejon Rei of the Myrdin-dai had inferred at court that this should mean that all of Rhonas Chas should weep with him—including the sky. It irritated the Sinechai of the Modalis that the beloved rain should fall simply because of the Imperial whim.

Sjei's booted footfalls splashed down the length of the narrow *Via Chiompasi*, turning to his right at the intersecting *Via Torakia*, which opened almost at once onto the *Paz Vitratjen*—the Plaza of the Unexpressed. A column of polished stone rose from the center of the ornate fountain, soaring nearly a hundred and fifty feet above the cobblestones and capped by a statue of Rhon flanked by smaller statues of Mnearis, the goddess of silent contemplation, and Anjei, the god of seeing the unseen and hearing the unspoken truth.

Fitting, Sjei thought as he crossed the wide plaza toward the myriad buildings comprising The Ministries to the southwest, that these should watch over the Plaza of the Unexpressed. Keeping the truth unspoken was the watchword of all Rhonas Chas, and contemplation in silence was the only way one could keep from quietly vanishing both from memory and existence within the Imperial City.

Sjei drew his thick cloak tighter about him against the rain as he quickened his steps toward the *Via Rhonas*. He had little time to make his appointment with the one woman in all the Empire with whom one could never afford to be late. It could not have been helped as the news he had received required verification before he could risk even mentioning the subject to his host, and his confirmations had only come to his ears minutes before.

Now, having been confirmed, this meeting was not only inevitable but also critical.

Sjei-Shurian quickly moved down the wide avenue of the *Via Rhonas* and across the God's Bridge, the rain drawing a veil around him as he crossed the island toward the Old Keep of the Iblisi.

"My dear Sjei! How kind of you to call."

Sjei smiled, mentally arming himself for the cut and thrust of the verbal engagement. Both of them knew that kindness had nothing to do with his presence in the Iblisi stronghold. "It was most gracious of you to agree to see me, Keeper, especially on such short notice. Your time is precious and not lightly granted."

"I only regret that this weather prevents us from meeting in more comfortable surroundings," Ch'drei pulled her lips even farther back into what should have passed for a smile but seemed more a hideous grin.

Ch'drei Tsi-Auruun, Keeper of the Iblisi, sat on her throne in her wide hall with the low ceiling beneath the courtyard of the Old Keep. She was an ancient-looking elven female, the skin of her face so tight that her sharp teeth seemed to hold a perpetually cadaverous smile. She stooped forward on her throne, gripping her *Matei* staff as though it alone was keeping her from falling to the floor. Sjei noted, however, that her black eyes were still shining and that she was not leaning on the staff nearly as hard as she would have him believe. As to her regretting the weather, Sjei would not have put it past her to have arranged it. "You need not be troubled, Keeper. Indeed, it is my concern for you and your honorable Order that brings me here today."

Ch'drei blinked. Sjei was being direct and the Keeper was uncomfortable on such open ground. "Indeed, your concern must be urgent to bring the Ghenetar Omris of the Order of Vash to me in such haste. Perhaps it has something to do with your cousin's daughter?"

Sjei braced himself but it was too late.

"Hers is a sad tale, is it not?" Ch'drei bowed her head slightly. "Returned from the Western Provinces, her family and honor lost. The makings of an epic were it not so tragic—though I suspect that 'epic' it will become in its telling should a few unpleasant details be omitted."

Sjei kept silent, refusing to give his adversary the satisfaction of an acknowledged hit. Parry and riposte, then parry again until the opportunity to strike presents itself. Turn the opponent's advantage to your own. He bided his time, offering up the truth to the Keeper of Truth until the time was right for the lie to be told.

"There is no point in denying it to you, Keeper. It is partially on her behalf that I have come," Sjei said. "This girl . . ."

"Shebin," Ch'drei said with quiet confidence. "You may use her name here where everything is known."

Not everything, Sjei thought. *At least, I fervently hope not everything.* Already he sensed he had given away too much. He had confirmed Ch'drei's suspicions about Shebin and their relationship. That knowledge could go badly for him in the wrong ears. Still, Sjei knew in this game that one should always use the truth until the lie was absolutely necessary. "As you wish, Keeper. Shebin Timuran of the House of Timuran is, indeed, the daughter of my unfortunate fool of a cousin. It has become a matter of honor in my House that we find the one who so terribly wronged her and bring him before Imperial justice . . ."

"Yes, yes, yes," Ch'drei waved her hand dismissively. "This slave named Drakis who has fled to the north. And I suppose you wish for the Iblisi to find this runaway slave for you?"

"No, Mistress Keeper."

Ch'drei moved as if to speak and then paused for a moment. "You do not wish us to find this slave Drakis?"

"No, Mistress," Sjei replied. "We have already done so. He is forming an army of rebellion in the northern provinces and the Legions have been dispatched to deal with the problem. That is not why I have come before the Keeper of all the Iblisi."

Ch'drei frowned. "What has happened that would occasion this humble Keeper of the Truth to be of service to you?"

Sjei clasped his hands behind his back. "I come with strange news, Keeper, and would hope that your wisdom would guide me."

"All the knowledge of the Iblisi is at your disposal," Ch'drei lied. "What news brings you here?"

"News of a battle, Keeper," Sjei replied. "A battle most gloriously won beyond the Northmarch Folds north of a place known there as the Whispering Hills against this same army of rebellion."

"The Shrouded Plain," Ch'drei said. "It is on the Ephindrian frontier, if I am not mistaken."

"You are most learned of all elves, Keeper," Sjei replied.

"And you have come to tell me you are troubled by this great and glorious victory against the enemy of your House?" Ch'drei said, impatience coloring her words.

"I have come to report that the victory was not as complete as the commanders in the field have reported to the Imperial Throne," Sjei responded. "The Blade of the Northern Will Legions were in pursuit of this Drakis rebellion; a large force of rebellious manticores and chimerians fleeing northward out of Northern Steppes. They all believe in some nonsense about this slave being a human legend though I can make little of it."

"Indeed?" Ch'drei answered, her smile having somehow managed to lessen slightly. "A human legend, you say?"

"It's of no consequence," Sjei said, smiling inwardly. "I am more interested in the reports that, after our warriors engaged these rebels on the very edge of this Shrouded Plain, they fled into the mists, and our forces were unable to either find or pursue them. Contact with this large group of dangerous rebels has been temporarily lost."

Another lie. Sjei knew exactly where they were—which was why he had come.

"An unfortunate result," Ch'drei agreed leaning back slightly. Sjei realized she was feeling uncomfortable being forced to stoop over on her chair. Ch'drei wanted to straighten up against the back of the throne but could not do so while Sjei remained or risk giving up her pretense of being feeble. "Word had reached our ears of such a battle, but we are sorry to hear that the outcome had not been as complete as we had previously heard. I regret that I am unlearned in the arts of war, Ghenetar Omris Sjei, and feel ill equipped as to how I might advise you on matters of marshal conflict."

"On the contrary, Keeper, you can be of great assistance to me," Sjei replied with a nod of his head. "The details of the final moments of this battle have only recently been made known to me. It seems that while our armies were on the verge of complete victory, one individual changed the complexion of the field of battle and allowed the rebels to escape."

Ch'drei stiffened on her throne. "A single person, you say?"

"Yes. An elf."

Ch'drei ran her long tongue over her thin lips. "And what, may I ask, did this singular elf do?"

She does know him, Sjei thought, a thrill of triumph running through him. *That leaves only one question to be answered.* "The details have not yet reached us and the reports we have are vague at best—but we believe that he used Aether magics to create a diversion. Some reports even say that this elf held office among the Iblisi . . ."

"That is not possible," Ch'drei responded decisively.

"No?"

"I know where all my children are to be found," Ch'drei replied again with a forced smile. "This elf, whoever he is, is not one of my Order."

"I am pleased to hear it," Sjei replied with a slight bow. "I suspect these reports are of an imposter on the frontier who has lied about his importance at the expense of the honor of your esteemed Order."

"Such an—imposter must not be tolerated," Ch'drei replied. "The honor of my House is challenged. It is our fervent hope that your Legions crush this imposter's corpse beneath their boots as well as all those who have sided with him in his rebellion."

Sjei nodded. The moment had come for him to tell the lie he had hoped to tell. "Then I am pleased to report that your honor is vouched safe. This imposter is already dead."

Ch'drei held perfectly still. "Dead?"

"Yes, my field commanders report that this elf who made possible the escape was killed before he himself escaped," Sjei said, clasping his hands in front of him and shaking his head. "The reports are, as I said, still incomplete but I have been told his body remained on the field."

"I am somewhat interested in this imposter," Ch'drei said with carefully crafted apathy. "Perhaps I could spare a few of my own Inquisitors and Assessia in recovering the body and determining this imposter's origins. I would gladly offer whatever assistance I could to . . ."

"Which was my purpose in coming," Sjei said, opening his hands. "I am as concerned about this imposter as you are, Keeper, but the Legions themselves are still in pursuit of these rebel forces, and determining the disposition of one corpse from among the thousands on a battlefield would be a disservice to the Imperial Will. Nevertheless, I assure you that I have made inquiries and should be able to report to you a proper location within the next two to three weeks. But if you could send some of your own Inquisitors to discover the body and retrieve it, then your generosity would serve us both in the Imperial Will."

The lie. The elf in question was Soen as they both well knew and was anything but an imposter. Ch'drei would never take his word for it that Soen was dead but she might consider the possibility enough to divert those who were looking for the living Soen to search a battlefield for a dead one. There were enough elven dead on the verge of the Shrouded Plain to keep them occupied for some time. Sjei just hoped that it was enough to buy him time to find Soen first as his armies pressed northward along the Shadow Coast.

It was only a matter of time before he caught up with Soen—and Soen would lead him to Drakis.

If he could keep the Iblisi looking in the wrong place.

Ch'drei drew in a deep breath. "Then this imposter is certainly dead."

"Yes . . . and may the gods grant your Iblisi their favor in finding him."

CHAPTER 18

The Ambeth

THE SUN WAS LOW on the horizon when Ishander steered their boats to the outside bank of a curve in the river. There, a stone carving jutted out from the surrounding ferns overhanging the river. The youth braced his feet wide on the platform at the back of the boat and reached up with his bladed staff, catching the carving. The boat swung around with the current but Ishander stood fast. Urulani, seeing what the young native was doing, moved to the back of the boat and reached up to catch the stone as well. The second boat passed Drakis, Ethis, and the Lyric, swinging with a bit more violence as its tether went slack and then suddenly tightened once more, pulling the bow sharply around against the current.

"Are we there?" Urulani asked the young man.

"No," Ishander answered. "We wait."

"Wait for what?" Ethis asked, but the boy gave no answer.

Time passed as slowly as the river drifting past them. Drakis had long since exhausted speculation and was never very good at small talk. The boy kept his staff lodged against the stone, holding them in this position, shifting only occasionally to keep his balance.

The sun was nearly setting by the time he spoke again.

"We have been welcomed by the clan," Ishander announced. "You may let go of the stone, lady."

Urulani raised her eyebrow slightly. Drakis could not be certain whether she was surprised or affronted by the remark but she let go of her hold, her dark arms falling to her sides, shaking them to relieve the aching.

"Did you see any signal?" Drakis whispered to Ethis.

"No," the chimerian answered quietly, "but not seeing one does not mean there was none. We must be close."

The boats drifted around the bend, running down a straight section of the river that moved swiftly before slowing again as it turned to their left.

"You are the guests of our Clan-mother, Audelai El," Ishander spoke without preamble. His voice was overly loud and carried a stiff, pompous quality. "As guests, you shall enjoy the privileges of our great city and the protection of its fortress walls. If you are to remain our guests, you will acknowledge the law of the Ambeth Clan as your own, our customs will be your customs and our justice your justice. Do you submit your will to that of the clan?"

"I do," Mala answered at once.

"And I submit myself even more than she does!" piped in the Lyric.

"Might I ask a question?" Ethis said as he raised one of his four hands.

Ishander looked momentarily troubled, as though someone had sung a wrong note in the expected melody of his song. "You . . . a question?"

"Yes," Ethis continued. "What if we don't want to submit our will to the clan?"

Ishander blinked. "What if you . . . what?"

"I mean, we don't know what the clan expects of us or what its rules are or whether we're breaking them or not," Ethis continued. "So what if we don't agree to this will of the clan?"

Urulani turned to cast a look of gentle warning in the direction of the chimerian.

Ishander stuttered for a moment before recovering, indignation blossoming in his features. "Well . . . you . . . you would . . . you would be horribly executed as cowards and enemies of the clan!"

"Oh, well, then!" Ethis said with an exaggerated shrug. "I guess we *do* submit to the will of the clan."

"What about the short one?" Ishander asked, pointing his pinkie finger at the second boat.

Mala reached under the covering tarpaulin at once and raised Jugar's limp hand. "So does the dwarf!"

"We all do, Ishander," Urulani said, her dark eyes fixed on the young man. "But will you teach us the ways of your people? We do not wish to offend your Clan-mother."

The young man smiled. "Of course! I am a Far-runner and I know the ways of many places and peoples—but I have never met anyone like you. Were you a Clan-mother where you come from?"

"Something like that," Urulani said. "I was the captain of a ship—like you—only my ship was larger and held all my clan."

The boy's eyes grew wide with wonder, but he managed to recover his composure and regain his studied, stoic expression.

"You gave your speech very well, Ishander," Ethis said. "Is giving that speech also part of the clan's law?"

"Yes," Ishander answered. "We Far-runners must learn it before we may leave our clan strongholds. It is to be given to all those the Far-runners bring from the outside into our city."

"And how often have you given this speech yourself?" Drakis asked.

The boy glanced at Drakis and then fixed his eyes back on the river. "Once."

"And that was to us?" Drakis continued.

Ishander ignored the remark, launching once again into his recitation. "Tremble before the wonder that is Ambeth! Clanhold of the Ambeth people and symbol of its might and glory! Look upon our wondrous works and despair!"

Drakis turned to look forward where the river again twisted, this time to the right, and caught his first sight of Ambeth.

His first thought was that the young man was making fun of him.

"Ah," Ethis said from behind him. "So this is what has become of the mighty human empires of the north."

As they came to the bend in the river, Ambeth appeared not so much a fortress as a stockade. Vertical logs had been driven into the ground to form a defensive wall. An attempt had been made to keep the jungle cleared outside the wall far enough from the stockade so that its defenders might see trouble coming before it was upon them, but the jungle was uncooperatively encroaching on the space. There were stockade towers erected on either side of the river and at intervals down the wall but these were barely twenty feet tall—not even as tall as the subatria wall that had surrounded House Timuran and that had been considered only for show.

Drakis craned his head, trying to see beyond the gap in the wall where the river ran between two of the watchtowers and was dismayed.

Ambeth was little more than a collection of low, thatched-roof huts scattered over a spit of land that formed a long, slow curve in the river. Here and there among the huts, the crumbling walls of what may have been a former settlement jutted upward in jagged defiance toward the sky but were generally ignored by the surrounding architecture of the hovels. There was a "Keep" of sorts—a second stockade wall atop the rise looking over the river that surrounded a single tower. Even that structure was a sad one, cobbled around the remains of a former stone tower now patched together with wood framing.

As they passed slowly between the watchtowers, Drakis took in the totality of the village of which Ishander had so generously boasted. On their right, the stockade wall ran a short distance up from the shore and then angled back toward the river at a watchtower. There, barely past the river's edge, the stockade wall abruptly ended, as though the river would protect the village and further extension was not required. To his left, the land rose gently from the river, creating a shallow beach toward which Ishander steered them. There were many boats on the beach and small homes beyond. Smoke rose from numerous chimneys and hung in a layer just above the village, turning blue and gray in the deepening sunset.

His warrior mind instantly conceived of a dozen different plans by which he could overwhelm the defenses of this village—the place where they staked their survival.

But it was the sound, at last, that attracted his attention.

The sound of children laughing.

Human children.

Drakis stared in wonder at the beach ahead of them. From the hovels and the homes, the dirt streets and alleyways, the broken ruins and the thick bushes and plants they came: humans. Young, old, men, women, warriors, and artisans, they came toward the beach.

The wonders he had seen, Drakis realized, the ruins of greatness and power that they had witnessed in Pythar were the legacy of these people. Their ancestors had built these ruins. They had been a great people—a people who had challenged the Rhonas Empire itself.

One question kept nagging at him as they pushed toward the shore and the line of guards quickly gathering there.

What happened that they should have fallen so far?

"All kneel before the Clan-mother of the Ambeth!" thundered the broad-shouldered human who stood a full head taller than Drakis.

Drakis had been considering what it might take for him to disarm the warrior and, on reflection, believed he could do it. Still, it would not be proper to insult the only hosts they knew within a thousand leagues who could supply them with food and water.

Drakis knelt along with Ethis and Urulani. Mala and the Lyric were behind them. The dwarf had, for good or ill, regained consciousness and lay again on his makeshift litter struggling to sit up.

"Where are we?" Jugar demanded.

Drakis pushed him back flat on the litter. "We're in Ambeth. Hold still."

"Ambeth?" the dwarf responded with a quizzical look on his face. "Where or what is an Ambeth?"

Drakis pushed Jugar back flat once again. "Hold still and listen . . . then perhaps we can all find out."

The Keep of Ambeth was, as Drakis first believed, little more than a shored-up repair of a tower that had existed here long before Clan Ambeth claimed it as their own. A lodge-hall had been added to the original broken foundation that joined with the tower walls. The tower itself had framing around it. Drakis was uncertain as to whether the ancient tower walls were holding up the framing or the other way around. Drakis and his companions had all been marched up from the shore through the town and directly across a wide square into the large room attached to the tower. The flanking soldiers did not seem interested in conversation although the streets were lined with the curious townspeople, all of whom were gawking, laughing, pointing, and chattering with each other as though the newcomers were exotic animals on their way to the forum for a match. The soldiers had positioned them in front of a large fire pit near the center of the lodge with the tower base on the far side.

A figure emerged from the shadows at the base of the tower. It was a woman of uncertain age. There were lines at the corners of her eyes, but her skin and her cheeks were otherwise smooth as was her high forehead. Her hair was long and cascaded down around her shoulders but there were streaks of gray in the rich black strands. Her eyes were a striking violet, bright and intense. She had a wide, generous mouth although one of her front teeth was slightly crooked. She wore a long robe whose colors were indistinct and faded while around her neck hung an eclectic assortment of so much different jewelry that Drakis wondered how she was managing to hold it all upright.

"I am Audelai El, Clan-mother of all the Ambeth!" the woman intoned in a deep, rich voice. She looked up toward the sky and brought her palms together in front of her. "Have the strangers accepted our ways?"

"The strangers have accepted the ways of the Ambeth, Clan-mother," Ishander said, his voice breaking slightly in his enthusiasm.

The Clan-mother raised her hands high above her head and spoke toward the ceiling. "Then the protection and hospitality of the Ambeth shall be with our guests and the laws of the clan shall be their laws until the fall of the sky!"

"The Ambeth are One!" shouted the warriors in the hall followed closely by Ishander.

The Clan-mother then lowered her hands and looked at Drakis. Suddenly, she smiled and winked, then started clapping her hands together in glee. Audelai El ran quickly around the fire pit and clasped Urulani by both hands, helping her to her feet. She moved among them, reaching down and helping them up as she chattered along. "Oh, this is too marvelous to have you here with us, really, it is! To think of it! Outsiders who have come to us from foreign lands and bringing knowledge of places that we have only considered in our dreams. I cannot tell you how excited I am personally to see you.

Anything that I can do for you, anything at all, I'll do if it is within my power to make it happen. I can only assume that you are on a great mission of some importance for we have heard of stirrings among the dragons of the Surgani Mountains and that danger is passing north-ward through the land, bringing change to the world."

Drakis stood as she took his hands. "Clan-mother, We are only . . ."

"Great people of destiny, you may bring the salvation of our people at last, restore the greatness of our land, and challenge the treachery of all dragons that was our doom," Audelai El said, smiling into Drakis' face. "You honor us by coming to our clan! There is always profit to be had in change, you know—all one needs to know is how."

Drakis was stunned. "Well, thank you, we . . ."

"How soon will you be leaving?" Audelai El concluded through her charming smile.

CHAPTER 19

Dark Wells

THE DWARF ROLLED BENEATH a particularly dense fern and
held perfectly still despite the pain shooting up his leg.

Mardosh staggered as he came up the dirt path the locals grandly
called Jurusta Road. Mardosh was his "clan-law escort"—a warrior
stooge assigned to him by the ever-loving Clan-mother to go with him
wherever he went in Ambeth and "assist" him with "advice" regarding
what was permitted under clan-law. This apparently also extended to
who he could talk to, what he could talk about, and which parts of the
town he was allowed to visit. Jugar had no doubts that Mardosh's duties also extended to reporting to the Clan-mother fully about all the
locations he visited and the details of every conversation he had. The
fact that everyone in their group was assigned a clan-law escort when
they left their quarters in the Keep only deepened the dwarf's suspicions. They were captives in a prison without locks.

Worse, for Jugar, was the loss of the Heart of Aer. The very
thought that he had lost the stone both sickened and enraged him.
Without it, he was largely powerless, almost bereft of magic. The
stone had been drawing upon Dunaea, the soul at the heart of the
world, absorbing its power from the surrounding stone. Jugar had
hoped to use some of that Aer to heal his leg though he had not decided whether to tell his companions about the mending. He rather
enjoyed being hauled around by these humans. But then the stone

was stolen by that Ishander whelp before he could magically mend the leg. He could feel it calling to him somewhere nearby and he was desperate to get it back.

But first he had to find it.

Jugar's frustrations were soon alleviated, however, when he discovered that he could easily outlast Mardosh in any drinking contest and that Mardosh was more than willing to let him try. So each afternoon, Jugar would grab his crutch, slowly and painfully lead his escort down Tyra Road to a ramshackle tavern at the intersection with Elucia Road and invite the hulking warrior to join him in a drink or two or three or however many were required. Then, when the time was right, the dwarf would slip out of the back of the tavern and make his way through the back alleys and narrow gaps between the shacks that comprised the town. His leg was still a problem but far better healed than he let on to anyone. He soon discovered that he could make good time up the roads, and that most of the locals were indifferent to his passage. So long as he avoided the notice of the occasional warrior—who seemed more interested in keeping order in the town than conducting warfare—he could move about freely. Then, after a few hours, the dwarf would dutifully find Mardosh, often exactly where he had left him and convince him that they had been together this entire time. Then the dwarf promised not to tell his masters about Mardosh passing out. But today Jugar had been impatient and Mardosh was trying to follow him, although his escort had a hard time catching Jugar as he made his hobbling dash up Elucia Road and onto Jurusta Road.

As if these human fools knew anything about building a proper road let alone who Jurusta—their own ancient goddess of spring, passion, and art—even was, Jugar thought as he lay beneath the fern. To them, it was just another name for the wandering breaks between the thatch-roofed hovels packed in some cases wall against wall in the tight space of the stockade enclosure. These may have once been true roads, Jugar knew, by the few patches of fitted stone roadway that remained, and perhaps these names that had passed down the generations once had meaning to the inhabitants of this place. But the great buildings had all fallen, and all that remained of the footfalls that once trod these spaces with such purpose were meaningless names of forgotten gods.

Jugar watched as Mardosh, bleary-eyed, stood uncertainly on the road looking back and forth and finding it impossible to make up what remained of his mind regarding a direction to take. Jugar decided to make up his escort's mind for him by pulling himself farther back into the brush and moving between the huts away from the road. He stood up slowly, picking up the carved stick he used for a crutch. He still favored the leg and it gave him considerable pain which the crutch alleviated most of the time. He could move quickly on it when occasion called for it, but a slower pace was more comfortable. He had decided to explore the north side of the town and try to discover where this Ishander made his home and get back his stone.

Jugar scowled as he pushed through the thick fronds of dense undergrowth. All these plants! He was a dwarf of the mountain and of stone. Plants in their place were fine, but he found their touch unnerving in this climate, wet and slimy. He caught a glimpse of one of the watchtowers through the leaves overhead and decided that it was as good a direction to take as any.

He was losing sight of the thatched buildings around him when the jungle opened up onto the broken stones of a circular courtyard. One curved wall remained standing, supported by three pillars on the far side, sheltering the statue of one of the human goddesses. The broken bases of several more pillars were set about the courtyard while the debris from the structure's collapse jutted out beyond the perimeter from the surrounding thick undergrowth. Jugar took all this in but pushed it aside as his mind fixed on the object around which the stones of the courtyard were symmetrically arranged.

It was an Aether Well.

And yet, it was not, Jugar thought as he examined it from beyond the rim of broken cobblestones. The stone was shaped like an Aether Well, but the material in it was a smoky gray color, dark and with unusual striations in the crystal structure. The stone jutted upward out of the ground as Jugar had seen in the Aether Wells of the elves, but the shape of the stone itself was different; more of a jewel-faceted dome than a dagger driven into the face of the world.

Jugar glanced around. The palm leaves of the trees rustled overhead with an afternoon breeze but the courtyard was still. Tentatively, the dwarf placed his crutch onto the smoothed stones, hopped once to stand on them, and then carefully made his way forward.

Jugar had studied the magic of Aer and Aether with a fanaticism fueled by desperation. Aer was the magic of the dwarves, the faeries, the dryads, the sirens, the goblins, the merfolk, and the pixies. It was the magic of nature that welled up from the soul of the world, flowing and connecting all creation. It was natural and blessed by the gods.

Aether was the magic of the enemy of nature. It was the magic of humans, of chimerians and, worst of all, of the elves. Aether drove crystal blades into the world and bled the Aer from it, sucking it from the wound and distilling it into focused power that was terrible and precise. That was the purpose of the Wells: to extract and refine the natural power of Aer into the potent magic of Aether.

Jugar had studied Aether magic as one would study the moves of an opponent before battle, trying to know the enemy better than the enemy knew himself. He knew the lattice structure of the crystals used for the Aether Wells, the nature of their linkage to other Wells, the loss of power over distance, and the dissipation rates of their charged devices over time. Contrary to what he had told the others, he knew a great deal about the use of Aether magic and the complexities of activating it. The best he had mastered related to the Heart of Aer, but that was because he was so familiar with the stone and its properties. His anger, after they had passed through the portal when the dragons attacked, had stemmed not from any lack of ability on his part but because the portal had been powered from the dragon's side. Perhaps it was some energy seeping into the south of God's Home Range from the elven Wells in Nordesia. All he knew was that there was no power on their side to activate the portal. It had angered and puzzled him at the time, but, with his leg broken and beasties threatening, there was no opportunity to look into the matter.

But he was a dwarf—he knew stone—and now he had the time.

Jugar moved carefully across the courtyard and slowly knelt before the human Aether Well. The stone was covered in part by a layer of dust, sticks, and dead fronds fallen from the jungle canopy overhead. The depths of the stone looked dark to him.

Jugar reached out with his hand to brush the debris from the Well.

His hand touched the stone.

Jugar suddenly drew his hand back as though the stone itself were white hot.

His bushy eyebrows rose in astonishment.

Carefully, he opened his hand and placed it cautiously upon the stone.

A great gap-toothed smile slowly spread across the face of the dwarf.

"Oh, my beauty," Jugar whispered and he looked at the statue of the goddess against the shattered wall. "I was so wrong."

"So you found an Aether Well," Urulani shrugged irritably. "I wouldn't be surprised if they were buried every hundred feet or so in this place."

"It would do you more credit if you broadened the scope of your understanding," Jugar sniffed. "It isn't the fact that I found an Aether Well—it's what the Aether Well told me that is important."

"So now the Aether Well is speaking to you?" the Lyric asked in breathless fascination.

Drakis rolled his eyes. He had spent most of the day with the Clan-mother, listening to her blather on about the greatness of her people, how glad she was that they were granting their hospitality to such gallant strangers all the while hinting at how happy everyone would be after Drakis led his companions beyond the stockade wall.

Now their escorts had once again deposited them in their "exclusive guest quarters" which, it turned out, were in the cellars beneath the Keep. There were individual cells with cots and straw in them that might have passed for a dungeon except that the town did not have enough iron to afford the fashioning of bars. Mala lay back on her cot while the Lyric leaned against one corner of the room, humming to herself until her interest had been piqued. Everyone else had gathered around the dwarf in the open space in the middle of the cellar.

"Thank you, Litaria," Urulani said to the Lyric before turning to Drakis. "Do you know what the dwarf is talking about?"

"No," Drakis sighed, rubbing the weariness from his face, "but I've learned mostly to let him keep talking and eventually it seems to make sense."

"I am honored, indeed, that our good friend Drakis should allow me to continue without interruption for, I assure you," the dwarf continued enthusiastically, "that everyone here will profit greatly by their attention."

"Just when is he supposed to start making sense?" Ethis asked Drakis.

"I shall use small words and illustrations for those who are challenged in the lingual arts," the dwarf frowned as he spoke. He knelt down on the packed dirt floor, pulling several stones out of the pocket of his vest and quickly setting them on the ground, arranging one large stone in the center and several smaller stones quickly around it. Gripping a small, sharp stone in his wide hand, Jugar pressed the edge of the stone into the dirt and drew lines from the outer stones toward the central stone.

"Think of these as elven Aether Wells," Jugar instructed. "All of these Wells are driven into the world, spikes that pull at the soul of the world."

"Soul of the world?" Drakis asked, scratching his head.

Jugar scowled. "Aer—the power of natural magic that binds creation and the world together."

Drakis squinted and frowned.

"Think of it as wheat or grains or fruit," Jugar said. "Things that feed you that come from the ground."

Drakis nodded.

"These outside stones represent Aether Wells," Jugar continued with exaggerated patience. "Think of these as a still for making ale."

"A dwarven metaphor, if ever there was one," Ethis observed."

"These Wells draw the power of natural magic out of the world— like taking the grains or fruits and putting them into a still. It transforms the mash in the still into ale. The ale is a good deal more potent and has a more powerful effect on you than just chewing on the grains or the fruit as I am sure you have experienced so many times in your life that its effects are apparently permanent."

"You've made your point," Ethis said. "The Aether Wells transform the Aer drawn from the world into Aether, which is the basis of elven magic."

"Yes, but here is where I have discovered something that I had not previously supposed," Jugar said excitedly. He pointed down toward the outer stones, flicking his hand from each toward the middle. "The Aether Wells provided only a small part of their refined Aether power to the households of the frontier. Most of the Aether they produced was directed inward through the connections between their Wells to the center of the Empire—to Rhonas Chas. Think of it: the power of an entire continent being drawn inward to satisfy the magic center of the Imperial Throne. It is what has kept the Empire in control down these dark centuries—the ability to deal with problems on its frontier from the powerful center outward."

"So what have you discovered that changes any of that?" Ethis demanded.

"We had always supposed that the elves had patterned their magic on the human system of Aether," Jugar said shaking his head. "But I touched the stone of that Well today—a Well of the fallen human ancients—and discovered that it works backward to the elven system."

"Backward?" Urulani exclaimed. "In what way?"

"That stone was designed *only* to emanate and deliver power, not to gather it," Jugar said. "The lattice structure within the crystal was specifically arranged to prevent power from flowing back down the linked structure."

"Drakis, he's not making sense again . . ."

"It means that where the elven Wells are designed to feed the magic *into* the center," Jugar said with carefully pronounced words, "the human system was designed to feed the magic *outward* from the center—disseminating the power of the human magic to the outlying regions from a central source. That is why the portal could not be operated from our side when we arrived here. That is why magic has completely failed in this land—it may even be the reason why the human empire fell to the elves in the first place."

"So," Drakis said, gazing at the ground. "It's like a river, flowing out from the center."

"That's right, lad!" Jugar smiled.

"And something in the center has stopped the river from flowing?" Urulani continued the thought.

"Exactly so!" Jugar said, tossing the stone from his hand to the ground in triumph. "If we were to find the source of this magic—open the gates that are preventing its flow—then who knows what wonders it might perform? The one thing I am sure of is that it would make their system of portals functional again; it could very well get us home. I tell you, when I looked up and saw that goddess looking over that Well, I thanked her out of sheer joy . . ."

"Goddess?" Mala said, suddenly rising from her cot. "What goddess?"

"Why, lass, I was so ecstatic at my discovery that I didn't stop to ask her name . . ."

"What did she look like?" Mala demanded, coming quickly over to where the dwarf knelt. "Did she speak to you?"

"No, lass," Jugar looked up questioningly into the intent gaze of the auburn-haired woman. "She was but a statue there at the edge of the courtyard. It's of no consequence . . . the point is that we need to find this place, this center of magic. I could do it, too, if I had back the Heart of Aer from that Ishander thief!"

Drakis glanced at Ethis, but the chimerian's face was as blank as ever as he spoke.

"You are right," Ethis said. "We should speak with this Far-runner about what he knows about, where this 'center of magic' might be found, the ruins downstream, and about your stone. Drakis, do you think you could arrange that with the Clan-mother?"

"Audelai El?" Drakis smiled. "Woven in the middle of all her polite speech were questions about whether we were warriors for another clanhold of humans sent to open the gates for their attack, disguised dragon-men, or mercenaries hired by the dragons to spy on her personally. She likes to keep her enemies very close. I think if I proposed *anything* that would get us out of her 'great city,' she would gladly help us fill our packs and shed a gracious tear while pushing our boats away from her shore with a firm kick of her sandaled feet."

Jugar stood to face Drakis. "Find me that stone, get us a guide to the center of their magic, and I might just be able to get us all home."

Drakis looked at Mala. "Then let's go home."

CHAPTER 20

Grandfather

"WHAT IN THE NAME of the gods was the point of that?" Drakis huffed as he stepped out of the audience hall of Ambeth Keep. Ethis was at his heels as they both followed Ishander out through the gate of the Keep's stockade wall and down the wide and uneven stone stairs. The locals called the open plaza before them Ambeth Commons, and in the escaped warrior's view, it was the first thing these people had named correctly. The Keep sat on a promontory overlooking a bend in the river and the Commons was a large open space behind it. The town's well was located in its center with some of the larger merchant or tradesmen establishments surrounding it. Not that there was much in the way of either merchandise or trade. Several roads led away from the plaza into the uneven angles of crowded huts and shacks that made up the architecture of the town.

"You mean our audience with the Clan-mother?" Ethis said as he followed Drakis down the stairs. "We got permission to speak with this Far-runner, didn't we?"

"The Clan-mother is wise!" Ishander said back over his shoulder with defiance as he strode across the Commons in front of Drakis and the chimerian toward Tyra Road. "She honors you by permitting this audience with the greatest of Far-runners!"

"Permission, yes . . . but just the two of us?" Drakis answered the chimerian as he picked up his pace to keep up with the young man leading them through the crowded streets of the town. "You deliberately made sure the others were left out. Urulani looked as though she were going to take you apart with her bare hands, and the dwarf . . ."

"Did you really want the dwarf along?" Ethis said, his usually blank features shifting to express astonishment.

"Well, I'm sure *you* don't!" Drakis said as they moved quickly down the gentle slope of the road toward the Elucia crossing. The street was crowded but the humans packing the roadway about them hastily moved aside at the sight of the four-armed creature with a barely discernible face. "Why didn't you just give him his Stone instead of making him fret over it?"

"Because it pleases me not to do so," Ethis responded with an honesty that Drakis had not expected. "He's far more manageable without it and besides, he doesn't trust me."

"Indeed?" Drakis rolled his eyes. "I wonder why not?"

"Keep up!" Ishander shouted at them although they were practically walking on his heels as it was.

"Besides," Ethis continued. "He already suspected I stole it once. How will it look if it appears in my hands?"

The street—Drakis still had trouble thinking of the uneven dirt path in those terms—meandered along the side of the gentle slope between the sawtooth placements of the structures on either side. Though every hut, hovel, or shop seemed to aspire to square corners, angles, and straight lines, none of them appeared to have had any success in the matter. Drakis believed he could count on the fingers of both his hands the number that managed to hold themselves together well enough to support a second floor. Each was fitted around, over, or between the crumbling ruins of their glorious and long vanished past—a legacy which appeared now to be more of an inconvenience to them than a loss.

"I don't know why you are so concerned about this," Ethis continued. "Because the dwarf was looking for the stone, he discovered the Aether Well and a possible means of getting out of this strange land. All in all, my *not* giving him his stone seems to have helped us far more than if I had just politely handed it over to him. Besides, I managed to get Audelai El to agree to call off her less-than-charming escorts as well by putting us under the charge of this most able warrior Ishander. I would have thought that alone would have been worth the price of letting the dwarf pull at his own beard for a while."

"I could have used his advice," Drakis huffed.

"What needs to be decided now does not benefit from protracted argument," the chimerian replied, a puzzled edge to his voice. "I thought you of all people would appreciate a few less voices in your head."

They followed Ishander as he turned right up Abratias Way, the widest of the streets in Ambeth that ran from the flat riverbank where the boats docked up the gentle slope toward the stockade wall. At the head of the rising street, he could see the Old Gate, as the locals called it, to the north that led into the more extensive part of the ruins. Ambeth had once been much larger than the present extent of the stockade walls. This morning the gates were open as the Hunt-runners passed through them as they did each morning, singing their song as they marched out of the town. They were followed by the Grass-walkers whose job it was to gather fruits and vegetables from the jungle as well as from several large farming plots outside the village. Each group sang their own song, but the melodies each interwove with those of the other group. It was a rather beautiful sound, Drakis thought, with the Hunt-runners and the Grass-walkers naturally taking up different parts in harmony as they moved into the ruins and the jungle beyond. Old men and women as well as young children cheered and waved as the parade of workers moved past them.

It all would have been a rather heartening scene if Drakis had not known that there was a good chance that a number of those singing as they marched resolutely through the gate would not be returning by nightfall. The Hunt-runners suffered perhaps the worst as the prey they stalked was as often stalking them. The Grass-walkers were not without their own dangers as the carnivorous beasts ranging beyond the stockade walls often lurked around the more fruitful regions on their own hunts. The once civilized lands of the human empire had grown decidedly uncivil.

As the Old Gate drew closed before them, hiding the deep ruins beyond, Ishander turned to their left where Jurusta Street crossed Abratias Way. Jurusta was barely a path here, snaking its way between homes. The street quickly dissolved into a labyrinth of huts and shacks so tightly jammed together that it was almost impossible to tell where one ended and the next began.

"This great Far-runner lives here?" Drakis asked in dubious tones.

Ishander, jaw set, turned so abruptly that Drakis nearly ran into the young man. "He is the greatest of the Far-runners! He has seen the farthest towers of the lost kingdoms and walked the streets of the gods! You will be respectful of him—for that is the law of the clan!"

"We accept the law of the clan," Drakis said with a slight bow and opening his hands wide before him. The truth was he was suspicious of the "law of the clan" to which they were expected to so dutifully be obedient. No one ever bothered to explain nor, indeed, seemed to know just what this law of the clan was until Drakis or one of the other "outsiders"— as they were called—broke one of their unspoken commandments. Drakis suspected that their captors made up the details of the law of the clan as they went along depending upon whatever the Clan-mother decreed from moment to moment. If anything, to Drakis, it seemed that the foundational principle underlying every application of rules was "if it can embarrass the outsiders or cheat them out of something—that is the law of the clan."

Ishander scowled, but Drakis had a hard time taking the boy seriously. He was not yet "in his beard" and despite his considerable bravado and unquestionable skill at survival while they were escaping Pythar, there was a greenness to the boy's manner and movement that the seasoned warrior now remembered seeing too many times in young Impress Warriors: eager, fearless, and all too often short-lived.

Ishander squeezed back between two woven reed mats that passed for walls. Any concept of a path had vanished altogether, and Drakis found the smells overwhelming. The young man stopped again.

"Remove your shoes before you enter," the youth commanded.

"Enter where?" Drakis asked.

"Honored ground," Ishander said with a look that, not for the first time, told Drakis that it was common knowledge to everyone but him. When both Drakis and the chimerian had loosened their sandals, the young Far-runner pulled back a woven mat and beckoned the outsiders within.

Drakis stepped barefoot onto the clean mat flooring and was at once confused and astonished. The room was small and had a low ceiling, but it was carefully organized and well ordered in complete contrast to the chaos outside its walls. Yet, even in its order, it was an explosion of contradictions. Low tables displayed a dizzying array of art alongside broken bits of mechanisms and intricate devices the purpose of which Drakis could only guess at. On one table there lay scattered a pile of small, metallic wheels with jagged edged teeth that seemed to have once fit together inside a bent, green-crusted metal casing. A box encrusted so thickly in rust that it seemed barely able to hold its shape sat in one corner of the small room. There were tubes of copper leaning against another corner beyond a set of carefully arranged pillows that were in a hopeless tangle. Several statues had been placed about the room. Some of them were partial and others complete. Some were so small as to be able to rest in Drakis' palm while one statue of an enormous winged creature with four legs and no head was far too large for the room with one of its wings sticking through the side wall.

But it was the large stone throne, the back of which ended abruptly in a jagged, shattered edge, that commanded his attention, for there upon it sat the master Far-runner.

He had no legs below the knees. He was an old man; the oldest Drakis had any memory of ever seeing. His carefully kept white hair had been pulled back from his forehead into a long, tightly woven braid that fell down his back. His body was strong but the tone in his muscles had started to fade. He had chiseled cheekbones and his pale eyes were unfocused, seemingly trying to look everywhere at once. He turned toward the sound of Drakis and Ethis as they followed Ishander into the room.

"Outsiders!" the elder Far-runner exclaimed, his face bursting into a smile of childish delight though his eyes did not seem to find them as they stood before him. "A human who smells of distant blood and a rubber-man! Oh, how wonderful!"

Drakis glanced at Ethis, but the shapeshifter's face remained impassive.

"Come to hear, have you? Come to see?" the old man cackled. "Come to be led by the runner who cannot walk?"

"We have," Drakis answered. "We need to know . . ."

"Of course you do!" the old man laughed, slapping his bony hands on his thighs. "You're running far, young man! Farther than anyone has ever run before. You have to know? Why, my son, you have to know better than any of us!"

"Sire, you're confused. I'm not your . . ."

"Sire be damned, you can save that for the clan-witch and her puppet show down on the point," the old man interrupted again. "My name is Koben Dakan, I'm the best damn Far-runner that ever lived, boy."

"But your legs," Ethis asked, "how could you . . . ?"

"And a chimerian!" the elder man exclaimed. "Never have met one of your kind before, though I've seen plenty of likenesses of your clan out in the Lost. Thought your kind were all made up by the lore-tellers but I guess I was wrong. Well, I'll tell you, rubber-man, why this great Far-runner is stumping around on what's left of his knees. I was running in the north, down the left branch as it were of the River Aegrain past the Divergence Falls. I had seen some markers that looked like an old road to Kesh Morain—the City of Delights as it was known in the Time Before—and was holding my path as close to the river as possible without losing the markers taking me farther into the . . ."

"Grandfather," Ishander grumbled under his breath.

The old man looked over at the youth. "Well, perhaps I'll tell that another time. The tail of the tale is that Clan Drevoll found me and thought I was poaching on their past. They had the idea that Shurih was their ruin to pillage and wanted to say so clearly to our clan. So they took just enough of my legs to make sport of me. But I got them back, you see, after I'd been there several months and gotten used to getting about on these stumps . . ."

"Grandfather!" Ishander snapped.

The elder man screwed up his face in disgust and turned back, his blank eyes looking toward Drakis. "He's my grandson, and yet he treats *me* like a whelp. You can just call me Koben as long as Audelai is out of earshot and you don't make me mad. So she sent you to me, did she?"

"Uh, yes," Drakis said, clearing his throat. He was beginning to think he would not be able to fit his questions edgewise between the elder's words. "We need to know . . ."

"What happened?" Koben said, his eyebrows rising. "What happened in the Time Before when the magic was stolen from the land, when the Citadels went dark and the plague from the south robbed the life from our land? Is that what you want to know?"

"Yes, Koben," Ethis said.

The elderly Far-runner nodded sagely, then sat back against the broken throne, pressing his long, bony fingertips together.

"Haven't the slightest idea," the old man said.

Drakis blinked. "But . . . we were told that . . ."

"Young man, I may not be much to look at now but I was the best in my day," Koben said. His blank eyes seemed to be looking onto a different place and a distant time. "I ranged across the Desolation. I've seen the canopy trees stretching over the borders of Armethia itself. I've scowered the Mnaros ruins and tempted the drakoneti of Pythar. I've climbed the God's Wall Mountains and seen the dragons on their crags. I've tread with quiet respect past the towers of Aegrain and left the ghosts to sleep there undisturbed. I've even seen the towers—those incredible, heart-breaking towers of Khorypistan still standing bright in the distance. No man has gone further, seen more, and been more disappointed than I. No man alive knows more than I do about the past, and I'm telling you that all I know is that it's gone . . . it's all gone forever."

"Then you have no idea what happened in the Time Before," Ethis said, deliberately frowning.

"Oh, there are the stories and the legends," Koben shrugged, opening his hands casually. "They tell of the time when the plague of long-headed demons came from the south and stole the magic out of the land. They say that men and dragons were brothers in the Time Before, together guarding the secret of the great magic that protected them both. There were some who, at least one legend says, took this brotherhood too far and tried to use that same magic to remake humans into a semblance of their dragon neighbors. That is the explanation we have of the drakoneti although we have no real knowledge of it. All this happened so long out of memory and the records were lost in the calamity when the Towers of Light went dark. The power of Aether—so the legend says—kept our land strong and the demons of the southlands in fear. The Fordrim down the east fork of the Tyra tell a story where the dragons betrayed their human brothers—I spent some time with them before the Drevoll took me—and that it was their betrayal that caused the Aether to be stolen from the land and the glory of humanity to fall in a single night."

"What if the magic were to return?" Drakis asked. "What if someone found a way to bring it back?"

The old man pondered for a time before he spoke. "That the Aether is gone is sure, and now there are none left who might use it even were it to return. Even so, who can say what might happen? The long-heads from the south believed that we were extinct and after they had their fill of feasting on our land, left it like a rotting carcass. Yet the fathers of our fathers before us—few as they were—still managed to survive. We are still here. We may be a flickering flame in the winds of terrible times, but we burn still. Who is to say what we might be if the great fires were rekindled among the Lost Citadels?"

"Can you tell us the way?" Ethis asked.

The old man smiled. "No . . . not even I can tell you that."

"I know the way," Ishander said, folding his arms across his chest.

The old man turned to the youth, a pained expression on his face. "No, Ishander! You must not. It is farther than even I have run. Your father was foolish to have tried . . ."

"I will take you," Ishander said, ignoring the old man and addressing Drakis directly. "I have seen the Towers of Light. I have walked the Lost Citadel. I know the way."

CHAPTER 21

Uncertain Ground

"IT IS A VIOLATION OF CLAN-LAW!"

Philida, a female Hunt-runner, stood before Urulani with her bare feet planted resolutely wide and firm against the track of packed dirt that ran its serpentine course through the thick jungle growth that all but obscured the collapsing ruins around them. It had previously been Armenthis Road, but once they had passed the Near Gate beyond the Ambeth wall, the ancient avenue had nearly disappeared altogether.

Philida was almost a full head shorter than Urulani but had a muscular build that reminded Urulani of Jugar. She was unquestionably strong, as she had demonstrated only three days before when she had found Mala and the Lyric walking up this same street toward the Near Gate through the town's defensive wall to the north and had summarily picked up both women and carried them back into the marketplace where, apparently, clan-law dictated they should remain. Her hair was a mousy brown, what little there was of it, since the woman preferred to keep it cut less than a finger's width in length. She had a strong jawline, which was often set in defiance of Urulani's wishes and small, gray eyes that peered at the Captain of the *Cydron* with perpetual suspicion. Her skin was deeply tanned and leathery from exposure, leaving it wrinkled and old in appearance. If the woman had a love interest, Urulani would have liked to meet the person just out of curiosity to see what kind of companion this woman could successfully bring to heel that she would bother with enough to keep.

"Violation of clan-law?" Urulani yelled back at the Hunt-runner. Her own people—the Sondau of Nothree—had little in the way of material possessions except those that they "liberated" from their gnome, goblin, or elven neighbors whenever the need arose. The Sondau were a happy people, living life on their own terms to come and go as they pleased; these Ambeth humans were plentiful, it was true, but seemed in a perpetual state of anxiety and desperation. They hunted but took no joy in the hunt. They brought in fruits and vegetables gathered from the forest but never seemed satisfied with what they found or how much they brought in. The Clan-mother counseled peace but beneath her words was a perpetual message of fear. Urulani's own people were dark-skinned sea raiders who had the sense to take only what they needed to live and spend the rest of their time enjoying the living of that life. These light-faced northern people seemed to have lost all their senses along with their color: they were afraid of everything, driven to have more of everything than any of their neighbors, and so busy getting everything that they had no time to enjoy anything. And all for what? So that they could fill their lives acquiring a hoard of possessions only to die and get no use or pleasure out of what they had spent their lives acquiring.

If this was the great human empire of the ancients, then it was no wonder they were nearly extinct.

And now Urulani was facing perhaps the most stubborn example of northern human thinking in the compact body of Philida Creve, the so-called escort assigned to Urulani, Mala, and the Lyric.

Only Mala and the Lyric had disappeared, which had made Philida more intractable than usual.

"Just which clan-law are you thinking is being broken right now?" Urulani seethed at the Hunt-runner who looked as though she were holding her breath. "The clan-law that says that we are all supposed to stay within your sight or the clan-law that says we must remain within the town walls? Or perhaps you're thinking of the clan-law that says guests must be kept safe from harm? Well, Mala and the Lyric have managed to get through the gate without you stopping them and they're out there . . . somewhere."

Exactly where in the somewhere had become increasingly difficult to ascertain. Their trail was easy enough to follow when Urulani or Philida picked it up, but it often led into the ruins and seemed to wander back on itself from time to time. Urulani felt sure that it had led her and their escort both no more than a few hundred strides beyond the town wall and yet Urulani had not been able to see the wall for some time and was feeling slightly confused by the tree canopy overhead that blocked her view of the sun.

"Their being out here is a violation of clan-law," Philida said. "*You* being out here is a violation of clan-law! You must go back!"

"I'd be delighted to go back," Urulani said, reining in her anger and trying to penetrate this woman's thinking by speaking slower. "As soon as we find the Lyric and Mala."

"No," Philida responded. "You are in violation of clan-law. You must go back now."

"But if I go back now, I'll have to leave you to do it," Urulani said with bridled fury. "And that would be a violation of clan-law, wouldn't it . . . being out of your sight?"

Philida puckered her lips in thought. It looked painful. "Then I will take you back."

"Ah, but if you take me back, you will be leaving the Lyric and Mala out here beyond the Ambeth wall," Urulani said. "That would put them in danger, and then *you* would be in violation of clan-law. Neither one of them has enough sense to survive on their own. Are you sworn to protect them?"

"It is my unquestioned duty!" Philida responded indignantly.

"Then let's find them quickly, get back inside the town wall, and then *no one* will be in violation of clan-law," Urulani said, pushing her way past the shorter Hunt-runner as she again followed the booted prints of Mala's feet and the smaller, bare prints of the Lyric back into the undergrowth. She could hear Philida following noisily behind her.

What kind of a hunter is she? Urulani thought. *Maybe her specialty is deaf beasts that have to be wrestled to death.*

Pushing past another fern, Urulani found the trail easier to follow

as the jungle gave way to a colossal ancient structure. The domed roof
had partially collapsed but the walls seemed largely intact. Urulani
wondered for a moment why the Ambeth had not used this structure
for shelter rather than rebuild at the edge of the river. The trail of the
two women led very clearly across the broken, dirty flagstones to a
wide set of stairs and a large arched opening.

The noise behind her had stopped.

Urulani turned to look back. "They must have gone in there. We
just need to bring them . . ."

The short woman was trembling, her eyes fixed on the ruin before them.

"Philida?" Urulani asked quietly. "What is it?"

"You go," the Hunt-runner said in a quavering voice.

Urulani opened her mouth, about to say something about it being
a violation of clan-law but stopped as she realized that Philida was on
the verge of fleeing. Instead she said, "All right. I'll go get them. You
stay right here and I'll be back."

"Yes," Philida gulped.

"I'm going to draw my sword now," Urulani said evenly. "Right?"

Philida managed to nod her head.

Urulani turned back, slipping her blade from its scabbard. It had
been made abundantly clear to her by Philida that "guests" of the
Ambeth clan were in violation of any number of clan-laws simply by
showing their swords uncovered anywhere at any time. The Sondau
woman, her smooth black skin now suddenly damp with perspiration,
moved quickly up the steps and into the open, arched portal.

Dim light filtered into the hallway that appeared to run along the
interior length of the wall before turning at the corners, the sagging
ceiling having fallen completely in several places. The floor was covered in debris. The walls featured faces, dim and indistinct in this
light carved in a frieze that ran down the length of the hall.

These lost humans had a fetish for face carvings, Urulani thought
to herself, following the clear tracks down the hall toward a passage
to her right.

"Li-li . . ."

Urulani froze, her eyes widening in the darkness. She shook her head, drew in a deep breath, and then continued. The tracks definitely led through to the right. She turned and paused again.

This was another hallway, but the walls were of wood. She could hear them creaking as she passed them, moving toward the intersection with another hall toward the end. There the halls turned left and right. She could see where these, too, continued deeper into the building.

"Li-li . . ."

She had definitely heard the voice that time. It echoed down the hallway so badly that she was uncertain as to its direction. She could not tell if it was Mala's voice or that of the Lyric, but it must have been one of the two of them. How either of them knew to call her by that name was a mystery that angered her. No one called her that anymore.

She hurried down the hall to her left, following it to the right and then stopping at another intersection. Two branching hallways went into the darkness on her left or her right while the one in front of her continued a while before also turning right.

Urulani gritted her teeth.

"A labyrinth," she muttered. "I hate labyrinths."

"Li-li!"

Urulani whirled about, but there was no one behind her. She was sure the voice had been close, so close that it she thought she felt the breath on her neck.

"Where are you?" she called out.

"Come, Li-li . . . Come and find me."

Urulani adjusted the grip on her sword. It must have been the Lyric, she thought, moving cautiously down the narrow hall. She and Mala playing their own little game in the ruins like children—too foolish and young to know that there are dangers in the world. What was she doing here, anyway? Charging in to rescue these two women who represented everything she hated. The Lyric who changed who she was and what she knew more often than the sun dawned. Urulani prized reason, tactics, and thought—while this woman placed them all in danger by her madness.

Worse for her, though, was Mala. She was a traitor whose trust was forever lost and her every action in question. She had betrayed them all and had a hand, no doubt in Urulani's mind, in the attack on Nothree and the death of uncounted numbers of her kinsmen. The Sondau captain would have tossed her overboard the night she was exposed, and they would all have been rid of her long before now.

And yet here she was, moving deeper into this maze and for what? To rescue two foolish women who could not even manage to keep within the barricade walls.

"Why have you come, Li-li?"

"I've come for you," Urulani shouted down the hallway. "We've got to get back to the town."

"No, Li-li," the deep voice said. The walls around Urulani groaned. "You did not come for the women—you came for *him*."

"I don't know what you're talking about," Urulani shouted, her hand suddenly shaking; she had to concentrate before it would stop. "We need to leave."

"You cannot leave," the voice said. It seemed to come from everywhere. "You came to find me . . . but you are lost and wandering. You do not know the way because you do not know what you want. You will never find it until you know what you seek."

"I'm looking for two women . . ."

"You do not want them . . ."

"But I *will* have them!"

"Because he would want it to be so."

"Stop it!" Urulani shouted.

A whisper came into her ear.

"You are lost, Li-li . . . you need to find the stars again. They have been hidden from your eyes, but you shall see them again, as you did when you were young. Come to Chelesta, Li-li."

Urulani turned toward the voice. The faces in the wall were those of a woman.

It was her own face carved in the wall.

The face slowly smiled at her.

Urulani roared, swinging her sword wide and connecting with the carved face. In an instant, the wall exploded into dust followed by the wall behind her and those at either end of the labyrinthine halls. Instinctively, Urulani raised her arms to cover her face.

When she lowered them at last, she saw that the entire maze had vanished, crumbling to dust around her. In the center of the now empty shell of the building stood the Lyric and Mala gazing up at a statue of a woman that had remained unscathed through the years and the fall of the maze.

Urulani quickly crossed the now open space, her footfalls kicking up thick dust as she ran. "Lyric? Mala?"

The women turned toward Urulani. Mala had an expression of surprise, but the Lyric was unfazed.

"So you came for her," the Lyric said with a smile and a vacant expression. "She said you would come when she called."

"Come with me," Urulani said, not wanting to think about what the Lyric was implying. "Philida is waiting for us outside, and we've got to get back inside the town before we're missed."

"Oh, I don't think anyone will be looking for us," the Lyric said with a smile. "They'll be dealing with far bigger problems. You're right, though; we had better hurry or we'll be caught outside. He has come. He's the beginning of the path but he does not comprehend its ends."

The Lyric looked up.

Urulani followed her gaze. Sunlight was streaming down in columns from the broken dome far overhead. Urulani could hear horns blaring in the distance.

A screeching sounded so loudly that it raised a pall of dust up from around their feet as a shadow rushed overhead, blotting out the sun in its passage. Its shape and sound Urulani had seen only once before, but it was unmistakable to her now.

An enormous dragon had come to Ambeth.

Two more shadows like the first crossed over them in quick succession before Urulani was finally able to run toward the open doorway of the structure, with Mala and the Lyric close behind. As soon as they were outside, Philida joined them in their mad dash.

CHAPTER 22

The Horn and Hand

THE CRASH OF A GONG resounded from the walls of Ambeth. Drakis started at the sound and the quick succession of alarms that followed it. He pushed his way out of the Far-runner's hovel just as the enormous silhouette of a dragon passed so closely over the town that he ducked instinctively.

"Mala," Drakis demanded of Ethis, who had followed him in his rush to the alley. "Where is she?"

"She was with Urulani and the Lyric," Ethis answered at once.

"Where!" Drakis insisted. "Where were they?"

"They were in the market plaza near the Keep," Ethis responded. Drakis' voice was closer to panic than the chimerian had ever heard before. The screams of the townsfolk were making it difficult to be heard. "I don't trust their handler, but Urulani will take care of them."

"No, we've got to find her," Drakis yelled as he ran down the alleyway toward Abratias Road.

"We've got to leave while we still can!" Ethis said, stopping Drakis just short of the road. People were flooding into the street, a river of panic as they tried every way to leave the town for the relative safety beyond the walls. All the gates were open wide but the sudden mob rushing toward them choked the openings. Children were crying everywhere, their panic spurred more by their parents gripping them in fear than their own concern.

"Why do they even *have* these walls?" Drakis said grimly as he tried to push his way along the edge of the panicked crowd. Ethis followed closely as they slipped, pulled, and occasionally pushed their way down the edge of Abratias Road. Drakis was sweating profusely by the time they reached the intersection of Tyra.

Ethis shouted something, but his words were swallowed up by the keening voice of the gray-mottled dragon as it rushed over the length of the town.

"What did you . . . ?"

"I said LOOK!" Ethis shouted, pointing down Tyra Road toward where the curving path rose up toward the Commons.

Drakis looked. The road was packed with panicked townsfolk blindly shoving their way toward them. A cart had overturned in the intersection in front of them, causing many of the terrified Ambeth to rush down toward the river bridge as well as in every other direction. All this Drakis took in even as his heart went cold in his chest.

Two of the dragons had landed at the far end of the road on Ambeth Commons while a third turned slowly overhead, seeking to land there as well.

"Mala," Drakis said, then grabbed the closest of the chimerian's four arms. "Come on!"

"And just where are we going?" Ethis demanded.

"To the river!" Drakis replied, charging across the street, dodging and shoving his way through the mindless panic. It was easier going with the fleeing host than against them. Drakis and Ethis quickly reached the river's edge. As Drakis had surmised, the villagers were intent on crossing the bridge or, in some cases, attempting to swim the wide river, leaving the shoreline far less crowded than the streets. They made their way quickly along the shamble of buildings and ruins bordering the shoreline.

"This is your plan?" Ethis said with an intense hoarse whisper. "To get *closer* to these dragons?"

"It's Mala," Drakis said as though that were the final answer to all arguments.

"Mala?" Ethis replied. "Haven't you learned anything? She sold your life's breath to the Inquisitors and you're still trying to protect *her*?"

Drakis did not even acknowledge the question, but continued moving along the southern end of Elucia Road where it followed the riverbank. The road soon turned back up the slope with the Keep on their right and the Commons at the top of the rise. The three dragons had all landed in the Commons, each sitting back with their wings folded and facing the Keep. They all seemed to be staring at something.

Drakis was suddenly shoved to one side, pressed firmly against the rough planks of a wall. He instinctively reached for his sword, but a larger hand encased his own against the grip, holding the blade firmly in its scabbard.

"Think, Drakis," Ethis said, pinning the human against the wall. "She's probably not even there! She's fled with the rest of the town, and if you're looking to save her, you should be looking for her *out there!*"

Drakis struggled with all his considerable strength but the chimerian held him fast. Rage filled his vision with red.

"You're not going to save anyone by dashing in and challenging a dragon with your sword drawn—let alone three of them at once," the chimerian said urgently. "You've got to listen to me!"

Drakis froze.

Come to the tears of the Ambeth lost
Come are the mighty of old
Where is the son come?
Where is the past found?

Ethis turned his head, his blank, featureless face twisting consciously into the image of concern. "What is it, Drakis?"

Drakis started to shake.

Where is the man whom the wise foretold?
He who is seeking the truth?
What does portend?
In treacheries ends?

"I hear them," Drakis stammered.

"Hear who?"

"THEM!" Drakis hissed through clenched teeth.

Ethis sharply turned his head and looked up the street, relaxing his grip.

When fell the towers of human right?
Why did their oaths they forsake?
Death came in calling . . .
Dark brought the falling.

"I don't hear a thing," Ethis whispered, more puzzled than alarmed. "In fact . . . it's uncommonly quiet."

Drakis turned his head to look toward the Commons. "One of them . . . the rust-colored one."

"What about it?" Ethis asked.

"It's . . . singing."

Broken the vow of the ancient kings,
Dead in the ground they now rot.
Where is the Seeker?
Where is the Keeper?

"They are making no sound," Ethis whispered again. "Do you understand them?"

Drakis squinted, trying to concentrate.

Come to us that we may know you
Come to the horn and the hand
Drakis returning . . .
Drakis in yearning . . .

"They . . . they're *asking* for me," Drakis said quietly.

"For you?" Ethis asked. "Are you certain?"

"Yes," Drakis nodded, gently pushing the chimerian's arm out of the way. "I can't explain it, but . . . but they want me to come."

Drakis began walking up the center of the deserted street.

"This can't be good." Ethis shook his head as he followed. Drakis knew that the chimerian was taking far more care than he was in moving silently along the buildings and finding cover between him and the monstrous beasts as he advanced. Drakis' own training sounded in the back of his mind reminding him that he, too, should be taking such elementary precautions, but there was something in the dragon's song that beckoned him onward with an understanding of inviolate honor and truce. It was not peace or even trust but something else that he was having trouble putting words to in his mind. Oddly, the fact that there were three of them was comforting to him although he did not understand why that should be true.

Drakis stepped slowly up the trodden clay of the road and onto
the deserted Commons. His sword remained in its scabbard and he
kept his hands far from its hilt. He moved gingerly between the
mottled gray dragon on his left and the yellow-and-green dragon on
his right. Both had reared back on their curled tails and sat upright in
the open space before the Keep, their wings partially extending from
time to time, flapping gently to help them keep their balance. Each
of these dragons was nearly forty feet in height, their great, horned
heads craned forward on their long, scale-plated necks as they
watched him imperiously through their reptilian eyes. Directly across
from where he stood sat the third dragon, a towering behemoth with
rust-colored scales almost a third again as large as the other two
dragons.

Drakis stepped carefully between them with light treads, his eyes
fixed on the great rust dragon before him.

The gray dragon suddenly hissed so loudly that Drakis flinched,
turning sharply toward the sound. The dragon's lips curled back, baring sharp teeth taller than the human's height. With a speed and agil-
ity far greater than Drakis could have imagined in such an enormous
creature, the gray dragon's head rushed toward him. Drakis fell backward, his hand reaching for his blade.

The head of the rust-colored dragon slammed into the onrushing
head of the gray dragon, knocking it to one side. The gray dragon
pulled its head upward, roaring with such a deafening sound that
Drakis dropped his sword just as he drew it, his hands rising instinctively to cover his ears.

The rust-colored dragon howled back, its neck curling down over
Drakis. The enormous body fell forward, and for a moment Drakis
thought it might crush him, but then the dragon spread its claws, ar-
resting its fall as its forepaw smashed into the ground only ten feet to
the human's right, gouging a deep hole and shattering the stones of a
section of ancient roadway. The scaled breast of the beast filled his
vision as the monster turned, bringing its own head down toward the
human.

Drakis clambered backward, tripping over the broken stones and
falling before he could get his footing. He glanced anxiously about

him, searching for his sword, but the colossal head was rushing toward him.

Then it slowed and stopped just above him.

Drakis lay staring at the beast for a while, neither of them moving.

Tell us the truth we are seeking
Come to the horn and the hand
Drakis returning . . .
Drakis in learning . . .

Drakis stared for a moment at the terrifying face staring back at him. Thick, leathery skin lay beneath the scales all of which were a deeper reddish color near their base but faded further out. The enormous teeth were yellowed with age, though how old the creature might be was beyond his guessing. One of the eyes was a milky color and probably blind and several of the multiple horns springing from its head had long ago been broken off and worn smooth by time and use.

The dragon turned its head so as to get a better look at the human with its good eye. Then it twisted its head downward, lowering the long horn, which emerged from its head just behind the eye, until it was within a few feet of the prone human.

Drakis smiled momentarily. It was like watching an old man crane his head to hear better.

Come to the horn and the hand.

Drakis slowly reached upward, laying his hand hesitantly on the surface of the horn.

His eyes widened and he drew in a sharp breath.

CHAPTER 23

Strong Currents

U RULANI THREW HER BACK against the village wall just to the left of the open North Gates. The villagers had fled into the surrounding jungle although Urulani knew that their safety there was far from guaranteed.

Mala dropped down next to Urulani, more out of a desire to remain close than to follow her toward the danger. She smelled of panic, Urulani thought, staying so close to the raider captain that she could barely move her elbows without hitting the traitorous female. Not that Urulani would have any personal concerns about hurting Mala if she got in her way. Indeed, Urulani rather relished the excuse as she had come to the conclusion that the woman should have been relieved of the burden of her existence ever since her treachery had been exposed some weeks before when they were still at sea. But Drakis had insisted on protecting her, and Urulani found herself irritated that she felt a desire to honor his proclaimed protection of this ridiculous excuse for a female.

Philida knelt on the opposite side of the gate, her face drawn and her eyes wide. She spoke in urgent, hushed tones across the deserted, open gate. "We should flee into the brush! Now!"

Urulani smiled across at the Ambeth Hunt-runner. "Wouldn't that be a violation of clan-law?"

"That *is* clan-law!" Philida hissed back.

"How can you say that?" Urulani replied, drawing the curved blade of her cutlass from its scabbard. "After you've worked so hard to get us all back into the village."

"We have to get closer," Mala said suddenly.

Urulani turned her face toward her clinging companion, her languid dark eyes set against the midnight-velvet complexion. "*You* want to get closer?"

"No!" Philida demanded emphatically. "We stay here!"

"It's all right, Philida," Urulani smiled grimly back at their escort as she turned in a crouch toward the gate. "You stay here. The Lyric will protect you."

Philida looked up. The Lyric was standing behind her, her pale face grinning vacantly as she examined a large butterfly that had landed on her arm.

Urulani sprinted through the gate, silently dashing down the right-hand roadway—Heritsania, she thought it was named—and following the cobbled-together buildings on the south side between her and the dragons to the south. Just ahead of her, the road turned southward, and she knew it sloped down from there toward the Commons. It would afford her a good view into the plaza where the monsters had settled while still affording her the benefit of a little distance and cover behind which she might hide.

Not, she thought, that she had any real idea how far from these creatures was far enough or what cover might be effective.

She was just coming to the corner when something caught her foot, causing her to stumble.

"Sorry," Mala exclaimed in a hoarse whisper.

Urulani gritted her teeth and choked back the words she longed to say. She knelt, sword in hand, at the wall of a bakery that stood at the corner where the road turned southward. The shutters remained open above her and the smell of baking bread drifted out of the windows and down around her.

Urulani's face was blank; her eyes focused as she slowly leaned forward to take in the street and the Commons at its end.

The road descended as she remembered, a gentle clear slope leading directly to the open area in front of the Keep, which the locals called the Commons. The street was completely deserted. Doors swung slightly in the gentle breeze. The three dragons looked hunched over, each of them towering above the surrounding buildings. The Keep was almost completely obscured by the monstrous forms though some of the eastern parapets surrounding the Keep were visible. Two of the dragons were smaller in stature—although the term smaller had little meaning in this case, Urulani thought grimly. All three of them seemed intent on something below them in the Commons. One of them, the gray-scaled dragon, snapped its head downward in sudden ferocity but the largest of the three—the rust-colored dragon—threw its own head into its smaller companion and pushed it aside.

There was a human moving among the dragons.

Urulani's jaw dropped.

"Drakis?" Mala murmured next to her.

"It can't be," Urulani said in wonder.

The enormous rust dragon lowered its head. It looked to Urulani as though the monster were somehow bowing to Drakis.

"Closer!" Mala urged. "We have to get closer!"

Urulani glanced at the former slave once and then nodded. "I think you may be right."

Urulani dashed to the other side of the street and then down along the open and now vacant buildings, trying to keep herself inconspicuous as she approached. The idea of attracting the attention of these creatures terrified her. Her crew had been decimated the last time they had fought just one of these dragons, and they had only defeated it because Ethis had closed the fold portal on the creature's neck. Now there were three, and she still had no idea what tactic might actually prove effective against them in battle.

They came to where Heritsania was crossed by Jurusta Road. A smithy shop on the corner provided them with some protection. Urulani could see a maze of alleyways winding back among the hovels and the animal stockade beyond them. She knew that those alleys eventually would wend their way to the Commons and provide them with better cover as they approached—but she suddenly questioned why they were here at all. Why even come this close since they obviously had no idea what they would do about these dragons even if they did get close enough to them to strike. Yet Drakis was there, standing in the middle of them, and there was something in that which filled Urulani with the desire to be there with him, somehow, and not let him face these behemoths alone. Maybe that's why Mala was insisting that they get closer . . . so perhaps, she thought, the warrens would allow them to approach unseen.

Urulani reached her hand out for the wall, to pull herself forward into the alley.

"Wait!" Mala breathed. "Look!"

Each of the dragons stretched out its wings, the sound of their leathery surfaces rustling loudly in the morning air. With enormous power, first the gray, and then the green dragon with yellow markings pushed downward, the flapping raising a sudden hurricane in the middle of the village. Doors slammed, pottery crashed, and loose objects of all kinds flew through the air with every beat of their wings as each took flight. Last of all, the enormous rust-colored dragon raised up, the downdraft of its wings greater than those of its companions as with raw power the dragon drew itself into the sky with raw strength. Then, airborne at last, the rust dragon pulled itself forward, gaining speed in the air with its two companions following behind. Together, the three wheeled once over the town and then struck off toward the south.

Urulani jumped up and was running down Heritsania Road even before the dragons had made their turn above the town. She could see that it was, indeed, Drakis in the middle of the Commons, sitting on the ground and slumped over forward. Urulani dropped her sword on the ground as she reached him, falling to her knees and gripping Drakis' shoulders before he fell over. Mala was with her, stopping next to them and looking down as she stooped over them.

Drakis' head fell back, and his eyelids fluttered opened.

"Am I back?" Drakis asked, blinking and trying to focus his eyes.

"Yes," Urulani said with the sudden flash of a smile. "A better question might be if you know where you've been?"

"HAIL DRAKIS!"

Drakis frowned at the sound as he struggled to his feet. "What in the name of the gods . . ."

"HAIL DRAKIS AND THE HEROES OF AMBETH!"

Mala and Urulani turned toward the sound. It was coming from the wall of the Keep at the edge of the Commons. A figure stood atop the parapet, hands raised overhead and shouting out over the roof-tops of the now vacant town.

It was the Clan-mother, Audelai El.

"All hail to the victorious warriors who have saved our village and our people from the dragons of the south!" the Clan-mother continued. "Sound the bell and blow the horn! Call all the people of Ambeth that they may hear the glorious deeds done this day—of Drakis and his heroes who have saved all Ambeth from the dragons' wrath!"

"Can't we get her to shut up?" Mala sniffed.

"I suspect it would be against clan-law," Urulani offered dryly.

The gongs were sounding on the village walls in the distance. The villagers were returning and making their way toward the Commons. All the while Audelai El continued her praise of Drakis, recounting how he and his brave companions had rid the village of the dragons.

Drakis glared at the dwarf standing next to Audelai El on the parapet.

"Not again," he growled under his breath.

"But I swear to you, by Thorgrim's Beard, that it wasn't me," Jugar protested.

The Clan-mother had gathered all the strangers back into their assigned quarters while she arranged for a special celebration over their deliverance of the town. Now Ethis stood leaning against one corner of the room, both sets of his arms folded across his chest. Mala stood nearby, quieted by the confrontation while the Lyric waited in a statuesque and disapproving pose next to her. Urulani sat on a bench nearby, resting her chin on her fist as she watched the argument unfold. The dwarf's face was beet red, holding his ground against the unbridled frustration of the human warrior.

"Not you?" Drakis raged. "It's *always* been you!"

"Now, lad, that's not exactly true . . ."

"No?" Drakis countered. "Who was it that told tales of the glorious prophecies after House Timuran fell?"

"Well, aye, that was me to be sure, but . . ."

"And I suppose you had nothing to do with telling the faery queen about these so-called prophecies either?"

"Never! I would never have given that woman so much as the time of . . ."

"And in the city of the mud gnomes?" Drakis shouted, his fists planted on his hips. "What about the speech you made there?"

"Sure, I have to admit that in that particular case I may have had something to do with . . ."

"And now you've got Audelai El, the slippery Clan-mother of Ambeth crowing about it, too!" Drakis seethed. "And she's got this village believing it now."

"And I believe it," Urulani said quietly.

Silence fell in the room.

"No, Urulani, you don't understand," Drakis said, trying to rein in his temper. "This whole prophecy nonsense has nothing to do with . . ."

"I believe it," Urulani said, standing up. "I was there today. I saw the dragon bow down before you."

"Please," Drakis said with a weary sigh. "That's not what happened."

"I saw one of the dragons try to attack you," Urulani continued. "The great one protected you from him and then bowed down to you."

"No, that's not what happened," Drakis said, his anger spent. "Abream—the gray dragon—it was his brood-brother that we killed at the fold portal. He only wanted revenge for his brood-brother's death. Pharis was just keeping me alive so that I could . . ."

Drakis stopped speaking.

Ethis pushed himself away from the corner. "How is it that our friend Drakis knows the *names* of the dragons who came calling today?"

Drakis looked away.

"Indeed," Ethis continued. "How is it that friend Drakis even knows the kinship of these monsters?"

"Because I spoke with them," Drakis said, still looking away.

"Spoke with them?" Ethis pressed, moving around so he could look into the human's face. "And how is it that this ordinary man, who claims to have no important destiny, can speak with dragons?"

"I don't know," Drakis shrugged. "It has something to do with the Dragon Song. I heard it when the dragons came—all vague and rhythmic and frankly not making much sense. It was only after I touched the creature's horn that . . ."

"Go on," Ethis urged, an insistent, commanding tone underlying his voice.

"It was as though both the dragon and I went to a completely different place," Drakis said. "I can't really explain it except that it was beautiful and quiet. I could still see the town around us but it was different—perfect, somehow. They weren't the broken down, temporary buildings the town is made of but elegant and shining. Even that linen shop on the corner was, I don't know, a *perfect* linen shop."

"And . . ." Ethis urged.

"Well, in this place there was only this dragon and myself, and I could suddenly understand what he was saying." Drakis' gaze fixed far beyond the walls of the room. "He told me his name was Pharis, Prince of the Eastern Sky. He apologized for Abream and introduced Marush—the green-and-yellow dragon. He said they were glad to have found me in time."

The large eyebrows of the dwarf went up. "In time? In time for what?"

"He said that Queen Hesthia was looking for us and that it was best that he had found us first," Drakis answered. "I took it from him that there were a number of dragons who were upset about her rule. Many of them suspect that she came into power only because the drought of magic weakened all dragons and that she would do anything to prevent us from restoring Aether to the land."

"Is it possible?" Jugar said, barely hoping for the answer. "Could the Aether Wells of Armethia flow once more?"

"According to Pharis, that's what this Queen of Dragons fears," Drakis said. "It was the loss of Aether that caused the Citadels to fall and allowed the elves and their armies to lay waste to the entire kingdom. The dragons believe that it was the humans—who were in control of the Citadels—that caused the Aether to fail and who broke their vows with all dragonkind."

"And, according to the Far-runners, the humans believe that it was the dragons who broke their vows," Ethis said, his face forced into the semblance of a thoughtful frown. "Neither seems to know what happened."

"Pharis would like us to find out," Drakis said.

"How?" Urulani asked.

"He said that we would be going down the river," Drakis frowned. "There we would find Chelesta—the city of the lost Citadels. There, he said, we would find the truth."

"Audelai El has already offered to outfit a journey," Ethis said. "Supplies, boats . . . even a guide."

"If we could restore magic to the land," Jugar said, his eyes shining, "then we could use the fold again. We could get home, lad."

Ethis nodded. "Even if we *don't* restore the Aether Wells . . . we'll be closer to home down the river than we are now."

"It's perfect," Drakis said, then shook his head. "There is something about it being all so perfect that feels wrong to me . . ."

Mala stepped forward, taking Drakis by the arm.

It was Urulani who looked away.

"You promised me, Drakis," Mala said, looking up into his face. "This is my way home."

CHAPTER 24

Divergence

BY THE MORNING of the third day, everything had been quite neatly arranged.

The entire village had turned out along Quabet Road and along the boat landing shoreline. The bridge that crossed the River Havnis between Abratias Way and the tannery buildings on the south side of the river was packed so tightly with people that the Lyric fretted over one of the children at the railing being pushed off. Exuberance was in the air. The Hunt-Runners and the Grass-walkers had remained within the stockade walls this morning, occasionally breaking out in songs of praise or wild cheers whenever one of the members of Drakis' expedition to the Citadels of Light glanced up from securing the provisions on their boats.

Drakis tried to look up as little as possible.

"Are we ready?" Ethis asked with frustration in his voice as he walked quickly up to stand beside Drakis. In all his confused memories, the human Impress Warrior could not recall the chimerian sounding so impatient.

"Nearly," Drakis answered, jerking his head toward Urulani on his left. "Our Lady Captain rearranged the supplies twice in these first two boats. They're both secure. She's repacking the third boat now. Once that's done, we should be ready to leave."

"Not soon enough," Ethis said, clearing this throat. "The dwarf is getting set to make a speech."

"Oh, not now!" Drakis groaned, throwing the end of the braided rope violently against the hull of the boat.

A short way inland from the river's shore, Jugar leaned on a crutch he had fashioned for himself. Mala stood next to him, fidgeting and uncomfortable. She had tried to help tie down the supplies in the second boat, but Urulani had chased her away with harsh and occasionally colorful words expressing her less than approving opinion of Mala's efforts at rope handling. On the other side of the dwarf stood the Lyric, her face held high and a look of haughty condescension on her features. Her hand rested on the shoulder of the dwarf as though he were speaking for her. The dwarf had found, borrowed, or stolen a bright red strip of cloth, which he had tied around his waist. The colors of the rest of Jugar's clothing had become muted and stained over the course of their long road, but Drakis was suddenly reminded of the outrageous costume Jugar had worn when he first encountered him in the depths of the dwarven halls seemingly a lifetime ago.

"Our good friends of Ambeth," Jugar shouted, and the cheers of the crowd forced him to pause as he flashed a broad, gap-toothed smile.

"Do you think he's ready to leave?" Ethis could barely be heard over the noise.

"Him? With this kind of audience?" Drakis shouted back. "We'll be fortunate if he's ready by next month!"

Jugar held up one hand to quiet the crowd, but it took nearly a minute for them to still enough for him to feel confident that his words would be heard. "On behalf of myself and my companions on this perilous quest, I wish to offer to the good citizens of Ambeth— heirs to the greatness of all Drakosia which is that hidden knowledge of the ancients and the glory of which is prophesied to return and bless you, this valiant people—it is to you that we offer our grateful hearts, our unwavering devotion, and a pledge of the might of our strength and steel!"

A roar erupted from the assembled townsfolk.

Drakis rolled his eyes just as Urulani hurried up to him at the second boat.

"If only he'd broken his jaw instead of his leg," Urulani grumbled.

Drakis couldn't hear her over the din. "What?"

Urulani just shook her head then continued as the applause started to die down again. "The weight in that last boat is now more even and I've secured everything. It will float level now and that should help if we run into any shallows. Most of the supplies are in that third boat. We'll tie the boats together once they're all launched. I'll pilot that last boat at the back of the string while that local whelp . . . hey, where's our boy-guide?"

"Ishander?" Drakis frowned. "I haven't seen him."

"Do you think he's going to join us," Urulani asked with a dismissive sniff, "or does he plan on just telling us where to go?"

Drakis raised his eyebrows as he turned to look at Urulani. "Is something troubling you?"

Urulani glared back at Drakis, her dark eyes suddenly daring him to look away. "I am a sea raider of the Sondau! I ride the waves of vast seas and two oceans! I speak and at my word warships steer into the face of storms! Coastal towns in Nordesia dare only whisper my name . . . and I am now captain of a raft full of fruit waiting on a dwarf who is short on stature and long on wind!"

The sound of the crowd had died down sufficiently for Jugar to continue. "We seek the Citadels of Light—those great and terrible places of the ancients—and there we will brave the dangers of its cursed streets and doomed towers! There, on behalf of you, good friends, we shall . . . we shall . . ."

The dwarf faltered in his speech. The Lyric, her hand still resting on Jugar's shoulder, bent down and whispered into his ear.

The dwarf brightened. "There we shall discover the truth of the past and the fall of the Lost Empire!"

The Lyric whispered again.

"And restore the glory that once was!"

The dwarf frowned, uncertain about his last words as he glanced over at the Lyric.

The Lyric only smiled confidently at the dwarf and nodded in reassurance, even as the crowd roared in tumultuous approval.

"Well, I think we've heard enough," Drakis said to the raider captain and the chimerian standing on either side of him. "Where is that Far-runner who is supposed to be our . . ."

"He's here," Ethis said, nodding to their right.

The young man swaggered toward them. He was barefooted and wore a loincloth. Drakis had come to understand that this was the traditional attire of the Far-runners. He also wore the traditional vest, but this particular one was crafted out of fitted pieces of polished metal that seemed to mimic the pattern of scales Drakis had seen on the dragons only a few days before. The youth also wore a towering and, in Drakis' opinion, ridiculous hat of long feathers and barbed sticks pointing straight up. He seemed disdainfully unconcerned, however, as he strode through the parting crowd to the cheering accolades of the villagers around him. His long braid swung back and forth down his back as he moved to stand facing the dwarf. Then he turned, his chin held high, as Mala ducked to avoid being hit by the tall hat. Ishander held both his hands high in the air.

The villagers quieted at the sign.

"I am Ishander, son of Pellender, the son of Koben Dakan! We are Far-runners of the Ambeth. We outrun the wind and rivers. We slip in silence from death's chill grasp. We fly before the dragon on the wing and the drakoneti on the hunt, and none stop us in our flight!"

The crowd cheered once more.

"Is he saying that they run from a fight better than anyone?" Ethis chuckled.

"Maybe," Drakis said with a quick snorting laugh.

Ishander held his arms up again, his voice demanding. "Who is there who will keep my soul while I fly from Ambeth?"

Drakis furrowed his brow. *What was the boy talking about?*

Koben Dakan emerged from the crowd. He moved with great difficulty on the shortened stubs of his legs, each capped by hardened leather fittings. The elder Far-runner could barely stand on his own but refused two of the village guards their offer to help him. The old man's wispy hair flew about his face in the breeze coming up the river, his blank gaze seeming to search in front of him. In the old Far-Runner's arms lay the young man's leather vest.

Behind him, Audelai-El, the Clan-mother, followed. She was clad in a robe of the same metallic scales and crowned with a towering headdress of dried reeds. In her outstretched hands, she held a weathered wooden box.

Ishander stepped toward the old man and the Clan-mother, removing the tall, feathered hat.

"May the sights seen by my eyes be ever with the clan. May the words that I hear be ever with the clan," Ishander said, handing the tall headdress to his grandfather. He then removed the metallic vest, which clanked as he exchanged it for the leather vest. "May the soul of my body be ever with the clan."

Koben Dakan's eyes were filled with intense pride as he handed the simple leather vest to Ishander. "The Ambeth honor you always. Your name is sung always. Your soul is with us always."

The villagers erupted in wild cheering.

The Clan-mother held up her arms and the crowd quieted. "I, Audelai-El of Ambeth, bestow the *Akumau* . . . the seal of people's runner on this great quest."

An excited murmur ran through the crowd. Drakis gave Ethis a questioning look, but the chimerian only shrugged with all four of his shoulders. Ishander stood tall, his head held high in anticipation.

"This *Akumau* was last worn by Pellender, Far-runner of our Clan," Audelai spoke over the murmur of the crowd, quieting them. "Before his last journey, he left it to me—asking that I bestow it upon the one chosen by the gods to bear it next in the name of the Ambeth!"

Ishander took a step forward, his chin raised in pride.

"The female called Mala of the Strangers will bear the *Akumau*," Audelai said in a clear voice.

The assembled clan gasped, their eyes all turning toward a suddenly very uncomfortable Mala.

"No!" Ishander yelped. Hurt, anger, and horror all passed over his features. "I am the Far-runner! My father bore that seal. It is mine by right!"

"It is *not* your right," Audelai said firmly into the stunned silence. "It is the Clan-mother's right to bestow this seal on the god's choice of bearer—and the gods have chosen the woman called Mala."

"But it was the *Akumau* that my father wore . . ."

"And now Mala will wear it . . . the gods have decreed it; it is clan-law."

Mala stammered. "But . . . but I don't want . . ."

"It is clan-law!" Audelai said firmly, the old woman's jaw set. Drakis realized that the crowd did not like what was happening any more than Ishander did. Nevertheless, Audelai reached into a small box and, opening it, presented it to Mala.

Inside was a small, polished gemstone set in an ornately patterned medallion less than a thumb's length in diameter. The engraving was of two heads of a dragon intertwined and facing outward, both set on a background of dragon wings around a polished green gemstone. The piece was suspended from a narrow, golden chain.

Mala took up the chain, drawing it over her head. The necklace hung around her neck and she bowed slightly to a smattering of clapping from the crowd, who remained stunned at this turn of events.

Jugar scowled in obvious disapproval.

The Lyric beamed.

"Her?" Urulani spat at the ground. "A traitor who would sell our lives without a second thought, and they honor *her*?"

Drakis kept a gloomy silence.

Ishander turned back to face Jugar, the Lyric, and Mala as he put on his leather vest. He eyed each of them for a moment, glaring at Mala with contempt, and then abruptly said, "It's time to leave."

Ishander strode past the trio and walked directly toward the boat grounded ashore next to Drakis, Urulani, and Ethis. He barely glanced at Drakis as he spoke, "You three tie these boats together right now—about six arm's lengths of cording between them."

"It would be better for us to launch the boats now," Urulani said, "and tie them off when we get afloat."

Ishander turned on the dark woman. "You know nothing about it! Do as I tell you and do it now!"

Urulani lunged toward Ishander with the clear intent to do harm. Drakis managed to block her at the last moment. The rage drained from Urulani's features, and she stepped back, turning to the last boat and quickly securing a line with considerable vehemence.

"Ishander," Drakis called after the young man. "Urulani knows what she is doing. You don't have to . . ."

The boy stopped, turning quickly to face Drakis. "I am the Far-runner! I am the guide! The black-skinned woman knows *nothing* of the river. You and the four-armed one will push me and the dwarf off in the first boat after they are all tied together. Then you will join the women in the second boat. The Urulani woman will steady the third. We are leaving at once! It is clan-law!"

"Of course," Drakis said quietly. "Clan-law."

"Come, dwarf . . . you ride the river with me." The young Far-runner grabbed the dwarf by the shoulder.

Ethis' face was featureless as he stared at the young Ambeth Far-runner stomping off toward the first boat. The chimerian scratched his head with his third hand as he spoke. "He seems to believe he is in charge."

Drakis glanced at Ethis, then began securing a second line to the prow of the middle boat. "He can believe what he wants, and I'm perfectly willing to let him believe it until the time is right."

"And when might that be?" Ethis asked.

"Probably when you give the dwarf back his stone," Drakis replied quietly.

Ishander climbed into the first boat along with the dwarf. Ethis and Drakis managed to push it off of the sand. The young Far-runner instructed everyone else to get into the second boat except Urulani, who grudgingly took her place on the third. Ishander held the first boat against the current, pushing farther and farther out into the river. Then, suddenly, he pulled up his river pole, releasing the first boat into the current. The rope snapped taut, yanking the second boat off the shore. Ethis, Drakis, and the Lyric all lost their footing while Mala nearly fell over the side into the river. Urulani watched as both boats gained speed in the current, the rope between her boat and the second drawing up its slack at an alarming rate. Urulani gripped the raised tail of her boat with both arms as the rope suddenly tightened. The third boat leaped from the shore. This caused Drakis and Ethis, who were just then regaining their footing in the boat to come crashing down again. Urulani's boat scudded into the water so quickly that the rope slacked again, and the third boat nearly collided with the second, sending a wave of water up from between the boats to drench the occupants of both.

Ishander stood at the prow of the first boat, guiding it under the wooden framing of the Abratias Bridge, acknowledging the cheers of the crowd on the bridge above and seemingly oblivious to the disarray in the boats trailing behind him, each bumping awkwardly against the pylons supporting the bridge.

Drakis dragged himself to sit up in the boat, his back against the gunnels.

"So the heroes of Ambeth set off on their quest," he muttered, wiping the river water from his face.

Audelai-El was nowhere to be seen.

Audelai El could hear the distant sound of the townsfolk still cheering as she walked carefully among the ruins. Each step was taken with distaste, as she hated being in the wild. She preferred things all neatly ordered around her. Broad avenues and clear, open spaces to look out across and see trouble coming from a distance—that was her idea of a pleasant place. The jungle was just too unpredictable and filled with things that were simply out of place.

She came at last to the great ruin of the temple. She had forgotten to which god or goddess it had once belonged. Elucia, perhaps . . . she could not recall though she thought someone had once told her. It was the best of the ruins outside the stockade with its walls intact and large sections of the dome still standing. The villagers all believed it cursed; she supposed she did too, so far as curses went. Nasty, broken-up old things, these ruins. She had no desire to enter them.

But the temple did serve one function very well that was to her interests.

It was easily spotted from the sky.

A gale of hot air suddenly encompassed the Clan-mother from behind. She yelped in startled surprise, turning at once.

The enormous head of the dragon Pharis lay largely hidden by the mammoth ferns of the jungle floor. Audelai El reached up to touch her heart, wondering all over again how it was that a creature of that size could possibly hide so well in the brush.

Audelai El reached out carefully and touched one of the dragon's unbroken horns on the right side of its head.

The world vanished around them. Suddenly they were on a bright, grass-covered plain where everything was nicely arranged. The flowers grew in perfect rows and the trees were all uniformly shaped. Even the dragon lay in perfect symmetry.

Audelai sighed in relief.

"Have they gone?" the dragon said to her. He always spoke to her in this place, and it was one of the things that she loved about talking with the dragon.

"Yes, Pharis," Audelai El replied with a smile. "Just as I promised you they would."

"So they are off chasing the Lost Citadels," the dragon murmured.

"Indeed, I believe they said they were searching for the truth about their past and what happened to the magic," Audelai El replied cheerfully. "It is exactly as you had suggested, O mighty one."

"And the talisman," Pharis continued. "You gave it to Mala?"

"As you instructed," the Clan-mother answered. "Although why is a mystery to me. She is the weakest among them."

"Weaker than you know," Pharis chuckled. "I learned much about her when I communed with the man Drakis. He is brave and determined but not yet disciplined enough to guard his mind. She betrayed his love for her before—she betrayed them all. It is only fitting that she do so again."

"Mala?" Audelai El frowned. "I would have thought that one of the others . . . any of the others . . ."

"Would Drakis wear the talisman beyond the first bend in the river, let alone long enough to be of any use to us?" Pharis rumbled. "Their Lyric is unpredictable; their dwarf too scheming, their chimerian too clever and the warrior woman too savvy. Among them, Mala is the only one vain enough to want to wear it. It will serve us well; Drakis will not leave her side."

"I told them Pellender had returned it to me," the Clan-mother said, smiling at her own cleverness. "None of them suspect the truth."

"You have done well, Audelai El," the dragon responded.

"It was the only way to keep everyone safe," the Clan-mother replied. "You said so yourself. All Ambeth was in danger from the Dragon Queen had we let them remain. Hestia would have discovered them here and everything would have been undone! The dragons under her sway would have destroyed us all."

"She is a treacherous Queen," Pharis hissed. "She must not learn where Drakis and his companions have gone, or she will hunt them."

"The villagers know they have been here, but I have taught them not to trust the Dragon Queen," Audelai El said confidently. She was enjoying the perfect smell of the flowers in their perfect rows. "They flee from all dragonkind, so their coming will remain between us and the dragons in your company."

"For a while," Pharis said. "But these . . . heroes . . . Hestia is seeking them, and it is only a matter of time before she discovers them. She fears what they may learn. She fears what they may do . . . or undo."

"I do not understand you," Audelai El said, doubt playing at the edge of her mind.

"You need not worry. You have fulfilled your bargain," Pharis replied, flicking the tips of his enormous leathery wings in his pleasure.

"Then you will keep my village safe from Hestia's wrath?" Audelai El prompted.

"It shall be as I promised," Pharis said.

"And the heroes . . . our Far-runner and the others?" Audelai El continued. "You will watch over them on this journey until the very end?"

Pharis smiled. "Until the very end."

Pharis hated the temple, and his reasons were deeper than those of the Clan-mother. So it was that Marush—the yellow-green dragon of Pharis' flight—having learned of Pharis' rendezvous the previous day, felt perfectly safe in quietly sliding into the temple ruins undetected several hours in advance. The temple would mask his presence even from Pharis, so he waited with patience honed over centuries.

He watched Audelai El touch the horn of Pharis. Once the bond was made, however, it was easier for Marush to overhear the conversation between them. The bond is a loud thing, to a dragon's understanding, for the dragons themselves communicate more by their thoughts than through their restricted voices.

For dragonkind this is easy, but with humans it is far more difficult; it requires the dragon to have more control in the bond, and often it results in the mental equivalent of shouting. Indeed, it even requires the human to physically touch the dragon's horn for a proper bond to be made: otherwise humans tend to hear only the subconscious patterns of dragon thoughts—what humans often refer to as Dragon Song. It was in no small part the concerted effort to project these thoughts that called this Drakis human from the southern lands. It is what has always called humans to dragonkind—but understanding thoughts of humans comes only through the bond with touch.

Once made, however, the loud mental exchange between dragons and humans can be overheard by other dragons—especially those with talent.

Like Marush.

It was because of his talent and through long and careful effort that he became accepted among the Dragons of the Eastern Skies and, in time, became the companion of Pharis the Prince of the East. And now, as was his duty and the purpose of all the plans long laid, he overheard the conversation between Audelai El and this ancient dragon, their bargain, and the story of this Drakis-human.

All that was left was for Marush to patiently wait for Pharis to leave and then find a way of telling it to Hestia, his Dragon Queen.

Book 2:

MISTRALS

CHAPTER 25

Braun

SOEN PUSHED HIS WAY forward between the pilgrims. He knew his opportunity to get close to the brilliantly lit figure at the crest of the small hill was rapidly ending as the throngs of humans, manticores, and other races converged on the spot.

Soen's black, featureless eyes squinted against the dazzling rays darting through the air, but he had barely advanced a few steps before he realized that it was *his* staff that he was approaching.

Some human was wielding his own Matei staff!

Soen bared his sharp teeth in a grimace, shoving his way through the crowd. That he had lost his staff among the strange phantoms in the surrounding fog was embarrassing enough.

But to have it retrieved and *used* by a human was a humiliation beyond tolerance.

The elf could now see several other figures standing about the human; the unmistakable silhouette of a manticore and several elves. There appeared to also be at least one chimerian among them, but it was becoming increasingly difficult to see them through the crowd of pilgrims pressing toward the light, blocking his way. In moments, Soen was in the surging mass of the multitude, pressed on all sides by the desperate procession. The massive throng became a river of creatures, taking on a motion of their own. Soen was swept up by them, being pushed forward involuntarily now toward the hilltop.

Soen drew in a fierce breath, the nostrils of his pointed nose flaring.

He recognized the human wielding his staff. He had seemed such an insignificant creature, barely worthy of his notice when he met him on the Panaris Road just the day before—the mad Proxi of the insignificant Captain Shuchai.

He remembered the human's name . . .

Braun.

Braun turned his broad, swarthy face, looked directly at Soen across the immense crowd, and smiled. The stocky man then turned with the staff, planting its tip into a crumbling set of foundation stones behind him.

The light of the staff flared, and to Soen's astonishment the bright glow of a fold erupted above the stones. The glow at its edges was a deep blue color and spherical. That it was a fold was unquestionable since he could see an altered and shimmering landscape beyond it, but the form of it was unlike anything he had seen before. Pushing back the surrounding fog, it grew in size, expanding beyond its pedestal base.

Its existence was impossible.

Soen searched his memory for some explanation. Folds had to be established between two points—it was a fundamental law of the Aether governing their construction—so these stones must have been linked to another location in the past. If a fold had been established here on the Shrouded Plain, it must have predated the War of Desolation. That conflict had been largely expurgated from the histories of the elves. It was the first time the Rhonas Legions had suffered a devastating loss in warfare and had been pushed back from their objective of conquest on the borders of Nordesia. Not that the Legions left the land quietly. There were stories told of human settlements cut off from their armies on the Mistral Peninsula who fled southward along the Mournful Mountains only to be surrounded by the retreating Legions at Panaris. Panaris itself had been a beautiful plains city but it was an easy place for the retreating elven Legions to exact revenge for their frustration. Their cold and merciless destruction of that city had resulted in the cursed plain where not even elves cared to conquer.

The refugees that fled here were said to have traveled the Mournful Road but all the writings Soen recalled referred to it as a physical road. Now, perhaps, he believed they were wrong: could this be the Mournful Road—a human-built fold still functioning? If that were true, then he would have to place the establishment of this fold over four hundred years ago—predating the elven use of Aether by nearly a hundred and fifty years. That it was a fold supported by Aether magic was obvious as this human Proxi was powering the fold using his own *Matei* staff.

His own staff, Soen fumed.

The crowd flowed toward the still opening fold, urged onward by the manticore Grahn Aur. Soen forced himself forward and across the flow of the onrushing mob, trying desperately to reach Braun and his staff. He glanced up and caught his breath. The sphere of the ancient fold had continued to expand, the glowing wall of its magic rushing over Soen and the pilgrims crowded around him.

Now inside the haze of the fold, Soen had nearly reached Braun. The elves around him had stopped with their arms extended toward the staff as Grahn Aur stood with his eyes fixed on Braun, his arms crossed.

Vendis was standing next to him, his blank face turned toward Soen.

The renegade Iblisi broke free of the crowd, lunging toward Braun and his staff.

The fold collapsed.

Soen fell heavily against the ground, his long hands locked around his *Matei* staff. Within a beat of his heart, he had pushed himself up from the ground into a combat stance, his staff swung level in his grip and pointed alternately in rapid succession at Braun, the Grahn Aur and Vendis. His arm was still numb from his encounter with the Drakis Shade, and Soen gritted his sharp teeth, trying to steady the top of his *Matei* staff as it wavered slightly.

The Grahn Aur turned slowly to face Soen.

The world paused in silence to hold its breath.

Soen became aware that the chill of the Shrouded Plain had vanished. Warm sunlight beat down upon his back and the world was suddenly bright. He stood upon a crumbling foundation of stones as he had moments before, but the air was vastly different.

He could smell the seashore. He heard the sound of birds cawing in the distance.

A roaring cheer erupted all around him, the sound startling him in its complete shattering of the silence that had reigned moments before. The thunderous noise rolled across the landscape, shaking his bones with its deep resonance. He had heard such sounds in the great arena in Rhonas and once on the field of battle.

It was the sound of triumph.

It was the sound of validation.

Soen stood rock still, his staff shifting quickly from target to target on the platform.

It was Vendis who stepped toward him, raising his four arms high above his head, urging the pilgrims to quiet.

Soen shifted his staff, aiming it at the center of the chimerian's body mass, rehearsing in his mind the way to separate Vendis' parts most effectively. The feeling was returning to his arm and with it the nearly overwhelming enormity of the pain from the touch of the Shade. Soen pushed it aside in his mind, concentrating on Vendis.

The crowd closest to the platform saw Vendis and grew quiet. An anticipatory silence radiated back across the multitude.

Soen fingered his staff, and a chill deeper than the Shade's touch filled his mind.

There was no Aether remaining in his staff.

The power of its magic had been completely drained.

Vendis addressed the surrounding multitude in a loud, clear voice. It carried across the mass of silent pilgrims straining to hear his words.

"We have been tried in our pilgrimage!" Vendis shouted, his arms still raised. "The Legions of Rhonas have sought our destruction! We have followed the Grahn Aur northward to find the man of prophecy—he who will free us once more! And Drakis has brought to us this renegade elf—an enemy of our enemies—who has turned his back on his vile nation and, through the power of his magic delivered us this day from the Shades of the Panaris Follys!"

Vendis turned to face the elven Inquisitor, pointing at him with both of his left arms. "I give you the Hero of the Shrouded Pilgrimage . . . the one who has defied Rhonas and saved us this day from its mighty Legions . . ."

Soen's hand still shook. Braun stood next to the Grahn Aur, beaming at him. The manticore, too, was watching him although Soen could not be certain whether his gaze was cautious or predatory.

Vendis shaped his face into a grin as he spoke, turning to face the still shaking elf. "I give you . . . Soen Tjen-rei!

Soen's blank, black eyes shone with hatred.

The multitude of pilgrims, now numbering almost sixty thousand strong, once again erupted in cheer.

The Council of the Prophet convened that night within the walls of the Grahn Aur's tent. Gradek had stationed guards not only outside the tent itself but in a perimeter nearly a hundred paces from the stakes holding it to the ground with instructions that no one outside the council and those specifically invited by the Grahn Aur were to be allowed any closer.

The question of Soen Tjen-rei was being debated.

Soen stood in the center of the tent, surrounded on all sides by the seated council. The Grahn Aur sat on his high-backed throne with cloth chairs situated in a wide semicircle around Soen. To the Grahn Aur's left sat the human Braun, who gazed on Soen with an oddly blissful expression. Next to him sat an elf looking intently at Soen through narrowed eyes, followed by Gradek the manticore Captain of the Watch. To the right of the Prophet sat Vendis, followed by a cheery-faced mud gnome and a bored-looking female goblin picking at her teeth. The shadows of a phalanx of guards outside the tent shifted listlessly across the fabric.

Not that they would do much good, Soen thought to himself. *If I willed it, most of this council would be dead before the guards were aware anything was happening within.*

"Council of the Prophet," the Grahn Aur's voice was warm and easy. "May I present to you Soen Tjen-rei . . . formerly Inquisitor of the Order of the Iblisi. It is not who he was but who he is now that is the issue before this council."

"I disagree," said the frail, nervous-looking elder elf seated two chairs to the left of the Grahn Aur. "Who he was—truly, who he was, is of supreme importance to this council."

Vendis groaned. "Must we hear again a litany of the terrible crimes of the Rhonas state? We've all experienced them, Tsojai Acheran."

"I'd like to hear it again!" chirped the mud gnome seated to the right of Vendis.

"You would, Neblik!" Vendis retorted.

"House Acheran?" Soen said quietly. "I know that name. It was a House in the Western Provinces, was it not?"

"You know *nothing* of my House, Iblisi!" the elf spat the words as though they were venom. The frail elf barely reined in his anger as he continued. "My House was of the Second Estate, Inquisitor. I was raised in Rhonas Chas and summered on the Benis Coast with all the privileged class. My father was Khal-rei Acherana, Grand Guildmaster of the Paktan Order. But I was tutored by one of your own Order, Soen Tjen-rei, and came to know the truth of the Empire. I saw how bankrupt the Empire had become—devoid of any real glory and only serving itself with lie upon layered lie!"

"Is there any way to stop him from talking?" said the bored female goblin seated next to Neblik on the far right of the Grahn Aur.

"Hush, Doroganda," the Grahn Aur said quietly. "Let him finish."

"Grahn Aur," Soen asked. "Am I permitted to speak?"

"You already have," the manticore replied with a deep chuckle. "But, yes, you may speak here."

"Sha-Acheran," Soen said, turning toward the elf. "I recall that you *were* a House in the Western Provinces. A House listed as the Fifth Estate . . ."

"Banished!" Tsojai answered back. "Disgraced! In Rhonas Chas I was an elf of enlightenment—with a vision for a better future for our race. It was not just me . . . there were many more of us. We found each other, spoke of change. We learned of the elves of Oerania and

Exylia—of Museria, Brendabria, and Lyrania—across the Aergus and Meducean Seas. Places where elves struggled to live in freedom and peace. We wished the same for the elves of Rhonas. We hoped to change the Empire from within."

"The Emperor did not share your vision," Soen said. "And so he banished you."

"No, he did more than banish us," Tsojai replied. "He put us under Imperial Devotions. Surely, the great Soen Tjen-rei, was aware that the Empire was not above enslaving its own citizens through the Devotion altars? It wasn't enough that humans, chimerians, and manticores be put under House Devotions and kept docile to do the labor of the Imperial Will. Why stop there when you can pacify your own citizens at the same time?"

"Is this true?" Gradek asked in astonishment. "Does the Empire work its slave magic on its own as well?"

Soen drew in a deep breath. "Yes, Gradek . . . it is true."

"You see!" Tsojai exclaimed. "So, yes, Inquisitor Soen, my House was in the Western Provinces when the Wells failed . . . but that freed more than the slaves of my House . . . it freed *me*, too! I remembered what the elves could have been but for an Empire drunk with Aether and the power it gave over every other thinking being. *That* is whom you serve, Soen of the Iblisi. The very existence of your Order is to discover the truth and hide it from the world. Why should this council hear your words? Why should we trust anything said by such a servant of the Emperor?"

Soen nodded. "You should not give me your trust."

Doroganda looked up in sudden interest. "What did he say?"

Braun folded his arms across his chest. "He said we shouldn't trust him."

"But," Neblik raised his hand. "If Tsojai says we shouldn't trust what he says . . . and he says we shouldn't trust him . . . does that mean we *should* trust him because he's lying about how we shouldn't trust him?"

Braun nodded. "That makes sense."

"Neblik, that makes no sense!" Tsojai responded with exasperation.

"Look, Tsojai," Neblik replied. "It's my job here to keep a record of the story. I just want to get it straight!"

"Then let's ask for some clarity," the Grahn Aur said. "What did you mean, Soen Tjen-rei?"

"I meant, Grahn Aur," Soen said, addressing the council as a whole, "that this council should give their trust to no one. I am an elf of the Empire—the same Empire that hunts you hunts me as well. Whatever their reasons—or whether reason is involved or not—we are, for this time, traveling this same road together. Trust is not something you should give . . . it is something that can only be earned. I tell you that my purpose here is not to harm you, this council, or your people. But our fates are woven together for a time . . . and I need that time to earn that which you should not give too easily."

Soen knew the stars had risen above the tent in which he sat. The canvas had grown darker with the passage of time, and the evening breeze had pulled the smell of the shore away from the encampment. The air temperature had fallen slightly but not precipitously and so he knew the weather had remained clear.

So the stars were out though he did not see them.

Soen squatted, instead, inside the tent, holding and shifting his now-drained Matei staff, rolling it again and again across his finger-tips. He had never before held a staff so completely devoid of Aether life. Even in the Benis Isles campaign, when he held out for six weeks with the garrison at Sh'dakya Keep against the assault of six Legions of Lyranian elves and thought this magical weapon exhausted of all power—even then it had more life remaining in it than the all-but-dead shaft of polished wood and its crystal headpiece now contained.

And so he squatted here in the tent they had provided for him, rolled his staff, and contemplated the options remaining to him.

He was a Hero of the Pilgrimage now.

That, he reflected ruefully, would mean that he could not go any-where among the pilgrims without attracting attention. Even as he was escorted here, everywhere he glanced there was another human, manticore, or mud gnome praising him, thanking him or, worst of all, wanting to touch him. He was perhaps the most highly skilled Iblisi of this age, he dispassionately commended himself, and yet his very ability for anonymity had been stripped from him.

Worse, he could not doubt that word of the "Hero of the Pilgrimage" would all too soon find its way down the coastal trade routes—with his name and his location being all too soon whispered into Ch'drei's ear.

Of course, he reflected, all of that could be fixed. There were entire chapters of history where blunders, atrocities, and mistakes had been obliterated from memory and history. He had done so himself on numerous occasions. All it really took was a judicious application of controlled information, the retelling of a plausible alterative tale, and the eventual expurgation of troublesome facts from the official record. Soen knew better than anyone that the most evil of despots could be remembered as benevolent so long as the right people were in charge of the record.

The trick, he thought to himself, was to outlive the truth until the lie could be properly established. His problem, however, was now having to outlive both the truth AND a lie—the whopping lie of being a delivering hero to thousands of pilgrims.

Even that could have been handled to his advantage . . . if Vendis had not somehow known his true name. Soen's eyes closed in frustration. How *had* the chimerian known his name?

Soen heard footsteps approaching outside the tent. He continued to play with the staff, shifting it expertly in his hands. He had been among the elite of the Iblisi and use of the Matei staff was only one of his many skills. He was a dangerous creature even without its power but one of the primary tennets he adhered to was to choose carefully when to act. There were far more answers to his questions to be had among this pilgrim horde, and it remained to his advantage to learn those answers before he acted.

So it was that when the tent curtain opened, he remained calmly squatting in the center of the tent and rolling the useless staff in his long hands.

The Grahn Aur entered the tent first, his large manticore frame nearly pushing his mane-covered head into the canvas above him.

"Soen Tjen-rei," the manticore said quietly. "It is better that we should meet this way."

"Grahn Aur," Soen said, not looking up. "You honor me . . . too well."

A single, deep chuckle came from the manticore's throat. "Too well, indeed."

"And as it appears that I have saved your rebellious horde from the depths of the Shrouded Plain," Soen continued quietly. "Perhaps you could tell me just where we are now . . . in case someone asks me where I saved them *to*?"

The Grahn Aur nodded. "We are between the Willow Reaches and Glachold—some forty leagues north of the Mournful Mountains."

Soen looked up sharply, his black, pupil-less eyes fixed on the manticore. "That is impossible."

"Nevertheless," Grahn Aur said. "We are here."

"No, you lie," Soen replied, shaking his head. "I know Glachold, and I've walked the Shifting Pass through the Mournful Mountains. That's nearly three hundred and fifty leagues from the Shrouded Plain. We would have had to pass through a dozen folds—powered each of them separately—brought the horde through each one before conjuring the next. The loss of Aether alone over such distances would have made it impossible to achieve."

The Grahn Aur stepped closer, folding his legs under him as he sat down in front of the disgraced Iblisi. Soen considered this. The manticore was deliberately putting himself in a position where it would be easy for Soen to attack. Was it a gesture of trust, underestimation, or arrogance?

Hunter or hunted?

"Impossible now, perhaps," The manticore spoke again. "But perhaps not always before."

Soen frowned at the thought. He had been in the service of the Iblisi for so long, had covered up so many lies, and been the keeper of truths locked and hidden away for as long as he cared to remember. It had never occurred to him, as a keeper of the truth, that there might be truths others kept from him—that some of his own truths might be lies as well.

"Your coming was a blessing of fate to us," the Grahn Aur continued. "We had learned of you and your journey since the fall of Nothree and have been most anxious to have you find us. It is why we sent Vendis out to bring you to us. He thought it much easier to have our quarry come to us than to run about the countryside searching for you."

Hunted it is, then. Soen drew in a breath, turning his staff again in his hands. "Chimerians are a people of many talents."

"They are useful if somewhat mercurial," the Grahn Aur agreed. "Vendis, in particular. Did you know that he was recruited as a spy for the Modalis?"

Soen stopped turning his staff and looked up again. "You surprise me, Grahn Aur."

"A compliment," nodded the manticore, "as I understand that surprising you is not easily accomplished. Yes, he told me all about it and has been most helpful in securing information regarding the movements of the elven Legions and the continuing search by the elves for a certain renegade Iblisi who seems reluctant to vanish as so many of his brothers and sisters have done before him."

"And now you've made me a hero to your rebellion," Soen observed. "That will hardly ingratiate me to my Order, let alone the Imperial Throne."

"It was fated, Soen," the Grahn Aur shrugged. "It seems it was fated that Braun should find your staff in the haunted mists of the Shrouded Plain. It was fated that the gateway to the Mournful Road should present itself. Do you not see the hand of the gods in these events?"

"I do not believe in the gods," Soen sneered.

"And yet you served their purposes today."

"I did *not*," Soen snapped. "It was that strange Braun human who found my staff and opened that impossible fold!"

The Grahn Aur chuckled again. "Braun was always that way . . . especially in the end. We all thought we had lost him at the Ninth Throne—believed he had cost us the prize when he actually showed us the way. Drakis didn't understand—perhaps he still does not."

Soen caught his breath.

"Yes, Soen," the manticore smiled, baring his own sharp teeth. "We have been looking for each other. Grahn Aur is my title . . ."

"But your name is Belag," Soen finished.

The manticore nodded and then stood. "And I have come to ask for your help."

Soen stood up as well, his dead Matei staff on the floor at his side. "You want *my* help?"

"Yes," Belag said. "We need you to find Drakis."

CHAPTER 26

Hospitality of the Khadush

"I'VE DEALT WITH A great many manticores in my life," Soen said, tilting his elongated head slightly to the left as he considered Belag with his cold, black eyes. "I do not recall meeting any with such an odd sense of humor."

"And I have never met an elf that *had* a sense of humor, let alone one who could recognize one when he saw it," Belag returned through a wide smile that bared his teeth. "And yet here we are; me entertaining in my own tent the Iblisi assassin who tried so desperately to hunt me down, and you the Inquisitor wondering why the very slave he sought to destroy has offered the protection of his tent and the request of his services."

"Something like that," Soen said with a slight nod, and then turned back to studying his dead Matei staff.

"It is because we both need the same thing," Belag said. "We both need Drakis—and we both need each other to find him."

Belag stood up slowly and walked to the side of the large tent. An ornate, low table sat there, several large pewter mugs carefully placed at one end while at the opposite end a half keg filled with snow surrounded a tall glass carafe. The manticore pulled the carafe free and poured clear water into two of the mugs.

"One of the older Khadush boys overheard me one day as I reminisced fondly about drinking cold, clear water from a high mountain stream," Belag said as he picked up the mugs and turned back toward the elf. "It was only three days later that this appeared in my tent. Imagine it: young manticores charging across the landscape and up to the tops of the high mountains, gathering the ice and snows from their summits and the water from their glacial lakes only to charge back over forty leagues—their prized snow melting all the way—to set this water here just so that I might drink it while it was still fresh and cold."

Belag offered one of the mugs to Soen.

"I've tried to get them to stop—told them it is unnecessary and wrong," Belag continued. "But they keep doing it anyway. Why is that, do you suppose?"

Belag continued to offer the mug to the elf, but Soen remained where he squatted, his black eyes staring up at the manticore. Belag shrugged, then set the mug down in front of Soen. He again sat down cross-legged in front of the elf, drinking with long satisfaction from his own mug.

"Well, I like to think it's because they finally have something in which they can believe," Belag continued, answering his own question. "They are filled with energy and enthusiasm. They hope to be part of something better than themselves and meaningful. They are looking for purpose in their existence—so they fulfill my idle wish whatever the cost."

"Then you are just another master to their slavery," Soen replied. "They've only exchanged one tyrant for another."

"I am not their master," Belag said with a quiet rumble in his voice. "I serve them."

"A servant of the masses, then?" Soen sneered. "So sounds the first note of every tyrant's song who ever strutted upon the stage of history."

Belag gazed at the renegade Iblisi for a time and then said, "I would have thought even the elves better mannered than to insult their host in their host's own tent. However, as you have not attempted to kill me thus far, I must assume that we do need one another after all."

Soen ran his tongue over his sharp teeth, considering. "You would be foolish to think that my bite was found only in this staff."

Belag smiled and nodded. "And you would be foolish to think that I was ever truly alone."

Soen nodded in his turn.

"We can help each other," Belag said. "We may have different reasons, and we most certainly have different objectives, but whatever ends we have in mind, we both want Drakis back."

"I assume you have a plan," Soen said.

"Yes," Belag answered, standing up once more. "I must leave you now, but Vendis will explain it to you."

Soen bared his teeth as he looked up, his long, pointed ears flattening back against his head as he spoke. "I would be delighted to have Vendis explain a few things to me."

Vendis held open the flap with both his right arms, as he invited Soen to step out of the Grahn Aur's tent.

The Iblisi outcast blinked against the sudden brightness around him as his eyes adjusted to the wide, open sky that stretched overhead. Only a few, wispy clouds marred its vibrant blue as it stretched over the landscape of gently rolling low hills. The Grahn Aur's tent had been pitched on the tallest of these, giving a magnificent view of the countryside.

Soen turned around slowly, taking it all in. To the south, he could see that they were about half a league away from the crumbling fold platform they had arrived on the night before. Beyond that, far in the distance, stood the deep purple, haze-obscured peaks of the northernmost tip of the Mournful Mountains.

Everywhere else . . . for at least five leagues in every direction . . . the hills were dotted with tents, wagons, temporary stock pens, and the ebb and flow of manticores, gnomes, chimerians, and even elves and humans.

Thousands upon thousands of them.

They were, for the most part, made up of children and the elderly, but there was no mistaking in Soen's mind what he was looking at.

This was an army—or at least the potential for one—which the Legions of the Emperor's Will would never allow to survive.

"I see you are still carrying your staff," Vendis said, his elastic face consciously pulled into as pleasant a form as possible.

"Force of habit," Soen offered though he knew better. The Aether may have been completely drained from the staff, but in his hands it could still be a most effective weapon. The elf lifted his chin toward the sprawling encampment around them. "How many are there?"

Vendis gazed out over the hills. "Fifty thousand . . . perhaps closer to sixty-five thousand by now. More are arriving every day, and it is proving impossible to keep an accurate count."

"Accurate count or not, you're a victim of your own successes," Soen said. "How long can you feed this rabble?"

Vendis did not answer immediately, apparently considering what or how much he should say.

"How long, Vendis?"

"Three . . . perhaps four weeks with rationing."

Soen nodded. "The Imperial Legions are wasting their time. They don't need to come north to destroy you . . . they only need to let you starve yourselves to death."

"We have been negotiating with the Nordesian goblins," Vendis said, "but they are reluctant to move against Rhonas. Their city-states are governed by local warlords and their allegiance to each other is only bound by their mutual hatred for the elves—no offense."

"None taken," Soen sniffed.

"Still, they are practical enough to know not to start a fight that they aren't absolutely sure they can win," Vendis continued. "We get the feeling they're watching—waiting for something to change before they choose sides."

"No doubt they're also watching Ephindria," Soen said casually. "You chimerians have not been entirely forthcoming about your own position regarding the Rhonas Imperium."

"Our nation is our family," Vendis replied.

Soen smiled inwardly. It was the uniform response from any chimerian whenever they were asked about anything taking place within their own borders. Ephindria had drawn itself into a deep isolation from the rest of the continent and seldom engaged in any trade, commerce, or communication beyond that which was absolutely necessary to be left alone. Chimerians were found to be relatively common throughout the Empire, even in Rhonas Chas itself, but universally they were silent about anything going on within the opaque borders of their homeland.

"So it seems we have found the 'prophet' after all," Soen continued.

"It is what you wanted," Vendis said with a nervous laugh.

"And what is it that you want from me," Soen asked. "That Braun Proxi managed a rather impressive feat by plucking most of your fellow pilgrims out of the Shrouded Plain and dropping them here—thanks to his borrowing my staff . . ."

Vendis' face fell slightly at the mention of Braun's name. Soen noted the chimerian's uncertainty about the human. Vendis seemed as uncomfortable with the thought of Braun as Soen was himself.

". . . But I cannot see that it has done your cause much good. You cannot hide over sixty thousand beings in the open and not be discovered. The Legions will find you—and most likely will be preparing to obliterate all traces of you within two weeks at the most. Even if the Legions decide to forget their campaign entirely, you'll all most likely starve to death within a month without help."

"We have a plan," Vendis offered.

"Ah, yes . . . which, no doubt, is where I come in."

"We've been negotiating with the goblin warlords of Nordesia."

"To do what?"

"Cross the Erebus Straits," Vendis said quickly. "We'll flee northward into the lands of Drakosia—where Drakis has gone."

"You're going to leave Aeria for the northlands," Soen said with skepticism. "Sixty thousand of you? Just how many ships do you have?"

"We're negotiating for fifteen—maybe more."

"If you're using trade galleys out of Thetis Bay," Soen said as he considered the problem out loud, "then they will probably hold about a hundred, maybe a few more in transport across the straits. Then, too, you'll have to find a suitable landing where you can set up and survive. I make that out to be about two crossings per ship each month not accounting for weather and losses."

"That seems about right," Vendis agreed.

"Then, by my figures, it will take you only a year and a half to transport your entire pilgrim band to your new world," Soen said. "And, simplifying your problem further will be the fact that all of your passengers will be *dead* long before the year and a half is over. Think of the savings. None of them will have to eat during the voyage."

Vendis shook his head. "No. We can live that long if we have the help of the goblins in Nordesia."

"Nordesia?" Soen laughed. "You must be joking!"

"We have reason to believe they will shelter us and barter for supplies long enough for us to make the crossing and establish our own crops," Vendis said. "They like the story of Drakis and would like to support us . . ."

"But . . ." Soen urged.

"But they need proof that this Drakis exists," Vendis continued. "So, while they may not be willing to openly side with us, they *will* trade to outfit a ship for you, a crew, and provisions."

"And just where is it that you want me to take this expedition?" Soen asked.

"You were tracking Belag before with the help of beacon stones," Vendis said. "The ones that led you to follow Belag eastward out of Nothree."

"Yes," Soen sighed. "What of them?"

"I have since learned that they were dropped by someone in our company—a type of slave they called a *Seinar*," Vendis continued. "The elves tell me that such a person is compelled to continue dropping those stones until the last three remain with them. Is this not so?"

"Yes, so far as it goes," Soen answered. "The beacon stones do not work on the water."

"But you could track them once they made shore again," Vendis said.

Soen considered for a moment, continuing to turn the drained and powerless staff in his hands. The chimerian was right and it galled him. He needed the help of these delusional fanatics if he was ever to recover Drakis and sort out the quagmire he found himself in. The question for the elven Inquisitor was just how much deeper into this mess he would have to sink before finding his way back out.

"Yes, I could," Soen said, turning to look at the chimerian. "But I would need the staff recharged before that would even be possible."

"Which would require an Aether Well," Vendis nodded. "You are an elf of tremendous talents, Soen. We can get you into Port Glorious. We can get you across the Straits of Erebus and into Drakosia. Belag said that was where Drakis was being called by the Dragon Song when he left. You get back onto land in Drakosia—and I've no doubt that you can take care of the rest from there."

Soen considered again for a moment. Port Glorious was anything but what its name implied. He had never been there and from what he did know about it, had hoped never to go. The farthest northern outpost of the Rhonas Imperium, Port Glorious was little more than a collection of elven dwellings crammed within the walls of a fortress on the northern shore of Mistral Bay. No folds terminated there or anywhere within five hundred leagues of its gates. The port was supplied largely by sea via the occasional and entirely irregular arrival of Imperial ships from Port Dog or Shellsea. It was, above all, the place where the Emperor sent the most loyal of his citizens whose names he wished to forget.

"So your plan is to have me walk into an elven fortress, recharge my staff, sail across the straits to a different continent and just— 'find'—Drakis and bring him back?"

"Essentially . . . well, yes."

"And if I were to kill him when I found him?"

"You need him alive—and you need us to get there and back again."

"And what if I don't come back," Soen said.

"Oh, I'm sure you'll come back," Vendis said. "You're an elf of honor who will keep your bargain."

Soen laughed. "You really don't know elves very well at all, do you?"

"Oh, I'm not worried about you remembering our deal," Vendis said, his blank face contorting into a smile once again.

Soen restrained the urge to rearrange the chimerian's rubbery features. "Indeed, and why not?"

"Because," Vendis said through his smile, "I'm going with you to make sure you don't forget. We should be ready to leave within three days' time—then there won't be a moment to lose after that."

"Another well-thought-out scheme," Soen said dryly, "Three weeks. One week to get there. Perhaps another week to get back. That leaves us an entire week of our own to find Drakis on a different continent."

Soen looked across the vast assembly around them and wondered if he were looking at the dead who had not yet realized that they were already doomed.

"You had better hope that Drakis likes the seashore," Soen said.

CHAPTER 27

Cascade

JUGAR REACHED DOWN with his crutch as he lay in the boat, his back against the reed side, and tried desperately to get at the spot that itched underneath the splint on his leg. He did not dare sit up higher in the little craft on the planks lashed as benches across the two sides of the boat as the others used them. Being aboard Urulani's ship had been hazardous enough but these small boats were outright dangerous in his mind. They felt as though they would overturn at a mere suggestion. His temper was not helped by the fact that water had come into the boat over the sides when he and the chimerian boarded from the little spit of an island where they had made camp the night before. Ishander seemed to know where the islands were on the river and had stated a clear preference for spending the night in the middle of the river rather than on either of its shores—a suggestion with which the dwarf heartily agreed. But the water in the bottom of the boat was now sloshing most uncomfortably around his buttocks, renewing his discomfort with every rock of the boat.

How had he, Jugar, come to this? He had seen the advantage clearly enough on the verge of Vestasia. All he had to do was promote this Drakis human as the great one of the prophecy, convince enough gullible people that it was so, and allow the chaos to happen without drawing any further attention to himself. He relished the idea of keeping himself as anonymous as possible in all of this because, as the old dwarven saying went, vengeance is forged best on the heels of astonishment. They had come all the way to ancient Drakosia on that Urulani woman's boat, but Jugar had figured it would all add to the myth, so he endured the voyage. Then they would come to the God's Wall—if they found it at all—poke about, and return to Nordesia or Vestasia or pick any other country ending with an "a" and Jugar could pick up the tale again—adding a wonderful bit about returning from the ancient land of the humans as the prophecies had clearly foretold.

But then everything went terribly wrong; they had actually *found* dragons.

Jugar frowned as water sloshed up his rump again.

It was Ethis the chimerian who had put him in this situation and ruined all his lovely plans.

Jugar looked up at the chimerian, who knelt in the front of the boat, leaning against the upturned curve of the reed prow. They were paired again in the middle boat. Drakis sat in the front with Mala and their Far-runner guide—a whelp of a boy whom Jugar suspected had plans of his own. Behind them in the trailing boat, Urulani stood at the stern while the Lyric sang an endless series of nonsensical songs. These seemed to make the warrior woman's features more dour than usual. Shouting between the boats was discouraged, and no doubt with good cause, as there was far too much movement among the shadows of both riverbanks for the dwarf's liking.

The water splashed beneath him again.

It was just his run of luck, Jugar decided, to be stuck in this boat with the least talkative member of their not all that merry band.

This was the final torture for Jugar. He was gregarious, even for a dwarf. He loved the sound of his own voice and believed unabashedly that his stories, tales, anecdotes, and views on any subject were far more interesting and engaging than anyone else could offer. Moreover he loved conversations—even if they tended to be a bit one-sided—and the challenge of discussion and exploring ideas.

The silence was as annoying as the water he sat in.

Jugar could stand it no longer.

"So . . . Ethis . . ."

The chimerian turned around expectantly.

Jugar blew out a breath and looked away.

"Yes, what is it?" Ethis asked.

"Oh, nothing, really, I just . . ."

The chimerian turned his featureless face toward the dwarf, holding to both sides of the river craft with two of his arms and folding the remaining arms across his chest. "Did you have a question?"

"No . . . Yes . . . I was just wondering . . ."

"Go on."

"Did you know there was a time when chimerians and dwarves were allies?" Jugar blurted out.

Ethis blinked. "That would have been a long time ago, indeed, as I recall."

"It was back in the Age of Frost, when the world was young and the stones of the mountains were fresh," Jugar said.

"You're talking about the Omrash-Dehai," Ethis replied, himself slipping down off the prow to also sit in the bottom of the boat.

Jugar suspected Ethis' move was a conscious effort on the part of the chimerian to establish rapport with him as they spoke but pushed his suspicions down for the time being. "Yes, I believe that was the name. It was said by the lore-keepers to be a time of peace."

"The name means 'The Peace of Reasoned Thought' in the chimerian ancient tongue," Ethis observed. "It is revered in our nation with days of memorial observance."

"Indeed?" Jugar said, with honest interest. "I was unaware that the Ephindrians celebrated anything at all."

Ethis pulled his head back slightly. "Our nation is our family."

"Yes, yes, yes," Jugar said, waving his hand. "My nation *was* my family, but now both appear to be gone, do they not? I know better than to ask a chimerian what happens behind the walls of his nation. Ephindria is a closed book, sealed and hidden away from the prying eyes of the rest of us. You chimerians are found nearly everywhere throughout the Rhonas Empire, and yet the rest of us know practically nothing about you. I really do not understand you or your people, Ethis. You watched the rest of the world bleed before the injustice of the elven dictators and said nothing—and by all appearances did nothing. Is it that you are afraid or that you do not care?"

Ethis kept his silence.

"Please, Ethis," Jugar urged. "Your actions, noble as they may have seemed to you at the time, stranded us in this forgotten end of existence. You broke my leg, and I've lost the Heart of Aer . . ." Jugar's voice caught at its mention. "You could at least give me some *reason* that would console me beyond your nation being your family."

"It is . . . it is not to be discussed with outsiders," Ethis said slowly. "We have long been a people at one with each other . . ."

The boat began to rock more urgently.

Jugar sat up, his eyes wide. "What is that? What's going on?"

'I don't know. The river is moving more rapidly," Ethis said, his body twisting nearly completely around, as he called to the boat in front of them. "Drakis! What is it?"

Jugar's eyes followed the tether that linked the prow of their boat to the high stern of the reed boat in front of them. The Ambeth boy was still standing there but was working his river pole with more agitation than Jugar remembered seeing before.

Drakis appeared next to the youth, calling back across the water. "Our guide says we're coming up on a cascade."

"A what?" Jugar shouted back.

"A cascade . . . fast, rough water and . . ." Drakis turned toward Ishander for a moment, engaging in an exchange which the dwarf could not hear before turning back to call across the water." . . . And some falls. He's going to steer us toward the shore. We'll walk the boats down the edge of the river until we get past them."

Jugar felt a twinge from his broken leg. *Just what I need,* he thought ruefully, *a nice long walk along a rocky bank of a treacherous river.* He reached down to adjust his splint, hoping that any change would alleviate the itch that still plagued him.

"Wait!" Ethis suddenly called out, pointing from the opposite side of the boat toward the nearing shore. "Drakis! Look!

Everyone on all three boats heard the chimerian's warning. All but the Lyric fixed their eyes on the riverbank.

It was moving.

Once, when Jugar was young, the dwarf had accidentally overturned a barrel of ground meal that his father had asked him to retrieve from their cellar. It turned out to be a fortunate mistake as cockroaches had made their way under the ill-fitted lid and had been feasting. The overturned keg caused the cockroaches to erupt from the barrel as a river of motion. Now, staring at the numberless shadows flowing between the trees with lightning speed, darting forward in the deep shade of the jungle canopy, Jugar was strongly reminded of those roaches once again.

"Drakoneti!" Ishander shouted, his voice suddenly higher than Jugar remembered it. The youth frantically began working his pole, pushing the lead boat away from the right-hand shore and toward the left.

The bank was beginning to slide past them faster and faster as the river gained speed. Whitecaps began peaking in the surface of the rough water, splashing over the sides of the reed boat.

Jugar arched his back, trying to get a better look down the river. He could see the river narrowing where it dropped down into a tight gorge.

The boat rocked suddenly against a wave, splashing water over the dwarf's face, blinding him. Jugar sat quickly back down in the boat, discovering that the water around him had grown considerably deeper.

"No!" Urulani's voice came from the boat trailing Jugar and Ethis. "That shore is crawling with them as well!"

Jugar craned around as best he could, water dripping from his beard and head. He drew his hand once again down his face, trying desperately to clear his eyes.

This time he could see them, their scaled bodies, their long, grasping hands, clawed feet, and tails. The woods seemed infested with them, all following the river's edge, their dreadful eyes focused on the three reed boats as they rushed to keep up with the increasingly swift river.

"I don't think that shore's any friendlier," Jugar offered.

"Stay down low in the boat," Ethis said emphatically. "Lash yourself to it if you can."

"Tie myself down to this bundle of sticks?" Jugar said with indignation. "Are you mad?"

Motion to his right caught Jugar's eye. Urulani was rushing from the back of her boat toward the prow, her hand clutching her dagger. She grabbed hold of the upturned bow with her left arm, slashing desperately at the line connecting the boats.

The boat rocked suddenly from side to side.

Ethis was cutting their rope to Drakis' boat. It split apart with a distinct twanging sound as the rope, relieved of its tension sprang away and fell into the river.

Jugar gaped. "Has everyone gone mad?"

Ethis stepped quickly back down the boat. His eyes searched about for a moment before settling on something. He reached down, pulling out the dwarf's war ax. Before Jugar could protest, Ethis thrust the handle into the dwarf's hands.

"Use the blade in the river," the chimerian ordered. "It will help steer the boat."

"Put my nice steel blade in *water*!" Jugar yelped. "I've spent my life trying to keep this blade *out* of water!"

Ethis was not listening. He picked up a river pole similar to Ishander's from its stowage place in the bottom of the boat. "We're about to go into battle, dwarf. Think of the river as your enemy."

The bow of the boat pitched up just as Ethis got to the stern. It rushed over the billowing swell, dropping down the other side in a sudden plunge that stole Jugar's breath from him. The world had, indeed, gone mad as the river before the boat suddenly looked like an angry wall of chaotic white reaching up to engulf the boat and the dwarf with it.

Jugar turned his ax over and, gripping it upside down, drove it into the whitewater over the side of the boat. The river tore at his grip, determined to wrench the ax out of the dwarf's hands but his grip was strong.

The bow plunged into the water on the other side of the swell, rolling over both Jugar and Ethis in a wave of blinding white before the reed boat shot through the other side. Jugar shook his head violently, clearing his vision in time to see a huge finger of rock jutting up from the riverbed. Water swept around either side.

"Right!" shouted Ethis. "Steer us right!"

Jugar grimaced as he turned the ax in his hand, then shouted victoriously as the bow of their boat swung to the right, shifting them into a chute that drove them with breathtaking speed into a spinning eddy drifting toward the top of a series of waterfalls.

Tree trunks and branches from either side of the narrow channel stuck out over the river, casting their shade over the sudden calm.

The dwarf laughed out loud. "Now THAT was a fine thing, Ethis! I might even get to like that!"

Ethis crouched at the end of the boat, gazing up into the trees.

"There's Drakis ahead of us," Jugar nodded. "I don't see Urulani or the Lyric. You don't suppose they somehow got ahead of us, too, do you?"

Ethis leaned forward, speaking quietly.

"Paddle, Jugar."

"What?"

"Paddle," the chimerian repeated with sudden urgency. "Paddle NOW!"

Jugar pulled his ax, swinging it sideways, and, with both hands, stabbed its head into the water next to the boat and pulled. Ethis set the pole and pushed with all four hands, scuttling the boat suddenly forward.

A screeching cry filled the air above them.

The trees were swarming with drakoneti.

Jugar drew his ax from the water, swinging it forward and plunging the blade into the river again. The boat was moving faster now, rushing headlong toward a cascade of falls whose roar was growing by the moment.

The drakoneti, seeing their prey escaping, leaped from their perches. Several of them splashed into the water around their boat, thrashing and screaming.

"We've got to get to the cascade!" Ethis shouted. "Keep paddling!"

"I AM paddling!" Jugar shouted back, his teeth set. "You're the one with four arms! I'd think paddling would be a better place for you than for . . ."

The boat suddenly shook with a thudding sound.

Jugar looked up.

A drakonet rose up, gaining its footing on the cross planks between the dwarf and Ethis at the back of the boat. It smelled terrible to the dwarf, its scales flashing in the dappled sunlight through the overhanging trees. Its barbed tail flashed over the dwarf where he sat ducking down to avoid its sting.

Two more drakoneti missed the center of the boat but managed to grip the sides. One was struggling in the current beneath the boat but the other was pulling itself up over the side.

Jugar yelled, drawing his ax from the water and turning it in his hands. He swung first on the drakonet that had nearly pulled itself over the side. The pain shooting up through his leg was blinding, but his aim was true; the blade swept through the creature's joint cleanly severing the forearm. The drakonet howled and slid back down the side of the boat before sinking under its keel.

The second creature was clawing frantically at the reeds, but the dwarf would not allow it to get purchase. He twisted the blade again, slamming the flat of it repeatedly against the long, bony fingers of the dragon-man.

The monstrous face opened its wide mouth filled with razor-sharp teeth, howling in hatred and indignation, but as it shifted its fingers, the dwarf's tactic proved effective. The drakonet lost its grip, sinking quickly into the dark waters.

"That's two for me, chimerian," Jugar crowed though sweat was breaking out on his brow. The color had left his face and he was having troubling seeing. The pain in his leg was overwhelming. He could see Ethis at the back of the boat, fending off the drakonet who was shifting quickly from side to side, looking for any opening to attack.

"You'll be three," Jugar said raising his ax.

His footing dropped out from under him.

The reed boat rushed over the edge of the first cascade, plummeting down and crashing into the water below. Jugar fell backward, his head and shoulders wedging in the bow of the boat. His ax lay under him, pinned by his own body.

The drakonet lay on top of him, its face pressed close to the dwarf's own. Its eyes suddenly focused, its maw flashing open to engulf Jugar's face.

Suddenly the face jerked backward. The boat rocked precariously as Ethis wrestled with the drakonet, but the creature was too strong even for the chimerian. It shifted in Ethis' grip, its claws slashing at the air.

Jugar struggled up from the bottom of the boat, dragging his ax up with him. He could barely see and seemed to be having trouble catching his breath.

He pulled back the ax and swung with all the strength he had left.

Jugar felt the satisfaction of the blade lodging in his enemy.

Then the boat rolled at the crest of another cascade.

The dwarf knew that he had to get his ax back.

So he held on, dragged over the edge with his vanquished enemy, tumbling through the white, roaring air and crashing into the swirling waters of the river.

He wondered for a moment if dwarves could float . . .

There was the rush of waters.

The last thing he remembered were strong hands . . . and four arms . . . wrapping themselves around him.

CHAPTER 28

Shadows and Scales

E THIS DRAGGED THE DWARF up onto the wide sandbar just far enough to get Jugar's face out of the water before collapsing onto the sand himself. He lay there, drawing air into his lungs in deep gulps, coughing and sputtering for a time and contemplating the billowing clouds that drifted across the sun above him.

He turned his head. The dwarf was breathing, but barely. His normally ruddy skin color was returning, however, and this reassured the chimerian. Reluctantly, he rolled over on his side and pushed himself up to kneel on the shore and look around.

The bar stood at the fork in the river framed on all sides by steep cliffs. Across from the sandbar was the ravine cut by the river where he could see and still hear the cascades that had brought them here. The raging water tumbled down its course over a number of falls until it crashed into the whirling eddies of the basin, its anger spent by the time it lapped up against the wide sands. One fork of the river then continued through a cut to the north while the other wound eastward through a second, twisting canyon. The thick jungle crowded the crest of the cliffs overhead.

Ethis tensed, his eyes searching the tree line.

Nothing moved.

The chimerian's eyes narrowed in suspicion. Only minutes before, the jungle had been teeming with drakoneti. They were swarming through the dense foliage like a plague of locusts. He fully expected to see them spilling over the edge of the cliffs like a kicked-open nest of spiders, yet now they had seemingly vanished back into the jungle from which they had appeared.

He shivered, his elastic skin rippling in the motion.

Something was terribly wrong.

"Ethis!"

The chimerian turned toward the sound, which had been nearly muted by the roar of the cascades through the canyons. He staggered to his feet and waved his uppermost arms over his head in acknowledgment. "Drakis! We are here."

The human looked nearly drowned, his dark hair lying flat against his head and his tunic sagging from the weight of being permeated with the river. Drakis had a firm grip on the rope slung over his shoulder; the same rope Ethis had severed at the top of the cascades. It was still tied to the back of his reed boat, which listed slightly to one side in the gentler waters at the edge of the sandbar. Ishander and Mala stood in the shallow waters next to the boat, keeping it from grounding on the shore as Drakis pulled it up the beach toward where Ethis stood.

"Where's Urulani?" Ethis called.

"I don't know," Drakis replied. "I was hoping she and the Lyric were with you."

"We were separated up in the cascades," Ethis said. "We went one way around a rock and they went another and that's the last I saw of . . . wait! There they are!"

The reed boat was shooting down the cascades at a tremendous rate. Urulani could clearly be seen sitting with her back pressed against the back of the craft, her dark skin glistening in the bright sun as she gripped one of the cross planks cut from its place and now in service as an oar. The Lyric was there, too, her wispy, white hair now plastered against her narrow head as she knelt in the bow of the boat, her arms wrapped around the prow, her wide-eyed, hysterical laughter cutting over the roaring sound of the rapids. The craft plunged down the cascade, vanishing in an explosion of water, only to shoot up out of the water at the crest of the next falls and bounding again toward its edge. Urulani leaned hard on the board, shifting the boat sideways as it slid over the edge, dropping flat into the white water below it. The boat disappeared behind a rock outcropping for a moment before reappearing, its bow now aligned with the current as it shot down a chute and across a whirlpool before gliding out across the pooling waters at the base of the cascade.

Urulani hunched over where she sat.

The Lyric stood and began jumping up and down in the front of the boat, clapping her hands together in delight. "That was wonderful! Can we do it again?"

The look on Urulani's face suggested otherwise.

As Urulani guided her boat to the sandbar, Ishander nodded his head with approval. "You run the river well for a woman!"

"And it is amazing to me that you have lived this long," Urulani said tiredly in return as her boat whispered up onto the shore. She dropped the soaked plank, resting her elbows on her knees. "I count two boats. Where's the third?"

"Lost, I think," Ethis offered. "Jugar went over the side and I went with him. I'm not all that certain as to how we got here and I've seen no sign of our boat since partway down the cascade. Drakis, I think you were the first ones here, did you . . . Drakis?"

Drakis' eyes were unfocused. He was blinking as though trying hard to concentrate on something that he could not quite see or hear.

"Drakis?"

Mala rushed toward the chimerian, splashing up out of the water in her haste. "Ethis . . . everyone . . . we've got to hide!"

"Hide?" Ethis asked. "Where? There's nothing but this sandbar and the bare cliff face behind us."

"They're coming!" Mala said urgently. "We've got to leave! We've got to . . ."

A shadow fell over them.

Ethis looked up.

The enormous rust-colored dragon soared up over the tree line above the cascades, its leathery wings shivering as they pressed against the air, slowing the monster down precipitously. The dragon's neck craned forward, drawing the body and the wings down into a dive that skimmed just a breath away from the cliff face. It flew over the cascades and the large pool at the river's fork, the tips of its wings brushing the surface as it hurtled directly toward Ethis and his companions huddled on the shoreline.

Ethis reached for his sword instinctively . . . and found his scabbard empty. He bent down, grasping the dwarf by his collar with one hand and his belt with two others, trying to drag him toward Urulani's boat.

Urulani leaped up, drawing her own sword. Ishander crouched behind the boat, his back pressed against the craft's side. Mala rushed to stand behind Drakis, who held his hand up, palm open toward the dragon.

The Lyric did not even look up.

"Pharis," Drakis muttered. "What are you doing here?"

The dragon landed just off the sandbar, creating a wave that washed both Drakis' and Urulani's boats well up onto the sands. Its impact shook the ground beneath everyone, making it difficult to stand. Ethis dropped the dwarf while trying to keep his balance.

The wide head of the monstrous drake shifted quickly from side to side at the end of its long neck then moved quickly toward Drakis. Drakis lifted up his hand, reaching for one of the creature's horns on its head.

Pharis suddenly stopped.

His nostrils flared and he took in a quick, deep breath, then the muscles at the back of his jaw tightened, baring his long teeth on either side.

Was the dragon actually *smiling*? Ethis wondered.

Then the head craned skyward suddenly. In moments the enormous body of the dragon twisted around, its clawed feet plunging into the sands as it turned around. Mala screamed, trying desperately to stay away from the feet as the behemoth rotated directly over their heads. His wings extended with a great snapping sound, falling down around the boats and their crew huddling terrified next to them.

Then the dragon held perfectly still.

Petrified with fright, Mala knelt in the sand behind Drakis, the belly of the dragon not eight feet above her head.

Hide in the folds of my winged embrace.
Sheltered within my deceit
Dragons are seeking
Our ends they are wreaking . . .

She pressed her hands against her ears, but it did her no good. The song was thundering through her mind and she could not block it out. Worse, other songs were screaming through her mind, competing for the space in her thoughts and crowding out her own.

Where is the seeker of southern lands?
Answer the call of our horn!
Pay for your nation
Its doom's creation . . .

"Hold still," Drakis called out. "Stay hidden under his wings!"

Mala could see the sunlight still shining on the placid waters below the cascades, framed in the wings of the dark dragon standing above her.

An enormous shadow passed over the water . . . then another.

In moments, the sun was blotted out.

Answer the ancients of promised day
Come to the justice of truth
Tell us of shame
Tell us of blame . . .

Mala looked up. Beyond the trailing edge of the dragon's wing, she could see a patch of sky just above the top of the northern cliff.

A colossal golden dragon flew high above the cliff. Its scales looked somewhat tarnished but it was magnificent in the sunlight. It shifted its head from side to side, searching the ground below it.

Following in the path of its flight were smaller dragons of many different shapes and colors. Soon the sky was filled with these dragons, blotting out her view completely. The procession went on and on—thousands of the creatures soaring above the river.

The ground shook twice more in quick succession.

More dragons had landed on the sandbar, Mala realized. The trumpeting screech of their voices suddenly rebounded off the walls.

Found is the vessel of floating
Down on the north river's way
Hestia hunting
Pharis is coming . . .

The dragons screeched once again. The beating of their wings created a storm of sand on the beach as they lifted their mammoth bodies into the air.

Moments later, Pharis shifted as well, his own wings beating the sands around Mala and the others into an obscuring sandstorm. Mala covered her eyes against the onslaught and only lowered her arms when she felt the wind still once again and the sands settling around her.

Ethis was covering the still prostrate dwarf as best he could. Urulani, the Lyric and Ishander were all standing next to two boats, which the dragon apparently had pulled up even farther on land.

Drakis stared up in wonder at the retreating dragon as he spoke. "He hid us from the others. They're looking for us."

Mala turned to see the dark form of the dragon Drakis called Pharis laboriously pulling its ancient bulk into the sky.

Invisible is the traitor's road
Marked with the beacons of old
Smelling of magic
Betrayal tragic . . .
Find you the temples of ancient might
The key of magic fonts bright
There you'll be resting
Never confessing . . .

"We have to leave before they come back," Mala said suddenly. "We have to get down the river as quickly as we can."

"We now seem to have two guides," Ethis said, his expression conveying his skepticism. "And just which river do you think we should take?"

Ishander spoke up. "We will be taking . . ."

"Shut up," Ethis said, his words sharp and final. "I was asking the woman."

"The dragons are searching the northern fork," Mala said at once. "I say we take the eastern fork."

"Prudent choice if nothing else," Ethis offered. "And just what do you expect we'll find on this eastern fork?"

She looked up. The Lyric was already in the boat even though it was fully ten feet from the shoreline. She was looking directly at Mala, smiling and nodding at her.

"Home," Mala said. "The eastern fork is the way home."

CHAPTER 29

River of Sighs

THEY TRAVELED THE EASTERN RIVER. Ishander called this the River Tyra and asserted that it would lead them directly to Chelesta—the Citadel of Light—the ancient center of the lost human empires. The young Ambeth Far-runner maintained his arrogant demeanor through it all, treating Mala's assertions as mere confirmation of what he would have said if she had not spoken before him. That the dragons were searching the north fork of the river, the young Far-runner claimed also had no impact on his decision to lead them all down the eastern fork.

The narrow canyon of the cascades that ended in the diverging forks of the river proved to be a cut down through the edge of a plateau. Within only a few leagues, the towering walls of the plateau were behind them and the tempo of the river slowed as it widened and began winding its way toward the east through the lower points of an undulating plain.

Which meant that all they could see, Urulani thought ruefully, was an unchanging wall of the same jungle trees repeated over and over again. Each bend in the river seemed to bring another turn through the same unending procession of palm trees, ferns, and dense undergrowth. An occasional pile of stones or remnant of a wall would appear to bring some relief to the monotony but it was short-lived; there had not been enough of the original structures remaining in any of the places they had had seen thus far to spark more than a literally passing interest.

Well, Urulani consoled herself, *at least we're making good time into the middle of nothing.*

Urulani's dark, smooth arms dipped the long pole back into the still waters more out of habit than need. Their reed boat—the second of the two remaining—was near the center of the channel, and the river was doing most of the work. She stood at the back of the boat as she had seen Ishander do, with her back leaning firmly against the upturned stern that stood almost five feet above the keel. She realized that the boats had been specifically designed for this purpose so that the person controlling the boat would have both something to rest against on long journeys and, at the same time, better control of the boat along the way. Most of the effort on the pole was in resisting the river's force rather than supplementing it. A back planted firmly against the upward curving stern allowed for much better control in slowing down the craft and turning it against the current.

It was a different way of working the water and, in some ways, that knowledge made her all the more heartsick.

Urulani was a woman of the Sondau, a cunning tracker, warrior, and captain of the raider ship *Cydron* which she had led into more battles than she could count. She had been the embodiment of victory, confidence, and success for so long that she had begun to believe that she had a right to it; that somehow all the world revolved around her shrewd plans and skill with both speech and blades. She was a popular figure—perhaps legendary—among her people and held the unwavering loyalty and confidence of every man in her crew.

Her crew . . .

Now she had failed them. She knew of three at least who were dead because of her and their names continued to torture her. Gantau who came back because she told him he must only to die before they could retreat through the fold, Yithri who had died so horribly before the rage of the dragon, and Kwarae . . . who had been dragged silently into oblivion before she even knew that danger was still present in the darkness. Worse for her were her thoughts about Djono, Kendai, and Lukrasae—the three members of her crew that had been left on the other side of the fold before Ethis collapsed it and stranded them all here. Her last instructions to Kendai, her sailing master aboard the *Cydron* had been to get back to the ship and return with help. Did Kendai and his companions even escape the rage of the dragons that remained on the far side of the magical portal after it had closed and killed one of the monsters? If Kendai did escape, did he attempt to return and find her? She had seen her comrades die in battle before and knew well that such were the fortunes of warriors, but those deaths had been part of the risks taken by all the Sondau as they strove to keep their footing in the world. Such losses were to be honored for their service to the Sondau Clan but this was different. She had always taken comfort in being surrounded by the people of her clan, the crew of her ship, and her comrades in arms. Now, despite the fact that she had often tracked others on her own without any help, she suddenly felt alone and vulnerable without her crew. What purpose had those deaths served—except to make her the captain of this tiny boat in charge of two contemptible excuses for women, sailing down a river hundreds of leagues from the nearest ocean?

Urulani looked down at the two women seated in the boat at her feet. The Lyric had clearly lost whatever mind she may have once had although she at least had the courtesy over the last week of maintaining a single persona—strange though it might be. To Urulani, she seemed like a woman who had completely given up on herself, her mind drifting from one identity to another, which struck the warrior woman as disgustingly undisciplined.

As for Mala, Urulani was of the opinion that she should have died long ago and the Sondau woman was still inclined to correct that mistake. Mala had utterly and completely betrayed Drakis and, in the process, had called down death upon Urulani's own village of Nothree. Good people had died because of her, and the woman seemed oblivious to her responsibility for their deaths. Why the Ambeth should choose her, of all their company, to be given their medallion was incomprehensible. Why Drakis—an otherwise sensible human— remained in love with her was unfathomable.

And yet . . .

Mala seemed somehow different. There was a deeper sorrow to her, the pain of a hidden wound that was found at the corners of her thoughtful frown and her creased brow. It had started, Urulani thought, when she had wandered off in the Pythar ruins. Mala had experienced something there that changed her. Perhaps it was something similar to what Urulani had experienced in the temple outside of Ambeth when . . .

Urulani caught her thoughts up short. No, it must have been an illusion. Her mind was playing tricks on her in the humidity under the midday sun, and she must have been remembering it wrong.

Ahead of her, the boat carrying Ethis, Drakis, the dwarf—who for good or ill was conscious again—and Ishander drifted around another bend in the river. She could see Drakis and the chimerian rise suddenly in the prow of their boat just before it drifted out of sight around the bend.

"We're nearly to the Kesh Morain," the Lyric said, not looking up from where her hands were winding and unwinding a piece of thread over her index finger.

The sound of the Lyric's voice shook Urulani from her reveries. "What did you say?"

"Off to our left as we round the next bend in the river," the Lyric said without looking up, her voice suddenly resonant and sounding somewhat affected, "you will see the Kesh Morain. Kesh Morain meant 'Arms of Peace' in the original Drakonic tongue. It was fabled for its fountain park—a great promenade that ran through the center of the city from the waterfront nearly half a league to the Palace of Crystal Arts. The most famous of these fountains were the Fountains of Herithania—Goddess of the Way, Abratias—God of Justice—and Jurusta, goddess of spring, passion, and art. My personal favorite, however, was the Fountain of Elucia whose waters sprang dramatically from either side of the promenade and formed cooling arches and mists over the walkway between their grand carvings."

Urulani's boat swung around the bend of the river.

The sight took her breath away.

Here the jungle had somehow been kept at bay. Perhaps it was because the stones that formed the foundations of the city's core were so closely fitted that the jungle had not been permitted to find purchase to pull them apart. Perhaps there was some other power at work here that held nature at bay. Whatever the reason, spread before them was a city of the ancients that was largely intact.

Three jetties still thrust out into the river, their fitted stones having lost their edges and crumbled into the river over the passage of time. Between the jetties, wide steps almost entirely obscured by moss rose from the water to a wide promenade that followed the curve of the river. There was a line of buildings—three or, perhaps, four stories tall—on the far side of the promenade, the faintest hint of diverse colors remaining on their cracked facades. This line of buildings was split by two tall towers, the tops of which were curved in tiers to tall peaks. One of the peaks had fallen, its stones lying in a pile of rubble at the base of the tower. Between the towers, however, Urulani could see a long open space running back from the river to a building that leaned heavily to the right. A painfully bright flash of reflected sunlight occasionally shot toward her from the walls.

"The fountain park was lined with museums, shops, and academies dedicated to the disciplines of music, dance, frescoes, sculpture, theater, and storytelling," the Lyric continued in a calm, almost bored voice. "This reflected the primary exports of this city—its artwork and crafts—as well as its popularity as a vacation destination for families on holiday."

Nothing moved in the city as the boats slid past. Drakis and Ethis were gesturing to Ishander to make landfall on the steps between the quays but Ishander emphatically shook his head no. He said something to the chimerian that ended the argument. There was something forbidden—or deadly—about the city.

"Music of the featured players changed each day on the promenade, the sounds falling delicately over the boats in the river—as did the laughter of children as they played in the water on the steps, inviting all who passed by to join in the celebrations."

The air was growing oppressively humid. Dark clouds were gathering to the west, casting shadows over the city. The silence was unbearable.

"We invite you to return to Kesh Morain often," the Lyric concluded as the city drifted out of sight behind them, the dark clouds blanketing the ruins and the first rumbles of thunder rolling down the waterway.

Urulani shivered suddenly in the oppressive heat.

"Why have you come, Urulani?"

The warrior woman turned instantly toward the voice addressing her. "What did you say?"

"I was just wondering why you have come," Mala said, looking directly up at her. "What are you looking for? You didn't believe in Drakis when you first came looking for him in Vestasia, yet you came. You didn't believe in him when we escaped from Nothree but you brought him across the ocean to this continent and found the very dragons you didn't want to believe existed. So I was wondering why you came. Do you know what it is you are seeking?"

"Why are you talking to me?" Urulani said as she shook her head. "What is it that you want?"

Mala drew in a deep breath, considering her answer. "I want to find a home."

"I had a home," Urulani said, her dark eyes fixed on Mala as she spoke. "It was a beautiful and peaceful place until you came."

"I thought so, too," Mala answered quietly.

"And yet you brought those assassins into my home," Urulani said, her anger barely contained.

"I could not choose to do otherwise," Mala said.

"I will never forgive you for that," Urulani breathed.

"No, you should not," Mala said, turning away and gazing across the water toward the shore of the river as it drifted by. "No more than I can. So perhaps we are both looking for a home—or for a reason we should be deserving of a home."

"I have no home," Urulani said gruffly.

"Yes, you do," Mala said. "We both do . . . we just have not found it yet."

The rain broke over the river at once, a torrential downpour that seemed to draw a veil around them. It was so thick that Urulani could barely see that the boat only about a hundred feet in front of them was turning toward shore.

CHAPTER 30

Fordrim of Kesh Morain

DRAKIS PEERED INTO the gray torrent around him, rainwater coursing down through his hair. He wiped his hand over his face again and again trying to keep the water out of his eyes. The downpour was so heavy, however, that he was forced to open his mouth wide just to breathe.

"You're sure about this?" he called back.

"The Fordrim trade with my clan," Ishander spoke over the noise of the rain as though he were stating the obvious. "This is where we will find our last chance for shelter. The women will need rest."

Drakis turned to face forward again. He did not know about the women, but *he* certainly needed to stop and put his feet on land for a while. He had found the motion of this small boat entirely different from the *Cydron* and not much to his liking. He was feeling increasingly sick from its motion and desperately wanted to feel some stable ground beneath him.

"Can you see anything?" he asked the dwarf.

Jugar looked as pale as Drakis felt. "The eyesight of dwarves is, may I say, better than most creatures that grace our land and spectacular when compared to the narrower capabilities of humans with regard to a darkened space. It is said that dwarves see better in the dark than in the light—possibly because dwarves can actually see differences in temperature in the darkest of places well beyond the capabilities of humans to perceive."

Drakis stared at the dwarf. "So . . . what do you see?"

"Not a thing," the dwarf replied.

Drakis growled in exasperation and faced forward once again.

"It's this cursed rain!" Jugar complained. "It makes everything look the same."

Light exploded off to his left, diffused by the clouds and rain, and outlined the dark silhouette of an imposing section of ruined wall. The ghostly, looming shape vanished almost the moment Drakis saw it as the light died. Booming thunder shivered the boat immediately. The rain, shaken from the clouds, fell with increased vigor around them.

"We're close to shore!" Drakis shouted. Instinctively, his hand went to the hilt of his sword. He glanced back down the length of the boat. "Be ready!"

Jugar sat in the bottom of the boat, drenched, and with his arms folded across his chest in indignation. Ethis showed him three of his empty palms while the fourth shook his empty scabbard.

Then Drakis remembered; both the dwarf's ax and the chimerian's blade had been lost to the river at the cascades.

"Well, think friendly thoughts," Drakis muttered to himself and he reset the grip on his own blade.

Without warning, the keel of the reed boat slid heavily against the sand of the shoreline, causing Drakis and everyone else aboard the small craft to pitch forward. Drakis managed to grab the upturned prow and keep his footing under him, but only just. Then, with instincts born of his years of training as an Impress Warrior, Drakis leaped off the front of the boat, landing with both feet on the ground.

The sand was sodden beneath his feet. Drakis stepped forward at once up the shore and onto firmer ground. He heard Ethis' footfalls behind him followed shortly afterward by the crash and complaints of the women as their own boat collided with the shore.

The roar of the rain filled his ears. The ground beneath his feet had been cleared and was packed down with the rainwater running over it. He could make out patches of fitted stones much the same as he had seen in the roads of Ambeth—remnants of cobblestone roads long vanished. All else remained hidden behind the watery veil. Drakis paused for a time, uncertain how to proceed.

Lightning flashed again, twice in quick succession followed by a third bolt. With each came a moment's glimpse beyond the shrouding storm; the stark contours of gathered huts up a slight rise to their left, an ancient wall propped up to their right, and an old building ahead of them barely discernible at the edge of a flat pool bordering a wide field.

"Do you see anyone?" Drakis said, raising his voice to carry over the storm.

"No," Ethis answered back, his own voice straining as well. "But look over at those huts . . . no, farther down. See those baskets piled near the door? Someone lived here and quite recently by the looks of it."

Drakis nodded as he rubbed the water from his face again. He was soaked to the skin, his tunic clinging uncomfortably under his leather vest. He turned to look back toward the river. Mala and the Lyric had left the boat and were standing expectantly on the shore. Urulani was tying the bow of her boat off to a stone column next to the quay. Ishander was pulling his boat farther up onto the shore, aided by the fact that the dwarf could not stand another moment on the boat and was hobbling painfully away from the river's edge.

Ishander strutted up toward Drakis and Ethis, his chin held high. "The Fordrim hide from a Far-runner of the Ambeth! I will be generous and make no more demands upon them than we need for our journey!"

"Generous to whom?" Ethis said, folding his arms twice across his chest. "There's no one here."

"There is someone here," the Lyric blurted out so suddenly that it startled the human warrior. "He needs you, Drakis and he hasn't much time!"

"Mala, what is she talking about?" Drakis asked carefully.

Mala shook her head, uncertainty in her eyes.

The Lyric's countenance was strange. The rain had flattened her white hair down into straight strands around her face. Her eyes were wide open, however, her gaze shifting in wonder at the still buildings around her. "She was here, Drakis! Maybe she is here still . . ."

"Who?"

"He needs you . . . he's been looking for you for the longest time but you have to hurry." The corners of her lips curled up in a faint smile. "There is someone here we need to see."

"What we need is water and food so that we can go on," Drakis said. "Losing that boat two days ago left us short of both. Ishander, is there any other place we might resupply?"

"No," Ishander said. "This is the place where we may find food and water."

Ethis looked up into the deluge falling around them. "I don't think water will be an issue."

"Then perhaps you had best get to filling those water gourds in what remains of our boats as soon as you can," Drakis replied testily. He hoped it was only the chimerian that was getting on his nerves. There was an indefinable quality about this place that upset him. "Ishander, who are we looking for?"

"We are looking for the Citadels of Light!" Ishander proclaimed.

"No," Drakis said as he felt his patience fraying. Sometimes he thought Ishander's ego got in the way of his hearing. "Who do we need to barter with here for food?"

"Clan-mother—or Clan-father," Ishander said although Drakis thought he saw uncertainty cross the youth's face for the first time. "It is much the same with all clans."

"And just where do we find this clan-whoever," Drakis asked.

"Clan leaders are hard to find sometimes . . . we ask the Fordrim!" the young man declared. "Those huts, over there."

"Why is nothing moving?" Ethis asked.

"Maybe they don't like the rain?" Drakis suggested through his puzzled frown.

"I know that *I* don't," Ethis replied.

"Just get filling those gourds."

Drakis turned and followed Ishander up the slight rise toward the line of huts. The packed ground under his feet felt like clay and he slipped often while trying to make his way up the rain-washed slope. It was difficult finding good footing. Ishander stood at the top of the slight rise, both fists balled on his hips as he waited for the older human to catch up to him for a few moments and then, abandoning patience, the youth turned, stalking toward the dark, open doorway of the nearest hut and stepping confidently inside.

Drakis shook his head as he neared the top of the slick rise. He called out over the roar of the rain. "Ishander! Come back out of there."

There was no response from the dark maw of the hut's doorway.

"Ishander?" Drakis called as he finally managed to crest the rise.

A high-pitched scream cut through the rain from within the hut. The young Far-runner suddenly exploded backward from the doorway in a panic of arms and legs. Ishander slipped on the muddy ground, falling flat on his back and sliding to a halt at Drakis' feet. He scrambled to get his arms behind him and his legs under him again but the slick ground worked against him. His eyes were fixed wide and his mouth gaping open as if preparing to scream again.

Drakis drew his sword in a single motion from its scabbard, facing the pitch-black doorway. He set his feet as best he could for the expected onslaught but nothing emerged from the darkness.

With a glance at the Far-runner still shivering at his feet, Drakis moved cautiously toward the hut. The rain continued its merciless assault around him, the sporadic flashes of lightning diffused above him.

Rubbing the water from his eyes one last time with his left hand, Drakis took a breath and stepped inside.

The darkness inside was almost complete. His eyes were having trouble adjusting to the deeper shadows. There were shapes in front of him; some on the ground and some sitting up. He opened his mouth to speak.

A dim flash of lightning pulsed through the open window.

The image came at him all at once, burning into his mind.

It might have been a family once. The bloated shapes were of different sizes and still roughly human in form. Dark liquid was pooled beneath them, reaching toward the door.

The stench was overwhelming.

Drakis' eyes slammed shut as he ducked back out the door. He stood for a few moments with his back pressed against the hut wall, his breath coming hard and fast. He could not get the smell out of his nostrils. He glanced at the foot of the doorway.

The dark liquid from the bodies was mixing in with the rain—coloring the ground around Ishander and the slope they had just climbed.

His gaze went to the openings of the other huts down the row.

Black fluid was spreading over the wet ground from each of the dark openings.

"Back to the boats!" Drakis shouted, his words all but swallowed up in the downpour. He pushed himself away from the hut wall toward Ishander, pulling the youth roughly to his feet and shoving him down the slope. "Back to the boats NOW! We're getting out of here!"

"What's wrong?" Ethis called, all of his arms extended at once.

Drakis fell on the slope, sliding for a time before he managed to get his feet under him again. "Plague—or worse—I don't know! They're all dead."

Urulani grabbed Drakis' shoulder. "Dead? Who's dead?"

"*They* are," Drakis motioned back to the huts. "All of them. We've got to get away from here while we can. Ethis, you drag our 'guide' back onto our boat while I get . . . where's Mala?"

Urulani jerked her head toward the dark gray shape looming up through the rain past the huts. "She went with the Lyric toward that building. Something about someone needing their help."

"Why would they . . . never mind," Drakis said, the rainwater flying from his hair as he turned his head. "You and Ethis ready the boats. They can't have gone far. Ishander! You're with me. We'll bring them back."

"Sooner is better, Drakis," Ethis called out, but Drakis was already running, his form disappearing into the veil of the rain with their young guide at his heels.

CHAPTER 31

Sanctuary

DRAKIS' FOOTFALLS SPLASHED across the sodden ground. The heavy, obscuring rain relinquished its shadows reluctantly, darker shapes against the gray flatness of the downpour. He stumbled over a body, losing his footing. The shape startled him, causing him to draw his blade from its scabbard at once.

"Drakoneti!" Ishander exclaimed. "I have never seen them this far north before."

The creature lay facedown in the mud but the massive shoulders, scale-covered skin, and broken wings protruding from its back were unmistakable. The jagged, broken blade of its sword was still in its hand, half obscured by the mud. Drakis spun around in the downpour. More bodies lay motionless in the rain, some human but a good deal more drakoneti.

They were standing in the aftermath of a battle.

The rains lifted for a moment, revealing with reluctance more of the carnage around them. The ground was strewn with the dead, many of their carcasses badly bloated and disfigured.

Drakis shuddered.

Curling around the dark form of the tower was the monstrous, enormous shape of a dragon. The dread creature lay lifeless on its side, its neck twisted so that its maw gaped open toward the sky. Rainwater ran from the corner of its mouth, and its half-open eye was milky and lifeless. The body was still held fast to the ground by ropes and netting fixed to several of the many iron rings driven deep into stone and earth in the ground. The stench from the dead beast was overwhelming.

Mala stood by the dragon's head, rain matting down and darkening her auburn-colored hair. She was shivering despite the warmth of the rain, her hand resting on the dead dragon's horn.

Even through the rain, Drakis recognized the creature at once. It was the gray dragon that had nearly killed him in Ambeth . . . the dragon he knew as Abream, the companion of Pharis.

"Mala," Drakis shouted. "We've got to leave here now!"

"She led me to him," Mala said through her chattering teeth. "She knew he was ashamed . . ."

"Who?"

"The Lyric."

"The Lyric! Where is she?" Drakis thought to call out the Lyric's name but realized that he did not know what to call her. "Mala, who is the Lyric supposed to be today?"

"She . . . she called herself Rishan, then went that way," Mala said, pointing toward the base of the building shape before them. "She went in there."

Drakis could see a dim frame of light through the pelting rain—a passage of flickering warmth in the dead world around him. The edifice ahead of him towered upward, its top quickly disappearing into the gloom. He slipped slightly in the mud and then pushed on through the dead around him, towing Mala behind him as he rushed up the rain-slicked steps and into the open portal.

The short hallway was covered in ornate carvings, a delicate latticework arch over his head. It was broken in several places, the pieces remaining on the floor where they had fallen.

The hallway ended in a series of short steps leading down to the floor of a large circular room. The chamber was illuminated by fires burning in three big braziers of stone, each fixed atop a pillar carved in the shape of a dragon with their heads all facing the center of the room. Each had its head turned slightly to the left, exposing an eye socket that looked directly down on a dark and lifeless crystal nearly five feet across—a dead Aether Well!

Atop the crystal stood the Lyric, her wet hair glistening in the light, a long staff held across her body with both hands. She wore a thick robe of light tan trimmed in gold and silver, though the cloth itself was badly stained in places.

"Who did you say she was today?"

"Rishan," Mala answered. "Keeper of the Past."

"Keeper of . . . what?"

"The Past."

"Rishan," Drakis called out into the chamber in a voice that was remarkably calmer than he felt. He descended the staircase with Mala at his back. "We need to leave now. Be a nice Keeper and come with us now, yes?"

"I will not come!" the Lyric answered. "I am the Keeper of the Past and you are a stranger to our lore!"

"I don't suppose *you've* met this 'Rishan' before," Drakis muttered back toward Mala.

"Not yet," Mala replied.

"Pellender!" The Lyric cried out, gazing toward the top of the stairs. "You have returned!"

Drakis turned to follow the Lyric's gaze.

Ishander stood at the top of the stairs, staring back at the Lyric, the color having drained from his face.

"We had become concerned for you, old friend," the Lyric said with a broad smile, her voice lower than usual. "Did you find the Citadel of Light? Did you find the Key?"

"Well at least she recognizes you," Drakis said to Ishander.

"No," he replied. "She recognizes my *father*."

"Your father?"

"My father was Pellender," Ishander continued, warily descending the stairs. "This was the way he came to the Citadel of Light—he was a friend to the Fordrim."

"And now you have returned to us," the Lyric said joyfully. "All the Fordrim bid you welcome and offer you the hospitality of our clan. You shall want for nothing. We looked to the Koram Devnet, but we had begun to lose hope of seeing you again. It seems the knowledge that dragon gave you was accurate after all!"

"Dragon?" Ishander asked with sudden interest. "What knowledge did the dragon give?"

"Oh, what was its name," the Lyric's smile faded slightly with thought. She stooped as she moved as though her back pained her. "Pharis . . . yes, I believe that was the name you told me."

"Wait," Drakis said, "Did you say 'Pharis'?"

"Who are you of unnamed lands that I should speak to you?" The Lyric turned a suspicious eye on Drakis. "Pellender I know, but you are unnamed to me. Who are you to have come into my sanctuary?"

Drakis drew in a breath, trying to control his frustration. "I am Drakis . . . We all have to leave this . . ."

"DRAKIS!" The Lyric blurted out, her voice breaking, startling Mala and Ishander. The Lyric's large eyes keenly focused on the Impress Warrior, suddenly overflowing with tears. "Drakis! You've come at last! And, Pellender, you have *found* him! We've been waiting for you so long . . . so long . . ."

The Lyric dropped her staff and rushed forward. She reached up with surprising strength, grabbing Drakis by the rim of his leather breastplate and held on tight, her grip like an iron vise. Her eyes shimmered in the firelight. "Is the magic coming back? Did you find the key?"

Drakis pulled at the Lyric's hands, prying her fingers free of his tunic. "Let go of me!"

The Lyric released her grip so suddenly that Drakis fell backward, sprawling to sit against one of the dragon pillars in the room.

"I'm sorry! Please . . . forgive me, Drakis." The Lyric staggered backward toward the Aether Well. "We've kept it all, Drakis! Just for you! Just for your return! And they said you were coming. We were going out to look for you."

"Wait," said Drakis, his eyes narrowing. "Who knew we were coming? How?"

"Lorekeeper Xandos," the Lyric said, her eyes slowly losing focus as she spoke. "A dragon came to him . . . told him we were to look for your coming. We were to shelter you until the dragon returned. But another dragon came afterward with the drakoneti to stop us from finding you. The Lorekeeper told me to stay here. That I would be safe and . . . I . . . I am not well."

The Lyric dropped down to her knees.

"What dragon?" Drakis asked, pushing himself forward and crouching next to the Lyric. "Was it the dragon outside?"

"I don't . . . perhaps," the Lyric said, her face puzzled, her eyes fixed on a distance only she could see. "Maybe it was another dragon or maybe the first one came back. The dragons are not to be trusted. One offered us hope and another brought the drakoneti and attacked the village. The Lorekeeper told me to stay here, sealing me in the sanctuary. He said I would be safe—that I was to be the Keeper until he returned."

"He never came back, did he?" Mala asked softly.

"No . . . I waited but no one came until you opened the seal," the Lyric said to Mala. "But I didn't know you were Drakis. Forgive me, please."

"Yes, you're forgiven," Drakis said quickly, "but we have to leave this place. It . . . it isn't safe here."

"I cannot leave," the Lyric said simply. "I am the Keeper. I have to stay."

"You have to . . . what is your name?" Drakis asked.

"I am Rishan," The Lyric answered. "Last Keeper of the Book."

Ishander turned his eyes abruptly on the Lyric. "Book? What book?"

"The Book of Memory," the Lyric smiled. A thin trickle of blood ran down from the corner of her mouth. "The Book of the Before Time. I can go nowhere without the book."

"My father once spoke of such a book," Ishander licked his lips. "He said it spoke the secrets of the old ways and of magic."

"Fine!" Drakis threw up his hands. "Anything to get out of here. Get the book and let's leave."

"No," the Lyric said shaking her head, her eyes focused once more but feverish. "I am the Keeper now! I keep the book for . . ."

"For Drakis," Ishander said with a smile. "And now he is here. I think you do not know Drakis. You do not know the one of the prophecy!"

Mala groaned, shaking her head. "Don't, Ishander. She's sick. Please . . ."

"Everyone knows Drakis!" The Lyric snapped at the youth. "He came from the Citadel after the fall! He wandered out of the burning and the death and the ruin—the end of all glory—and told us the stories of its terrible betrayal and the elven demons' destruction of our nation!"

"So, this is Drakis, standing before you . . .

"Is this true?"

"He is Drakis," the Lyric answered fervently.

"Stop it, Ishander," Drakis said firmly. Only then did he notice the body lying in the shadows on the far side of the Aether Well. It was small and lithe, perhaps a boy or girl not yet fifteen. The stained cloth of the youth's belted tunic matched that of the robe the Lyric was wearing.

"You lie! Why do you think he is Drakis?" continued Ishander, ignoring Drakis.

"Because he said he would return!" The Lyric answered as though the answer itself was enough explanation. "That has been the task and . . . and promise of the Keepers for the generations of my father and my father's fathers before him. We were to keep the knowledge of Drakis and his return."

"Show him," Ishander chided. "Show him! Show him what you have kept for him!"

The Lyric turned, spun unsteadily in her place and then danced haltingly toward the stairs. She grabbed Drakis' hand, pulling him to his feet and dragging him toward the base of the nearest dragon statue. Her husky voice echoed into the vaulting space above the circular floor.

Summon the mystery's well of light.

Summon the light from within.

Hand to the heart,

Here we will start.

The rhythm of the chanting was familiar to him, but he had never heard it spoken aloud—only in his own mind.

The Lyric lifted up Drakis' hand and pressed it against the chiseled stones of the dragon's breast just over her head. The stone shifted slightly as he pressed against it.

A tingling pain shot through Drakis like an invisible fire from his hand down through his body and legs. He cried out more in surprise than from the sting, withdrawing his hand from the stone.

"No!" The Lyric grabbed his hand forcefully again. "The whispers of magic are deep. It takes time to call them from below. You must be strong to await the drawing of the world to come!"

The Lyric once again pushed Drakis' hand against the carved stone representing the dragon's scales. It shifted slightly at his touch, the tingling pain again coursing uncomfortably through him, but he held his place, throwing his weight into the hand on the statue. Soon, he was aware of a low humming coming from the statue, a single tone of sound that grew with each moment until it filled the sanctuary.

The Lyric, her arms shaking, hurriedly moved to Mala and lifted up her hand, moving toward the second statue. There was desperation to her actions. The Lyric's movements reminded Drakis of once seeing a sick dog who, in the last moments of his life, rushed to return to its corner of the Timuran household to die.

Hold fast the portal to living light
Open the doorway to might
Never releasing
Our power's increasing

The Lyric pressed Mala's hand hard against the dragon's carved breast scales. She cried out sharply in pain, but the carving shifted inward slightly with a grinding sound.

In moments, a second sound was growing in the arched chamber around the Well, emanating from the statue under Mala's hand. This tone was higher in pitch, becoming a harmonic to the first tone, matching it to create a dual sound in the room.

The Lyric grabbed Ishander's hand, pulling him toward the third dragon statue in the hall. The Lyric's voice was strident now, shouting over the dual tone in the hall and quivering as they moved.

Three human hands to the dragon's heart
Holding the Kingdom aloft
Three press together
The wellsprings forever . . .

The Lyric pressed Ishander's hand against the breast stone of the final dragon. It, too, shifted. Ishander gritted his teeth against the pain.

Drakis felt his arm going numb. He was unsure as to how much longer he could hold the shifted carving in place.

Ishander's statue slowly added its own third pitch, growing until it matched the other two. As it did, ripples appeared in the air from each of the statues, converging at a place above the dark Aether Well. The air twisted around itself.

Drakis shouted in wonder over the sound. "A fold!"

Slow as a feather, a darkly stained book drifted downward out of the fold. The thick cover was bound in tarnished metal over crackled leather, the binding warped. There was a luster, however, to the edge of the pages. The Lyric climbed up the darkened face of the dead Aether Well and reached up, just as the book settled into her arms.

The Lyric collapsed atop the Aether crystal, her arms still wrapped around the book.

Drakis pushed away from the dragon statue, rushing to catch the Lyric before she fell. As he released pressure on the plate the fold above the stone collapsed. The sound from each of the statues fell suddenly silent as Mala and Ishander gratefully pulled their hands free.

The Lyric's eyes flickered open, gazing up into the face of Drakis. She drew in a rattling breath.

"I knew you would come, Drakis," the Lyric said in a rasping voice. "I am the last of the Keepers. Did I do it right? Did I keep my promise?"

"You did it right," Drakis said softly. "You were a great Keeper. Your fathers and their fathers before them will be proud and honor you."

The Lyric smiled through her bloody teeth. Her eyes fixed on Drakis and then her chest stopped moving.

Drakis bowed his head and drew in a deep breath.

Something pulled at his arms and Drakis looked up. The Farrunner had both his hands around the book and was tugging at it with all his might. The book suddenly broke free from the grip of the Lyric and Ishander wrapped both his arms around it.

"Ishander!" Drakis said sharply. "What do you think you are doing?"

"The book is mine!" Ishander declared. "It is my right!"

"You must respect the dead," Mala said quietly. "Their souls are not far . . . they are listening."

"The woman is dead!" Ishander shot back. "She has no use for a book! *We* are alive. My father told the story of such a book among the Fordrim—a book that held the secrets of the old ways. He said it revealed where the Key of Magic could be found. We have our lives to live and darker waters of river ahead of us. Your dwarf reads the old ways. I have watched him from when first you were in Pythar.

This book will lead us to the keys of Chelestra but it is *nothing* to dead eyes. Tears for the dead are *nothing*!"

Drakis looked at the young Far-runner for a moment as though he had never seen him before.

"You were right before, Drakis," Mala said, "We've stayed too long."

Drakis nodded. He lowered the body of the Lyric back atop the Aether Well crystal, folded her arms across her chest, and then stepped back.

"You did well, Keeper," he murmured. "You did well."

"Did I?" the Lyric said, opening one eye. "What did I do?"

Drakis gaped.

"Everyone back to the boats, right now!" the Lyric commanded as she jumped up to her feet, tossing the robe casually toward the young corpse on the ground behind the well and striding toward the stairs, her jaw set as she spoke. "You've got what these people died protecting, Drakis. Now find a way home with it."

CHAPTER 32

Koram Devnet

"GREAT TREASURE OF the Fordrim . . . my dwarven ax!"
Drakis turned a grim face toward the dwarf. The rain had been unrelenting for the last three days since they'd left the desolation of the Fordrim. Ishander stood at the back of the Ambeth boat at his long oar, guiding the boat down the river, his wet hair plastered flat around his head. The youth mostly glowered at the dwarf and his increasingly disparaging pronouncements from under the oiled tarpaulin that sheltered both the dwarf and the Fordrim book—and which subsequently left everyone else on both of the remaining boats exposed to the rain. Urulani stood next to him at the back of the second boat. The river was moving so slowly that they had tied the boats together side by side which allowed everyone to enjoy the slow escalation of the dwarf's frustration with the book in which they had held such hope.

"What is it now, Jugar?" Ethis asked wearily from the bow. The river had passed into a towering forest on either side of its slow, winding passage and the chimerian would even welcome the complaints of the dwarf to relieve him of the boredom of his watch.

"Three days," Jugar responded, angrily jabbing his thick index finger at the open book that lay across his lap. "Three days I've been poring over this wandering, pompous, disorganized drivel."

"There has to be something in there," Mala said, her own frustration mounting. "An entire village died protecting it."

"Well, then they struck a very poor bargain, if I may be permitted to say so," Jugar huffed. He rifled through several pages and then stopped, jabbing his finger down onto the vellum page. "Here! A list of the genealogical line of the priests who watched over the dead Aether Well including, may I add, those who stood watch over it after it had died and there was no longer anything to watch *for*. There's a great deal of repetitive text about *who* was entitled to activate the Aether Wells—which they call 'Fonts' by the way—but there is nothing at all about *how* to activate them or what might have caused them to stop functioning in the first place. Or perhaps their prize was this section back here which contains detailed and explicit instructions on all the ways it is *wrong* to use a woman, a man, a child, aunts, uncles, cousins, and several kinds of beasts that I have never even heard of before. That section, at least, was amusing and—if I ever find a worthy dwarven woman—might have come in handy. There is even a section here which, so far as I can tell, contains cooking recipes that use the Aether magic as part of its preparation. Everything I've read thus far is about *how* to use the Aether that is already flowing from the Fonts—and absolutely nothing about how to restore its flow should it stop."

"There must be something in there about the fall of magic," Drakis said in frustration.

"The most promising section," the dwarf said, gazing with some distaste down at the open book, "is this passage entitled "Lamentation of Twilight." It is an epic poem or song or free verse or some such nonsense about the fall of Chelestra—the Citadel of Light—and the end of magic. It even talks about you, Drakis."

"Not me," the warrior said with a heavy sigh.

"Well, then *a* Drakis," the dwarf huffed. "He's a hero figure who came out of the destruction of the Citadels and told the story of the fall of the Citadel of Light. It also talks a good deal about the betrayal of dragons causing the Citadel to fall, the Keepers of the Citadel hiding the key to the Font of Aether to keep it safe from these scheming dragons, the subsequent collapse of the Fonts and the utter destruction of the cities in a rather depressing fashion reminiscent of stale dwarven opera. There are entire rapturous passages about this key—which go on and on seemingly without end of repetition—but absolutely nothing about where they hid it or how to use it even if one could dig up the old thing."

"But we got that Aether Well to work back in . . ."

"It's called a Font," the dwarf corrected.

"Right . . . so we got that 'Font' to work back in the ruin of the Fordrim," Drakis finished.

"Well, you didn't exactly get it to *work* . . ."

"Really?" Drakis said. This learned discussion was testing his patience. "It seemed to work when I was there."

"You did trigger the fold above the Font," Jugar acknowledged, "but you did so by channeling your own Aer energy into the Font."

"My *own* Aer energy," Drakis shook his head. "Now what are you talking about?"

"All living things have some modicum of Aer generated within them as part of their life-force," the dwarf explained. "By connecting yourself with the Font, you were able to channel some of the Aer within you into the Font. This allowed you to draw some pooled Aether deep within the Font up to the surface to trigger the fold but not enough to get the Aether flowing. As long as you were connected to the Font, you could hold it open and whatever was left below was pulled up. Of course, the Font closed again as soon as you let go—there being no flow from the central Font to sustain it. Ultimately, I suppose, when we find this great Font at the heart of Chelestra, we'll be forced to do something similar to get it flowing again—although that Font would be enormously larger and built to supply Aether to an entire continent. That's where this key comes in—once the Aether is flowing again, we would need it to hold open the Font permanently, unless you plan on standing there forever and holding the Font open."

"So that's what this key is about?"

"Whoever holds that key holds the power of an entire continent," Mala said. "The dragons desire it most of all . . . and fear it as well."

Drakis glanced quizzically at Mala. "Could that be true? Why would the dragons care?"

"Some might want it to bring the magic back and restore the old kingdoms or enthrone themselves as the masters of Aether," Mala shrugged. "Others may want to bury it forever. If this book can be used to find this key then . . ."

"But it can't! There's nothing in it about the location of the key." The dwarf slammed the book shut.

"So it's pointless?"

"It's a waste of time, Drakis," the dwarf declared, frowning as he looked over the side of the boat toward the rain-veiled shore. "A waste of lives."

Drakis pressed his eyes closed for a moment, wiping the rain from them as he considered. "Well, we're really no worse off than we were before. We still have to find this original Aether Well . . ."

"It's called a 'Font' here," Jugar corrected again.

"All right, Font, but the point is that we still need to find it," Drakis continued gloomily. "Once we're there, perhaps how to activate it may be more obvious even if it isn't in this book. It doesn't have to be open for long—maybe we don't need this key at all. Have you finished reading that book . . . all of it, I mean?"

Jugar shrugged. "No. There are a few more sections I've passed over as not being promising enough, and they were written in a dialect I'm not nearly as well versed in reading. Perhaps there is something in there that can help us."

"Drakis?" Urulani said from the back of the second boat. "There's something ahead."

Ethis turned quickly back to look forward from the bow. "I can't . . . wait! It looks like a tower."

"Keep reading," Drakis said to the dwarf. He crossed the gunwales into the other boat and moved forward into its prow next to Ethis. He peered into the rain, again trying to wipe the water from his face.

A slim, tall shape rose before them, seemingly in the path of the boats, silhouetted against the gray of the leaden sky.

"I can't see whether . . ."

Lightning arced through the sky, merging in brilliance with the top of the structure. As the flash faded, several more bolts ripped through the sky, their cracked radiance illuminating the spindle of stone piercing the clouds. Drakis recalled the towers of Rhonas Chas and the ache that their beauty had inspired in him—but they were nothing compared to this glorious monument. Impossibly narrow lines swept upward then curved into shapes that inspired in Drakis the image of two elegantly rendered hands reaching into the heavens, holding between them a globe as an offering, the tips of the fingers pressed together to form the uppermost top of the tower.

"By the gods!" Drakis gasped in wonder. He turned, calling to their guide at the back of the first boat. "What is this place, Ishander?"

The youth's gaze was fixed forward, his jaw set. "It is . . . just another ruin of the lost time. It is nothing."

"Nothing?" Drakis was incredulous. "Surely it has a name!"

"No name," Ishander said flatly. "We must go on."

"There isn't the equal of this in all the known empires and kingdoms . . . not in Aeria, Oerania or Exylia," Ethis said, a tone of suspicion slipping into his voice. "You have known the names of nearly every broken stone on the banks of the river from Pythar to the Cascades . . . and yet you do not know the name . . ."

"It is the Koram Devnet," the Lyric said cheerfully.

Drakis turned to the Lyric in surprise. The woman had sat silently in the bottom of the second boat for the last three days, not saying a word to anyone since her outburst in the sanctuary of the Fordrim.

"Koram . . . what?"

"Koram Devnet," the Lyric replied with a smile. "It was built by the Third Dynasty King almost two thousand years ago and would long ago have fallen to ruin except that the Aether defended it for centuries, holding its structure in place and protecting it from assault. It was a symbol of the unification of Khorypistan, Tyrania, and Armethia. In the ancient speech it means 'Unity at the Divergence.'"

"Divergence?" Jugar puzzled, his brows furrowed. "What divergence?"

"The divergence of the Rivers Tyra and Havnis," the Lyric answered happily.

"She's right," Ethis shouted, gazing from the bow. "The river splits near the base of the tower."

Drakis looked back at Ishander. "Which way do we go?"

Ishander stood still, his gaze fixed beyond the bow.

"Ishander!" Drakis barked.

The startled boy jerked at the sound.

"Which river do we take?"

Ishander blinked at Drakis, rainwater running down his face. "You are always asking me questions! I am not your keeper!"

"But you *are* our guide," Urulani said, her anger and frustration boiling out in her voice. "That is your station on this expedition— guide us!"

"Tell us which river," Drakis insisted, making his way quickly aft in the second boat, threatening to leap across to where Ishander stood. "Right? Left? Which one?"

"I am a Far-runner of the Ambeth!" the boy shouted in defiance. "You cannot speak to me with such insolence!"

Drakis stared across at the youth, understanding dawning on his face. "You don't *know*, do you?"

Ishander refused to answer.

"You were as much surprised to see this tower as we were, weren't you?" Drakis continued. "You didn't know its name, and you don't know which river to take . . . because you've never been here before—you've never even *heard* of it before, isn't that right?"

Ishander stood tall, but Drakis could see that his limbs were shaking visibly. "I am a Far-runner of the Ambeth! My father . . . my father was the greatest of the Far-runners. He traveled the rivers to the ends of the world! He sought the Citadels of Light . . ."

"Yes, he *sought* them . . . but he never found them, did he?" Drakis pressed. "Maybe he told you what he knew . . . as far as he had run and returned but then he left to 'run-far' and he ran too far and never returned."

"He would have returned," Ishander shouted. "He knew the river and the far-roads! He knew the way to the Citadels beyond the Fordrim clans! He told me when he left . . ."

Drakis called through the rain to Ethis at the other bow. "Is there a landing near the tower?"

"Yes!" Ethis called back. "It looks like a sand bar spit extending out between the rivers."

"Get us untied!" Drakis ordered. "Ethis, can you pilot that boat?"

"The chimerian got us down the cascade," Jugar answered before Ethis could speak. "He can certainly get us to some sandy shore."

Drakis flashed a grim smile at the memory. He turned toward Urulani. "Make for the tower. We'll put in there."

"And then what?" Ethis asked.

"And then I don't know," Drakis replied. "I don't think any of us know."

The dwarf had hobbled his way directly to the tower the moment he landed ashore. Now he stood in the rain on the hard, slick stone stairs, leaning heavily on the makeshift crutch and glaring up at the closed gates before him.

"Tantalizing, isn't it?"

The dwarf turned awkwardly on his crutch toward Ethis. "Aye, it is most certainly a delectable and frustrating invitation."

"You still cannot open the gates, can you?" The chimerian's words were less a question than a statement.

"I have, I will admit, been giving the problem considerable thought," Jugar mused, his gaze returning to the gates. They stood at the top of a set of broad stairs obscured by dead leaves and debris. The ornate doors were of stone, their hue darker than the stained, paler stone of the tower itself. The doors were carved with a frieze of men and dragons at war near the bottom, then laying down their arms in the central sections and, finally, engaging in peaceful pursuits at the topmost panels. The doorway itself formed a great oval, partially truncated at the bottom where it fit in a nearly perfect seal against the top of the approaching stairs.

"As fine a stone workmanship as I have ever seen," Jugar huffed. "Curse them!"

"Is there no other way inside?" Ethis asked.

"I've conducted a most thorough examination of the tower from its various aspects," the dwarf continued as much to himself as to the chimerian next to him. "There appear to be a number of openings near the top of the structure—about that area where the palms look to be pressed together and from that pearl as an orb held between them—but nothing so low that it might present an opportunity to even one of your unique talents. This appears to be the only opening, and it is sealed against us. If only I had my . . . oh, it's useless to consider."

"Had your what?" Ethis asked.

"My stone," the dwarf whined. "The Heart of Aer!"

"Your rock opens gates?" Ethis asked, affecting a casual manner.

"In this case, it might," Jugar growled. "See here, chimerian! These doors are one piece—or appear to be one piece, held in place by the mechanism within. *That* mechanism was given its motive force in a disgracefully wasteful manner from the Aether that once flowed through this land. But now that the Aether is gone, there is no means by which the mechanism may be moved. No magic—no door." The dwarf looked up at Ethis, seeing that the chimerian had folded both sets of his arms in front of him, apparently considering their dilemma. Jugar nodded behind them past the ruined lawn and overtaken garden toward where Drakis had set up camp by the river. "So, what about the rest of them? Have they made a decision?"

"About which river to take?" Ethis shook his head. "No. They aren't even sure which river is called Tyra and which is the Havnis—as though that would do them any good."

The two stood staring up at the tower for a moment, the rain falling around them.

"I'd best help with the boats," Ethis said at last as he turned and walked away. "Good luck with the tower."

The Far-runner of the Ambeth sat on a rock overlooking the river, his arms hugging his knees to his chest. He had turned his back on the great tower that rose up behind him, well above the trees. He had turned his back on the boats still being secured to the shoreline.

"Ishander?" Ethis said quietly.

"Go away," the youth said.

"I need your help."

Ishander shook his head. "I am no help."

"But you are," Ethis said, keeping his eyes averted. "We could not have gotten this far without you. We cannot go on without your help now."

"You lie, bendy."

Ethis chuckled. "No, I don't. You are a Far-runner of the Ambeth. Please, I need help and you are the only one who can do this for me . . . for all of us."

"What is this help you need?" Ishander asked.

"Ishander," Jugar said brusquely, "I'm rather busy at the moment so if you wouldn't mind going back to the boats and . . ."

"Old dwarf," Ishander said quickly. "If I were to ask your pardon, would you grant it?"

The dwarf looked up at the young human.

"You are a most curious being of your race," Jugar said with a frown. "Dwarves do not forgive easily but if you are willing to make amends, then I would feel duty bound, as your companion on this journey, to consider it in the balance."

"Then that will have to be my best hope," Ishander sighed. He reached into a pouch he had slung over his shoulder.

"I'm not sure that I am entirely following what . . ."

When he pulled out his hand, it held the black, faceted stone.

Jugar's eyes widened. He smiled in wonder.

"I am sorry," Ishander said.

The dwarf snatched the stone from the young human, grinning down at it as he stroked it in his hands. When he looked up at Ishander, a shadow of anger and suspicion tempered his joy, but Jugar held it in check when he spoke. "Oh, no matter now, my boy. You've done right by me after all."

"Will this help us?" Ishander asked.

The dwarf's grin broadened again. "Just see if it doesn't!"

Jugar struggled up the stairs, nearly pitching backward once when his crutch caught on one of the stone treads but Ishander quickly righted him. The dwarf stood up to the door, holding the mystical black stone in one hand and pressing against the door with the other.

The great gateway door made surprisingly little sound as it slid backward into the opening and then sideways leaving the oval open as though no door had filled it just moments before. The dwarf and the young human both stepped inside, the dwarf gleefully calling a glowing ball into existence at the tips of his fingers.

"Ah," Jugar murmured with satisfaction, "it feels good to draw from the stone once more."

Inside, they stood at the bottom of a great rotunda extending upward, the ceiling lying beyond the reach of the dwarf's lit globe. A grand staircase curved upward into the darkness around the perimeter of the rotunda.

"We shall have to make that climb and get our bearings," Ishander said as he tried to gauge its height.

"Perhaps," Jugar chuckled as he pointed. "But the treasure is down here."

The dwarf hobbled across the rotunda, his globe illuminating a collection of baskets, small wooden boxes and earthen jars. Some of the jars were broken, but a good deal more were intact.

"These can't have been here long," Ishander said.

"Long enough," Jugar replied, examining the markings on the boxes. "They are the very supplies we need. Some of it is spoiled, to be sure, but there should be enough salvageable."

"Enough to continue on!" Ishander crowed.

"Continue on . . . to where?" Jugar asked.

Ishander was grinning again. "See this . . . carving atop this wooden box. It says we're to take the right-hand fork of the river. That's where he went—and it tells that this way is where the Citadel is to be found."

"How is that possible?" Jugar said, peering at the carving on the box.

"Because all of these boxes are marked in his name," Ishander said, motioning around him. "Each one is marked 'Pellender.'"

"Pellender?" Jugar repeated in astonishment. "Your father?"

"Yes, he came this way and left these supplies," Ishander nodded with excitement.

Jugar grinned as well. "And we know one thing more about him, my boy—that he has been to the Citadels before."

"He has?" Ishander asked.

"Obviously! Because he left his supplies in *here*," Jugar pointed out. "And he would have needed to have *magic* to open the door and put them here!"

CHAPTER 33

Backs to the Sea

"WE HAD A DEAL," Vendis said in crisp, clipped tones. "It was agreed on the word of the Pajak of Krishu. Our bargain is as unbreakable as his word!"

Soen looked away with a slight smile. He sat cross-legged behind the chimerian and the rest of the Pilgrim delegation on one of the many rugs that had been spread over the ground and now formed the floor of the *Jhagi*—the goblin equivalent of the command tents, which the elves themselves used in the field. Vendis sat with his legs crossed as well, with all four of his fists balled up and resting on his hips. The idea that anyone would take the word of a goblin— especially a Pajak of any of the various Nordesian tribes—was the source of temporary, if unfortunately ironic, amusement to the discredited Iblisi.

The delegation seated just in front of Soen consisted of Vendis, Tsojai Acheran, and Braun. The Grahn Aur had invited Soen in case any discussion of the mission itself became part of the negotiation— his presence granted over the objection of Tsojai.

Not, it now appeared, that they would ever even get to that part of the negotiation.

The Jhagi tent in which they met was approximately the same size as most command tents which Soen had had occasion to visit during his many journeys on behalf of his Order but given the diminutive

size of the goblins themselves, the tent seemed extravagant and os-
tentatious. Small shields that barely qualified as a buckler to his elven
eye hung on each of the tent poles. There were curtained compartments all along the back of the tent, each dividing veil replete with
golden embroidery or colorful batik patterns. Ornate and elaborate
lamps hung from the pinnacle of the tent poles as much to be seen as
to illuminate. Elaborate tapestries were arranged on each of the walls
of the tent, most primarily ornamental, but others, Soen noted, were
detailed maps of Nordesia, Glachold, and Port Glorious.

Central to every aspect of both the tent and, it seemed, the encampment was the ornate throne of embossed gold and silver that sat
in the center. It was set at the apex of two phalanxes of goblin warriors; each of their brick-red-colored faces glaring at Soen and Vendis
in turn. There were perhaps two hundred of these warriors inside the
tent, each wearing the thick, black leather skirt, polished to a shine,
and the matching black leather breastplate over the crimson tunic of
the Wyvern Riders.

Several actual wyverns—ugly beasts to Soen's eye—were cor-
ralled inside the tent to one side. Wyverns had been the goblins' warrior mounts as far back as the Age of Mists. Flightless beasts with
too-small leathery wings, they nevertheless had powerful flanks and
long legs that carried them with devastating swiftness across terrain
the elves could barely navigate. Their lengthy, barbed tails gave a
painful sting, and their small heads at the end of long, scaly necks had
a snout filled with sharp teeth. There had been speculation among
the Iblisi regarding whether these wyverns were an offshoot of the
legendary dragons of the north or a different species altogether. What
was known about them, however, was that once trained they were
fearless in battle, could outrun man or elf, and were devoted to their
riders so completely that a trained goblin could ride his wyvern into
battle with both hands free to either fire his bow or wield his *Krish*—a
long-handled, bladed device that could be used as either a spear or a
cutting weapon.

In the center of all this, a goblin wearing a thick fleece vest sat
atop the throne, his face darker than its usual brick-red color though
his wide mouth was twisting into various forms of amusement as he
spoke. "The Pajak of Krishu is a mighty warrior who laughs at the

weak and does not deal with the dead. He says that you *had* a deal with him which you cannot enforce nor put to his advantage as you once claimed."

The fact that it was the Pajak of Krishu that was seated on the throne saying these words with such condescension did not improve the chimerian's mood.

"Does the Pajak understand that all the people of our nation have been moving toward the Mistral Bay on the understanding of the Pajak's bargain with us?" Vendis continued. "There are women and children among them who are in need of food and shelter. All their hopes for deliverance rest on this expedition to the northern lands across the waters!"

"The Pilgrims of the Grahn Aur run from their enemies," the goblin replied from his throne in a nearly bored air. "They do not deserve hope or deliverance."

"They will soon reach the waters of Mistral Bay," Vendis continued. "Then where shall they go unless the great Pajak of Krishu will lend them the aid that he has promised?"

"They would go nowhere," the goblin sneered. "They cannot continue toward the north, for it would only bring them into difficult lands and closer to the fortress of their elven enemies. Back across the low hills they cannot go, for the Legions of Rhonas pursue them there. Westward they will never go—for those are the lands of the goblin kings and we have vowed none shall cross our borders and live!"

"Then must the Pajak of Krishu fulfill his bargain and give us the ship and provisions that he generously offered," Tsojai said.

"No, the Pajak will not!" the goblin sniffed.

Braun opened his hands. "If it is a matter of the bargained price . . ."

"At no price," the goblin warlord yelled.

"Then the Pajak of Krishu has no honor!" Vendis shouted.

Soen winced visibly.

The ringing of two hundred *Krish* blades sliding from their cross-back scabbards resounded in the hall as the Pajak of Krishu stood.

"Insolent, thoughtless bendy!" cried the goblin warlord, his bony finger pointing down at the chimerian in disdain. "You come into the tent of the Pajak, enjoy the hospitality of his fortress, the protection of his warriors, the magnificence of his wyverns, and the magnanimous generosity of his compassion—only to insult him to his face? The Pajak of Krishu would be justified under the Law of Nashkan in having you pulled apart by the wyverns of his own house! And I would do so at once were I more certain that tying a bendy to my precious pets would not do them harm!"

Soen drew in a deep breath, thanked whatever gods were still listening to him that he had familiarized himself with the customs of the northern lands before he had started down this bad road, and then held both of his arms upright, the backs of his hands turned toward the enraged goblin.

The Pajak saw the gesture and stopped his tirade, turning his glaring, large green eyes on the elf. "And what do you want?"

"I beg to speak before the Pajak," Soen said, his pupil-less black eyes averted.

Tsojai spoke sharply. "Soen has no authority here!"

"I believe that the Pajak alone grants authority in his own Jhagi," Soen countered.

"At least *this* long-head has manners," the Pajak spat.

"And why should I listen to the insults of this quiet elf called Soen when the chimerian and his brother elf are doing so well on their own?"

"The chimerian," Soen answered in a calm voice, "is a fool and does not respect the riders of the wyverns' flight."

"Well said," added Braun.

Vendis gaped at Soen. "Are you *trying* to get us killed?"

Soen ignored the chimerian and continued as he lowered his hands back into his lap. "The Pajak is both generous and honorable. He had once agreed to furnish us with a ship to cross the northern waters. He had before agreed to give us aid in this journey. The Pajak remains a goblin of honored story and fame. But we are fools. Will the Pajak tell us why he will no longer accept our treasures in exchange for his generously offered assistance?"

The goblin's eyes narrowed as he pursed his thick lips. His head began to nod and he sat back down on his throne.

Two hundred krish blades quietly slid back into their resting places as well.

"The Pajak is honorable and generous," the goblin warlord said, relaxing back into his large and gaudy throne.

"And is this why the Pajak has generously determined *not* to accept payment for his aid?" Soen asked casually.

"The long-head is wise," the Pajak nodded.

"What does that mean?" Tsojai whispered to Soen.

The goblin on the throne glared contemptuously at the nervous elf.

"Let us speak clearly before our host," Soen said in a voice that was loud enough to carry through the tent. He enunciated with exaggerated clarity. "The Pajak of Krishu is both generous and honorable. I believe he is refusing the offering of our payment to his tribe because it would be stealing, would the noble Pajak agree?"

The goblin warlord's face split into a wide, sharp-toothed grin as he waved a hand in a magnanimous gesture.

"You see," continued Soen with one eye on the Pajak, "he knows that he cannot fulfill his bargain. To take our payment without granting us the agreed exchange would be theft—something which a noble Pajak would know to be against the Laws of Nashkan and would put a curse on his tribe. The Pajak is no thief."

"Nor my people," the goblin said in a magnanimous tone. "We are the Krishu."

"Yes," Soen bowed from where he sat. "But may this long-head ask the noble and generous Pajak of Krishu why with all the powers of his great people he cannot provide ships and provisions?"

"We are not a people of the water," the Pajak replied.

"What need have the goblins of Nordesia of the wide waters when they command the northern hills and all the land between them?" Soen said, smiling with his own pointed teeth. "But when the Pajak of Krishu made the bargain, he most sincerely believed he could fulfill it. Something, it seems has changed—for which the Pajak and his tribe are surely blameless."

The goblin considered from his throne for a moment.

"Will not the Pajak grant these poor fools the benefit of his knowledge and cunning?" Soen asked quietly.

The goblin warlord smiled once more. "The Pajak likes you, Soen. Your tongue is as smooth as any he has heard and no doubt you could charm eggs from a male wyvern. The Pajak cannot provide you a ship, Soen of the elves, because they were all burned in the water that held them two nights ago off the shore of Glachold."

"Glachold!" Vendis exclaimed. "We had heard it was all but deserted."

"It has reached the Pajak's ear that the garrison in Port Glorious got an unexpected arrival of two full cohorts—almost twelve hundred warriors—who have been on forced march," the Pajak replied, his eyes fixed on his guests. "They arrived in Glachold two days ago and have burned every boat they found down to its keel."

"We would be able to destroy the cohorts in Glachold," Vendis said. "It's not that strong . . ."

"The Pajak would ask what you would then do, having captured the wondrous port of Glachold?" the goblin warlord sniffed, shaking his head. "You would have your backs to the sea with no ships and the Legions of the elves from the south. Still, it is all hot blood and fancy. You will never reach Glachold."

"We will," Tsojai replied. "We are marching there even now."

The goblin shook his head and smiled once more. "The Pajak knows that the Legions are closer than you believe. They have the smell of your blood in their nostrils and will soon be upon you. Two days, perhaps three . . . no more."

"Then help us," Vendis pleaded. "You have your mighty wyvern riders! You could slow the Legions—buy us time to escape!"

"Escape?" the goblin shouted in derision. The goblins in the hall all broke into laughter. The Pajak joined them, and it was some time before they quieted enough for the Pajak to speak again. "You want us to fight so that you can *flee*? Your people who have never once yet obtained the honor of a victory in battle wish to appeal to the Pajak of Krishu to fight your battle for you? We are a noble and a great race! We have had victory in battle and earned our right to survive! And you ask us to pit our warriors against the might of all Rhonas when you will not risk it yourselves? We will watch your battle with amusement. When it is finished, then we will have your treasures after all, Pilgrims of the Coward Drakis."

"What does *that* mean?" the chimerian demanded.

"It means," Soen answered, "that he won't take your bribe for the boats he cannot deliver—but there is nothing dishonorable about stripping the dead on a battlefield. He expects us to die."

Book 3:

CITADELS

CHAPTER 34

Arenas

THE COLISEUM WAS a grand oval structure and the center of entertainment in Rhonas Chas. Situated south of the spires of the Myrdin-dai Abbey down the aptly named *Vira Coleseum* and overlooking the *Paz Vitoras* plaza across from the Nekara Fortress enclosure, the Coliseum had once been a combat training facility for the Legions of the Empire. It still served this function although its primary interest for the citizens of the Empire had evolved into its violent, often bloody and, through rare accidents, occasionally deadly pageants which were staged by the Nekara for the entertainment of the Emperor and his court, ostensibly under the guise of informational reenactments of battles from long past or even recent history. The Nekara had produced an entire series of such pageants during the War of the Nine Dwarven Thrones, proudly displaying captured dwarves dressed as warriors. The dwarves always lost, of course, each one engineered through their Devotions to faint three to four blows following any blow that made them bleed. Each of these impressed Devotional slaves would then be taken below the Coliseum to where the Nekara kept their healing beds and be repaired and placed under new Devotions in time for the next performance. They could thereby come back to die before the crowd again the next day—or die twice for matinees. Occasionally, something would go wrong during the performance and an actual fatal blow would be struck that was be-

yond the arts of the healing beds and the slave would be killed outright, if unintentionally. The owner of the slave was always handsomely
compensated for the loss and, if truth be told, the crowds returned in
part to see if such an accident would happen again. But now the
dwarves were no longer news, their kingdoms conquered by the Legions of the Emperor and the pageant of the Ninth Throne had com-
pleted its run. The public was getting bored with reenactments of the
Aergus Coast Barons' Rebellion or the Benis Isles Campaigns—this
was old killing.

The public wanted fresh stories and fresh blood.

Thanks to the recent actions of the Legions of the Northern Fist
and the rapidly spreading notoriety of the young elven woman by the
name of Tsi-Shebin Timuran, the public would have its wish fulfilled.
It was in her name, so the story now was told, that the Legions had
marched northward against the Drakis Slave Rebellion. On the
haunted expanse of the Shrouded Plain they met, and it was here that
a new victorious story had been forged by the Fist of the Imperial
Will. Tales of the victory had spread quickly through the Empire and
were at the heart of nearly every conversation in Rhonas. So it was
natural, indeed, anxiously expected—that the Nekaran Prefects
should stage a spectacle in the Coliseum reenacting that glorious
triumph as soon as permissible.

It was then, thanks to an idea forwarded by Liau Nyenjen, head
of the Ministry of Thought, that the Nekara were given a special dis-
pensation. For the good of the Empire, the Nekara would be permitted to *schedule* the death of one human at each performance. The
Nekara balked at this idea. First, they reasoned that a regularly
scheduled execution at every pageant would be an expensive proposition. The resulting escalation in human prices on the slave market
would prove a boon to many in the outer provinces where the occasional human slave found under House Devotions would soon fetch
their masters unheard of prices at the expense of the Nekara. Worse,
the public might come to expect—even demand—more and more
executions as they became hardened to the killings in the pageants,
causing further escalation in costs. However, when Liau mentioned
that Tsi-Shebin Timuran herself would perform each execution, the

Nekara could see their potential returns expanding far beyond the risks involved and the new, sensational pageant was created.

At each performance there would be one exceedingly unfortunate human who was crowned to represent Drakis in the battle as it was portrayed. His fate was sealed and well known to everyone attending—except, perhaps, to the unhappy human at the center of the pageant. These "enhanced reenactments" were so popular among the elven populace of the city that additional performances and matinees had to be scheduled, resulting in a serious supply shortage of human males.

The hopes of the Nekara for a quick profit by the staging of the most violent to date of their spectacles, however, could not have been dreamed of to the extent that they were now enjoying; for the seneschals of the court had announced that the Imperial Box was to be made ready. The Emperor himself was attending the opening performance.

No price was too high nor favor too dear that it could not be traded for a place in the Coliseum that day.

The face of the Emperor was on every coin of the realm, carved into the ornamentation of every building, and depicted on statues in every plaza, garden, and courtyard both public and private throughout the Empire.

It was not a good face.

It was privately joked throughout the Empire that the Emperor, whilst a child, had so often assumed the countenance of practiced disgust over everything that his features had frozen that way. His upper lip was drawn back in a perpetual expression of disdain, showing his sharp upper teeth even when his mouth was ostensibly closed. The upper eyebrows were thin lines drawn back from the dull black eyes. His chin was particularly sharp, accentuating the long, narrow point of his nose. He constantly wore the long crown of his office; a golden wreath trimming the central headpiece that completely covered his elongated head in an opalescent shell. That the crown was also rumored to cover the fact that the Emperor had no hair on his head at all was never spoken aloud by anyone higher than the Fourth Estate and, therefore, was never heard within a thousand steps of the Emperor's ears.

He gazed down on the combat taking place on the arena floor below him with placid contempt. The Impress slaves that were taking the roles of the Army of the Prophet were obligingly doing their part to fall unconscious as they bled at the hands of the advancing elven warriors representing his northern Legions. The slaves were putting on a good show of battle as they were being pressed into a line of ghostly spirits—or, at least, fine representations of ghosts provided by the graces of the Myrdin-dai—who fell to the ground whenever they were pushed beyond the line of what the narrator had called the "Shroud of Spirits." This part of the spectacle bored him. He had already heard the reports of the battle from several different representatives of the various Houses, Orders and Ministries who had been directly or indirectly involved in the attack. He knew the pageant below them to be largely true although, perhaps, the manticores in the actual battle fought harder than those being wounded now on the arena floor below him.

And, of course, there had been no actual Drakis in the battle at all. The Emperor preferred to think of the unfortunate human desperately struggling on the arena floor as being more of a symbolic representation of Drakis rather than any actual creature. All story, he decided, was largely symbolic and should be modified where the truth became inconvenient.

He certainly could not deny that the populace loved it.

The Coliseum was packed from one end of the tiered bowl to the other, every available space taken up by teeming throngs of elven citizenry. With every blow struck and every fallen enemy before them, they cheered wildly.

"Wejon?" the Emperor said with his usual sneer. "Who is this you wanted me to see?"

"She is coming, my august lord," Wejon Rei said to the Emperor from his seat just behind the Imperial throne.

"But the pageant is nearly finished." The Emperor shifted slightly on his enormous chair. "The enemy is nearly vanquished. What more is there?"

"Only a few moments more, O glorious one," Wejon urged softly. "I do not think you will be disappointed."

"I don't know why I let you talk me into coming to this," the Emperor said to the Myrdin-dai master. "So far, this has proved to be a waste of an afternoon. If you and Ch'drei had not been so insistent, I would have never . . ."

The Emperor was suddenly aware of a hush falling over the audience crowded into every available space of the Coliseum.

From the southern entrance, a single figure emerged. She was a young elf in a tattered dress who stepped barefoot onto the bloodied sands of the arena floor. She walked past all of the still bodies of the fallen "traitors." A single human struggled and screamed wildly, his arms and legs pinned to the ground by the long tridents of six elven warriors—each in resplendent armor. He was the last human remaining alive on the field and knew that his moment of drama was about to be fulfilled.

"Who is she?" the Emperor whispered, unwilling to break whatever spell the woman was casting over the crowd.

"She is Tsi-Shebin," Wejon whispered back.

"The *actual* Shebin?" The Emperor was genuinely impressed.

"Yes, my glory," Wejon said. "She plays the role herself at every performance."

"Indeed?" The Emperor raised an Imperial brow. "Every performance . . ."

Shebin strode over with reluctant steps, her face downcast, a picture of shame and despair. As she came upon the held human figure of Drakis, she picked up his sword from the ground. Then she stood over him, raising the blade high above her head and shouting to the expectant crowd.

"The traitors lie! You are *not* the Drakis who has taken our lands, our honor, and our future! The *real* Drakis has fled to the north, where he plots in darkness to return and take from all our nation what he has already taken from *me!*"

Shebin turned to face the quivering human on the ground below her. The crowd in the Coliseum held their breath in delightful anticipation.

"But you shall *not* take from us *ever again!*"

Shebin plunged the sword downward into the chest of the prostrate human. Her thrust was carefully planned and the response was always the same. Blood gushed up the sword from the wound as she turned the blade, coating her hands and forearms. Then, Shebin pulled the weapon clear of the dying creature, turned, and with her arms now falling to her sides and her head once more bowed in sadness, slowly walked off the field, reluctantly dragging the tip of the sword through the dirt behind her.

The crowd erupted in deafening cheers.

The Emperor watched from his box, his eyes fixed on Shebin as she continued to walk from the arena, holding her pose and never acknowledging the crowd or their thundering approval. She was a symbol of the war . . . and she played the part well.

The Emperor stood and with him all the attendants in the box rose as well.

"Wejon, I believe you petitioned me for a private audience," the Emperor said as he left the box. "That can now be arranged."

The great oval of the Emperor's throne room was completely deserted except for three individuals. Two were seated on large chairs set slightly to one side in the center of the hall. The third sat on a throne floating on a cloud just higher than the two set on the polished marble of the floor.

All three waited in silence. One of those seated wore the robes of the Fifth High Priest of the Myrdin-dai. The other, an older woman of frail and mean countenance, wore the robes of the Keeper of the Iblisi. The Emperor had not spoken from his floating perch on his cloud-top throne and thus neither of his companions, more earthbound, deigned to speak.

The gates of the throne room opened at the far end of the great hall. The figure of a young elf woman entered, her long hands held demurely in front of her as she walked; her slippers making a swishing sound as she made her way across the polished marble floor. Her elongated head was bowed as she walked; her black-eyed gaze cast down to the floor. The rim of her white hair was carefully coiffed upward around the bald crown. The dress she wore appeared to be torn in places but that was merely an effect of the cut and tailoring of the dress. The fabric was new and glittered slightly with silver threads woven into it. It had become all the rage in the Imperial City known as the "Shebin" for the woman whose tragedy and legendary sorrow had inspired it.

That Shebin being, of course, the young elf approaching the Emperor in the dress named after her.

An inlaid circle of red marble thirty feet across marked the center of the hall. As instructed, Shebin stopped in the center of this circle and waited though, unlike the two elves seated at the edge of the circle, she did not have to wait for long. The Emperor leaned forward on his floating throne almost at the moment Shebin came to a halt.

"Tsi-Shebin," the Emperor acknowledged, thus opening the conversation and allowing Shebin to speak by the usual elven protocol.

"Your Glory," Shebin answered quietly with a deep curtsy.

"Daughter of the Empire," the Emperor said through his sharp-toothed smile, "we have heard much about you and your troubles. You are given leave to look upon me. Let us talk to one another as friends may converse—with ease and confidence in one another."

Shebin looked up and smiled her most endearing smile.

"I hope you will indulge me today," the Emperor said, returning her smile though perhaps not as warmly. "I have asked two of my friends to attend us today. Wejon Rei of the Myrdin-dai and Keeper Ch'drei."

Shebin bowed to both, each curtsy measured carefully to recognize their relative stations to the Emperor. "Priest Wejon and I are already of some acquaintance. His efforts to support Your Glory's armies in the north have been a great comfort to me. I have not previously had the fortune to be introduced to Mistress Ch'drei as the circles of our associations have not previously intersected, but I am honored that she should find this young woman of interest to her most august calling."

Everyone smiled. Everyone knew it was a lie. Sjei Shurian had carefully managed to keep Shebin as far from Ch'drei as possible. Wejon had ambitions, however, that would place him in Sjei's seat among the Modalis, and he believed Shebin to be a sword that could cut with both edges.

"Indeed, my Glorious and Exalted Emperor," Shebin said, "I have heard news that may be of interest to the Keeper of Truth . . . news concerning the location and prosperous health of one of her Order familiar to Your Majesty: Soen Tjen-rei."

Ch'drei's right eyelid twitched ever so slightly as she spoke. "Indeed, child. I would be delighted to hear it."

Shebin turned to face the Emperor. "And I should be delighted to convey it as it concerns us all. I have come before you, Mighty Emperor, to offer my soul to you as a loyal and loving servant of the Imperial Will. All that is required among us here is to come to some accommodation one with another. Grant me the desires of my heart, Glorious Emperor, and all here may benefit by your magnanimous boon."

Ch'drei raised a single, plucked eyebrow.

"That is, Majestic Master, why we have come together today, is it not?"

"What did you have in mind, child," Ch'drei asked.

"That I deliver to my Emperor, at his will, the knowledge, power, and wealth of the Modalis—and, need I add, the goodwill of the adoring rabble who want only to right the wrongs done to me by this world," Shebin replied softly.

"And your price?" Ch'drei urged.

"Only to be seen as the most favored of the Emperor's Will," Shebin nodded.

The Emperor smiled once more.

CHAPTER 35

Dead Silence

DRAKIS STRETCHED THE STIFFNESS out of his arms and legs, then, placing his hands behind his head, lay still on the woven mat on which he had slept through the night and gazed up in satisfaction.

After Jugar and Ishander had managed to open the tower, they had all secured the boats and moved into it at once. They had left the doorway open—none of them willing to risk closing a magical gate without some assurance of it opening again—but the rain and weather had remained outside of its boundaries. Indeed, it had been something of a marvel to Drakis to see the rain driving against the space where the door had been, only to drop down in sheets at the threshold. Not even Jugar attempted to explain that phenomenon. Jugar suggested building a fire in the center of the hall, but the Lyric had argued against it on the grounds that it would be disrespectful to such an honored monument. Drakis was inclined to agree with her— though the thought that he was agreeing with the madwoman more frequently of late troubled him. So they had spread their mats from the boats, wrapped themselves in what cloaks and blankets they had brought with them, and prepared for the night.

Drakis took the first watch. While they felt reasonably certain nothing had gotten into the tower before Jugar had opened the door, that did not hold for some dreadful creature following them in now that the way was clear. Drakis had sat pondering into the night their next course of action as he found himself watching Mala as she slept, her chest rising and falling as she lay silhouetted against the occasional lightning flash in the distant clouds beyond the door.

He still cared for her. After all she had done—her betrayal of them to the very Empire that sought to take all their lives—he still found himself caring for her. He told himself that his feelings had been engineered and drawn out of him by false memories planted there by his elven masters, but it did not change the feelings that welled up inside of him each time he looked at her. Knowing it was wrong did not take away the yearning for her, but it did fill him alternately with dread, anger, and guilt. The torturous memories that had been restored to them when the enchantment over them was removed had driven many of Drakis' fellow slaves insane. Drakis had wished in his idle thoughts that it had done so to him, for if he were insane, perhaps the madness that was his reality would be lost in a madness of the mind and he would not hurt anymore. The things he had been forced to do—or was it induced or seduced, it mattered not—had been viciously hurtful to Mala and their memories felt unforgivable. And Mala in her turn had betrayed them all, leading the Inquisitors toward them at every turn in their flight. He blamed her, hated her for her betrayal. He reflected and reasoned that she had had no choice in the matter. He could not stop loving her—which made his hatred all the more bitter. Thus the storm raged through his mind and body like the storm outside as he sat so very still in the darkness of the ancient tower.

But then, in the night, the rain washed away the complex memories that tortured him and the lightning burned away his confusion. He had promised to take her home. Perhaps that was the answer for them both after all. He had wondered if he could live with the pain and realized that he didn't have to live with it. If freedom was so painful a thing, why not give it up for a life of blissful ignorance?

But the lightning cut through the thought. It would not change the beatings, the abuse, the horror of every waking moment—only dull the memory of it. Every day would be dreadful with the only solace he could take lying in ignorance of why the scars covered his body and his soul.

Pain, he realized, was better than living a pointless existence. He had promised to take her back because she could not live with the pain—but he realized that if he fell back into that painless oblivion of Impression, then he would never have her. He would forget everything they had gone through together and never even remember why he had sacrificed his free soul for her. No, he realized, he would take her back—find a way to put her under his own benevolent Aether Devotions, allow her to forget the past and then win her heart afresh.

Drakis knew in that moment that he could become the master of Mala—and with that power he could *keep* her secure in her ignorance, could ensure that she would love him because he would *make* her forget everything else . . .

Then Urulani had relieved him of the watch. As Drakis lay down, he realized that for him to ever truly know that she was his, he would have to risk losing her. He would have to take her back with him to the southern lands, help her heal as best he could—and hope that someday she would love him despite their past; love him as he loved her.

Now he lay on his back and looked up into the incredible vault of the rotunda above him. Morning light was spilling in through the great open doors of the tower, and for the first time he could see the incredible carvings that filled the rotunda ceiling. Sweeping columns rose upward, converging at the apex of the dome. Colored light also filled the space like a prism from stained glass windows between the columns, which he had not seen in the dark of the previous night. It was an inspiring space, one that seemed to draw him upward toward the realms of the gods.

He drew in a deep breath.

Maybe it wasn't about what had happened in his memories. There was nothing, Drakis realized, that he could do to change the past—but he could do something about right now and believed that there was something better to come. He did not for one moment believe in any of this prophecy nonsense or that he was some sort of fated hero who would free the world of tyranny. But, gazing up into the beautiful space above him, he realized that he was hoping for something better to come. He could, perhaps, have a little faith in something after all.

The sound of wood breaking open resounded through the hall. Drakis sat up at once.

Urulani was prying apart the most reluctant of the boxes at the side of the rotunda, just finishing her inspection of the cache. She stood upright, shaking her head, her lips curling in disgust.

"I see you are up for breakfast," Drakis said through a yawn. "Are you going to cook?"

"If I am, you wouldn't like it," the dark-hued captain replied, striding over toward Drakis. "The jars were improperly sealed so the wine in them has gone to vinegar. Still, I managed to clean some of them out during my watch last night and get them outside. They should be full of rainwater, so you might try some of that."

"Anything edible?" Drakis asked, nodding toward the open boxes of the supply cache.

"Some," Urulani replied, handing Drakis a strip of dried fruit. "There may be enough to get us through another week but . . ."

Urulani fell silent.

"What is it, Captain?"

"I wish you wouldn't call me that!"

"Sorry," Drakis corrected. "What's bothering you?"

Urulani faced Drakis. "Well, we have, if we're disciplined, a week's worth of supplies now to continue on but . . . continue on to where? Our guide is useless and all we have at this point are some instructions carved into the top of a crate by his father—who, may I point out, has not been seen since he apparently went in the same direction we're so anxious to follow."

"The dwarf thinks he can get the magic flowing again," Drakis shrugged. "If he manages that, then we should be able to use the old folds to get back to your people on the shores of Vestasia—or at least most of the way. He has his precious magical rock back now and he thinks he can use it to guide us to the source of the ancient magic. We need to find the source and that means finding this Citadel at some city called Chelesta."

"And we just open the Well when we get there, I suppose," Urulani said, folding her arms across her chest. "With the help of that miraculous book you discovered—the one that so far does not contain a single useful idea—and magically transport ourselves across the ocean and back into our snug beds."

"You are always so cheerful in the morning," Drakis replied dryly. "Where is everyone else?"

"The women went down to the boats with the dwarf," Urulani said, her voice curiously detached. "He had apparently spent much of the night using that rock of his to help heal his leg."

"And did he?"

"Did he what?"

"Heal his leg?"

"He's managing without his crutch this morning and says he has improved his temperament although I have not noticed any change," she said, looking toward the doorway. "I've managed to load what supplies were salvageable into the boats."

"What about Ethis and . . ."

"Ishander, our noble native guide?" Urulani finished with her eyebrows arched. "They both set off to climb this tower before dawn. Last I saw of them they were heading up those stairs. That was about three hours ago. Now that you are *finally* awake, I'll go see what happened to them."

"I'll go and find them," Drakis said, strapping his sword belt and scabbard back around his waist. He pulled the blade out to check it before sliding it back into place. "You stay here and . . ."

"No," Urulani said sharply. "I will go."

Drakis was picking up his leather cuirass and stopped. "What is it, Urulani? What's wrong?"

"Everything . . . everything is wrong," Urulani yelled. "I've lost my ship—my crew—and I'm piloting some fishing dinghy through the middle of a jungle following a . . . a fool's dream! And *I'm* the fool for following the fool!"

"Look," Drakis said, trying with effort not to rise to the argument and keep his voice calm. "I'm just trying to get us back home . . ."

"Whose home, Drakis? *Mala's* home?" Urulani yelled. "Her home is a *cage*—you know that better than any of us, yet all you want to do is go back to sleep in the lie again instead of standing up, facing the pain, and living. You're already halfway there, Drakis; you turn a blind eye to anything having to do with Mala. She's got that medallion thing hanging around her neck that Ishander's papa was supposed to have taken with him on some big expedition where he was lost—that medallion lost along with him—and yet it shows up in the hands of the Clan-mother and is hanging around *her* neck? *Someone* had to find it. *Someone* had to bring it back. Mala is poison, Drakis, and you think that holding your nose while you swallow will make it all right. You're better than that, Drakis! You have a better destiny than that!"

Drakis shook his head. "Urulani, you don't know who I've been . . . or who I am. Half of what I remember, I can't tell if it's real or made up."

"Look at this place, Drakis," Urulani said, her arms open, gesturing at the tower around them. "This is *real*. This was what our ancestors built . . . all this beauty, all this incredible wonder . . . and they threw it all away. We were a great people, once. I don't think I realized how great we were, and look at us now; either slaves who don't even remember who we are let alone what we have lost or . . . or hiding from the world so that we don't have to think about it. But we're *here*, Drakis and I've seen things . . . heard things . . . and I know what we've lost."

Urulani stepped up to Drakis, jabbing her long, elegant finger into his chest.

"And you *are* a man of destiny, Drakis, whether you like it or not!" she said. "You could make a difference in this insane world if you would just *choose* to do something with your sorry life."

"What?" Drakis was incredulous. "Now *you* think I'm this legend?"

"Yes! . . . I mean, of course not. Oh!" Urulani huffed. "Sometimes I think I'd really like to just knock you to the ground!"

"Are we interrupting something?" Ethis called, his voice echoing down through the chamber from above.

"No, not at all," Drakis replied, taking a step back from Urulani. "Just discussing our next move."

"We take the river to the right!" Ishander said. The young Farrunner was descending the steps quickly in front of Ethis. "We find Chelestra."

"If we do," Ethis added as he made his way down, "it would seem that these celebrated 'towers of light' are invisible. We were at the top of this tower at dawn and I made a careful survey of the horizon. There are no towers or structures visible of any kind as far as I can see; just the canopy of the rain forest."

"My father went down the right-hand river," Ishander said in a tone that defied contradiction. "That is the road to Chelestra."

"How can you be so sure?" Urulani asked.

"He learned it from one who had seen it," Ishander replied. "He told me so before he left."

"Another Far-runner?"

"No," Ishander said with a grin. "From Clan-mother—who got it from a dragon!"

Three days.

For three days, the boats drifted down the River Tyra into a silent, dead land.

Jugar had become their compass although initially there were problems with his using Aer to detect Aether. Mala emanated tremendous Aether power—so much so that it made it impossible at first for Jugar to discover any magic other than what radiated from her. The *Akumau* she wore, they decided, was the problem. Jugar was able to compensate for the effects of the medallion only after considerable effort.

The first evening brought them to a broad spit of sand at the turn of the river. There they made their encampment under a clearer sky and warm, moisture-laden air. There was only sporadic conversation— stopping and starting in fits—as everyone was occupied with his or her own thoughts. The dwarf grounded his mystical stone in the sands and managed to draw from the earth some modicum of its energy. He further healed his leg that night—announcing that there was no magic in the air after his examinations—other than Mala's irritating Aether trinket—and that if there were a city of magic, it was too far off for him to feel it.

The second day was long, muggy, and offered slowly mounting consternation. The lush jungle growth to either side of the river slowly evolved into sickly, yellowish foliage, and the trees were far shorter than those they had encountered the first day out from

Koram Devnet. Moreover, the nearly constant chattering, croaking, and cawing that had emanated from the jungle till now had suddenly stopped completely. The silence that enveloped them now was unnerving. Jugar started telling tales of the dwarven kings just to fill the air with the sound of his own voice. So anxious were his companions that they hung on his words—except for the Lyric who offered a running commentary and critique on each of the tales as Jugar told them.

Mala spent her time gazing down the river, a look of anticipation on her face. Drakis could not guess what motivated her to do so and, when he asked her what she was looking for, she only smiled and turned away.

Urulani, on the other hand, maintained a profoundly angry silence at the tiller of the second boat. She occasionally would work the tiller-oar and push her boat with the dwarf and the Lyric aboard ahead of Drakis' own craft, expending her energy through the small ship and, it seemed, feeling the better for it afterward, at least for a time.

Ethis continued to peer forward from the bow of Drakis' boat as though searching for something. Never one to waste words, he found no discomfort in the silence except, it seemed to Drakis, for the ominous change that it seemed to portend.

Ishander stood at the tiller of Drakis' boat, lost in his own thoughts. He, too, peered over the bow in search of what was to come and kept strictly to his own council.

The quiet was beginning to make Drakis itch.

At the close of the second day, they beached the boats on the left bank. A flood some years before had cleared the trees, leaving behind a patch of open ground. There, near the boats, they made their encampment for the night.

The next morning, Jugar shouted in triumph.

Holding the Heart of the Aer in his left hand and his right hand above his head, he proudly proclaimed that there was magic downstream. It was barely discernible but it was there nonetheless.

He was confident that they would reach it by noon.

It appeared almost all at once.

"By the gods!" Drakis murmured. "Is that . . ."

"Chelestra," Ethis nodded, his own voice quieted with awe. "The Lost Citadel of Humanity."

The river widened as they cleared the bend. There stood the angled walls of the city, jutting out into the river, the stones from their crumbled tops fallen in great piles at the water's edge. The vertical stone mountings of a water gate rose up to the broken tops, each set across from the other over three hundred feet apart. The gates and their mountings had long vanished, but the cuts in the stones where they had been attached were still visible—speaking to the incredible size of both gates and the enormous effort that must have been expended in opening them into the river.

"Jugar!" Drakis called. "Where do we go now?"

"Through those gates, lad!" the dwarf called back. The Heart of Aer was in his left hand once more as his right hand guided them. "It's through there!"

The two river boats of the Ambeth seemed smaller still as they passed between the towering, broken pillars. The world was silent as they moved across the still waters, the slap of a small wave against the boats' hulls the only sound.

Spread around them in an oval was a wharf nearly a mile long on either side constructed of white stone with hundreds of berths built out into the bay. The stone was stained, and moss encroached upon the base of the wharf stones from the river but declined to climb much higher than an arm's length above the waterline. The ruins of diverse buildings—what Drakis did not doubt had been warehouses, pubs, inns, trade businesses, and perhaps homes—littered the top of the quay. Many of the berths were tall, but toward the far end, Drakis could see several stone staircases leading down from the level of the buildings to smaller landings much closer to the water's edge.

"There," Jugar pointed with his right arm, his voice hushed yet sounding loud in the silence. "That landing is the one."

Ishander urged the boat forward with his long-bladed tiller. The prow connected with the ancient stone quay with a resounding thump, scraping momentarily along the side until Ethis managed to pull the hull parallel to the dock with all four of his arms.

Ishander leaped off at once, proclaiming, "I am the first! You all are witness to my being first!"

Drakis shook his head as he stepped over the side of the boat and onto the landing. The sun was high overhead and the air was still. The air was oppressive. Drakis moved quickly to the prow of the boat, pulled the mooring rope, and looped it around one of the short stone pillars that stood at intervals along the landing. As he made another loop, he stopped, staring down into the water.

Urulani, maneuvering her own boat toward the landing saw his look. "What is it, Drakis?"

"Nothing," he replied. "Come in and I'll catch the bow."

Urulani nodded, shifting the long oar with a twist that pushed the boat forward. Drakis caught the leading edge of the craft and then walked it down the landing until there was enough room to swing the side of the ship against the dock. Then he fastened the bow to one of the pillars as he had done with the first boat and helped Mala onto the dock. He offered Urulani his hand as well, but she ignored him, jumping from the upturned aft end of the boat directly onto the dock, her sword already drawn.

The dwarf jumped out on his own, the ancient book held tightly against his chest. Once on the ground, he slipped the large book into his pack before shouldering it.

Ishander was already running up the stone stairs to the promenade at the top.

"Stay with us, Ishander," Drakis called up.

"I am a Far-runner!" called down the young man, his chin raised. "I must find a prize to claim my honor!"

"You are our guide," Drakis said in reply. "That, too, is part of your honor."

Ishander shrugged but remained at the top of the stairs.

"What was that about?" Ethis asked as he helped the Lyric from the boat.

"I want him to stay close," Drakis replied in a quiet voice, turning his back to Ishander as he spoke. "I am concerned about what we will find and how he will react."

Drakis nodded down over the edge of the dock.

Just visible several feet beneath the surface could be seen the sunken outline shape of a third Ambeth boat.

CHAPTER 36

The Altar

THE STREETS LEADING AWAY from the oval-shaped harbor were largely choked with rubble from the collapsed buildings on either side. There was a devastating sameness to the landscape, the undulations of five low hilltops surrounding the city apparently also carpeted with the same coarse jumble of ruins. What few walls remained were seldom higher than the level of Drakis' eyes. Here and there a corner of a building reached upward as much as twenty feet but these were a rarity. It appeared as though every effort had been made to flatten the stonework of the city back into the ground on which it had been built.

"Am I mad, or is it even quieter here than on the river?" Drakis asked, his voice hushed and yet still carrying through the silence around them.

"I cannot speak to anyone's sanity here," Ethis replied, his own words hushed. "But not even insects appear to want to visit this place. And, here, look at these cobblestones in the roadway."

"What about them?" Drakis asked.

"There isn't so much as a blade of grass coming up between them," Ethis answered quietly. "In the midst of all this jungle—with the flora of the surrounding lands teeming with life—none of the plants have encroached upon these ruins. In Ambeth, it was all they could do to keep the growth outside the walls and that was with concerted effort. Here, however, these ruins have remained undisturbed for centuries, without the encroachment of either plant or animal."

"Just us," Drakis observed.

"Indeed, just us," Ethis acknowledged.

"We're close!" Jugar called out, his voice sounding harsh and loud among the ruins. "This way!"

The dwarf led them down a broad avenue to the right-hand side at the end of the bay. The white-and-gray shattered marble lay in jumbled piles across the roadway, making their passage difficult. Drakis and Ethis followed the dwarf but not nearly as closely as their guide. Ishander looked like an anxious puppy, scampering here and there, peering into the ruins and then dashing back to the other side of the shattered street, climbing up a low pile of stones and staring into the acres of crumbled walls beyond. Urulani remained as their rear guard, shepherding the Lyric and Mala along as they moved away from the harbor.

"How will we find anything in this desolate place?" Urulani asked.

"I'm just following the dwarf," Drakis replied, finding it impossible to locate a bare patch of cobblestone in his path. He was forced to climb over a three-foot stone block. "Jugar, what is it?"

"An obelisk," the dwarf called back. "There's a clearing at the end of the street—an old park or square, perhaps. There appears to be a marker stone in the middle of it. There's very strong magic there."

Drakis peered over the rubble. He could see the towering stone, its top apparently sheared off, pointing toward the sky from a clearing ahead of them.

Ishander scampered ahead down the street, scrambling over the piles of stone and disappearing over the other side.

Ethis turned toward Drakis as they made their way down the remains of the avenue. "It is hard to even recognize any of the structures; the destruction is so complete."

"It was a war," Drakis said, his eyes scanning the jumble of stone around them. The quiet had left him nervous once more. "What would you expect?"

"Not like this," Ethis continued. "This is not the ruin of an army trying to conquer a city or even the destruction that one might expect of a siege. This was a determined effort to make the memory of the place vanish—to erase the city and everything that it . . ."

A horrific howling cry shattered the still air.

Drakis jumped at the sound, the shock of it surging through his body, his senses suddenly alert. Ethis tensed beside him. Both of them broke into a run, their swords drawn as they rushed over the rubble toward the wailing sound that continued unabated from the clearing in front of them.

"Mala! Urulani!" Drakis called out as he dashed forward. "Stay close!"

The center of the circular plaza was nearly devoid of broken stones and debris. As Drakis ran across the open space, the fitted stones underfoot gave way to dried and matted dead grass. He could see that it was not just the top of the obelisk that was broken; the stone was shattered, cracks radiating from a single impact point near the base. Ishander lay on the far side of the stone, fallen to the ground, facedown, as his howling cries continued. The dwarf was ahead of them, making his way toward the obelisk as quickly as he could, but his leg was still giving him pain, and both Ethis and Drakis quickly passed him in their rush.

Ethis and Drakis rounded the stone, their swords at the ready. Both froze.

The impact hole on the far side of the obelisk was far larger than evidenced on the side facing the harbor—a curved puncture nearly a foot wide plunging into the stone. But it was what lay at the base of the column that caught their attention.

The remains had barely held together. Most of the flesh had long since vanished, and only the tatters of the leather loincloth and vest remained. The bones of the rib cage were broken and splayed both in the chest and just to the right of the spine. A short-bladed sword lay rusting on the ground near the figure's right hand.

Ishander lay on the ground before the skeletal form, his knees drawn up under him as he wailed his grief into the dried grass beneath him.

Drakis' gaze settled on the tarnished medallion that hung around the neck of the corpse. Twin dragon heads intertwined against a pair of dragon wings surrounding a single green gemstone.

Urulani arrived with Mala and the Lyric at her heels.

He turned to face Mala. She stood staring at the medallion, fingering the matching talisman hanging around her own neck.

Jugar limped quickly around to join them and then gasped. "By the gods! What is this?" he murmured.

"So ends Pellender . . . father of Ishander and the son of Koben Dakan," Drakis sighed. "He runs no more."

Urulani whispered. "What happened?"

"A dragon, by the looks of it," Ethis said kneeling down to examine the remains more closely. He pointed toward the broken bones in the rib cage. "See this and through the back. Given his stature, he would have been standing in front of this stone—back to it as the claw pierced both him and the stone behind him. Here he died. Here he fell."

"There's your magic, Drakis," Jugar said, lowering his hand. "That's what I've been following."

"So it was Pellender's medallion you've been reading," Drakis said standing upright.

"No, actually. Strange enchantment that," Jugar said, moving closer to examine the medallion. "You would think that the medallion would contain the magic—and it probably did once—but it seems the device has transferred its powers into the bones of poor Pellender."

"You mean you've been following the bones?" Drakis asked.

"Will you have a little compassion?" Urulani shouted, kneeling down next to the sobbing Ishander, her arms around his back trying to comfort him. "This was the boy's father!"

Drakis let out a long breath. "I . . . I'm sorry, Ishander. Ethis, Jugar come with me. We should . . . I mean . . . Urulani, if you'll take care of Ishander for us?"

She glared back at Drakis, but nodded.

Drakis walked away from the pillar, leading the dwarf and the chimerian to the edge of the dried grasses and back onto the cobblestones of the plaza. They stood in a tight circle.

"We may have a problem . . ." Drakis began.

Mala stood staring at the medallion around the dead man's neck.

As she stood there, the obelisk, the dead Far-runner, Urulani comforting Ishander, and the vast ruins surrounding her all vanished, falling away from her eyes. She was standing once again in the obscuring, warm rain of the Fordrim village, the purple-hued dead all around her, the palm of her hand once again resting on the horn of the dead dragon as it had four days before.

"He is not yet dead," said the Lyric. She stood beside Mala in the rain, her white hair soaked and laying flat against the delicate, narrow features of her face.

"No," Mala replied. "Not yet . . . but soon."

"What did he show you," the Lyric asked.

Mala drew in a deep, sad breath. "A beautiful land of shining towers and contented creatures. Families gathered in the sunshine. Children at play. Dragons filled the skies, and the sky was at peace."

"They are all dead now," the Lyric said as softly as the rain. She took Mala's hand.

"Yes," Mala replied with infinite sadness. "Dead and gone."

"Why are they gone?" The Lyric asked.

"Because the magic fell and their world was at an end."

The Lyric looked around. "The world is at an end for this village, too. Did the dragon know why these people had to die?"

Mala drew in a halting breath.

"Because of us," she said at last, the rain falling around her from the weeping sky. "Abream knew we were coming here . . . and that the Fordrim had instructions from the Dragon Queen Hestia to hold us until she returned. Pharis could not allow us to fall into the claws of Hestia—and so he sent Abream to make certain we would not be captured. He had not intended to destroy these people, but neither could he fail Pharis—and the drakoneti proved too difficult to control. In the end he could not stop what he had begun—and died with his regrets."

"And all these died," the Lyric said as she gazed into the torrential rain, "the Fordrim families, young and old, the dragon Abream and these drakoneti as well, just so that you might come to Chelestra on the promise of home. So that you could come to a place so far removed from all eyes that no one would know if you lived or died—

especially, where no one would know *who* granted you mercy or *who* did the killing."

Mala turned toward the Lyric.

The Lyric pointed to the *Akumau* hanging around her neck. "The hunt is always easier when you know exactly where your prey is to be found."

"I don't know what you mean . . ."

"That medallion around what remains of Pellender's neck is the twin of your own medallion," the Lyric replied with a gentle smile. "It was given to him by the Clan-mother of the Ambeth. But no one asked where the Clan-mother got it or why . . . least of all Pellender. And now you have one just like it from the same Clan-mother and now you are asking why and, I should think, the three warriors now in conference are asking why as well. But you, of all people here *know* why, don't you, *Seinar?*"

Mala's eyes widened. The music that had filled her mind beneath the dragon's wings at the foot of the cascades filled her mind again.

Invisible is the traitor's road
Marked with the beacons of old
Smelling of magic
Betrayal tragic . . .

Mala reached up, fingering the medallion around her neck. Deep within her recognition stirred. It was all too familiar . . . she knew that she was being followed. She had again become the *Seinar*. She had betrayed them all once more.

Find you the temples of ancient might
The key of magic fonts bright
There you'll be resting
Never confessing . . .

"The dragon knows the scent of its own magic—even when it was forged in ancient times and is all but lost to the world," the Lyric said sadly as she gazed at Mala. "And now it reeks in your very bones. The dragon will track you, too, as he did before and he will get what he has sent you to retrieve for him. He wants the key of the Font—that is what Pellender promised him and failed to find. Now he has you to find it for him—you and your companions. And when you do, Mala, when you have the key and can deliver it, the dragon will gladly offer you any wish and make any promise you ask so that he might hide his shame and his folly for all time."

"But I don't know where it is!" Mala cried out as lightning rolled through the clouds overhead.

Thunder shook the ground around them, but the Lyric did not flinch.

"You already know where it is," the Lyric grinned. "You have the book."

"But there's nothing *in* the book," Mala shouted into the rain.

"It's not what's *in* the book," the Lyric replied. "The secret *is* the book!"

Mala opened her mouth to speak but then stopped, comprehension crossing her face.

The Lyric looked up into the rain and then back to Mala. "They're talking about you."

Mala shuddered. "Who?"

"Drakis, Ethis, and Jugar," the Lyric said. There was a peaceful serenity on her face. "They are trying to decide what to do about you. But you need not worry, Mala. Though the chimerian and Jugar will both warn against you, Drakis—the ever-devoted lover of the woman who betrayed him—would rather die than make you leave."

"And it is up to you," the Lyric whispered into Mala's ear, "whether he will get his wish."

The horror of the Fordrim village began at once to dissolve around her, falling apart like a mist blown to shreds in the morning light. Only the Lyric remained, her grin and features the same although her hair was once again the explosion of white chaos that she was accustomed to wearing.

The ruins of Chelestra once again lay in all directions and the sobbing of the Far-runner came into her ears.

"Drakis!" Mala shouted at once, running over to where the warrior stood with the dwarf and chimerian still talking in hushed tones together. She grabbed Drakis by the arm, shaking him for attention.

"Mala! What is it?"

"We have to hurry!" she said, looking into his face in earnest. "We have to find the Font in the Citadel right now. We're running out of time!"

"Are you sure this is the way?" Drakis said as they scrambled as quickly as they could through the rubble, the frustration clearly underlying his voice.

"As sure as I can be," Jugar said huffing with exertion, his right hand again raised in the air. "There seems to be magic everywhere, but it is stronger in this direction."

The plaza was behind them as they raced through the ruins. The road to the east was completely blocked by a fallen tower whose rubble was impossible to pass. At last they found a tortured route around the wreckage and regained some semblance of an avenue, only to come to a cross street. Drakis could see the wheel ruts that had been etched in the cobblestones ages ago. He wondered who those people were who had brought their wagons this way centuries before and what had become of them.

The road led them north, frustrating the dwarf who insisted they needed to find some passageway that would take them farther to the east. But the avenue proved to be a boon as it led them to a large, oval-shaped plaza with numerous streets leading away from it. In the center of the plaza was the remains of a large reflecting pool. In the center of the pool was a wide field of broken mosaics that had once been accessed by seven footpaths, only three of which were still intact.

"Now THAT is a sight that gives me hope!" the dwarf exclaimed with a wide grin.

Arranged on the mosaic field were a number of fold platforms. Each was dark and devoid of any Aether magic, and less than half of them appeared intact.

"Do you think they will work?" Ethis asked the dwarf.

"Aye, I should think that they will once I'm finished with them," the dwarf grinned. "That, my chimerian companion, is an exchange—a grouping of folds for long-distance conveyance. If there be any place that we could discover to assist us in returning to the lands of our civilized acquaintance—this would certainly be it."

Drakis drew in a breath and turned to Mala. "There is your way home, Mala. All we need now is . . ."

Mala looked up at Drakis.

It startled him.

Her eyes were soft and sad. The anger and the hatred that always seemed to be caged behind her countenance were somehow gone.

"Mala?" he asked with a hesitant smile.

"I'm happy, Drakis," Mala said with quiet wonder in her voice. "The ghosts are going to rest after all. I'm going to be at peace. We both will."

"I promised you," Drakis said. "I promised to get you home again."

Mala nodded, then smiled at him the way he always remembered her smiling before the House of Timuran fell and their innocence was lost. "And you are, Drakis. You are going to bring me home very soon."

"Drakis!" Jugar called out. "I've found it! Down this eastern road . . . no more than a half a league!"

"Let's hurry, Mala," Drakis said.

"Yes," she replied. "I only wish we had more time."

CHAPTER 37

The Battlebox

S HEBIN QUIVERED IN ANTICIPATION.
It was the first time she had returned to the council chamber of the Modalis since her most gratifying initial performance. Since that time, Tsi-Shebin Timuran had been quietly celebrated, circulated on the wings of her tragedy through a cycle of all the most fashionable and powerful families in and around the Imperial capital of Rhonas Chas. Instinctively, she knew her part in the events unfolding behind the doors of the Emperor's Court and played it with perfect pitch. With every party, dance, gathering, or social event, Tsi-Shebin was the embodiment of the fear at the heart of every elven Estate. She was the heartrending victim of escaped slaves—the personification of the ideals that demanded retribution and the establishment of the Imperial Will now being exacted in the Northern Campaigns. All Rhonas cheered the armies of the north, looked anxiously for their posted reports of conquest and justice imposed by the Emperor and his Legions of Rhonas—and it was all being done in the name of Tsi-Shebin and for the sake of her lost House and stolen innocence. It was not true, but it certainly was good business, Tsi-Shebin often said with a laugh when no one but Sjei was around to hear her, and she took wicked delight in playing the role. Her "peculiarities"—fits of violent temper and often sadistic retribution at the most innocent of slights—were carefully explained away as being,

in part, due to trauma from her awful past. Thus, even Shebin's bad behavior became part of her celebrity and only served to elevate her status in the sympathetic eye of the upper Imperial Estates. She had the hearts of the Third Estate and even the notice of the Second Estate who had only recently begun to include her at social gatherings. She was the martyr of the Western Provinces, the heartrending personification of cruel fate, and her mere entry into a room could evoke sorrowful bows in recognition of her pain and her shame.

Shebin relished all of it.

She had fame, power, and riches being lavished on her far in excess of anything that she had on many occasions expounded upon as her loss. Her father had dragged her out into the Western Provinces with the idea of elevating the status of their House; how delightful, Shebin reflected, that in his death he had achieved his objective to a degree that not even he could have imagined. Her mother was a loss and Shebin endeavored every few days to feel sorrow for her passing but was almost immediately comforted in each instance by the thought that Tsi-Timuri would have wanted all this for her only daughter. Even the loss of her home and family wealth was of little consequence. What use did she have for some provincial backwater outpost when the glories of the Imperial City were laid at her feet?

No, there was only one thing in her perfectly delightful life as a victim of tragic fate that kept her nights sleepless and drove her every move.

Drakis.

She was obsessed with his death.

In her more reflective moments—such as they were—she could even acknowledge that her elevated status and current fortunate position might actually be attributed to the human slave that had brought down her House and been the cause of her family's murder. For that, she might have been grateful except for two sins for which she could never forgive him and for which he must pay before she could have any peace. Of all the evils she had accused him of and for which an entire nation was now moving toward war, these two were known only to her.

First, he knew the truth about what had happened between them. That it was she who had forced herself on him. If that knowledge were to be generally known, it would undo all the power and wealth she had acquired at his expense. Yet even this was not the worst of his offenses in her mind.

He had chosen to leave her behind.

He had walked away from her! After all she had done for him and how she had taken care of him and been good to him and treated him better than any of her other slaves . . . he had just abandoned her there in the middle of nowhere to die as if she were just anybody else. Everyone loved her in the House of Timuran—she had made sure of it and woe to anyone who did not. Yet this *human* had rejected her and just run away.

No, he had to die and she could not rest until what little remained of his corpse was laid out in front of her. She had to smell the stench of his rotting flesh, longed to see it decaying in front of her and feel the breaking of his dried bones under her feet.

"One corpse at a time," she reminded herself. She giggled. "Or a thousand is even better."

"Tsi-Timuran," came the echoing voice rolling the length of the polished floor of the long corridor.

"My most honorable Ch'dak Vaijan," Shebin replied with a grace-ful bow. "I am humbled to be met by so illustrious a member of your council."

"We are honored in turn by your presence," Ch'dak responded. "All is nearly made ready, Tsi-Shebin. I should be grateful if you will allow me to escort you to the Battlebox."

Shebin extended her hand graciously through the offered arm of the Minister of Law. "Battlebox, my lord? Is this something you open like a present or one climbs in like a litter?"

Ch'dak chuckled. "Neither, my lady. It is a chamber beneath the council room here in Majority House. You are, indeed, most privi-leged, as this is the first time anyone from outside our brotherhood has been allowed access to this special room."

"Then, by all means, lead on, good Ch'dak," Shebin cooed. "I long to see something new."

"Not new, my lady . . . it is very old indeed," Ch'dak replied. "But I can promise you, it is unique."

Ch'dak stopped, turning them both to face a section of the cor-ridor wall.

"Please follow in my footsteps and do not tarry too far behind," Ch'dak cautioned. "The bridge beyond is part of our defense."

With that, Ch'dak stepped through the wall and vanished.

Shebin drew in a breath and followed. Once the illusionary wall had passed around her, she stood for a moment in the darkness, her featureless black eyes struggling to adjust.

It was an obscene vision. The continuous oval of the walls and ceiling were ribbed like a gullet descending steeply downward. A narrow staircase followed down its curving plunge into the depths. The stair led directly into the gaping maw of an obsidian mouth with jagged teeth both above and below. Two similar mouths lay beyond it, a dull red light glowing from below and silhouetting Ch'dak before her as he descended.

"This way," the minister admonished her to follow. "Stay close and they won't bite."

Shebin's black eyes narrowed as she proceeded down the steep staircase, her gown sweeping along each tread behind her. The stairs seemed clean enough, she thought—if a bit theatrical. She followed Ch'dak through the first two maws, stopping short of the third where the minister had stopped. He turned to Shebin and indicated the left wall.

"So we turn left before the third set of teeth?" Shebin asked.

"That is correct . . . for today," Ch'dak answered.

Shebin turned off the stairs and stepped through the wall of the staircase throat.

The Battlebox proved to be a low gallery surrounding a small, square arena filled with sand. Seated in the surrounding gallery were most of the Modalis. Sjei nodded in acknowledgment as she entered the room, as did Kyori and Liau. Arikasi was trying to engage Wejon Rei in conversation but the Fifth High Priest of the Myrdin-dai was too preoccupied with the box of sand to pay any attention to the Minister of Occupation.

"This is the Battlebox," Ch'dak said, his sharp teeth grinding with satisfaction and pride. "The room derives its name from the recessed sand table in the center."

"Sand table, my lord?" Shebin was fascinated but did not wish to appear too anxious to the minister. The more innocent she appeared, she believed, the more he would tell her. "What is it for?"

"It is a new development by the Myrdin-dai," Ch'dak was all too happy to explain. "It is a magical means by which we can oversee battles in distant lands."

"They look like toys," Shebin observed. Numerous small figures stood on the undulating contours of the sand. Each was arrayed in military formation similar to those she had seen her father's Impress Warriors practice in the fields during the summer months. She smiled playfully at the minister next to her, baring her sharp teeth and bowing her elegant, elongated head in his direction. "Do you play games here, Lord Ch'dak Vaijan?"

"The best of games," Ch'dak replied. "This is a game that will crush the Drakis Rebellion."

"Indeed?"

"This table—this Battlebox—shows what is happening a thousand leagues distant to the north," Ch'dak explained. "See those glass beads?"

"Above us? The ones on that brass shaft?"

"Yes, Tsi-Shebin," Ch'dak nodded in approval. "The white ones on the right tell us how many folds stand between us and the battle in Nordesia."

"Thirty-seven by my count," Shebin nodded. "Is that correct?"

"Very good, young woman," the minister answered. "Now there are also three red ones on the right as well and a number of additional red beads on the left. Those are military folds having to do with tactics during the battle . . . you need not concern yourself with those."

Shebin had known of the use of military folds in combat since her father pounded the knowledge into her when she was barely old enough to talk. She had understood battle strategies most of her life thanks to the fact that her father had no son and she was therefore the only one to whom old Timuran could display his knowledge of battle. She had resented it at the time, but it had come to serve her well. She could affect an air of female ignorance of combat and apply its lessons on the unsuspecting.

"Then what are all the little men in the sand for?" she asked, batting her black, featureless eyes.

"I'll not bore you with the details . . ."

"Oh, please do."

"Well, the Proxis of each Octian are all connected by the power of Aether magic with their war-mage—an elf commander—who issues orders to his warriors through the proxis. The proxy becomes the eyes and ears of the war-mage on the battlefield. What the Myrdin-dai have managed to do is link all the war-mages with Aether magic to a Battlebox like this one. The contours of the battlefield terrain, its features, and the positions of the warriors of both sides—are then reproduced in miniature on a table for the war-mages so that the entire battle can be observed at once."

"Ingenious," Shebin acknowledged, "but how is it . . ."

"That we can see the battle as well?" Ch'dak finished for her.

"Well, yes."

Ch'dak nodded, inordinately pleased to have Shebin's attention to himself. "The Myrdin-dai also created a means of linking the magical box through their own folds using message batons. They then run a constant cycle of batons to update our Battlebox here so that we can view the battle as it progresses. There is a delay, of course—it takes five minutes or so for the batons to pass completely through the system—but for all intents it is as close to being there and seeing what is happening as possible."

"I am most impressed," Shebin smiled once more. "So you have invited me to watch you play with your toys, then?"

"If I may," Sjei said, stepping up to where Shebin and Ch'dak stood. "This game may hold a special interest for you, Tsi-Shebin Timuran."

"Ah," Shebin smiled warmly. "Sjei Shurian. And how does this game hold a special interest for this humble servant of the Imperial Will?"

"You see the valley running down the center of the sand?" Sjei said, gesturing toward the Battlebox.

"I do."

"It is a rather obscure place known locally as the 'Willow Vale.' It is a depression that runs down to the sea west of a place called Glachold. Those brown-and-yellow figures near the end of the depression represent the armies and people of the Drakis Rebellion."

Shebin's nostrils flared at the sound of the name. "Indeed?"

"The rebels and their families are backed against the sea—the waters of the Straits of Erebus," Sjei continued. "To the east is Gla-chold which we have now secured with a garrison. To the south, these green figures arrayed at the end of the valley depression represent the Imperial Legion of the Northern Fist who, last night, caught up with the revolutionary forces."

"What about those rust-colored figures on the western slope?" Shebin asked.

"A goblin army," Sjei replied. "They have come to enjoy the show—as shall we. But perhaps of more interest to you, my lady, will be that bright red figure in the midst of the brown figures of the re-bellious camp."

"A single figure, my lord?" Shebin asked.

"That is one very important figure," Sjei nodded. "That is the only elf I know that could find Drakis . . . and though he does not know it yet, he is about to be a prisoner."

CHAPTER 38

Signals

"**B**Y THORGRIM'S BEARD," Jugar breathed. "Have you ever seen the like?"

The broad, ancient roadway ended abruptly in the massive ruin of what once had been the Citadel of Light. Most of the walls had collapsed and the upper stories were completely gone, yet here and there among the jumble of stones were glimpses of the glory of what had once stood here. Elegant carvings of coiled jade dragons wrapped around red marble pillars jutted upward in a jagged line on either side of the wide passage that once might have been the entrance from the avenue behind them. The base of one of the gate towers remained, its spindle peak now fallen next to it, flattened and cracked like an ancient eggshell. The foundations looked as though they had been half a league square.

Urged on by Mala, they followed a meandering and often bewildering path through the ruins, but from the beginning their goal seemed obvious: a towering set of buttress stones that arched over a region roughly in the center of the ruin. At last the narrow path led them between two walls and onto the outer edge of a wide circular plaza. The arches of stone—sheared off at various heights—curved overhead from the edges of the plaza. Broken foundation walls could be seen in a peculiar pattern of circles radiating from the center of the stone floor. Yet even its magnificence was overwhelmed at once by the vision greeting them from the center of the plaza.

Three statues of dragons stood in a circle, crouched down as though bowing to the dome of crystal. They reminded Drakis of the statues on the Sea of Sand that had brought them all to this place seemingly ages ago, except that these were somehow grander in scale, majesty, and beauty. The wings, which on two of the dragons stretched back and upward from the ground, pointing toward the arched buttresses overhead, were broken off of the third dragon statue and lying next to it on the ground. All were dulled by the dust and mud of time yet even in their fallen state they conveyed a glorious and inspiring visage.

"The Font of the Citadel," Jugar crowed. "You are ours now, my beauty!"

The dwarf dashed forward, immediately followed by Drakis and the rest of their expedition. The morning sunlight beat down on them in the open space as each marveled for a moment at the intricately carved statues towering above them.

Drakis turned to the dwarf. "Jugar! They are incredible!"

"Aye, they are that lad," he replied, climbing up onto the raised stone shelf surrounding the dark, mud-splattered crystal. It was twenty feet in diameter from the portion of the stone that was visible above the surface of the surrounding cobblestones. The curvature of its surface, however, only rose to about three feet above ground level at its highest. "If this particular stone is a globe, it's a mighty large piece of Aether Well! I should think it will take a mighty effort to get it flowing again."

"But can you do it?" Ethis asked.

"Starting it, aye, that we can do," Jugar said, his eyes squinting as he considered the enormous crystal in front of him. "Keeping it going . . . well that may be a different tale altogether."

The dwarf pointed. "Can you see that fissure in the top of the stone?"

"No, I don't see . . . you mean that crack?" Drakis asked.

"That is where the key is supposed to go," the dwarf replied.

"There?" Drakis was astonished. "I couldn't fit the edge of a knife blade in that let alone some sliver of a key!"

"It may look insignificant to your eyes," Jugar said with a thoughtful frown, "but placing that 'sliver' completes the matrix of the crystal.

That is the object that will hold the Font open and keep the Aether flowing throughout the land of your ancestors for the eternities . . . and especially until we can get a few of those folds activated and our cheery selves out of this realm of your destiny."

"What the dwarf is saying," Ethis said, clearing his throat, "is that we need a key to make all of this work; a key that was hidden over four hundred years ago in order to prevent exactly what we are attempting to do now—open the Font of magic. There is an alternative, however, Drakis, and I think we should consider it. We could continue down the River Tyra, follow it to the seashore and then find a more traditional means of crossing the Straits of Erebus."

"He's right, Drakis," Urulani said. "Maybe we could find the ocean and then . . ."

"I know where the key is," Mala said in a loud and firm voice.

Everyone turned toward her.

"What did you say?" Drakis asked.

"I . . . I know where the key is," Mala said clearly, not looking Drakis in the eye. "I can get it for you but you have to open the way."

"Mala, you're not making sense . . ."

"The secret is the book, Drakis," Mala said.

"Lass, I've looked all through that book from front cover to back and every word scrawled betwixt and between," the dwarf said, shaking his head. "There's naught there about where to find this key or . . ."

"It isn't *in* the book," Mala shouted. "It *is* the book! It's how the book was hidden . . . that's how they hid the key! The priests or wizards or whoever was in charge of the magic would not have stopped it until the last possible moment. There wouldn't have been a lot of time to hold the Font open and hide the key. So they put it somewhere convenient—somewhere nearby—where no one could get at it until the Font was opened again."

Ethis nodded in appreciation. "They put it in a fold."

"Yes," Mala urged.

"It's ingenious," Jugar said with a wry smile. "Everyone was looking for the key to open the Font when you needed to open the Font in order to get the key. And it would take quite a few people all working together to open the Font . . . a Font located in a place where few people were likely to come at once."

"And I know where to find the fold that they put it in," Mala said in a rush. She turned, pointing to a ruin set atop a rise to the northwest. "There is a temple . . . on top of that rise . . . and a tower there—or there used to be a tower. If you can open the Font while I'm there, then we can recover the key."

Drakis shook his head. "How could you possibly know . . . ?"

"I knew about the drakoneti attacking in Pythar before it happened," Mala said, desperation in her voice. "I knew about the river that brought us to the Ambeth before anyone. I know how the key was hidden and I know . . . I know where it is, Drakis. Please, please believe me this one time."

Drakis looked at her, anguish in his eyes. "Mala, you have to understand. I can't . . ."

Urulani pushed the Lyric aside and stepped between them, her hand on Drakis' chest. "She is going for the key . . . and I am going with her."

Urulani paused and then looked around, her eyes falling on the dwarf's red sash tied about his waist. The raider captain stepped over to Jugar and snatched the sash loose, spinning the dwarf about as it unwound from around him.

"Urulani," Jugar protested. "That is the finest article of decoration I have left!"

"This is our signal," Urulani said, stepping back in front of Drakis and brandishing the bright red sash in his face. "We will put this somewhere you can see it when we get there. Then you finish activating the Font and we will bring you back this precious key."

"How can you possibly believe her?" Drakis asked heatedly. "After all she's done to you . . . to your crew . . ."

"I believe her because I must," Urulani said, her eyes flashing. "Because after all that has happened, she has come to see the truth."

"Then go with her," Drakis snapped, turning toward the dwarf. "How long will it take us to open this Font?"

"That's a most difficult question, indeed . . ."

"How long, dwarf!"

"Perhaps half an hour," the dwarf shrugged. "Perhaps longer."

"You have half an hour to get to that ruin and signal us," Drakis said to Mala and Urulani. "If you do not hear from us by the time the sun reaches noon, then return to the harbor and we'll try to meet you there near the boats. Understand?"

Urulani nodded. Mala just watched him as he spoke.

"Then, one way or another," Drakis said, "we are all going home!"

"One way or another," Mala said through a soft smile. She turned and ran from the plaza with Urulani at her heels.

Soen Tjen-rei stood grimly at the door of the Grahn Aur's tent and surveyed the valley below him.

Belag had placed his tent after the elf fashion—atop the knoll of a hill looking back up the Willow Vale. It was a mean rise of rock, with sand and tough, stubborn brush clinging to it near the southern shores of Mistral Bay. Its only virtue was its height, which afforded a view back up the broad expanse of the Willow Vale and, at the moment, of the pending catastrophe that was about to befall the followers of Drakis and turn the valley into a slaughterhouse. Unlike the elves, however, Belag and all his officers preferred to command the battle near the front. This left Soen gratefully deserted and alone on the singular mount of stone as he considered his next move.

Across the valley, the manticores had, under Belag's direction and those of the army commanders beneath him, arrayed themselves once again in their classic battle lines. They were prepared to meet the elves in battle as they had fought their wars for centuries. They did so with trepidation. The warriors knew all too well the horrible defeat and routing that had had been their fate during their last battle with this same Legion on the Shrouded Plain. Yet they once again lined up in their ranks and formations and prepared for the inevitable charge that would signal the beginning of their fated defeat. The manticores were fierce and determined warriors and would have adjusted their tactics if they had any answer to the flexibility of the Rhonas folds and the Proxis who were as effective as they were disposable.

Soen could see the goblins on their strange wyvern mounts lining the top of the western ridge. They were here only for the spectacle—having made it clear to Soen and Vendis both that their interest in the impending battle was merely a sporting one and largely running along the lines of how long it would take the Legions of the Northern Fist to crush every living soul in their path into oblivion.

At the far southern end of the valley and stretching partially along the eastern flank were arrayed the Rhonas Legions who were biding their time in attacking. It was the strangest part of the whole affair for Soen. They had all been in place since dawn and yet they had not made any move against the Drakis forces.

The Drakis forces! Soen sneered at the thought. There was the real folly in all of this. He had begun all this hunting for an insignificant runaway slave who had somehow slipped his Devotions. Now two entire Legions of the Empire—sixteen thousand trained warriors—were being committed to the extermination of over sixty thousand men, women, and children—and those same sixty thousand followers were equally committed to defending their faith—all because they believed in the story of a man they had never seen and who, if he was somehow still alive on the wild northern continent, would never even know of their sacrifice in his name. Soen's own Order was seeking to snuff out not only the lives of both himself and his prey but to obliterate all knowledge that either had ever existed as well.

All this pain, turmoil, and death because of a story that someone told years ago to people who were just gullible enough to believe it and pass it on to others.

He had tried to avert such a disaster at every step, and if Ch'drei had been bolder or had understood his vision of how to make use of this slave and his legend, then perhaps things would have turned out better for everyone. Now here he was with his back to the sea and a massacre about to unfold around his feet—which might well include his own death.

It was definitely time to leave. He had learned all he thought he could from this Belag. He would find his own way across the Straits of Erebus and track down this foolish human slave if he could. Then he would drag him back and gift him as a present to Ch'drei— although exactly how he would do that to his best advantage would have to be determined later. He had several delicious ideas that he occasionally savored in his mind when time permitted.

All that would have to wait until he was clear of the battle. The goblins seemed reasonable enough so long as Soen bent his pride a little and honored their customs. West, he decided, then around the Goblin Peaks and in search of a ship that equated more coins with fewer questions.

Soen returned to the tent, shouldered his pack, and then reached for his staff.

It was not there.

Soen frowned, baring a few of his sharp teeth. He was in a hurry and having to search through the tent for his staff was irritating. He felt certain that he had left it there against the traveling trunk Belag used but his recollections of the night before were a little hazy. The strategy meeting had fortunately been short but was overcompensated for by the imbibing of a great deal of fortified wine. Soen was no stranger to the drink but its effect on him had been stronger than he had expected.

He pushed aside a number of boxes, baskets, and urns, but the Matei staff stubbornly refused to appear.

Soen ran the long fingers of his hands through the sparse hair rimming his elongated head. He pinched the pointed end of his right ear trying to remember what he had done with the staff but the memory refused to dislodge.

"Soen!" It was a voice from outside the tent.

Soen groaned. It was Vendis. Soen was trying to slip out of camp quietly. Attention was the last thing he needed.

"Soen! I've found something!"

Soen set down the pack. "What is it?"

"Come out! It's the signal! You've got to see this!"

Soen turned and strode out of the tent. If he could deal with the chimerian quickly then . . .

Light exploded around him and his feet left the ground. Soen spun instinctively, readying himself for combat but there was nothing to fight, as he was held weightless in the air. A hazy glowing sphere surrounded him just beyond his reach. He stretched his arms and legs carefully to steady himself and looked down.

Below him, Vendis knelt on the ground gazing up at him with a wide and vicious grin on his otherwise featureless face.

In his hands he held a Matei staff, its base planted against the ground as its Aether magic held the Inquisitor in a stasis bubble twelve feet overhead.

"My own staff?" Soen seethed through his sharp, clenched teeth.

"Recharged, as promised," Vendis nodded. "Did you not know that the chimerians were the ones who first *sold* Aether magic to the Rhonas elves?"

Soen was trapped with no Aether of his own and nothing within reach that he could leverage to attack Vendis and reclaim his staff. The entire purpose of the stasis bubble was to render the opponent inert but the drain on the staff was severe. Soen relaxed.

"You can only keep that up for about six hours," Soen observed. "I can wait that long to tear your heart from your rubber chest."

"No, you can't," Vendis replied. "My friends will be here to claim you long before then. You see, the battle has begun. The signal has already been given."

Soen raised his head. Already the Legions were moving down the slope and into the valley.

"And please appreciate the beauty of this," Vendis continued. "You *are* the signal!"

CHAPTER 39

Mala's Choice

MALA RAN.

Urulani was both frustrated and amazed. The tan slave woman with the reddish hair was flying through the ruins as though death itself was at her heels. Urulani was a trained and skilled fighter, a woman of the Sondau Clans who had led raiding parties and had run long scouting sorties across the wide savanna of Vestasia but even she grudgingly admitted to herself that she was having trouble keeping up. Mala's red hair bobbed ahead of her, vanishing around fallen marble walls or shattered statuary. It was as though the woman had wings. Urulani followed her down the debris-covered avenue back to the enormous plaza where they had found the fold platforms. The warrior woman was having trouble believing that anything that old or that broken could ever bring them hope of deliverance, but Drakis had said it was so and she had come to believe in him even when he did not believe in himself.

Mala, however, did not even slow her pace as they approached the platforms. Her attention was set on the hilltop still visible to them on the northwest side of the city and the cascade of rocks that, if Mala were to be believed, was once a temple and tower.

If Mala were to be believed . . .

How could she have put her faith in her, too? She was a traitor who deserved death or worse for what she had done to Urulani's crew, let alone what she had done to Drakis and her own companions. How much blood was on Mala's hands—and Sondau blood at that—and yet there was something in Urulani that drove her to believe—to hope, perhaps, that if someone like Mala could be forgiven, then perhaps Urulani could be, too?

Was that what this was about? Urulani thought grimly to herself as she leaped over a masonry stone lying in shards. Who was Urulani chasing through these ruins? She thought for a moment that it might have been herself and, at the thought, smiled grimly.

You can never outrun yourself, she realized, but your past can catch up with you.

"Mala!" Urulani shouted. "Wait!"

"There's no time," Mala responded as she raced around the southern side of the dark and foul-smelling pools surrounding the broken folds. "They are coming! *He* is coming!"

"Who?" Urulani called after Mala. "Who is coming?"

Mala gave no reply as she continued past the far end of the fold plaza and dashed down the broad, rubble-choked avenue beyond. It was more difficult for Urulani to see her through the jumble of stones. The street rose gently toward the distant hill that seemed to get no closer. Still she ran, frustrated that her long strides were bringing her no closer to Mala. Her own breath was becoming labored with effort. What was driving Mala, she wondered, that she should run with wings of the wind?

Glimpses of auburn hair continued to taunt her, driving her through the ruins. The way was growing steeper now, the streets narrower, and the way more confused. They were drawing higher above the city with every step toward the crest of the hill. The hilltop was near now—perhaps less than three hundred good strides—and she could clearly see the winding road that led to the ruin at its summit.

Urulani's eyes widened as the rubble opened again onto a wide plaza of perfectly fitted stones.

In the center of the plaza stood the feet and legs of a great colossus. Their form was breathtaking in its perfection but it was the head, torso and left hand that lay at the feet of the statue that captured her awed attention.

The face was stern yet passive, with a squared, dimpled chin and a narrow jaw. The bowed lips were small and supple and the brow furrowed over perfect eyes set looking to the left. The hair was curled and substantive, framing the face elegantly. The neck, shoulders, and arm were bare and the single arm was raised with an open palm bent away from the wrist, the fingers splayed as though the figure were either asking a question or beckoning. Urulani had seen sculptures before—the Hak'kaarin were often carting them from place to place across the plains and telling stories about them, but there was something so perfect about this statue that the raider captain found it was beyond definition by mere words or thought. It was the most beautiful thing that Urulani had ever seen—now lying amid the crumbling stones of the dead empire of humanity.

She stopped in her tracks. Tears welled up in her eyes. She bent over as the weight of the lost past settled on her shoulders—her own lost past reflected in the dead eyes of the fallen statue.

"Go back, Urulani," Mala said. She stood next to the statue's head, stepping up toward the raider captain. "Drakis needs you and they are coming!"

"No," Urulani said with a rough voice. She found it difficult to take her eyes away from the fallen colossus. "I'm coming with you."

"You can't," Mala said, her soft voice rolling across the silence of the plaza. "I have to go alone."

Mala reached out, taking the long, brilliant red sash of the dwarf from Urulani's hands. Mala carefully rolled up the sash in her hands, cradling it in her arms like a child as she walked around the statue toward the opposite side of the clearing.

Urulani at last took her eyes from the stern, sad face of the statue, gazing across its ruin to Mala on the far side. "She is up there, isn't she?"

"Yes," Mala said through a sad smile, her eyes fixed on the rolled, red sash. "And she is taking me home."

"We're going together," Urulani said, drawing herself upright.

Mala shook her head slowly, her eyes fixed on the sash cradled in her arms.

Anger welled up suddenly from deep within Urulani. "I am . . . I am the captain of this expedition! You will do what I say! I am . . . I am in command . . . I command . . ."

Mala shook her head again, looking up with her sad smile. "I have always been a slave, Urulani. You have run the open plains and conquered the winds and the sea—your life is as far from mine as the stars from the ground. All my life—what I have managed to remember of it—I have been a slave to other people's will, other people's choices. The elves enslaved me the day I came from my mother's womb. They stole my choices from me and made them for me. Then I thought I was given back my choice when the Well failed a lifetime ago in House Timuran. I didn't want the gift—I wanted other people to make my choices for me. And they were *still* making them for me because they had broken my mind years ago and made me a slave to my own confused thoughts and memories. Fear made my choices for me then—fear of the elves, fear of freedom, fear of having no one take care of me, fear of having to choose. Now *you* want to make me *your* slave by commanding me. Drakis wants to make me *his* slave by taking me back to the south and helping me forget. He thinks it would be a kindness but it would just be another form of slavery and—benevolent as his intentions would begin, it would destroy us both."

Mala drew in a breath.

"Now I choose for myself," she said. She nodded back down the ruined road behind Urulani. "Run back to him. He will fail without you. When the key is found, then I will go home. We will all go home."

Urulani turned to look back down the road behind her. From their height, she could more easily discern the layout of the city as it must have once been; the broad avenues in spiderweb lines that converged first at the fold platforms and then at a large structure behind that must have been the palace of the draconic lords. Farther past the fold plaza, forming the third apex of the triangle, was the ruin of the Citadel of Light where Drakis and the rest were awaiting their signal.

Urulani's large, dark eyes narrowed.

Something was moving across the dead city, like a slow tide from the southern edges of the ruins. Its flow had shifted to the left and right as it converged toward the ruined Citadel of Light.

"Drakoneti!" Urulani growled turning back to face Mala. "You knew they were . . ."

Mala was gone.

Urulani turned back to face the south, frantically gazing down on the ruined city spread below her. What had Mala said? "They" were coming. "He" was coming.

The drakoneti were flooding into the city by the thousands, moving to encircle the ruined Citadel. Over the river to her right she now could see the dark shape of a dragon, its wings barely visible in the sunlight as it flew directly toward Urulani . . . and the ruined temple behind her at the top of the hill.

Urulani roared in anger and fear.

In that moment, Urulani knew that Mala had betrayed them all, had led the dragon to them and would, she had no doubt, hand over the key to the dragon to save her own worthless skin at the cost of all their lives.

"Not if I can stop her," Urulani vowed, drawing her sword as she rushed past the fallen colossus and charged up the winding road toward the ruined temple.

She was halfway to the top when she saw the red banner of the dwarf's sash unfurl from a stone peak of a fallen tower near the crest of the hill.

"That's it!" the dwarf yelled. "That's the signal!"

"Now what?" Drakis shouted over the low hum filling the air around the Citadel courtyard. The pain in his arm was unbearable. He had been holding the plate stone of the dragon statue in place for what seemed an eternity. The stone pressed back with increasing force, vibrating under his hand. The glow in the ancient statue's eye had steadily increased but the pressure needed to keep his hand against the carved scale was unendurable. Still, he could not remove it until all of the dragons had been made active and, according to the dwarf, Mala and Urulani returned with the key. Letting go would mean starting over from the beginning and he did not think he had the strength for it.

"Now we activate the last dragon," Jugar yelled. "Then Mala receives the key."

Drakis gritted his teeth. Ishander was pressing against the second dragon, which left one remaining. "Then do it!"

The dwarf stepped over to the final statue. It was a reach for him but he stretched up and pressed his wide hand to the carved scales of the dragon statue.

Nothing happened.

The dwarf pushed harder.

Nothing.

"What's wrong?" Drakis shouted.

"It isn't working," the dwarf frowned.

"I can *see* that!" Drakis yelled.

Ethis stepped forward quickly, pressing one of his own four hands against the stone.

No change.

"I don't understand," the dwarf whined. "We used your hand on each of these statues before we started and this one was working just fine then! And it's working fine for Ishander."

"Human magic," Ethis said. "Perhaps it requires humans."

"Of course," the dwarf said. "Safe magic. All we need is one of the other humans . . ."

"*Which* other humans?" Ethis asked at once.

"Well any of the other . . . say, where is the Lyric?"

Drakis looked around frantically.

The Lyric was gone.

"We have three statues and *two* humans to activate them," Drakis shouted. "NOW what do we do?"

Belag roared in frustration.

The battle commanders of the Army of the Prophet were trying to fall back before the onslaught of the Legions of the Northern Fist. Each time they would re-form the line, reengage the enemy, and inflict losses on their attackers. Then the attackers would retreat. The manticores would pursue the enemy only to find themselves flanked by more Legion Impress Warriors pouring through folds established behind their lines. The manticores, gnomes, humans, chimerians, and even elven elements of the Army of the Prophet would then regroup with more losses, falling back behind their original lines and reforming the battle line once more. It was an attempt by the manticorian captains to address the traditional tactics of the elves and was far more successful than the usual manticorian charge that tradition dictated in the lion-men's tactics of battle. But the result was equally catastrophic: the back and forth of the battlefield resulted in a slow but continuous loss of ground for the Army of the Prophet and was a grinding mill of death on both sides of the line.

Belag damned the elven magic for the horrors it had unleashed on the world and on his pilgrims in particular.

And where was Soen and his magic when Belag needed it most?

"Retreat!" Belag bellowed as a new fold opened up behind him and more Impress Warrior troops of the Legions poured from it. Belag had been one of them not that many months before and knew how effective they could be. Yet he had no choice but to keep fighting even as he watched his army being ground down into the blood-soaked earth around him along with his dreams for his beloved Drakis and the promised freedom of the prophecy.

"Retreat and regroup!"

Urulani charged up the broken stairs curving toward the fallen cupola, her sword in hand and tears streaming down the smooth, dark skin of her face. She had allowed herself to believe. She had allowed herself to be weak. She had allowed herself to have a hope in the gods that her clan had honored from a dead and legendary past. Her heart had been betrayed, and Mala would pay for that treachery.

But not before she got what Drakis had come for; not before she obtained the key to the Font. She would deprive Mala of that prize.

The cupola stood atop a dome that had fallen with the collapsing wall and now sat like a broken eggshell at the edge of the temple rubble. The small circular structure had somehow survived the collapse and remained largely intact, the seven pillars still supporting a small cone that formed its roof. Even in ruin, the hilltop provided a panoramic view of the ruined city and the blanket of jungle forest stretching to the hazy horizon.

Urulani's eyes were fixed on the figure of Mala standing between the pillars, her arms folded across her chest, the dwarf's sash streaming from her grip down over the edge and draping on to the broken dome at her feet.

"Urulani," said a quiet voice behind her.

Startled, Urulani turned, sword across her body ready to strike.

It was the Lyric.

The dark woman shifted the sword, its tip pointing threateningly at the madwoman. "Stand aside! I'm taking the key."

The Lyric smiled. "It's not here . . . and you should not be either, Li-Li."

"Don't call me that!" Urulani growled.

"You have to run now," the Lyric said, gripping the blade of the sword with her right hand and gently pushing it aside. The blade slid through her palm as she did so, cutting it deeply with both edges. Her blood ran down the sword but the expression on her face did not change. "You have to take this fragile woman you call the Lyric with you. You are in great danger here."

Urulani felt a shiver run through her. "Who are you?"

"You know me, Li-Li," the Lyric said, blood dripping from her cut hand. "You have just forgotten me is all. I must go now but I won't be far from you . . . and you will remember me again. But for now—you might want to hide."

The Lyric gave a final smile . . . and collapsed onto Urulani.

The raider captain dropped her sword, catching the Lyric in her arms. The Lyric's head lolled back and then the woman screamed in pain and fear.

"Who are you?" the Lyric cried out.

"I'm Urulani," the captain responded as she always did to such requests from the Lyric. "And who are you today?"

The Lyric stared at Urulani in wild-eyed panic. "I don't know!"

Urulani blinked. "What do you mean, you don't know?"

"Please help me!" the Lyric cried out as she stared at her bleeding hand. "I'm . . . I'm hurt . . . and I don't *know* who I am! Please . . . please help me . . ."

Urulani heard another shrieking sound behind her. She turned.

The wings of the rust-colored dragon were beating the air as it approached the cupola at the top of the broken dome.

Urulani picked up the quivering Lyric in her strong arms and dashed behind a broken fragment of wall. She set the Lyric down, peering around the corner.

Urulani could see the red sash of the dwarf flailing in the wind created by the dragon's wings.

She could not see Mala.

CHAPTER 40

Shaken Foundations

"**WHAT CAN WE DO?**" the dwarf shouted back.

Drakis grimaced. The throbbing in his arm was excruciating, the thunderous rumble coming from the dragon statue next to his hand overwhelming.

Ishander raised his chin from where he stood, his hand pushing painfully against the carved scale set in the dragon statue's chest. "Do you hear that?"

"Hear what?" Ethis asked.

Ishander's eyes widened. "The drakoneti! They are coming!"

"Drakoneti?" Drakis yelled. The noise was making it difficult to hear. "How many?"

"I've never heard so many!" Ishander answered through clenched teeth.

Drakis shifted his stance, but a glance at the dwarf made him stop.

"Don't move!" the dwarf bellowed, both his hands held up in front of him. "The Font is nearly open! If you release that statue now, we may never have another chance at this!"

"So we just stand here until the drakoneti come and eat us?" Drakis demanded.

"It's just one more!" Jugar bellowed in frustration. "We've been shoulder-deep in humans for weeks and now we can't find *one* more?"

Ethis turned from where he stood near the dwarf and strode at once toward the third statue. He raised one of his four arms.

"But you're not human," Jugar called after him.

"Not yet," Ethis answered.

Before their eyes, the chimerian's form began to change. His two lower arms withdrew slowly inward, vanishing at last into the ripples of the shapeshifter's form. The long legs contracted and the body shortened. The surface of Ethis' body shifted colors, the folds shifting in the air like clothing. Parts of it hardened into the likeness of a leather cuirass. The ears, the ragged dark hair, the jawline of the face . . . everything molded quickly until the rough figure of Drakis appeared to be standing at the base of the third statue.

Ethis' eyes concentrated on his outstretched remaining right hand. The pigment, the form, the hairs on the back of the hand were all rendered in detail. He reached out for the breast scale of the final dragon statue, then pushed hard against it.

The duplicate figure of Drakis quivered, partially losing its shape as Ethis threw back his head and screamed.

The eye of the third dragon began to glow, the rumble from beneath their feet increasing with every passing second.

Ethis shifted his head to face the hand pressed against the stone. The duplicated features rippled, re-formed and then sagged again.

"It's working!" shouted the dwarf. "Drakis! Can you see Mala?"

Drakis turned, facing north and west across the ruins. He could see the distant hill, the long red cloth of the dwarf's sash flicking at a sudden wind. "No but I see the sign. She's ready as soon as . . . NO!"

A rust-colored blur soared through the achingly blue sky. Enormous leathery wings locked stiff in the air, wheeling the banking dragon in a spiraling circle around the distant hilltop.

Mala's hilltop.

"We have to do something!" Drakis cried in anger and frustration.

"We *are* doing something," Ethis called in response, his words slurred as he was having difficulty maintaining the shape of his mouth.

"All of this will be for nothing unless we get the key," Jugar said. "Keep going! We're almost . . . !"

Light flared out from the eyes of the dragon statues; brilliant beams that nearly blinded Drakis before he could turn his head away, slamming closed his eyes. Squinting against the brilliant light, Drakis turned to look over the great crystal stone of the Font to where the beams converged.

The air shifted, twisting on itself.

"It can't be!" screamed Drakis.

A long shard of crystal floated slowly down out of the fold. A silver handle was fixed around the end of the shard, gleaming brightly in the rays from the dragons' eyes.

"The key!" Jugar shouted. "It was here all along! Everyone stay where you are! I've got to get that key placed in the top of the Font stone!"

"But if the key is here," Ishander called, "why did that Mala woman . . . ?"

Drakis turned his gaze to the distant hilltop. "Mala! What have you done?"

She stood at the edge of the cupola. Her green eyes gazed languidly out over the ruined city, down the long avenues beyond the fold plaza to the ruins of the Citadel. Drakis was there, she thought. Mala was sorry that she was going to have to hurt him once more, but she hoped he would understand in time.

"I am here," she said aloud as she reached up with her hand and touched the amulet that still hung about her neck. "I am waiting for you."

The enormous figure of a dragon swooped past, suddenly obliterating her view of the city. It was a blur of rust-browns and reds barreling by in a roar of wind. Its shadow felt cold on her shoulders but was gone in an instant.

Pharis is here, Mala thought, with resigned calm.

She reached down and held the amulet in her hand. It was not metal after all, she realized, though part of the charm cast upon it was that it should appear as such. No, this was made of rarer stuff; the carved horn of a dragon and not just any dragon, she knew . . . but the dragon whose spirals were closing about her even now.

"Horn to hand," she whispered to the amulet she held. "Then bone to bone . . . my bones to yours, is that not true, Pharis?"

"It was the ancient way," came the words hissing into her mind. *"Forgotten to all but my kind. You have done well, Daughter of Humanity."*

"I have done what I must," Mala answered as she stepped to the edge of the cupola.

The wings of the enormous dragon shifted, catching the wind as it turned toward Mala. Pharis landed with his claws digging into the broken edge of the fallen temple dome, his gigantic head craning toward the red-haired woman standing between the columns. *"Where is the key?"*

"Hidden," Mala replied. "Hidden where you—a creature who cared nothing for the help of others could never find it. The humans never betrayed the dragons. The dragons did not betray humanity . . . it was only you."

"I betrayed no one!" Pharis snarled in her mind.

"You betrayed your own kind," Mala said quietly.

"The dragons betrayed themselves!" Pharis decreed, his wings flexing open in a show of might. *"Hestia and her court! They called her Queen! They were pets—docile and domesticated by the soft cage of human dependency!"*

"They were the friends and partners of humanity," Mala said.

"They were slaves made fat and lazy by the magic humans dredged up from the heart of the world!" Pharis' words thundered through her mind. *"Dragons once hunted the wilds of the Far Steppes! Their wings carried terror and respect across the skies. Their roar shook the earth and froze the hearts of their prey. We were the masters of all below us and above. We had a destiny—stolen from us by a human empire that ruled not by right but by virtue of ease! Without the corruption of magic we would have been a great race—a conquering race dependent on no one!"*

"And so you brought down the human empire," Mala sighed with understanding. "For the good of the dragons."

"Yes . . . for their good," Pharis' words blared through her mind even as the dragon before her roared to the sky. *"The magic of the humans had made us weak like cattle! Without it, our kind would be free once more to fulfill our destiny—as I am about to fulfill mine! Give me the key, Mala, and you may yet live through this day!"*

"So that all hope for humanity may be buried at last," Mala smiled. "And the evidence of your own offenses? And tell me, great Pharis, in the centuries since the fall of human magic, what great destiny have the dragons risen to fulfill? Where are your race's mighty achievements? Show me what the lives of this empire have purchased in the mighty rise of your freed dragonkind?"

Beyond the wings of Pharis, Mala caught a flash of brilliant light from the ruins of the Citadel.

Mala smiled sadly as she turned her back on the dragon and stepped into the cupola.

"Give me the key!" the dragon raged.

"I cannot," Mala answered stepping slowly across the broken floor toward the open arch on the far side of the cupola.

"You will serve me!" Pharis bellowed in her thoughts.

"But I do not have it," Mala replied. "It is not here."

"But you told the others . . ."

"I said that I knew where it was," Mala continued, not turning back. "And now it is too late for you to stop them from using it."

She took another step. She thought she saw the shadowy silhouette of a woman, tall and beautiful, standing between the pillars. Her arms were open. It may have been a statue but she thought she saw the arms widen to welcome her.

"Good-bye, Drakis," Mala said, smiling sadly as she took another step. "I know my own way home."

Searing flame exploded about her.

"NO!" Drakis screamed.

Fire from the maw of Pharis engulfed the distant hilltop, the red sash vanishing in the flames. The cupola atop the fallen dome shattered with the force of the dragon's breath, cascading downward over the fallen ruins.

"Stay where you are, you fool!" Jugar shouted. He had run as quickly as his still troublesome leg would allow to where the Key of the Font had come to rest. It had not fallen straight down and into place as the dwarf had hoped but had slid down off the exposed curve of the Font crystal and lay to the side. The dwarf now had the key in hand and was struggling to climb the slippery curve of the Font to its apex.

"Hurry!" Ishander urged. "Look!"

The drakoneti had come into view, their horrible features chattering in anticipation of catching their prey. There looked to be more than a thousand of them charging down the ruins of the roadway leading from the Fold Plaza.

"Even if we activate the Font," Ethis slurred his words, his figure growing more formless by the moment, though his concentration on his reproduced human hand remained intact. "How will we get past them to get to the folds?"

"And the dragon is coming," Ishander observed. "He flies directly for us!"

The dwarf continued to carefully crawl his way up the face of the crystal. He was near the apex of the stone. "One desperate act at a time, boy!"

The screech of the dragon cut across the ruins. The drakoneti raised their arms in excitement as they ran toward the ruined Citadel, their howling voices joining in a threatening chorus.

The stones around the Citadel rotunda shook with the force welling up beneath it. The sound was deafening as brilliant, blue light gathered in the Font crystal at their feet.

"Well," Jugar said loudly as he reached the apex of the Font. He could see the brilliant outlines of the fissure at the top of the stone and aligned the key to match it. "Let's see what *this* does!"

The dwarf plunged the shard into the stone.

Aether was the lifeblood of ancient Drakosia. It came from the Citadel of Light and flowed throughout Khorypistan, Tyrania, and Armethia. It was the underlying blessing beneath the united societies of humanity and dragonkind. Its use was ubiquitous and as varied as human thought could devise. There was not a single aspect of human or draconic life that was not directly empowered and improved by the application of Aetheric force. From the improvement of crop yields to transportation folds to dental hygiene or performance art, Aether was found at its foundation.

One of its most important applications, however, was in the strengthening of its cities. It allowed for magnificent architecture that would otherwise have been impossible using normal techniques of stonemasonry or construction and, equally important to the besieged humans of their age, to reinforce those same walls in the event of attack. Thus, each wall and structure of ancient Drakosia was strengthened by the force of Aether magic—an omnipresent, simple, and persistent spell which drew on the Aether to remember where the stones of the entire city were originally placed and to provide force enough to keep them there even when the force of an enemy was applied to it.

It was the collapse of this most elemental of spells that was the doom of the human empire—for when the Font went dark and the Aether stopped, the spell failed the architecture. A very few impossible structures failed on their own, but it was a trifle compared to the destruction visited on the cities by the invading elves who were bent on obliteration rather than conquest.

So the fallen stones of fortification walls, buildings, and towers lay in ruin and the cities were forgotten.

But the faint tendrils of magic once imbued in the stones remained—and the spell remembered.

Drakis was thrown to the ground.

The flood was rolling beneath him. He tried to get back to his feet, concerned for a moment that he had let go of his statue and somehow caused all this. The stones under him continued to buck, and he fell back down on all fours. The dwarf was sliding down the blazing crystal dome head first, rolling over the edge and onto the rotunda floor nearby. Drakis tried to crawl over toward him, but the stones moving under his hands and knees were making even that difficult.

Drakis looked again at the stone of the Font. It pulsed brilliantly, emitting a blinding column of light skyward.

"Jugar!" Drakis cried out. "What's happening?"

"It's working!" Jugar yelled.

"I *know* it's working but . . . the stones!"

The broken pieces of masonry scattered about the rotunda floor were rising up from the ground. Slowly, the broken fragments of walls, columns, arches, and ceiling were drifting purposefully upward.

"By Thorgrin's Beard!" the dwarf shouted over the terrible cacophony of grinding, crashing sound that thundered around them. He pointed toward the hilltop where Mala had given them their signal. "The city! It's . . . it's coming back!"

The blackened fragments of the burned-out cupola were rising back into place atop the fallen dome on the distant hill, followed by the slow resurrection of the dome itself, heaving upward, rising to where it had once stood magnificent watch over the city. The temple that had stood beneath and behind it was rising, too, its stones re-forming the walls and flying buttresses of the elegant sweeping structure. Beyond the walls rising around him, Drakis could see more towers lifting up from the dust, piercing again into the skies they had once graced.

But not perfectly, Drakis realized.

Many of the stones remained where they lay. Sections of wall were missing, and in some cases entire halves of buildings remained lying on the ground. Several of the towering spires assembled their striking spindly tops to hang in the sky without any visible supporting tower walls beneath their jaggedly re-formed centers. In the rotunda around him, several of the surrounding columns appeared to float in the air, attached neither to the ground nor to any arch above. Only part of the circular wall surrounding the citadel rotunda had rebuilt itself and only a small section of the entrance portico had assembled itself to float solidly toward the northwest. It was a dead city being raised by its own ghostly memories, trying to take on the substance long since passed away.

And the drakoneti could be seen still rushing toward them, although they appeared to be having some difficulty navigating the still shifting terrain underfoot. Weaving between the risen towers, flying with mighty beats of his wings, Pharis drove through the sky directly toward them.

The chimerian lay senseless on the ground on the far side of the Font, his form disturbingly nondescript. Ishander had his arms wrapped around one of the pillars, holding on to it firmly with his eyes closed.

"Quickly, lad," Jugar shouted. "We've got to get the key!"

"I thought we *had* the key!" Drakis said angrily. "You were the one who put the key in the Font!"

"I put the shard in the Font," Jugar yelled. "It's that tool I used to do it with that's the key. It's still holding the shard. If your friend Pharis gets a grip on that, he can remove the shard and close the Font. And I'm guessing at the speed he's coming, we don't have much time!"

The Font of the Citadel flowed, drawing upon the magic from within the world for the first time in centuries.

But the Aether magic that had protected all of the cities of the human empire awoke to its touch. Stones must be put back, walls reassembled, towers rebuilt, roads smoothed, and statues gathered back to their intended forms. A few such repairs and reinforcements—even in times of battle—would not have demanded much of the Font that supplied them, for such sustaining power would have been localized to the point of conflict.

But as the magic awoke, it called on the Font from everywhere at once. All across the ancient kingdoms of humanity—Khorypistan, Tyrania, Armethia, Pythar; in the Kesh Morain and a thousand other ruins across a continent; from the boundaries of the Siren Coast on the Charos Ocean to the Bay of Ostan off the Lyrac Shores—the magic that had failed to preserve the great cities and towns of humanity awoke and called upon the Font of the Citadel of Light to provide whatever Aether was needed to rebuild the ruins as much as possible.

And the Font answered by drawing as much Aether as was demanded to rebuild an entire empire at once.

CHAPTER 41

Slaughter

SJEI SMILED, baring his sharp, pointed teeth.

The shifts of the figures in the Battlebox promised a complete victory. Three Cohorts were pressing an attack against the enemy units who had been falling back in their positions for the last hour. Now they were neatly boxed in on three sides with their backs to the sea. Casualties among the front line Impress Warriors had been heavy, but they had consistently been pushing the rebel lines back—establishing gate symbols as they moved. The Army of Drakis—as he understood they had fashioned themselves—had learned at last not to press their advantage after the gate symbols had been inscribed but it had cost them ground and, for that matter Sjei thought ruefully, the ability to win. Unable to press any advantage they had merely been able to protract the battle but not, he knew, to change the inevitable outcome.

"Well, Sjei! It seems that the Emperor shall be given another victory this day." It was the cloying voice of Wejon Rei near his ear. The man had been a problem from the beginning, and now that victory was all but assured his support of the northern campaign would, no doubt, be remembered as one of eternal support. "I am gratified that our Battlebox should be so useful in the support of this campaign. Indeed, it is our own forward sequence of gates that brings the blessed Aether to support this noble campaign."

"We all strive to fulfill the Imperial Will," Sjei nodded without commitment. Wejon had arranged the audience for Shebin with the Emperor—one that had brought her to pass dangerously close to the circle of Ch'drei and her Iblisi obsession with truth—not that the Emperor cared one way or the other about the truth except as a tool for his own wants. Wejon was becoming a "loose stone underfoot" as the elf saying went—something small that can cause you to fall. Sjei would have to find a way to rid himself of this loose stone but his voice betrayed no such intention as he spoke. "Each contributes what he can and in his own way to his greater glory."

Wejon bowed slightly. "Indeed, as is the duty of every citizen to . . ."

The Aether globes lighting the room suddenly dimmed, flickering twice before brightening again.

Everyone in the Battlebox room froze in surprise.

Aether globes never dimmed.

Bang!

Sjei started at the sharp sound, his attention drawn at once toward the source of the sound.

An explosion of red glass flew through the room. Sjei instinctively raised his left arm to protect his face and eyes.

Bang . . . bang, bang, bang . . .

A succession of concussive sounds followed quickly. White glass now shot through the room. Cries of pain and surprise echoed between the columns supporting the ceiling.

Again the Aether globes dimmed, flickered and then died for one long, breathless instant before brightening again.

Then there was silence.

Sjei lowered his hand hesitantly.

The sand in the box before them was flat, no longer representing a model of the distant battlefield. The figures remained on the sand but they lay on their sides in their last positions and no longer moved.

Sjei looked up at the brass bar overhead.

The red glass beads were completely missing, blown to dust it seemed. Their only remnant was a slight rosy cast over the sands at one end of the box. Of the thirty-seven white beads that had been on the bar only moments before there now remained, by Sjei's count, twenty-eight and of those only nineteen remained on the right side of the bar.

Sjei reached down, grasping Wejon's tunic and hauling the Fifth High Priest of the Myrdin-dai to his feet. "How far are nineteen folds?"

"What . . . what has happened?"

Sjei had no time for dithering. He shook the elf to get his attention. "How far north is fold nineteen?"

Wejon came to himself, trying to break Sjei's grip on his clothing without success. "How *dare* you put your hand to the Fifth High Priest of . . ."

Sjei wheeled Wejon around, pointing up toward the remaining beads on the brass rod. "Where is that? Where is fold nineteen?"

Wejon's eyes were suddenly fixed on the brass rod. His mouth was slack with astonishment.

"How far?" Sjei insisted.

Wejon swallowed. "It's . . . that fold is somewhere near the Chaenandrian border . . . the southern end of the Northmarch folds, I think."

"The southern end?" Ch'dak Vaijan, the Minister of Law, had joined them in staring at the remaining beads. "That's over four hundred leagues south of the battle!"

"Almost our own border," Arikasi, the Minister of Occupation, sputtered in astonishment.

"No," Sjei said, his lips curling back from his sharp teeth. "That's as far as the gateway folds fell but whatever happened reached us here in the Imperial City."

"Impossible!" Wejon declared.

"They're your folds, Wejon!" Sjei snapped, wheeling on the Fifth High Priest. "We all saw the globes dim. Get them operational, Myrdin-dai, and right now! We've got to find out what is happening in the north!"

Sjei released Wejon with a firm shove then turned back toward the useless Battlebox.

"It could be weeks before we know what's happened!"

"Fall back!" Belag roared.

The forward lines of the Legions were surging against his own lines. The ground beneath the manticore's feet was churned into a mixture of dirt and blood, and though his warriors were holding the front line, a break in the right flank had allowed three Octia to charge behind their lines. They had been quickly dealt with but not before several gate symbols had been established and propagated behind his lines. It was only a matter of moments, Belag knew from long experience, before folds would open over those symbols and warriors would pour out of them against the rear of his battle line.

"We've nowhere to fall back to," shouted Gradek in response, his own sword clashing against a manticore Impress Warrior of the Imperial Legion.

Belag looked behind them. It was true. Their own lines had been pressed back almost to the encampment—the battle was on the verge of including the children and elders they were sworn to protect. He glanced up on the western ridge. He could see a dark line at the crest—the entire goblin army—watching and waiting. They were positioned on the right flank but Belag knew that they would do nothing. His troops were on their own.

"Braun!" Belag shouted. "Confuse those folds! Keep them from opening! Keep them from . . ."

Braun stared back at Belag in amazement. A fool's grin split his face. "Belag! Wonderful news!"

"What is it, Braun?" Belag asked. The manticore was suddenly aware of a change in the air. The sounds of battle had diminished.

Braun rushed over to the Grahn Aur, holding open his hands. "Look! I can't use the magic!"

Belag shook his head. Braun did not always make sense to him on first hearing. "How is that *good*?"

"Because," Braun answered with a vicious grin, "neither can the Empire!"

Belag's head snapped at once to gaze over the battle lines. His own troops had obeyed his command as best they could, falling back from the line of battle but the Legions had not pressed their attack. The front lines stood facing them uncertainly, their eyes wide. Cries of anguish erupted from behind the battle line in numerous places.

All down the line, in Octian after Octian, Impress Warriors were suddenly reacting strangely. Many fell to the ground screaming. Others fell to their knees. Many of the manticores lay facedown on the ground, their knees pulled up under them and their hands stretched out in front of them.

"Think of it," Braun said with fire in his eyes. "No Proxis to give commands or make gate symbols. No folds. No control."

As Belag watched in amazement, the Legions of the Northern Fist dissolved before him. The well-ordered lines melted into a confused mob. The sound of sword against sword erupted among the ranks of the Imperial army as Devotion spells failed. The madness struck the Imperial ranks. The Legions were tearing themselves apart. The greater part of the elven army turned away from the battle line in a sudden panic, running to the south away from the Army of the Prophet.

"Where are they going?" Belag asked in wonder.

"Nowhere," Braun answered with a malevolent smile.

Belag understood.

"Gradek!" he shouted.

"Here, Grahn Aur!"

"Bring all the manticore warriors to the line at once!" Belag drew his own sword and stepped forward. "We wear the armor of our ancestors. For the Honor and Pride of Chaenandria . . . today we charge!"

The stasis bubble collapsed.

Soen, suddenly freed, hurtled down from the sky toward Vendis, who was still gripping the now useless staff.

There were a dozen ways to kill the chimerian and none of them required the use of Aether. Each one passed swiftly through Soen's mind as he fell but he discarded them all. He had better plans for Vendis . . . more interesting and entertaining . . . but each required that the "bendy" be at least marginally alive.

Soen fell upon Vendis with fury, tearing the useless Matei staff from his grasp and flinging it far away. Pummeling blows would do little to damage the pliable chimerian but could be a threat to the elf. *Best to eliminate any weapons from a battle that do not serve your side,* Soen thought.

Both rolled together down the rocky slope, coming to a jarring halt against an outcropping a few yards down from the summit. Vendis' fist just missed Soen's head as the former Iblisi shifted suddenly and grasped the chimerian's hind leg. Bracing against his opponent's back, Soen pulled hard on the leg, feeling the bones slide and shift as he did. This would barely bother the chimerian, Soen knew, whose physiology was build around shifting bones. Soen spun quickly, the leg still gripped in the crook of his arm.

Another of Vendis' fists shot up. The chimerian had twisted completely around at the waist, his upper torso now on his back while his hips still faced downward. Soen had anticipated the move, however, catching the upward thrusting arm and deftly wrapping it around Vendis' own pulled leg in a simple knot.

Bind a bendy on himself, Soen thought as he jumped off Vendis, scrambling back up the slope toward Belag's tent. He yelled back down the slope toward the struggling chimerian. "Come on, Vendis! Come on!"

The chimerian picked himself up. Soen had bound the leg and the arm together tightly and it would take Vendis some time to work himself free of that but chimerians are versatile as well as flexible. Vendis began clambering up the slope using his free leg and remaining three hands to propel himself with amazing speed toward Soen.

The elf Inquisitor positioned himself before the tent door. All he needed now was for Vendis to take him through it.

"You're quite a miracle, aren't you, Vendis?" Soen taunted. "You take money from the Empire to spy on the Pilgrims then you spy for the Pilgrims to make a little on the side there as well. You're probably spying for Ephindria for all I know. So what's it about this time, Vendis? Who bought you today?"

"It's about you," Vendis answered as he shifted his strange, contorted form from side to side, looking for an opening to attack.

"So it's Ch'drei, is it?" Soen laughed.

"Ch'drei?"

"The head of my Order," Soen continued, backing toward the tent. "She bought you."

"You idiot!" Vendis laughed, displaying a wide grin on his malleable face. "Me work for that dried-up husk? She's nothing compared to . . ."

"The Modalis," Soen finished. "Of course, who else would find so gullible an agent and be able to arrange a war of convenience all for their own profit. Still, I wouldn't count on their help getting out of here."

"They will be here for me soon enough, Soen Tjen-rei!" Vendis countered. "They will be here for us both!"

"I think not," Soen replied, nodding past Vendis toward the battlefield beyond.

Vendis turned.

The Legions of the Northern Fist that had been so carefully organized and pressing their attack had evaporated into a panicked mob running away from the battle.

It was all Soen needed. He ripped the tent pole from the ground, thrusting it completely through the torso of the chimerian and driving it into the earth.

Nothing in their experience could save them.

Every battle tactic developed by the Imperial Legions had been based around the use of Aether magic. The doctrine of advance, gate symbol marking, retreat, and then Octia folding behind the battle lines had become so fundamental to every military campaign and so consistently victorious that no other possibility was ever considered. When faced with an unexpectedly resilient foe, the Legions could always utilize those same folds to retreat more quickly than their enemy could advance, regroup at a safe distance, and add what additional forces were necessary. All that was required to reengage the enemy then was to utilize the same gate symbols established during the failing battle, return and become victorious once more.

No one—from the *Octian* Impress Warrior to Sjei Shurian, the Ghenetar Omris of the Order of Vash standing in a dark room in distant Rhonas—had ever considered or prepared for the failure of Aether during battle.

The Legions fled southward in panic. Many were driven mad from the dissolution of their Devotions. Others were simply overwhelmed by panic. Some few managed to place themselves in a position to surrender but for the most part, they fled from the field of battle in the only direction they knew where they might find safety; directly toward the command encampment of the elven war-mages.

This, however, was exactly the kind of battle that manticores had fought for over a thousand years.

The lion-men stepped to the front of the battle line. Many of them had worn their family armor that morning, the rest managed to grab and wear at least some piece of their ancestral armor in the short time left to form the line four deep. Then, as one, four thousand manticores fell forward onto their hands, looked up and pressed back against their haunches. Each had a weapon slung across his back— some older than their grandfathers. Each breathed deeply in anticipation.

Silence fell down the line as gnomes, humans and elves watched in awe. The cries of the fleeing Legions were growing distant in their ears as a warm breeze drifted over them from the sea at their backs.

"For Drakis!" Belag cried.

"For Drakis!" returned four thousand voices rippling down the line in either direction.

"For Freedom!" Belag shouted.

"For Freedom!" answered the four thousand.

"Forever!" Belag bellowed.

"Forever!" the four thousand thundered back.

With a great roar, the front line charged. Each successive line bounded after it, their hands gripping the ground in front of them, pulling them forward. Their charging strides rushed them forward like a great wave across the blood-soaked ground, bounding over the dead and dying, shaking the world with each footfall.

The fleeing Legions heard them coming, felt their approach through the soles of their own feet. Panic claimed the Legions. Many of the Proxis in flight stopped and tried to inscribe a gate symbol but the patterns they scrawled in the ground were dead and useless. Warriors of the Empire, desperate to escape, began dropping their shields, weapons, and anything that might hinder their flight. A few

Octia formed up in Centurai, mostly elven warriors or those who were under the direct command of elves, to make a stand and form some semblance of a defensive line.

The raging manticores' reason fell to the passion of the hunt. The forward elements of the charge crashed into the ragged elven line with their swords drawn and battle rage in their eyes, smashing the lines and rolling through the warriors like a scythe at harvest. Those whom they did not kill in their first assault they left for the three lines of manticores that followed on their heels. By the time the forth line had passed where the elves had made their stand, nothing remained alive.

On the ridge overlooking the valley, the Pajak of Krishu gazed down on the battlefield and began to chuckle softly. Then his chuckle turned to a chortle and soon to peals of laughter.

"Great Pajak!" Hograthaben, the newly appointed (earlier that morning) General Field Marshal of the Krishu Wyvern Raiders and brother-in-law to the Pajak, addressed his leader. "The Rhonas Legions are in retreat!"

"The Pajak is most amused!" The Pajak responded through his laughter. "I suppose you want to collect the five coins of our wager, eh? Well, aye, Hogra, it was worth it just to see those haughty elven dead-eyes have their big heads handed to them for once on a battlefield!"

"But does it please the Pajak to allow the long-heads to escape?" Hograthaben asked.

The Pajak frowned. "Why would the Pajak allow that?"

"Surely the Pajak has noticed that the elven commanders are fleeing to the south," Hograthaben said, bowing deeply. The Field Marshal had to be cautious in his new position. The Pajak did not like his wife all that much.

The Pajak looked down toward the end of the valley. The command tents of the elven encampment were still standing but the elves that had occupied them along with what the Pajak estimated at three Cohorts of ceremonial guards had abandoned their positions and were moving quickly to the south.

"Surely," the Field Marshal said, still in his deep bow, "the Pajak will not allow the manticores alone to claim the glory of victory."

The Pajak turned his eyes on his brother-in-law. The elves had been an irritation and a threat to him and his family as long as he could remember. If these manticores and their strange religion could crush them, so much the better for him. The Pajak always liked to back a winner especially if winning benefited him personally.

"Field Marshal," the Pajak intoned in his most serious ceremonial voice. "You will take my army of wyvern raiders, and you will cut off the retreat of these cowardly elves. The manticores have shown what they can do in a charge—let us show them what goblins on wyvern-back can accomplish!"

Marshal Hograthaben bowed again, his brick-red face split by a grin and his long ears quivering with excitement. "In your honor, Great Pajak!"

The goblin Field Marshal turned to mount his wyvern.

"Oh, and Field Marshal?"

Hograthaben stopped to look back at the Pajak.

"Kill them all . . . all except one," the Pajak commanded.

"All . . . except one, Great Pajak?"

"Of course," the Pajak said through a sharp-toothed smile. "We need one left to tell the tale!"

CHAPTER 42

Scales

THE LIGHT WAS BLINDING.

Drakis had managed to force his way up to the top of the Font but even with his eyelids tightly held shut the brilliance around him was painful. He reached forward with his hands, feeling for the grip of the key. Why the dwarf had left the key connected to the shard in the first place instead of removing it angered him. That he had to be the one to retrieve it angered him further still. Maybe the dwarf could not remove it. Maybe it had the same magic about it that required humans to open the Font. Maybe the dwarf had simply made trouble for them all once again. There had not been time to ask let alone answer any of those questions as the drakoneti were converging quickly on the resurrected ruins of the Citadel and the dragon was racing through the skies to reach them at the same time.

Besides, the anger burned through the horrible, hollow despair that had opened in his chest. Mala was gone and the awfulness of the loss was held at bay by his rage.

In the blazing radiance, his hand caught on something.

Drakis wrapped his fingers around it. He could feel the cool polish of the metal under his hand, the rolling contours of the grip and the jewel set in its pommel pressing against his wrist. For a moment, he panicked, uncertain as to how to cause the key to release the shard. He did not dare pull for fear of removing the sliver of crystal and shutting the Font once more. But he discovered that it twisted easily in his hands to the left and, within a few turns, it fell into his hand.

At once Drakis turned to sit, sliding back down the curve of the Font with the key in his hand. He only opened his eyes when his feet connected with the edge of the Font, rising uncertainly to his feet. He blinked furiously, trying to see.

Drakis dropped the key at his feet, instantly grasping the hilt of his sword and drawing it.

The partially reassembled rotunda of the Citadel was filled with drakoneti. They stood at the edges of the circle, hundreds of them, their barbed tails coiling and uncoiling about their feet. They shifted listlessly from one clawed foot to the other. Their spike-boned faces were fixed on Drakis, swaying back and forth as though waiting.

Ethis was struggling across the floor toward Drakis. Ishander stood uncertainly holding his sword next to the dwarf wielding his ax.

Now is the triumph of dragon's might
Now is the end of the light
The future turning
The past is burning.

Drakis looked up. The dome was nearly complete with a large circular opening at its apex. A column of light shone down through the aperture but was occluded by the silhouette of Pharis alighting on its edge, his enormous rust-red head craning down through the opening. The dragon suddenly released his perch, falling from the ceiling to land on all four of his legs with a thunderous shock onto the floor on the opposite side of the Font. Drakis staggered slightly from the impact, the tip of his sword shaking in his hand. The dragon more than filled half the space of the Citadel.

Drakis snatched the key off of the ground with his left hand and backed several steps away from the dragon, keenly aware of the wall of drakoneti behind him. Jugar and Ishander closed ranks with him. Ethis, trembling and having trouble holding his form, quivered on the ground at their feet.

Pharis hissed. His eyes fixed on Drakis.

Now is the destiny long denied.
Now comes the end of the past

Our future making
The key now taking . . .

Footsteps scraped across the stone behind Drakis.

Drakis spun around, his sword raised.

One drakonet stepped from out of the horde. It was enormous; a full head taller than most of the other drakoneti. Its facial bones swept back from its face into a series of broken spines and horns. One eye was milky and useless but the other stared at Drakis with a brilliant, intense blue color. Its scales had a polished sheen that shifted colors as though oiled. Its shoulders were wide and its arms enormous.

The drakonet stopped, its barbed tail coiling behind it.

Drakis could hear his own heavy breathing. He raised his sword with his right hand, its tip wavering slightly in the still air. The left gripped the key.

The massive one-eyed drakonet began working its jaw. A horrible, choking sound croaked from its maw, its sharp teeth scraping against one another. It reached out with its right hand, the long, broken claws of its fingers opening toward Drakis, palm up expectantly.

Drakis lowered his sword.

"No, lad!" the dwarf croaked. "Don't do it!"

"It's over, Jugar," Drakis sighed. It had all been a horrible bad joke. So many sacrificed—Mala, Urulani, the Lyric—so many gone—and for what? All because they wanted him to be someone he was not.

The creature shrugged its shoulders, its jaw working again, a guttural rumble now emerging from its throat.

Drakis slid his sword back into its scabbard.

"No! Drakis, listen to me!" Jugar shouted in desperation.

The one-eyed drakonet raised its head.

"No, Jugar," Drakis said, transferring the key to his right hand. He held it up in front of him, gazing at it. "No more words."

He stepped forward, stopping in front of the huge dragon-man towering nearly a foot and a half over him. The monstrous creature was staring down at him with its vibrant blue eye, its wide jaws working as it muttered.

Drakis held the key out in front of him for the creature to take.

The rotunda fell into shadow.

The one-eyed drakonet looked up. Drakis followed its gaze.

Dragons were settling on the edge of the opening at the top of the dome, their shapes blocking out the sky beyond. There were five crowding the opening of various shapes, colors, and markings, all illuminated by the column of light above the Font. One was more striking than the rest, its scales a polished, golden hue burnished to a bright shine.

Pharis looked up as well, his neck recoiling as he hissed at the dragons perched above him.

The drakonet *spoke*.

Drakis turned to face the creature in front of him. For a moment, Drakis was not sure what it said but his eyes widened in astonishment as the word became clear in his mind.

"*DRA'AKISSSSSSSS . . .*"

The human's eyes went wide in astonishment.

In that moment, the drakonet reached forward. Its open hand plunged past the key and instead grasped Drakis' arm.

Drakis cried out in pain.

The world shifted. The rotunda was suddenly whole and restored: a beautiful vision of perfection. The arched buttresses rose to the complete dome, the columns stood in symmetry beneath the arches of the colonnade circling about the Font where the light of its Aether shot up through the opening like a beacon of hope.

Gazing down from above, the silver-burnished dragon spoke, its head arched down and facing Pharis as it spoke.

And Drakis *understood*.

". . . discovered what you have done, Pharis! Since the time the Darkness Fell you have told the lie of humanity betraying dragonkind. You were the Guardian of the Font. Yours was the charge to protect the Aether and our oath with humankind!'"

"My loyalty was to dragonkind, Hestia!" Pharis roared. "It is a loyalty and a duty lost among many of us!"

"We swore an oath!" Hestia answered from her perch above.

"An oath of servitude!" Pharis snapped. The dragon circled the

Font. "An oath that sold the birthright of dragons to the soft life of human pets! Listen to me! We had a destiny! We could have been a great and noble race that ruled the sky and land! We were the embodiment of Aer—the magic of the land. It welled up through the stones of our lairs and into our bones. We were one with the Aer! But the humans offered us an easy path, a seductive path! The Aether made us soft, complacent, and weak. We traded our eminence for soft rest and easy feasts. We forgot the wild sky and the touch of hard stone. Humanity made us tame and servile! They stood between us and our better selves!"

"And so you rid us of them?" Hestia asked in a hissing voice. "Thinking higher thoughts than the Ring of Five, higher still than all the oaths of the Dragon Elders who vouched for each clutch, you alone determined to break the oath, to sunder the magic and pull the darkness down upon us all?"

"I said nothing of the Dark Fall," Pharis replied. "The humans brought this on themselves."

"And yet when the human Drakis came—presented himself at our borders," said Marush, the green-and-yellow dragon that perched next to Hestia on the rim of the dome, "you kept him hidden from the eyes of our Queen—even as she heard word of him and searched the wildland for him."

"Not true," Pharis hissed back, circling the Font. "Marush, what have you to gain by lying so? Do you covet my title so that you would lie to our Queen?"

"Where is this Drakis?" Queen Hestia trumpeted.

"Here, Great Queen!"

Drakis turned to look at the drakonet gripping his arm who had just called to the Queen. He was astonished. The massive drakonet had been transformed in his eyes. The worn and broken horns of his head were complete and perfect. His bony face had taken on an indefinable elegance in nobler, smoother lines. The barbs on the tail were rounded and the creature wore a striking robe of crimson trimmed in gold brocade. His blind eye now matched the blue of the other, both giving a softer look to the face.

"Speak, Theodris," Hestia commanded. "Too long you have been without a voice."

"Too long since the Dark Fall," Theodris answered. "Too long since our adoption to dragonkind by the power of Aether and the long night of our dimmed minds and barbaric half-thoughts. We were immortals condemned to roam the world as little more than animals when the Aether fell. We have lived a waking nightmare these long years."

"And found you Drakis?" Hestia said.

"This is Drakis, Queen Hestia," Theodris said, still gripping the human's arm.

"The Drakis of old?" Hestia replied, her eyes narrowing.

"I cannot say, Queen Hestia," Theodris answered. "But he restored the Font and fulfilled the oath of humankind."

"And what say you of Pharis?" Hestia asked.

Theodris spoke clearly into the hall. "He enslaved us, bade us first that we might kill this Drakis before you had discovered him. When this failed, he turned us to a new purpose—to seize him in the wilderness. He wanted him taken but for himself alone and in a place far from the eyes of Your Majesty's loyal friends. At last he determined as he had done before to follow them to this fallen place and attempt to retrieve the Key of the Font."

"For what purpose?" asked the purple-hued dragon in a high, fluting voice.

"That he might recover the Key of the Font—and hide it from Your Majesty . . . and the world." Theodris answered.

"Not true!" Pharis shouted. "A conspiracy of lies!"

"Pharis," Hestia intoned. "We are beings of the Aer and so we existed before the human Aether . . . and so we have existed since. By the power of the Aer we breathed our fiery breath. By the power of Aer we could lift ourselves into the sky. Now the darkness is lifted by the hand of a human and powers that once were mine are mine again."

Pharis coiled back.

"As you had taken the Aether from us," Hestia declared, "now we take the Aer from you . . . and leave you to the justice of humanity's heirs here among us; the drakoneti."

Theodris released Drakis' arm. The perfect form of the rotunda vanished at once, replaced by the strange incompleteness of the suspended ruins. Theodris once more assumed his monstrous visage

Pharis leaped upward, his wings extending as Hestia and the four dragons with her drew in their breath. Pharis beat his wings once, twice . . . pushing frantically to get through the opening of the dome, but it was too late. Hestia's breath and the breath of the dragons about her spewed from their gaping maws, encompassing the rust-red dragon in a gray mist as he rose into the dome. Pharis beat his wings again, trying to push past them through the opening but the mist remained behind, holding the dragon's form in the air for a moment behind him. Pharis faltered in the air, wings flailing, desperate to support his weight, but the power of Aer had been pulled from him.

"Out of the way!" Jugar shouted, pushing at Ishander. Ethis managed to stand, staggering toward Drakis.

The dragon fell out of the ceiling, crashing down atop the Font. Pharis scrambled to get his footing on the stones, clawing at the dragon statues to find a purchase but the drakoneti were already swarming toward him. The dragon-men rushed from the surrounding walls, leaping upon the dragon, clawing at the membrane of his wings, tearing at his scales.

Pharis howled in pain, thrashing his great claws about, but the drakoneti would not be denied. The crippled dragon managed to roll onto his feet, charging between the suspended columns of what had once been the entrance hall. The drakoneti cheered and abandoned the rotunda, streaming out in pursuit of the fallen Pharis.

The din of the mob receded and silence again filled the hall. Four of the dragons had left their perches atop the dome to witness the end of Pharis—inevitable now that he could no longer fly or breathe magic—but Hestia remained, looking down from above. Theodris, too, had remained, standing near Drakis as though waiting for something.

"Drakis?" Jugar said quietly. "What's all this about? Where did all those monstrosities rush to in such a hurry? Are we going to be eaten or worse?"

Drakis was gazing blankly at the Key of the Font still in his hands. His voice sounded far away in his own ears. "No, Jugar. I've spoken to them. They won't harm us."

"Drakis, lad, you've *done* it!" Jugar's shout echoed among the ruins, his voice startling in the silence. The dwarf brandished his ax. "Now if these beasties don't mind, we can get to those fold gates! Maybe now we can go home, eh?"

Home. The word rang in Drakis' mind. House Timuran had been home but it was lost. Urulani's village could have been home before the Iblisi had destroyed it looking for him. Home was where Mala wanted him to take her . . . where he had promised to take her.

But he knew now that home *was* Mala.

"Drakis!"

Drakis raised his head sharply at the sound. A woman's voice echoed down the entrance hall. He could see her running toward him, holding another woman in her arms. His eyes brightened, widened, hoping . . .

"You wish home?" the drakonet said with a heavily slurred tongue.

Jugar looked up at the enormous beast in surprise. "Why . . . yes . . . yes! Can you assist us in getting back to our native soil?"

Drakis stepped toward the hall in anticipation. The women were drawing nearer.

"Hestia say dragons honor still ancient oath to humankind," the dragon-man said. "Come to aid and defend as oath to fulfill. With Aether their strength is new. No gates or fold. Dragons carry you home to southlands."

Home. He had promised to take her . . .

Urulani rushed into the hall carrying the Lyric, whose arms were wrapped around her neck. "There's something wrong with her, she's . . ."

Drakis' face fell in anguish.

"Mala?" he asked.

Urulani shook her head . . . could not meet his gaze.

Drakis' comprehension of Urulani's simple motion drove him to his knees, the Key of the Font rolling from his open hands.

"Can you believe it?" Jugar shouted joyously. "We're going home!"

Drakis threw his head back and released a cry of anguish that came from the great emptiness within him. It came again, the sound of his overwhelming loss ringing beneath the broken dome above.

And again . . .

And again . . .

And he knew that the sound of it would echo endlessly in his gutted soul.

CHAPTER 43

Recompense

VENDIS SAT ON THE FLOOR of his cage, the fingers of both pairs of his hands intertwined in front of him, his face a blank as he looked back at the Council of the Grahn Aur arrayed about him in Belag's tent.

Belag sat in front of the caged Vendis on an ornate throne of silver inlaid with jewels, liberated, it was said, from the command tent of the Rhonas Legions—the same Legions that had been trampled into the bloodied ground of Willow Vale. It had been presented to him by the Pajak of Krishu as a gift of honor, the rightful spoils the Pajak had taken from his victorious obliteration of the fleeing Cohorts of the Legion command.

The Pajak himself sat on his own throne to the right of the Grahn Aur. A number of jewels—also liberated from the seized elven possessions—had been hastily added to the gold embossing of the Pajak's throne by the goblin smithies so that it might shine more gloriously than that of the Grahn Aur. There had been some concern earlier in the day that the Pajak would, by nature of his four-foot stature, have his head lower than that of the towering manticore Prophet of Drakis. The quick application of several soft pillows to the throne and four hastily carved blocks of wood set beneath the Pajak's throne had solved the crisis of diplomacy. Now the Pajak leaned forward, his long hands knitting together and his large eyes narrowed in anticipation of the traitor's judgment on the word of the elf, Soen Tjen-rei.

Soen himself stood casually to the left of the Grahn Aur, his arms folded across his chest. The rogue Iblisi's black eyes were fixed on the prisoner and impossible to read. Some who were in the tent would later describe it as malice, while others thought it more like amusement or satisfaction. Most, however, were correct in believing that Soen's look was a careful and deliberate study in conveying nothing at all. Soen again wore the robe of an Iblisi as everyone present—indeed, in the entire encampment—now knew that he was once of that Order. It was an awkward and uncomfortable position for Soen, who preferred to remain as anonymous as possible. He had hated being known at the Imperial Court and now he found himself in the same position in the court of the rebellion. Soen knew that fame brought with it many problems in his work but that it could also be used to his advantage . . . as it was at the present moment.

Braun, the human Proxi turned wizard, stood to the right of the Pajak. He now wore a robe that looked as though it had once belonged to an elven war-mage. Soen could still see the faint outlines of the original owner's House markings in the fabric from which they had been removed. He also held a Proxi staff in his hands, the steel point at its base polished to a bright shine for the occasion. The crystal in the staff's headpiece held a strange purple glow that Soen had never seen before. It was a color difficult to look upon.

Next to Braun stood Gradek, the manticore warrior now made Commander of the Armies. He had been a believer before the Battle of the Willow Vale but it was not until now that he had any real hope for their future. He held his head high with the pride of one who has passed beyond belief to conviction.

Seated beyond Gradek was Tsojai Acheran, the frail and nervous elf who had been brought to the council to represent the small elven contingent of converts and had been saddled with the responsibility of correspondence and intelligence. Soen believed Tsojai had no capabilities for either function. Tsojai had a deep-seated distrust of the renegade Iblisi that had not been diminished by presenting Vendis as a traitor. As far as Tsojai was concerned, they should *both* be in the cage. He sat as far from Soen as possible, while still being considered one of the council.

Neblik, the Hak'kaarin gnome, sat on his small rug to the left of Soen, taking in everything that was said and done. He would be spreading the story of this council to the rest of the encampment through his fellow gnomes as soon as the proceedings were finished. The goblin Doroganda sat beside the gnome, prepared as soon as the opportunity presented itself to condemn the chimerian to a number of different deaths she had devised for him.

Hegral stood guard behind the cage. He was a manticore of tremendous strength and courage but he also benefited from an important skill: Soen had taught him how to stun a chimerian long enough to kill him properly.

Beyond Hegral the tent was packed with representatives from as many of the different camps as could fit inside, and many more were gathered just outside. The question of how to deal with Vendis—or anyone who had betrayed the cause of Drakis—was of some debate among the members of the encampment. Some believed that faith in Drakis was a personal choice and that those who no longer believed should simply be banished from the community. Others believed that a rejection of Drakis was an attack on the faith and should be met with punishment. Betrayal of the faith to an enemy, they believed, should exact a swift and final punishment.

Everyone looked to the Grahn Aur's judgment of Vendis as a guide for their future.

And, at that moment, the Grahn Aur was looking at the caged Vendis.

The cage itself had been built to Soen's specifications. It was wrought of a woven lattice of iron rods with no opening between them more than three inches wide. These formed a large cube seven feet on a side with rings mounted to the exterior through which carrying rods could be inserted to transport both the cage and the prisoner inside. But it was the second cage built within the outer cage and suspended by rods at the corners to be positioned exactly one foot away from all the outer cage walls that secured the chimerian. This iron-woven box within a box was five feet on a side. To the humans it looked as though it would be an inhumanely cramped space, but Soen explained that the unusual physiology of the chimerian would allow him to contract with reasonable, if far from luxurious, comfort. Soen had further explained that the particular spacing of the bars and the one-foot interval between the outer and the inner box combined with the spacing of the woven sides would make it impossible for the chimerian to use his bendable talents to escape. A matching set of locked doors—also constructed of the same woven bars—allowed access from the outside through the outer cage into the inner cage. In all, the arrangement allowed for Vendis to see out of his cage and, more importantly, for those outside to keep an eye on Vendis within.

"Vendis, you have heard the statements given before this council," Belag said in a voice that carried beyond the confines of the tent. Belag wore the ceremonial robes of his office as Grahn Aur. "Charges have been made against you—that you secretly aided the enemies of Drakis. That you aided the Legions of the Northern Fist and the Empire of Rhonas in following the course of our pilgrims through the wilderness, and that you colluded with them in an attempt to capture Drakis and deliver him to the Rhonas Empire as well as assisting them in their attempted destruction of the believers' armies and families. That you willfully detained a member of our followers . . ."

Vendis scoffed at this, shaking his head. This part of the charge was about Soen.

". . . with the intention of delivering him into the hands of our enemies. What have you to say to us in this matter?"

Vendis stood up. "Well, quite a bit, actually."

The Grahn Aur gestured for the chimerian to begin.

"Since I came among this people, I have come to know and accept the faith which had driven each of us to . . ."

"Oh, let's kill him and be done with it," Doroganda chirped from the far end seat of the council.

"She makes a fine point," said the Pajak at once. He had never seen a chimerian killed and would very much like to know how it was accomplished.

Belag held up his hand. "This is the first time our council has been forced to sit in judgment on one of our own. What we say and do here will echo down through our generations to come. We must deliberate properly, weigh the different points of view, and listen in earnest to his defense before we kill him."

Soen coughed quickly rather than laugh.

"Has our judgment already been made?" asked Tsojai in his high-pitched voice. "Are his words to mean nothing in our ears? He was a trusted member of this council once. Is this the same fate that awaits us all should we be accused on such thin evidence as one person's charge?"

"You are right, of course," Belag nodded "We must hear what he has to say before any judgment is made—please make note of that point, Neblik!"

"May I speak now?" Vendis asked.

"Of course," Belag said with a wave of his enormous hand. "Please proceed."

"As I was saying," Vendis started again. "Since I came among this people, I have come to know and accept the faith which . . ."

"Grahn Aur!" A young manticore had burst into the tent, yelling excitedly as he pushed aside the spectators near the entrance. "Grahn Aur! I must find the Grahn Aur!"

"I am here, Jegak!" Belag stood with annoyance. "We are in the midst of council! What do you mean bursting in on our . . ."

"He is come!" Jegak shouted breathlessly. The young manticore's chest rose and fell rapidly from his exertions.

"Who?" Belag asked. "Who is come?"

It was then that they noticed the sound. It was a rising cheer, shouts and the bedlam of a thousand, thousands, tens of thousands of voices rising up from the encampment.

"Drakis!" the youth shouted. "Drakis is come!"

The Grahn Aur glanced sharply over at Soen whose own normally impassive face expressed surprise equal to Belag's own.

"How do you know it is Drakis, boy?" Belag demanded of the young manticore.

"Because he comes on *dragons!*" The boy was nearly faint from lack of breath but the excitement drove him on. "See for yourself, Grahn Aur! He comes on *dragons!*"

Belag rushed past the cage. The spectators in the tent were already pushing their way out the opening, many of them making their own exits. Soen rushed to follow on Belag's heels. The council rose at once, heedless of the complaints of the Pajak, who was forced to be the last of the throng to exit the tent.

The cheering beyond the tent walls washed over Vendis, who was left forgotten in his cage.

Forgotten but not entirely alone.

Braun remained.

Vendis gazed at the former Proxi from the center of his special cage. "And what of you? Are you not going out to greet this godlike human of the prophecy?"

Braun shrugged. "I've already met him."

"You've . . . what?"

Braun stepped casually over toward the cage, pressing his grizzled face against the outer bars. "Don't you worry about a thing, Vendis. I have a great number of acquaintances. You wait here. I know just the person who can take care of you."

They came from the north, from across the Straits of Erebus and over the waters of Mistral Bay. The names of the dragons—Marush of Drakis, Wanrah of Ethis, Pyrash the Patient of Jugar, Kyranish of Urulani and Ephranos of Karan the Lyric—each would be noted in chronicles made by the gnomes, told and retold throughout the encampment. How their wings shone in the sun of the bright sky, how the wind was carried beneath them as they landed on the shores of Willow Vale west of Glachold and the weeping joy that accompanied them as the companions of Drakis slid down the sides of each dragon's lowered neck to return again from their quest in the north as the prophecy had foretold.

Later they would learn of Ishander and the drakoneti, of the end of Pharis and how Ishander remained in his own land to help the drakoneti redeem the Lost Citadels of the North.

But on that day the story was told of Drakis dismounting from Marush, his face drawn and careworn from the journey and the trials of his quest. He stood beside his dragon as though his thoughts were elsewhere. The Grahn Aur stepped up to Drakis then, casting aside his ceremonial robes, and grasped him with great joy by both shoulders.

"You have returned," said the Grahn Aur. "My friend, you are home!"

Drakis, it was written, offered no reply.

The sounds of laughter, music, and joy filtered up through the folds of the Grahn Aur's tent and into the head of the chimerian, now completely alone and forgotten amid the revelries that had erupted throughout the encampment.

"Is anyone out there?" the chimerian shouted for the hundredth time, but to his surprise, this time there was an answer.

"Yes, someone is here."

Vendis turned, but the relief he felt kindling in his soul was snuffed out at once. "YOU!"

Ethis bowed slightly with all his hands behind him after the chimerian custom. "Yes, Thedis of Salashei. What a strange fate that I have come to find you at last."

"Thedis, then. I have not had use for that name in a long time," Vendis said. "Perhaps you could tell me what happened to Thuri?"

"I found him and he was dealt with although in a rather circumstantial way," Ethis said. "It cost me more than he was worth . . . far more . . . but then you would know all about that, wouldn't you?"

Vendis held his silence for a moment before he spoke. "So Drakis has returned."

"But you don't really care, do you?" Ethis said, stepping closer. "The Salashei family has been hunting the High Council in Exile rather effectively for some time. The High Council ruled the families of Ephindria, keeping the meddling elves at bay. With the complicity of the Hueshei and Whylin families for trading rights with the elves, you took over the governance of most of the provinces. Did you really think that the High Council would simply let the trade families bleed them without exacting blood in return?"

Vendis raised his hands in front of him. "Listen to me, Ethis. We're both tradesmen—we each have our skills to sell. You sold talents to Lady

Chythal and the High Council in Exile. I sold mine to the Salashei, but that's no reason why we cannot strike a bargain between us."

"Indeed?" Ethis said.

"These pilgrims—fanatics—they're doomed," Vendis said. "I know! I've lived among them. They had a victory, true, but I'm a wizard. I know that the Aer has returned to the land these last few days. Perhaps it is not as strong as it once was, but it is back. How long can this rabble survive against the Legions supported by Aer? The Council in Exile has been preaching the fall of Rhonas for so long that they barely believe it themselves. *We* are the future, Ethis; the Salashei saving the family of Ephindria by allying themselves with the elves . . . and you can be a part of it, Ethis! I can see to it!"

Ethis drew in a long, considering breath. "First, tell me: why were you pushing that Iblisi elf to come to Drakosia? Surely not to look for the fabled Drakis!"

Vendis shook his head.

"You were coming for me?" Ethis asked.

"Yes," Vendis answered quickly. "I was coming to find you . . . to ask you to join with us."

"Of course," Ethis smiled. The chimerian reached up for the lock on the outer cage. He deftly picked it and opened the latch.

"Don't you worry about a thing," Ethis said, reaching in for the second lock on the inner cage. "I want you to deliver my answer personally."

It was late when Hegral returned to the command tent, remembering that they had left the chimerian there in the excitement of the dragons' arrival.

He found Vendis dead in his cage, both the inner and outer doors still locked. There seemed to be no violence done to the body, though it sagged horribly in death.

"Humph," Hegral said, straightening up. "Saved us the trouble, eh? Well, good riddance!"

They waited in the Emperor's Court of the Cloud Palace at the center of the Rhonas Empire.

The enormous room with the sweeping pillars reached to the dome overhead. There, the mystical sun shone down from above, burning with the power of Aether gathered in from the ends of the Empire. It reflected off of the carefully angled oval panels overhead, softening the light and casting just the perfect shadows across the Emperor's features as he sat on his glorious throne on the platform floating on a cloud above the polished floor.

All around the Emperor's Court stood the ordered ranks of the various powers that struggled with one another to fulfill the Emperor's Will. Daramonei workers, Paktan guildleaders, the war-mages of the Orders of Krish, Nekara and Vash, Ch'drei and a contingent of Iblisi were all prominent as well as a plethora of individuals from the thirty or so ministries that made up the governance of the Rhonas Empire. Even their arrangement in the hall had been carefully determined and, in many cases, delicately arranged.

So it was that Sjei-Shurian, the Ghenetar Omris of the Vash was standing conveniently next to Kyori-Xiuchi, the Tertiaran Master of the Occuran as they both waited in the hall.

That they were both members of the secretive Modalis was, of course, no accident.

"I note that the Myrdin-dai are not represented at court today," Kyori spoke quietly into the hall without turning his head, but his words were just loud enough to reach the ears of Sjei standing next to him.

"The Myrdin-dai have fallen from the grace of the Emperor," Sjei said, likewise without turning his head from the magnificent spectacle of the Imperial throne. "Word of the failure of the Aether causing the loss of one of the Emperor's most beloved Legions in the northern reaches of the Empire was laid squarely upon the shoulders of your brother Order."

"And Wejon Rei has not been seen among us of late," murmured Kyori.

"Who?" Sjei said casually. "I don't believe I recognize the name."

"Indeed," Kyori replied with a slight smile. "Now that you mention it, neither do I."

"Which puts me in mind," Sjei said, "we appear to have an opening in the council of the Modalis."

"Have you someone in mind?" Kyori asked smoothly.

"I believe I do," replied Sjei. "Someone who has the Emperor's ear . . . someone who can move easily among the many Ministries and for whom access is eagerly granted."

The great doors to the throne room opened with a stately motion. All eyes turned toward the portal.

Resplendent in a flowing gown, Shebin walked across the polished floor. The scarlet-colored dress had been carefully tailored to fit Shebin's figure, the collar framing her elongated head and ears perfectly. The red train fanned out behind her, brushing the floor as she floated on a smaller rendition of the Emperor's cloud. She floated upward, higher and higher, the train lifting from the ground as she approached the Imperial throne and the welcoming smile of the Emperor.

"I understand her procession started on the Isle of the Gods," Sjei said quietly.

"In our own temple," replied the master of the Occuran.

"It seems your Order is in favor once again," Sjei nodded.

"Indeed, the Emperor smiles upon us and our service to his will," Kyori smiled pleasantly as he spoke. "Services which he will need now more than ever before."

"Has the Aether been restored in the north?" Sjei asked.

"It has," Kyori's smile fell slightly as he spoke. "There are problems, however, which we will soon correct. We have taken control of the Northmarch Folds from the Myrdin-dai but . . ."

"Go on," Sjei urged.

"Nothing of concern," Kyori said quickly. "Aether is flowing northward at a troublesome rate. I'm sure we'll have it corrected soon."

"I, too, trust that your Order will correct the problem soon," Sjei remarked. "Now that the Emperor has adopted the symbol about which we shall forge a truly great—and profitable conquest. Not a bad story, is it, Kyori? Poor little orphaned girl from the Western Provinces taken into the benevolent grace and household of the Imperial family?"

"A moving story indeed," Kyori agreed.

Shebin floated across the boundary of the Imperial cloud, coming to rest at the foot of the steps leading up to the Emperor's throne. The Emperor stood to the sound of trumpets filling the hall, reached down, and took Shebin's hand.

The assembled crowd, noting their cue, erupted into applause and cheering. The sound of their cheers echoed through the Imperial halls, floated out of the Cloud Palace and onto the Garden of Kuchen below where the Third Estate citizens had gathered in anxious anticipation of this moment. The cheers in the garden erupted and, like a wave, spread through the throngs in the streets of Rhonas Chas, a chorus of approval and support.

"Cheer on, citizens," Sjei said, applauding wildly. "We have our war!"

THE END OF BOOK TWO